Entitleme...

Branden Blinn

Entitlement
Revised Edition published in 2025.

Published by ACACEA, LLC
www.williambrandenblinn.com
www.brandenblinnnarrativefiction.com

ISBN Paperback: 979-8-9936458-0-3
ISBN Hardcover: 979-8-9936458-1-0
ISBN eBook: 979-8-9936458-2-7

Book Launch by: Ink to Impact Publishing

Illustrations by: Branden Blinn

Editing by: Buddy Thornton

Printed in the United States of America.

This book is a work of fiction/non-fiction. Names, characters, places, and incidents are either products of the author's imagination or used fictitiously. Any resemblance to actual events, locales, or persons, living or dead, is purely coincidental.

For information, bulk orders, or speaking engagements, please contact: **tbbmgfilmguy@gmail.com**

Dedication

For SEB
I hope you see the truth inhabiting reality beneath, between,
amidst, and around all these words.

"Still"

Acknowledgments

It seems that all young men need mentors, especially in this day and age. Thankfully, I have had a few, but none have been as important to me as William Cronshaw, who graced my life just as I was stepping into the truth about who I am, what is important to me, and why.

He provided me with stability regarding integrity, honesty, clarity, and a commitment to self-expression. He perceived my creativity buried deep within me when I could not. He fought to help me recognize it and bring it forward.

Most importantly, he honored me when I began to unleash it and gave me the courage to fortify it in every way I could, regardless of how others might receive or perceive it. I feel like I owe him everything.

I also want to thank Jack Law, Timothy Williams, Mike Fuller, and Sharon Hayden for continually supporting me in all the ways only they can and have over all these decades.

Mostly, I have to thank my dear, dear, lifelong friend Jack Eiman. For so many things, in ways too profound to name, that I don't even know where to begin.

Finally, I want to thank Sherry Gideons, Natalie McQueen, and especially Buddy Thornton for pulling me across the finish line.

About the Author

Branden Blinn is an award-winning filmmaker and LGBTQ content creator whose work has reached more than 45,000,000 viewers worldwide.

Best known for his short film *Thirteen or so Minutes* and the YouTube viral favorite *Triple Standard*, he has written, directed, and produced over thirty episodes of web-based content, most of it for YouTube and HERE TV.

With *Entitlement*, his debut novel, Blinn brings the same emotional honesty and cinematic storytelling that have defined his films to the page, exploring themes of love, identity, and the courage it takes to live authentically.

The rural Virginia meeting room, bustling only minutes before, now stood in stark contrast. Tables were dismantled with the clatter of folding legs, and a group of local teens stacked chairs. Their banter about sports echoed faintly, a thin veil of normalcy over the tense atmosphere.

By the door, Daniel Eiman stood silently beside Andrew Steadman and Charlie Atwood. They were young, mid-twenties at most, yet their expressions carried the weariness of those who had fought too long for something that still felt unfinished.

Harvey lingered a few feet away, still engaged in conversation with the council members. The faint rustle of papers and muted laughter from the teens created a strange juxtaposition to the unspoken tension in the air.

The outer door creaked open, and a gust of cold air swept through. Brent Evans stepped inside, shaking off the chill. "The coast is clear," he said, his voice low but steady. "They seem to be gone."

As Harvey approached, his steps slow and hesitant, Andrew's tone lightened, though it couldn't hide the edge beneath. "Harvey, where's your car?"

Harvey gestured vaguely toward the back of the building, his gaze darting toward the windows as though expecting someone.

Daniel, breaking his quiet demeanor, offered a warm smile. "We'll walk him over there."

Andrew nodded. "I'll pull the truck around front."

Not missing a beat, Brent added, "I'll come with you."

Andrew turned to Daniel with a grin. "Give me your jacket."

Daniel hesitated, pulling the collar tighter around himself. "It's freezing out, dude," he protested, but relented with a sigh, handing it over.

"Exactly," Andrew said, smirking into the jacket. "I'll take that hat too."

Before Daniel could react, Andrew plucked the hat off Daniel's head and removed the black O.U.T. binder from Daniel's grasp. Leaning in close, he whispered for Daniel's ears alone, "Be nice."

Daniel shook his head, watching Andrew and Brent enter the cold. "Turn the heat on full blast," Daniel had called after them.

Harvey, flanked by Daniel and Charlie, watched as Brent and Andrew exited. Charlie pointed at the side wall where the skinheads had been standing, then turned to Harvey. "Who were those guys?"

Never saw them before," Harvey replied, his voice tinged with unease.

As Daniel, Harvey, and Charlie reached the back exit, the tension in their conversation lightened considerably. Daniel's voice was warm and genuine as he turned to

Harvey. "You were great up there, Harvey. How long have you lived here?"

"All my life," Harvey replied with a small, proud smile. "Except for college and medical school."

"Wow," Charlie said, clearly impressed. "They must all be really proud of you here."

Daniel rolled his eyes, but the corners of his mouth twitched upward.

Charlie had reached up and wrapped his arms around Harvey. "We'll get them the next time, buddy. We'll get them the next time."

Before Daniel could respond, the gymnasium doors burst open behind them with a deafening bang. A teenager stumbled in, his face pale, his words tumbling out in frantic gasps.

Daniel didn't need to hear the specifics. His body moved before his mind could catch up, his legs propelling him across the gym and out of the main entrance. The frigid night air hit him like a wall, yet he didn't stop. Charlie and Harvey followed close behind, their footsteps echoing in the silence.

The night smelled faintly of pine and exhaust, the hum of a distant highway drifting through the trees. Daniel's breath came in clouds as they rounded the corner toward the lot. What he saw stopped him dead in his tracks.

The metallic sheen of wet paint, garish red letters slicing through the night like an open wound.

"Faggots die!"

The red words stood in sharp contrast as they dripped down the side of Andrew's white truck, their venom still fresh, staining the air with the acrid tang of spray paint.

*****

Daniel's eyes snapped open. Six years later. He shot up in bed, gasping for breath, sweat running off his face, soaking into his shirt.

His hair was shorter now, and the lines around his eyes had deepened, sharpening the blue that had only grown more vivid with time.

Hearing the familiar scratch at the door, he opened it, and Jupiter bounded in, tail thumping the floor, oblivious to the storm in Daniel's chest. Daniel sank to his knees, burying his face in Jupiter's fur.

Had the nightmares returned? Had they ever truly gone away? Three years had passed since the last one, but now they were back, vivid, merciless, unrelenting, scrawled across his mind with the clarity of something that had only been waiting for permission to surface. They tore through the walls he had spent six long years meticulously erecting, barriers that had once seemed strong enough to hold the past at bay, which now only loomed larger than ever.

*****

The Morning light poured through the large classroom windows, illuminating the floating dust motes like tiny dancers. The worn wooden desks, etched with the marks of countless lessons learned and forgotten, glowed faintly in the sun. Daniel stood at the front of the room. His gaze, usually warm, carried a heavier depth today as it swept across his students. The fine lines at the corners of his eyes made his expression even more earnest.

Everything that haunted him, everything that evaded him, everything that eluded him was right there before him, reflected in his students' faces. He had learned how to focus, how to bring himself back, how to remain present to what mattered.

Even so, as he had done so many times before, Daniel summoned the presence of mind and the quiet strength of spirit to stay here, now, with them, to keep teaching, to keep going, to keep drawing from the depth of what he knew was right, from the being within him that would not let him go.

Despite the hyperactivity of the teenagers sprawling across the desks, fidgeting, doodling, whispering secrets, Daniel felt for the quiet within him and found it, steady and familiar. It showed in his stillness, in the unhurried way he carried himself; his pressed khakis and crisp button-down shirt standing timelessly against the ripped jeans and band tees favored by his students.

He wasn't trying to be one of them but rather a lighthouse in their sometimes stormy teenage seas, a living extension of the stillness that had become his daily practice to keep alive within himself, one day, one step, one moment at a time.

Today it took more effort than usual, but he gathered himself, drawing again on the quiet discipline that never failed him.

"Alright, class, let's talk about Salinger," Daniel said. His calm, measured voice carried easily through the room, steadying even the most restless students as he settled into the familiar rhythm of the work he had come to love.

Moving to the blackboard, he picked up a piece of chalk and wrote the names Holden, Franny & Zooey in neat, controlled strokes across the center of the blackboard. The rhythmic tapping against the slate echoed in the sudden hush that had fallen over the room. Years of activism had instilled in him an almost theatrical sense of timing, knowing when to command attention and when to yield the floor. The cadence steadied him as he sank into the territory he knew best, and into the quiet remembrance of why he had chosen this school, this class, in the first place. Or perhaps, why it had chosen him.

"What do you think motivates these characters? Why do they feel such conflict within themselves and the world around them?" Daniel asked, inviting his students. Hands shot up across the room, a forest of eager limbs waving for his attention. Daniel's lips twitched into a small smile, silently acknowledging their enthusiasm.

Three years earlier, when he first entered Leominster High School as a substitute teacher, he discovered a passion for teaching. A year later, after accepting a full-time position, he began to wonder how such a rewarding career had evaded him for so long.

Now entering his fourth year of teaching, this year's class of incoming freshmen had quickly become one of his favorites. As he scanned the room, his gaze settled on a young woman near the center, known for her thoughtful observations, who had partially raised her hand.

"Please," Daniel urged her to share.

She hesitated for a while, but then began in a soft yet clear voice. "Do you think their privilege shapes their perspective on culture and society? Like, because they come from wealthy backgrounds, they might not understand the struggles of others?"

It was not lost on Daniel, or perhaps anyone in the class, that the question had come from the daughter of one of the wealthiest men in their predominantly working-class town.

"That's an interesting observation. Yes, for sure," Daniel remarked, carefully choosing his words as he scanned their faces. "These characters do hail from privilege, which undoubtedly colors their perspective. The disillusionment with society could partly stem from the sheltered environments in which they were raised. Thank you," he concluded, giving her a smile and a nod.

Daniel couldn't help but feel a tug of memory as he spoke. The mention of privilege and societal perspective triggered those faint echoes from his past, where discussions of privilege and power had been a daily part of his life. He pushed back the memories, working to keep a neutral expression while focusing on the students before him as he continued.

"It's also important to recognize that these narratives not only highlight unique social and economic backgrounds and present specific social and cultural perspectives, but they also vividly capture the experience of growing up influenced by, and possibly influencing, the world around us, regardless of the time period or economic circumstances of our upbringing."

The students seemed to be taking it in, their faces reflecting varying shades of thought. Daniel felt himself slipping back into that familiar, comforting space. Realizing he had a little more time, he asked softly, "Anyone else?"

Daniel couldn't help but notice the typically boisterous and vibrant center of the freshman football team sitting quietly in the back row with his teammates. Today, he uncharacteristically raised his hand with care, waiting to be acknowledged before asking his question.

"Go ahead, Mark." Daniel encouraged.

Mark Slate glanced at his teammates, and after a few moments, they nodded in support. He faced the front of the room and posed his question.

"I want to know what *you* think about these books, Mr. Eiman. You keep wanting to know what we think. But what do you think about them? They're clearly written in a completely different era, and they don't seem to me to be terribly relevant - No offense or anything."

Daniel shook his head, smiling to himself. "None taken."

While considering how to manage the apparent provocation, he observed the boy seated next to Mark in the back row. The boy's hair was a chaotic tangle, mirroring the confusion in his mind. His constant, growing restlessness had drawn Daniel's attention. When their gazes finally locked, Daniel unintentionally heightened the boy's increasing agitation by merely stating, "What!"

Usually preferring to stay quiet and in the background, Daniel and most of the class were shocked by what came out. "I think they're depressed! Clinically! All of them!" The boy's blunt comment, along with the abrupt way he delivered it, made half the class erupt into laughter, prompting the center of the football team and the other boys surrounding him to join in with their own disparaging comments.

Daniel's response was both immediate and genuine. "Unquestionably," He nodded to the class, signaling his agreement as they settled down. "But why? Why are these characters so depressed?"

Daniel paused, letting the question sink in.

Just as he was about to break the silence and continue, a popular girl, always the last to enter class and the first to leave, muttered to herself, but loud enough for a specific boy in the back row to hear, "Maybe he's depressed because he's playing too many video games, and his life is totally wasting away."

The boy sitting across from the disheveled boy, to whom the comment was clearly directed, shouted back. "Or maybe she's depressed from scrolling through Instagram, endlessly, constantly, all day long, comparing herself to a bunch of loser TikTok influencers she'll never be able to emulate in a million, trillion years!"

Suddenly, pandemonium erupted in the classroom as the girls surrounding the popular girl began shouting at the boys seated in the back. The boys, on the other hand, wasted no time retaliating with their own jibes, caricatures, and insults.

Daniel, along with the rest of the class, watched in amazement as the room devolved into complete chaos.

Daniel was instantly catapulted back into his own stormy youth, where his four brothers clashed with their girlfriends, and his mother joined the fray of relentless, fiery arguments. Each one fiercely protecting their own limited perspective, relentlessly dismissing or vehemently opposing anything and everything that came out of one another's mouths.

Witnessing the escalating disorder in his classroom, he could only shake his head in disbelief at the utter chaos that engulfed his class.

These incidents seemed to be happening more frequently, not just in his classroom but throughout the entire school. Young men were becoming increasingly reactive to harsh criticism and verbal jabs from young women, who appeared more visibly fiery and combative than ever before.

Daniel, both astonished and bemused by the whole scenario, silently shook his head, turned his back to the class, grabbed the chalk, and began writing on the blackboard. Above Holden, he wrote 'Luke Skywalker,' above 'Franny,' he wrote 'Princess Leia,' and above 'Zooey,' he wrote 'Han Solo.' Above their names, he wrote 'Obi-Wan Kenobi' and then next to him, 'Darth Vader.'

Over to the side, next to the Star Wars characters, he wrote 'Dorothy,' 'Scarecrow,' 'Tin Man,' 'Cowardly Lion,' and above them, he wrote 'Glinda,' the 'Wicked Witch,' and the 'Wizard of Oz.'

The steady rhythm of chalk against the blackboard clashed with the noise swelling in the back of the room. The boys' jeers, once playful, had sharpened into something harsher, aimed at the girls in front, who were now shrinking beneath it. The air turned volatile, on the brink of boiling over, when Mark Slate, eyes fixed on Mr. Eiman, sprang to his feet and cut through it in the way only he could: "Hey! Hey!! Hey!!! Hey!!! Hey!!!! Hey!!!!!"

The outburst jolted the room into silence. Even Daniel turned, eyes fixed on him, startled by the sheer audacity of it. With every face turned toward him, Mark said what was, to him, simply obvious: "I want to hear what he has to say."

The girls, with their cheeks reddened, eventually turned to face the front as the boisterous boys gradually calmed down. Before long, everyone's gaze was directed forward, though a few boys in the back couldn't help but exchange whispered comments, which drew soft chuckles from their friends and disapproving looks from the girls in front.

After offering Mark brief but silent acknowledgement, Daniel turned back to the blackboard and wrote 'Yoda' between the junior and senior Star Wars characters.

When he finally turned to face them, the students were exchanging glances, curious to see which surprising path Mr. Eiman would lead them down next.

Daniel maneuvered around his desk, stepping closer to them. For a moment, he and Mark shared a look, and in that simple, quiet exchange, a calm took hold, spreading until it enveloped the entire class.

"Look, Holden, Franny, and Zooey are fictional creations, and yes, these books were written during a different time, portraying what could be viewed as an outdated culture. And I had to ask myself: Why am I going to teach these now? How are they relevant today? Well, just look at yourselves," Daniel said. "Seriously, pay attention to how you're treating each other right now, this minute. It's not terribly different. The only difference is that women speak their minds instead of suffering silently."

"Franny may be thinking it," then, gesturing to the girls on the side by the door, "but you are all speaking it."

Then, eyeing the back row, "And you boys are reacting the same way, just using a different syntax."

"Syntax?" One of the boys in the back shouted out.

"Language structure, pattern, way of delivering your message." Daniel shot back.

Daniel paused to gather his thoughts before going ahead. "When I chose to introduce Salinger's work to this class, I had to reread these books myself. To my surprise, I discovered a significant theme I hadn't noticed the first time I read them at your age. An essential theme that completely eluded me until I revisited these books two months ago to prepare for this class."

Daniel nodded to the class, intentionally meeting the eyes of those who would look back.

"And I wondered, will they get it? Should I even try? Now, I may be twice your age chronologically. Still, in the grand scheme of things, I'm not that much older, not even a full generation," he added, nodding to them. "I'm not young enough to fully grasp the rapid pace of technology you all handle so easily. I am just old enough, however, to see the impact that it's having on you. To see what it's doing *to* you. You might not realize it now, but these themes that Salinger masterfully illustrates are still pertinent today. In fact, I believe they're more relevant now than ever before."

Daniel stepped back to the blackboard and picked up his pointer before turning back to the class. "Yes, these books were published a decade apart, starting in 1951. They will transport you to a different era when society and culture functioned in completely different, if not somewhat suppressed, ways. The canvas that Salinger paints is very different from what we experience today. But the underbelly of what these characters grapple with: depression, alienation, disillusionment, the search for meaning if not distraction, is all very real."

"Listen." Daniel deliberately made eye contact with everyone present, holding the gaze of those who returned it and, this time, lingering longer on those who tried to look away. When he spoke again, his voice became even gentler.

"Holden, Franny, and Zooey exhibit behaviors and thoughts that indicate they are grappling with deep and painful issues. Great literature reflects real-life challenges, and Salinger excels at portraying the intricate thoughts and emotions of young men and women."

All eyes remained glued to Daniel, listening, waiting; teenagers deep in thought. When he spoke again, his voice rounded into a tone he was hoping would convey his genuine empathy and understanding for each and every student in the room.

"It's not weapons and wars at our doorstep today. It's artificial intelligence, social media, TikTok, and, yes," he deliberately directed his comment to the boys in the back, "video games. What is your attention on and why? What's engaging your imagination and why? The dawning of the Industrial Age was exciting. The dawning of the information age was overwhelming. Whether you want to face it or not, what's happening here and now at the dawn of the AI age or cognitive era is downright terrifying. It may not seem so to you, but only because you have no idea what's been happening to you."

Daniel gestured to the blackboard. "Do these characters make more sense to you?"

The majority of the students returned his nod, while the boys seated at the back appeared to calm down, genuinely interested in what he would say next.

He pressed on, "What truly matters to you? Why? Where do your struggles lie? Why? Are you feeling down, and if so, why? What if the antidote to Artificial Intelligence is you? What if the solution to Artificial Intelligence is humanity itself? Are you prepared? Are any of us truly prepared? Do you even want to be?"

Daniel used his pointer to tap on Dorothy. "Centuries ago, Pliny the Elder told us that home is where the heart is. Where is home for you? The house I grew up in felt like a war zone, much like what just occurred in this classroom five minutes ago! It didn't feel like home to me. I had to find '*home*.'"

Daniel gently slid the pointer from 'Dorothy' to 'Yoda,' as he concluded. "I had to find *home inside* myself." After resting on 'Yoda' for effect, he purposefully slid the pointer back to 'Dorothy.'

After giving it time to sink in, he continued. "All of us, at some level, including Salinger and all of his characters, are trying to find - *home*."

Everyone in the room was focused on him. His passionate mix of compassion, authenticity, and genuineness had somehow successfully recaptured their attention.

He gently tapped Dorothy a couple more times before deliberately sliding the pointer to Scarecrow, then to Tin Man, and finally to Cowardly Lion as he continued, respectively, "What are your brain, your heart, and your courage focused on?" Then, pointing to the Wizard, he asked, "Is someone or something attempting to or successfully manipulating you from behind a curtain? Are you even aware that such a possibility exists? And if so, how? How might a wizard be manipulating you? Who are the wizards of today?"

With his patient nod and steady gaze, Daniel became the calm center of a swirling storm. Never had something seemed to matter so much to him. Never had he cared more.

"The question you want to be asking yourself is," he continued, "is this thing doing something *to* me? Or is it doing something *for* me? Is life doing something *to* you? Or is it unfolding *for* you? Are you even aware of such notions?"

Strategically moving his pointer over to Luke Skywalker. "Do you have the strength and the ability to draw the force to face your foes?" Then he pointed to Obi-Wan Kenobi, "How do you face your foes?" Next, he pointed to Darth Vader, "Who are your foes? Do you even want to face your foes? Do you even care?"

Just as Daniel was about to finish, the shrill ringing of the bell seemed louder than usual, startling half the class, all of whom were just sitting in their seats, staring up at him.

Once the bell's piercing shriek subsided, an all-consuming silence enveloped the room. A silence so complete that even the smallest sounds seemed loud, including the groaning of the aged wooden window frames and the soft creaking of chairs as students shifted in their seats without rising.

Daniel continued even softer, "Salinger has the answer. It's buried in these works. I want to see which one of you is savvy enough to figure it out and tell us. If you want. If not," he gestured to the popular girls, "enjoy Instagram, TikTok and," pointing to the boys in the back row, "your video games. The choice is yours. That is, if you even have a choice. Do you? Do any of us? And if we have a choice, where does that choice exist?" He then maneuvered the pointer back and began tapping over and over on the printed name of 'Yoda' as he repeated, "Where does that choice exist?"

Usually, the ringing of the class bell triggered a swift shift from minor commotion to major chaos, with students scrambling over one another and their desks to escape the classroom. Today, however, was different. Today, his students were captivated by the front of the classroom, their eyes darting back and forth between Daniel and the name 'Yoda' in print. Many were completely immobilized, caught in a state of utter disbelief.

Daniel's intense gaze melted as he softened, and a genuine smile spread across his face. He opened his arms, a gesture of acquiescence. "Okay, you can go now. The bell has rung. Class dismissed. Go on, get out of here."

Daniel chuckled quietly as he observed the surprise on his students' faces gradually shifting back to their typical, albeit slightly more subdued, expressions. The sounds of backpacks being zipped, chairs sliding on the floor, and soft conversations slowly became livelier as they gathered their belongings and exited the classroom, murmuring to themselves and each other as they left.

Daniel turned his attention back to the script on the blackboard, carefully erasing each name one at a time and leaving 'Dorothy' for last. After slowly erasing her name, he returned the frayed eraser to its ledge, shaking his head with a smile.

Engrossed in deep contemplation and introspection, he was closing his satchel when he suddenly noticed someone standing in front of his desk.

The classroom had emptied, but a fourteen-year-old boy, awkwardly lanky with octopus-like limbs, a face dotted with acne, and a mouth full of braces, was standing in front of his desk.

Usually acutely aware of anyone in or near his immediate vicinity, Daniel was shocked to realize that not only had Benjamin McCray been standing there, but he appeared to have been patiently waiting the entire time.

"I'm sorry, Benjamin, I didn't realize you were there. What's up?"

Benjamin's mouth opened and closed a few times before he found his voice. "Is it...true?" Benjamin stammered, his voice barely above a whisper. "You used to be in some sort of... politics?"

Daniel remained motionless, unable to meet Benjamin's gaze, as he was hurled back into his past for the third time in less than an hour. This time, he felt powerless against the surge of memories that yanked him to that period he had spent the last six years attempting to purge from his heart and soul. It felt like trying to halt a torrent of water with just his hands as he desperately battled against the unyielding current pulling him back. At the same time, memories burst through the fragile defenses of his closely guarded, not-so-distant past. It was no longer his nightmare. It was his reality, one he was beginning to realize was never going to leave him.

*****

It was high noon, and the grand marble steps of the Capitol Building shimmered under the bright Washington sunlight. People poured out of the doors; Congressional aides, lobbyists, and politicians alike, swarming like bees around a flower. At the center of the buzz stood a younger Daniel Eiman, just twenty-six, his long hair brushing the collar of his shirt. He soaked in the attention like a natural-born politician, his face alive with energy as he shook hands and exchanged congratulatory slaps on the back.

To his right, Marty Chambers, brash, sharp-witted, and always looking as though she had just stepped off a 1940s movie set, stood with a cigarette dangling from her fingertips. Despite her femininity, there was something unyielding about her, a fierceness that kept people at arm's length. She surveyed the crowd with detached amusement, her gaze drifting down to the parking lot below.

Leaning against his dusty white truck was the object of both their affection. Tall and muscular, with sun-bleached hair, Andrew Steadman exuded a quiet strength. The kind that came from being raised in the aristocratic social elite. He stood with his arms crossed, watching the spectacle with indifference as if none of it mattered to him. This seeming indifference seemed to dampen Daniel's spirits until supporters in the crowd enveloped him once more, highlighted by Charlie Atwood, a fireplug of a man, all stocky muscle and uncontainable energy, wrapping an arm around Daniel and pulling him into a mock headlock.

"Daniel, my man! Unbelievable. Congrats, bud." Charlie bellowed, his voice loud enough to cut through the crowd's din. Brent Evans, a former teammate of Daniel and Andrew, who was now a stunningly handsome, Eurasian lawyer-turned-activist, joined in. "You did it, man! You're a miracle worker!" Brent said, ruffling Daniel's hair like an older brother would. Daniel laughed, his shirt becoming increasingly disheveled as more people fought to congratulate him. It was a victory lap of sorts, and he basked in it.

That was up until Marty Chambers, always the realist, turned her full attention to him. Her face darkened as she blew cigarette smoke into the sky, purposefully just missing his face. "It's unethical, Daniel. Digging into people's private lives like that," she said, her voice sharp and cutting.

Daniel's expression hardened as he straightened his shirt, which was continually being tugged and grabbed by well-wishers. "You need to quit smoking, Marty. It's unladylike!"

The two had squared off, the tension between them palpable. "It was a win, Marty!" Daniel couldn't have been more direct.

"At what cost? She flicked ash toward the marble steps. "You dug into his private life."

Daniel straightened his tie. "He's a public figure."

Marty stepped closer. "He's a person."

It hit; of course, it did, coming from her, but he didn't back off. If anything, it clarified things. "And the public has a right to know," he said, his voice quiet but confident.

Marty studied him. "Be careful, Daniel. Sometimes the truth burns everyone."

There was a certain brashness reminiscent of Lauren Bacall about this sophisticated creature whom Daniel had somehow come to love and respect. As the prodigal daughter of Massachusetts' first female governor, albeit Republican, there was much to admire about Marty, aside from the fact that they were staunch political rivals.

Andrew loved her almost more than life itself, and Daniel had often wondered if they might have become a thing had Marty gotten to him first.

Andrew always insisted, "Never!" But Andrew and Marty sure did love and respect each other. It was, after all, Daniel who had introduced Marty to Andrew.

"You're gay?!" Marty's shock at learning of Andrew's proclivities had genuinely stunned her.

"Yes!" Andrew had responded emphatically.

"What a waste! What a complete and total waste!" Marty had retorted. Then, pointing to Daniel, "And him? Why him?"

Daniel could only shake his head. It was just as big a mystery to him, if not more so.

"Oh yeah," Andrew had said as he pulled Daniel closer, planting the wettest, juiciest kiss on Daniel's mouth that he could muster.

Utterly embarrassed by the entire exchange, Daniel tried to wipe the excess saliva from his mouth discreetly, but to no avail. Andrew, who seemed to exude excess fluid from all his orifices, had grabbed Daniel and kissed him even wetter. Proudly for everyone to see.

Daniel could have done without much of Andrew's public displays of affection. However, it was Andrew's way of marking his territory for the whole world to see, and it was a small price to pay for all he had received in exchange from Andrew.

But here, Daniel and Marty were again, face to face, this time on the steps of the Capitol Building. More than anything, Daniel wanted to ease the sting that the whole scenario was causing.

But before he could offer an olive branch, Marty turned on her heel and descended the steps with a cool elegance that only she possessed, heading down to Andrew. Daniel watched as Marty greeted Andrew with a kiss on one cheek, affectionately patting his other cheek before striding away.

The radiance of Daniel's hard-earned win slowly diminished as he watched Andrew make his way around to the driver's side of his truck. Neither looked back nor uttered a word. The crowd may have continued to press around him, celebrating the victory in their own way, but Daniel's thoughts remained with Andrew until he managed to pull away from the chaos and head toward the truck, following Andrew's lead.

As Daniel and Andrew left the Capitol parking lot, the late afternoon sun dipped below the Washington skyline. The bustle continued behind them, but the euphoria of a political victory rapidly faded for Daniel, like the last rays of light descending towards their fate beyond the horizon.

The drive home felt longer than usual, even though the streets of Georgetown were not far from the Capitol. They traveled through the familiar routes, past the grand old houses with their brick facades and ivy-covered walls. Then they passed the historic rowhouses that gave the neighborhood its charm.

Daniel sat in the passenger seat, his eyes shifting between the passing scenery and Andrew's stoic profile. The hum of the engine and the rhythmic thumping of the tires against the asphalt filled the silence, creating a steady backdrop for the thoughts swirling in Daniel's mind.

It wasn't the first time they had sat in silence after an event like this. But this time, something felt different, heavier. The streets, usually bustling with joggers, dog walkers, and students from nearby Georgetown University, seemed eerily still. Daniel could feel the tension tightening in his chest, an invisible thread pulling at the space between him and Andrew. He shifted in his seat, wanting to say something to bridge the growing chasm, but the words wouldn't come.

For six years, Daniel and Andrew had been inseparable. Since the moment they met, really.

Billionaire Myles Steadman had insisted that his son be allowed to commute to campus from their Central Park West brownstone, but Columbia University wouldn't permit it. The university accepted that one of their wealthiest alumni's sons could live off-campus during his freshman year; however, the swimming coach refused to grant Andrew special treatment, no matter whose son he was.

Andrew couldn't have cared less. He'd had roommates at Groton, and as far as he was concerned, he could easily share a room or two at Columbia. It might even be fun. He'd never cared for the pampering his self-made father insisted on. As the only boy in a household of six children, Andrew had been doted on by maids, a governess, tutors, and his mother, until her sudden, unexpected death, along with five older sisters, the youngest of whom was seven years older than he was.

Once all concerned parties agreed that it would be acceptable for Andrew to have one roommate on campus for the first semester, with the caveat that he would be allowed to live wherever he wanted afterward, a deal was crafted. Everything went according to plan until that first day when Andrew walked into his new dorm room to find Daniel Eiman unpacking.

Andrew had just stood there, staring across at Daniel in a way that made Daniel incredibly uncomfortable.

After several moments, Andrew warmly extended his hand. "I'm sorry, Andrew. Andrew Steadman. Nice to meet you."

Andrew's grip caught Daniel off guard. It was firm, firmer than usual, and Andrew's hand felt hot. Not just warm, but heat-generating hot. And more than a little sweaty.

Daniel didn't want to be rude, so he waited to wipe the sweat off his hands until Andrew looked away.

But in a flash, Andrew turned back and stared at Daniel for what felt like an eternity.

"Should we go eat?" Andrew finally offered, breaking the awkward silence. "I'm starving."

Daniel looked at his watch, trying to figure out exactly how to respond. Eventually, he eased out, "Don't we have practice in like half an hour?"

Andrew quickly looked at his watch, chuckling to himself and shaking his head. "Oh, right, of course. My bad."

Andrew just kept staring. Daniel went back to unpacking until he found the courage to face Andrew again.

"Dude, you are ridiculously handsome. Like stop-me-in-my-tracks handsome," Andrew had blurted out.

"Ummm, thanks. I guess." The statement had genuinely caught Daniel off guard. "Ahhh, you're very handsome yourself." He offered back.

"You don't have to say that." Andrew countered.

"Well, you really *are* very good-looking as well," Daniel smiled back.

"Thanks." Andrew nodded as he spoke. Then he clarified, more for himself than Daniel, "I mean, I'm not gay or anything. But there's just something about you. Do you believe in past lives?"

"Ummm…" The question seemed totally out of the blue, completely catching Daniel off guard. He could only shake his head and shrug, saying, "I don't know; never really thought about it."

In the awkward silence that followed, Daniel nodded, shrugged again, and returned to unpacking his suitcase, trying to conceal his unease. As the middle child of five sons, Daniel had never felt that he stood out to anyone, nor had he ever understood what exactly Andrew saw in him over the years. But it felt good to receive the attention; that was for sure.

Andrew swam only the butterfly stroke; it was the only one that interested him. Unlike Andrew, Daniel specialized in the backstroke but also competed in the individual medley. Although his breaststroke was weak, his backstroke compensated for it. Over time, he gradually improved in all strokes, gaining both skill and confidence.

It always helped to have Andrew within peripheral vision. They each swam their respective strokes in the medley relay, and from the moment they met, it felt as though Andrew never left Daniel's side.

Andrew gripped the steering wheel tightly, his knuckles whitening under the strain. He wasn't angry, Daniel knew that much, but disappointment radiated from him in waves. It was the kind of quiet disapproval that didn't need to be spoken to be felt.

As they approached the familiar stretch of M Street, lined with upscale shops and boutiques, Daniel finally spoke. His voice was low, almost swallowed by the sound of the truck's engine. "Andrew, can you tell me what's going on?"

Andrew didn't answer right away. Instead, he stopped the truck at a red light, where the late afternoon sun cast a faint glow across his face. His expression remained unreadable, and his eyes were focused straight ahead. After what felt like an eternity, Andrew's response was measured and calm. "I just don't want you to lose sight of what matters most to you, Daniel. This... all of this... It's starting to consume you."

The light turned green, and the truck lurched forward once more. Daniel turned his head, watching as the storefronts blurred past outside his window. He recognized that Andrew was not wrong. The politics, the power plays, and the endless meetings had a way of creeping in, taking more than they contributed. *But wasn't that the price one paid for trying to change the world? For standing up for something?*

They turned onto the quiet side street leading to their brownstone, where the old brick buildings cast long shadows across the narrow road. Andrew parked the truck in its usual spot, the tires crunching over the loose gravel of the driveway. For a moment, neither of them moved. The engine ticked softly as it cooled, and the familiar creak of the house settling into the evening echoed faintly in the stillness.

That evening, in the cozy bedroom of their Georgetown brownstone, the soft glow of the bedside lamps bathed the room in warm light. The space perfectly blended Andrew's love for Southwestern decor with Daniel's eclectic taste in art. Their oak branch bed stood proudly against the exposed brick wall, while framed photographs of their six years together were scattered across the room: hiking in the Rockies, laughing at a bonfire, winning a local charity competition. It was their sanctuary, filled with memories.

But tonight, it felt different.

Daniel sat on the edge of the bed, his face buried in his hands. Standing just in front of him by the window, Andrew stared into the quiet streets below, his back to Daniel.

Daniel gathered the courage to look up. Then, speaking to Andrew's back, "For six years, it's been all about you, Andrew. For once, something's finally happening for me. Can't you be happy about it?"

Andrew turned and stared across the silence at Daniel.

"Andrew, I know I'm usually very good at reading your mind, but for some reason, right now, I'm having a problem with it!"

Andrew stepped into Daniel's face. "My point exactly!" Andrew's words felt like a sucker punch to Daniel as he dejectedly shook his head.

"Look, it was my idea that you become an activist, Daniel. And I was right, you're good at it. Hell, you are great at it. People bend over backward for you and don't even know why. Now, I know this feels like life and death to you, these rights that we're fighting for. I want them too! We all do. It's just… don't let it get bigger than you are. It's all starting to go to your head."

Daniel fought with every ounce of energy not to burst into tears and start sobbing. He stared down at the floor, fighting back the flood of emotion that clawed at his throat.

He didn't even notice Andrew had slid onto the bed beside him.

"Let it come to you, Daniel. And it will. I promise. Everything you want will come to you."

"I don't have your life, Andrew."

Andrew circled Daniel's heart, waiting until Daniel's eyes met his. "Everything."

With that, Andrew vaulted back to his side of the bed, stripped, and slid under the covers. He pulled back the bedding on Daniel's side, motioning him over. "Just a quick nap. Tonight's going to be long and arduous."

"Yeah, well, duty calls, right? What time are you heading out?" Daniel asked, trying to lift the mood as he began undressing. He froze mid-motion when Andrew said, "As soon as the council meeting ends."

"No, Andrew, you're not coming to the council meeting." Daniel shot across at him. "You're going to your sister's birthday party!"

Andrew met Daniel with that mischievous smirk that signaled something seemingly sinister that always turned out to be fun. "Change of plans."

"Andrew, I promised them! I promised them you would go. Becky is finally warming up to me after all these years, and I promised her. And you did, too. I heard you promise her!"

"And I will go. As soon as Harvey makes his statement, I'll leave. Nothing is going to start before 9 or 10 anyway. It'll be fine. Becky will be fine."

"Andrew, please!"

"No! Let it go, Daniel! This is one of those times you need to let it go!" Andrew insisted.

"I promise I'll be gentle with Harvey." Daniel pleaded. "You don't have to supervise me."

"I think I do." There was an increasing edge to Andrew's tone.

Daniel shook his head, staring across at Andrew in utter disbelief.

"Just please let it go." Andrew reiterated, "Everything's going to work out perfectly." Then, softening, "I'm on your side, Daniel. I'm always on your side. Do you trust that I'm on your side?"

"No! Not at this moment. It does not feel like you're on my side." Daniel's words, meant to harm only, softened Andrew.

"I'm on your side. I will always be on your side." Although meant to be disarming and reassuring, Andrew's words only made Daniel worry more. He shook his head as he stripped naked and slid into bed next to Andrew.

Andrew pulled him close.

Daniel closed his eyes, surrendering to Andrew's embrace. The day's weight lifted momentarily as the world outside disappeared.

*****

Meanwhile, back in Daniel's Leominster High School classroom, Benjamin McCray stared at him. Daniel's eyes were open, but they appeared glazed over. Benjamin had no idea where he had gone, but suddenly, it felt like Mr. Eiman wasn't even there.

Daniel was still lost in the memories of him and Andrew in their Georgetown brownstone six years prior. As dusk turned to night, his eyes snapped open. Reaching for the clock, he flew out of bed. "Oh my God, I'm late." Andrew sat up in bed, trying to get his bearings as Daniel threw on his clothes, tripping and almost falling in the rush.

"What's going on?" Andrew climbed out of bed, caught up in the chaos, trying to get his bearings.

"I'm late. I'm going to be late. You and your fucking naps!" Daniel struggled to collect everything he needed.

"Shit!" Andrew flew into motion, reaching for and pulling on his clothes.

"You're not coming with me, Andrew!" Daniel was emphatic.

"Daniel, you have to let this go."

"You're such an asshole sometimes."

"I love you, too!"

Daniel grabbed the One United Territory binder and flew out the door, Andrew on his heels.

Night settled over the rural Virginia town like a heavy blanket, cloaking the makeshift auditorium in shadow. The structure, cobbled from aged wood and corrugated metal, stood like a lone sentinel beneath the star-streaked sky. Lanterns glowed dimly at the entrance, casting uneasy shadows across the cracked pavement.

Daniel, Andrew, Charlie, and Brent moved with quiet purpose, their footsteps crunching on gravel the only sound in the stillness. Ahead, four associates, two men and two women who had stood with them at the Capitol, led the way, still offering congratulations for Daniel's victory. To any onlooker, their faces would have read as one: focused, determined, ready.

Just as the eight of them rounded the sidewalk, the roar of an engine shattered the stillness. A black SUV, sleek and menacing in the moonlight, screeched into the parking lot, its tires spitting gravel. The car's polished surface gleamed ominously, reflecting the cold light of the stars. Five rowdy skinhead college boys tumbled out, their raucous laughter cutting through the night like a knife. Their faces were flushed with a toxic mix of arrogance and alcohol, and their eyes gleamed with cruel intent.

"Hey, watch where you're going!" one of them shouted, his voice dripping with mockery as they nearly collided with Daniel and Brent.

Daniel's jaw tightened, his muscles coiling like a spring. Without a word, he uncharacteristically shoved the boy closest to him away, his eyes blazing with fury. The boy stumbled back, surprise and anger flashing across his face. Sensing the impending explosion, Andrew stepped between Daniel and the skinheads, his posture protective and unyielding. The tension was a palpable force that held everyone in its grip.

For a moment, it seemed violence was inevitable, but the skinheads, perhaps recognizing the danger in Andrew's gaze, backed off, muttering insults under their breath.

Inside the auditorium, the atmosphere was thick with anticipation. The room was a contrast to the outside world, a hub of quiet tension and whispered conversations. Dark eyes darted behind black-rimmed glasses, assessing the room with a mixture of caution and curiosity. Harvey, a local physician turned volunteer politician, stood at the center of this storm. At forty-seven, Harvey was balding and sharply groomed, his stiff white shirt and bow tie giving him an air of meticulous authority. He surveyed the room, intentionally avoiding Daniel, who had stepped in front of him with a determined expression. Andrew stood behind Daniel, a silent pillar of support. Just beyond them, Brent, Charlie, and their four associates chatted among themselves. Their conversation was a low murmur against the rural voices surrounding them.

The room was filled with purposeful men and women clustered around a head table. Aged steel microphones glistened under the harsh fluorescent lights. Meeting participants navigated through, embodying the community's easy, down-home charm. It would take an avalanche to excite them, even if a sense of anticipation hung heavy in the air on this night.

Daniel stepped closer to Harvey, gesturing sweepingly toward the room. "I think those are some of the friendliest faces I've ever seen, Harvey," he remarked, his voice tinged with irony.

Harvey's eyes wavered with uncertainty. He was a man caught between two worlds: the serene life of a rural doctor and the turbulent waters of local politics.

The meeting room participants gathered around the head table. Rural throwbacks to another time, they greeted each other in a slow, down-home way that spoke of long-standing community ties.

Daniel's voice softened, but his determination did not. "You're not just their councilman, Harvey. You're their doctor. You went to Harvard. You're their star. Their bright and shiny star."

Andrew's voice, an intense whisper, cut through the unspoken growing tension between them. "Daniel."

Daniel turned to face Andrew, whose expression had taken on an edge. Daniel changed his tone but not his tact. "They're trying to outlaw you, Harvey. They want to outlaw you but don't really know you, do they?"

"Daniel!" Andrew's voice was sharper now, urgent.

Harvey, glistening with sweat, extracted a handkerchief and swiped it across his brow. The room seemed to close in around Harvey. The weight of expectations and fears pressed down on him heavily.

In the meantime, unbridled passion had Daniel by the throat, a sharp contrast to Andrew, who stepped closer to Harvey, softening the exchange and becoming gentler. Easing himself between Daniel and Harvey, Andrew's words were both gentle and firm. Andrew was facing Harvey but talking to Daniel, "Don't worry about it, Harvey. We'll do it another day. Whenever you're ready," he said, his eyes now fixated on Daniel. "Whenever you're ready."

Harvey headed towards the front, his footsteps echoing in the hushed room. As he got out of earshot, Daniel turned to Andrew, his frustration boiling over. "He's ready now!"

"Keep your voice down," Andrew cautioned, his tone steady but firm.

Rural eyes lingered; the exchange piqued their curiosity. Daniel turned his back on the room, his face a mask of barely suppressed anger. "That man has lived here for thirty-five years, Andrew. His whole life. He is their hero."

Andrew's voice was calm and measured. "When he's ready. That's our deal. He's not ready!"

"Yes, he is!" Daniel insisted, his voice rising.

"No, he's not!" Andrew's retort was equally forceful.

The tension between Andrew and Daniel crackled like a live wire. They crossed to the back of the room, where Charlie, Brent, and the four associates had saved chairs for them.

Despite their effort to dress down and blend in, their city styles stood out, sweltering through the rural backdrop. Up front, Harvey took his place behind the center microphone, his posture tense but resolute.

Charlie made room for Andrew and Daniel, who wound up between the two women. Brent leaned in, his curiosity evident. "When's he going to do it?"

Andrew's response was terse. "He changed his mind."

Charlie's eyes widened in disbelief. "What do you mean he changed his mind?"

One of the female associates gestured across the room, where the five skinhead college boys leaned against the wall, their eyes fixed on the eight city slickers with predatory intensity.

Andrew scanned the room. Volleying looks between Andrew, Daniel, and the skinhead boys. Wary locals looked back, exchanging uneasy glances among themselves and with each other.

Andrew's voice was low but insistent. "Maybe you guys should head back now. We'll meet you at O'Sauls at ten."

"No, you won't be going to O'Sauls, Andrew, because you're leaving for your sister's birthday party right now!" Daniel glanced at his watch, a trace of worry spreading across his face. Then he turned to the others. "I'll meet you at eleven," then, putting his full attention on Andrew and insisting, "because Andrew's leaving right now."

Charlie, his stubbornness evident, shook his head. "I'm going to hang."

Brent nodded in agreement. "Me too."

"I'm going to hang, too!" Andrew retorted.

Andrew watched as their associates reluctantly exited. Their departure telegraphed a quiet concession to the escalating tension. He then looked across at the skinhead college boys who also had their eyes on the departing city slickers. All of this gave Andrew pause.

Daniel glared across at Andrew, who responded, "Something's not right here. I'm not going anywhere. Let it go."

Exasperated, Daniel turned away, shaking his head.

An hour and a half later, as the meeting ended, participants poured out. The room was empty, save for a handful of teenagers bantering about sports while they dismantled tables and stacked chairs.

By the door, Daniel stood silently beside Andrew and Charlie, their expressions a mix of anticipation and exhaustion. Harvey lingered a few feet away, still engaged in conversation with lingering council members. The faint rustle of papers and muted laughter from the teens created a strange juxtaposition to the unspoken tension in the air.

The outer door creaked open, and a gust of cold air swept through. Brent stepped inside, shaking off the chill. "The coast is clear," he said, his voice low but steady. "They seem to be gone."

As Harvey approached, his steps slow and hesitant, Andrew's tone lightened, though it couldn't hide the edge beneath. "Harvey, where's your car?"

Harvey gestured vaguely toward the back of the building, his gaze darting toward the windows as though expecting someone.

Daniel, breaking his quiet demeanor, offered a warm smile. "We'll walk him over there."

Andrew nodded. "I'll pull the truck around front."

Not missing a beat, Brent added, "I'll come with you."

Andrew turned to Daniel with a grin. "Give me your jacket."

Daniel hesitated, pulling the collar tighter around himself. "It's freezing out, dude," he protested, but relented with a sigh, handing it over.

"Exactly," Andrew said, smirking into the jacket. "I'll take that hat too."

Before Daniel could react, Andrew snatched the hat off Daniel's head and pulled the black O.U.T. binder from his grasp. Leaning in close, Andrew whispered for Daniel's ears alone, "Be nice."

Daniel shook his head, watching Andrew and Brent enter the cold. "Turn the heat on, full blast," Daniel had called after them.

Harvey, flanked by Daniel and Charlie, watched Brent and Andrew exit. Charlie pointed at the side wall where the skinheads had been standing, then turned to Harvey. "Who were those guys?"

"Never saw them before," Harvey replied, his voice tinged with unease.

Charlie's uncertainty deepened, but Daniel shrugged it off, his bravado masking his own conflicting emotions.

They crossed toward the rear side door, Daniel forcing a semblance of good humor. "You were great up there, Harvey. How long have you lived here?"

Harvey's smile was faint but genuine. "All my life. Except for college and medical school."

"Wow. They must really love you here," Charlie said, his tone admiring.

Daniel rolled his eyes at Charlie, who ignored him as he wrapped an arm around Harvey. "Next time. We'll get them next time, Harvey."

Just as they reached the side entrance, their conversation was cut short as a teenager burst through the door. His face was plastered with horror. The boy's eyes were wide, his breath coming in sharp, panicked gasps.

Daniel and Charlie, sensing something was terribly wrong, tore across the hall and past the boy out into the cold night. The boy stared after them, his horror mirrored in Harvey's eyes.

As Daniel finally succeeded in dragging himself away from the brink of the looming chasm, Harvey's perplexed gaze shifted to Benjamin's bewildered eyes. The gymnasium, which had been repurposed as a meeting room, was transformed into his classroom, and he was once again able to concentrate fully on the here and now.

He was most struck by the afternoon sunlight streaming through the tall classroom windows, casting a glow just behind Benjamin. As he concentrated on the suspended particles of chalk dust drifting within it, Daniel felt his frazzled nerves gradually begin to settle.

He paused briefly to gather his thoughts before focusing entirely on Benjamin. Despite feeling like it had all happened only yesterday, what came out of his mouth was, "That was a lifetime ago, Benjamin. Right now, I'm your English teacher."

Benjamin McCray was also fighting to reorient himself. His unruly hair, slightly too long for his age, hung over his forehead as he shifted nervously from one foot to the other.

Daniel watched as his gaze dropped to the floor, then back up, gathering his courage. His words stumbled over themselves as he tried to form the question hanging in the air between them: "I—I... Are you...? Are you...?"

Daniel tilted his head slightly, watching the boy. He wasn't impatient, but he could feel Benjamin might need encouragement to get out whatever it was he was fighting to.

Stepping around his desk, Daniel gently placed his hands on Benjamin's narrow shoulders, his touch light in his silent attempt to offer encouragement. He waited until Benjamin's eyes met his before leaning in closer, offering more reassurance by gripping his shoulders just a little tighter. "Am I... what, Benjamin?"

Benjamin's face flushed red, his eyes darting to the open windows across the illuminated rows of blond wood desks, where all day, students had been feverishly scribbling notes. Now, the desks were empty, and the room had fallen into a quiet stillness, save for the muted sounds of teenagers cavorting in the schoolyard outside.

Summoning courage, Benjamin looked back, searching Daniel's eyes, "Are you... are you gay?" he finally blurted out, his voice still barely above a whisper.

The question hung in the air like a stone dropped into still water.

Daniel immediately yanked his hands off Benjamin's shoulders and stepped back. For a split second, his eyes shot to the classroom door, checking if anyone had seen or overheard. The clock's ticking on the wall echoed loudly in their sudden tension. Outside, a group of students seemed to have gathered just outside Daniel's classroom window. They were laughing, their voices carefree, seemingly oblivious to the weight of the question inside.

Daniel tried his hardest to look composed. Then, taking a long, drawn-out breath, he inched closer to Benjamin again, hoping to mitigate the effects of his sudden and abrupt reaction. "What's going on, Benjamin?" Daniel asked softly.

Benjamin's face flushed deep crimson. "I... I'm sorry. I'm really sorry." Without waiting for a response, Benjamin turned on his heel and rushed out, leaving Daniel stunned and standing alone in the quiet classroom.

Daniel's eyes remained glued to the door as it closed behind Benjamin. Afterward, he surveyed the classroom's desks and chairs as if answers would somehow magically appear from them.

He then realized that the chatter outside in the schoolyard had stopped. Daniel intentionally focused on the group of students he had seen earlier outside. This time, he noticed that one of them had angled his phone to record the activities occurring inside.

Daniel's mind began racing. Were they filming them? Had they seen what was happening inside? "Fuck!" Daniel thought to himself.

Daniel nervously collected himself and his satchel and headed for the staff room, slipping through the door as inconspicuously as possible. Thankfully, his friends and coworkers were engrossed in their daily routines, entirely unaware of the mounting concern that continued to brew inside him.

The English composition teacher hunched over a desk piled high with essays. Her red pen darted across the pages, leaving a trail of corrections behind. An improvised fence surrounded her personal space, which included a stack of textbooks with spines old and cracked from countless semesters.

The science teacher stood by the window; his boisterous voice and lively movements filled the small space effortlessly. He and the gym coach were engaged in a heated argument, interspersed with playful shoves and fits of laughter. Daniel quietly moved through them to his own corner: a tiny nook tucked between a shelf full of paperbacks with ear creases and a dusty filing cabinet.

The alcove reflected his style, featuring a weathered wooden desk, an easy yet supportive chair, and a few necessities: a well-used laptop, a stack of notebooks filled with his scrawled handwriting, and a cracked mug bearing a passage from To Kill a Mockingbird.

With a faint thud, Daniel placed his leather satchel down beside him and slid into his chair. The familiar creak seemed to offer him a soothing presence. He delved into the bottom drawer for a file, only to feel something unexpected beneath his fingers.

Daniel pulled the object out. A sudden wave of shock briefly stopped his breath as he realized it was a faded, tattered picture of Andrew, his arm wrapped around a younger version of himself, as the proud pair stood in front of their Harlem brownstone. His iconic broad smile split Andrew's face as they posed for the camera.

Another cherished photo was stuck behind it. Andrew and Daniel had been captured in an unguarded moment of pure joy at a friend's dinner party. Their faces crinkled with delight and laughter.

"Hey, Daniel, everything alright?" The English comp teacher's perceptive voice sliced through the veil of distant memories, snapping Daniel back to the present again. He looked up to find her peering at him with a concerned frown etched on her usually friendly face.

"Yeah, just... old memories," Daniel replied, forcing a smile as he tucked the photos back into the drawer, hoping he'd successfully masked the tumult now beginning to gnaw at him. He closed the drawer with a soft click as if sealing away a time capsule.

The science teacher looked over, briefly diverted by the interaction. "Everything alright, Daniel?" he inquired, his tone genuine but still tinged with a bit of playful teasing.

"Just some old photos," Daniel offered, his tone casual, hoping to deflect any further attention from himself. "Just some old photos," he repeated, more to himself than to anyone.

The staff room continued to reflect the usual end-of-day energy. But Daniel was somewhere else, his mind caught in the web of memories he had spent the last six years desperately trying to forget actions taken and not taken as a result of his enthusiastic, seemingly uncontrollable impulsiveness. Andrew's voice echoed in Daniel's mind, "Do you think you could maybe think before you leap? Just, you know, maybe once in a while." The thing Andrew loved the most about Daniel also seemed to be the thing he disliked the most about him. Daniel found himself engulfed by a flood of unwelcome memories until the English Composition teacher suddenly jolted him back to reality once more.

"See you tomorrow, then," she called out as she headed for the door.

"Yeah, see you. Safe travels," Daniel called after her, offering a small wave as he packed up for the day and headed toward the hallway himself. The school was quieter now; the chaotic setting had been replaced by the distant hum of cleaning staff and the occasional echo of a closing locker.

Daniel made his way to the parking lot. Each step suddenly felt like a minor effort. His automobile, an ancient black Saab, stood alone in the bright sunlight of the late afternoon. As he arrived, he paused briefly to absorb the tranquility of the nearly empty lot. The car door creaked slightly when he opened it and slid into the driver's seat. The familiar scent of worn leather and subtle remnants of days gone by offered some consolation.

Daniel turned the key, hoping the quiet hum of the engine would soothe his mind, but it did not. As he drove out of the parking lot, he replayed the day's events. The classroom conversation had been stimulating and reminded him of why he enjoyed teaching so much. However, he had clearly left the class in shock, and he wondered if he had perhaps taken it all a bit too far. Then, the encounter with Benjamin added weight to an ever-increasing sense of responsibility. *Was he ever going to learn to pull back? Why had he touched him? Why?*

Seeing those old photos of Andrew and recalling the day he was so intent on forgetting triggered emotions he hoped were long gone. *Had those kids seen his interaction with Benjamin? Could they have recorded it?*

Daniel navigated the winding road, longing to silence the increasing chatter that filled his mind. "Deep breaths," Andrew used to always say to him. "Just close your eyes, imagine me lying next to you, and take deep breaths until it passes. Let it pass, my sweet prince. Let it pass." God, he missed Andrew.

The strong afternoon sunlight illuminated the colonial-style homes, emphasizing the white fences and well-kept lawns. They would soon be filled with leaves beckoning toward autumn as mid-September approached. He tried to shake off the multitude of unwanted thoughts and replace them with more comforting ones, like reminding himself of one of his favorite aspects of teaching: getting off work early in the afternoon.

The breeze blew gently along the road. Tall maple trees swayed softly as their leaves danced with the balmy afternoon breeze. On either side, the walkways were lined with tiny, quaint stores. Their windows displayed a smattering of faded beach and pool toys, now on clearance, alongside mannequins wearing light sweaters and jackets, hinting at the arrival of the cooler weather Daniel always appreciated.

Breathing as deeply as he could, imagining Andrew's presence right by his side, was not working. No matter how beautiful the scenery was, despite mid-September's reach toward October being his favorite time of year, Daniel's mind was far away, battling the demons of his past.

Had he done it again? Had he crossed that line? Had he let his passion take control? What was he thinking? Had he even been thinking? He only wanted to help. Did his kids understand the layers of everything he was trying to convey to them?

Slowly approaching the turn where the oak-lined trees would usually guide him back to Amherst, he turned instead onto Route 2 and headed towards Boston.

Brent Evans always knew what to do. Even though it had been three years since they last spoke, Daniel was sure Brent would help him; after all, Brent had always been the kind of person Daniel could rely on in times like these.

Lost in the noise and commotion of Storrow Drive, Daniel's Saab headed toward Cambridge. Shortly after, as he turned onto a familiar street, reality hit him.

He loved his teaching job. Could something as simple as this cost him his position? Certainly, they would understand. Would they? He probably shouldn't have put his hands on Benjamin. That likely wasn't the right thing to do. He tried to shake it all off, but past experiences wouldn't let him.

By luck, there was a parking spot right in front, just behind the handicapped space. The front window proudly displayed the arched lettering: Brent Evans, Attorney at Law. The once-newly installed handicapped access ramp still looked as tasteful as Daniel remembered. He often thought about how well Brent had designed it, or perhaps it was Rebecca.

He parked and headed up the steps. Surprisingly, the door was open. The polished mahogany wood of the hallway glimmered under the soft overhead lights as Daniel made his way into the reception area.

"Daniel! Oh my God," Rebecca sprang out of her chair, rushing around the desk to hug him. "We've been so worried about you!" She held his face in her hands, gazing into his eyes before pulling him into an even tighter embrace.

"I've missed you, too," Daniel replied as he wrapped his arms around her, letting himself relax into her embrace.

Rebecca took in the sight of Daniel, noting the lines etched onto his face and the remnants of sadness in his eyes. Yet, she couldn't deny that he still looked handsome to her, especially in the old leather jacket he always wore. "Handsomer than ever!" Rebecca exclaimed, giving him another, even warmer hug.

Daniel shifted uneasily. Never quite comfortable with receiving compliments, even from Rebecca, he gently tried to steer the conversation in another direction. "Um, is he in?"

"He's not here right now. He has therapy this afternoon," Rebecca responded, placing a reassuring hand on Daniel's arm. "Do you want some coffee or …?"

Daniel interrupted her, his genuine concern clear, "Is he still getting therapy?"

"The other kind of therapy," Rebecca clarified. "He's almost back to his normal self. Well, as normal as can be expected. I'll text him and let him know you're here."

Daniel immediately shook his head, "No. No, please don't."

"I know he'd love to see you, Daniel! Please wait. He should be back in an hour or so," Rebecca pleaded.

Daniel checked his watch, suddenly feeling guilty for having just arrived unannounced. Struggling with this and Rebecca's enthusiasm, he gestured his intention to return perhaps another time, "I'll just..."

"Please wait," Rebecca insisted. She knew Daniel well. She also knew she wouldn't let him leave town without at least seeing Brent, no matter what the circumstances.

After a moment of hesitation, Daniel finally agreed to wait for Brent to return from therapy. "I'll tell you what, I'll come back. Will he stop by here after therapy before going home?" he asked.

"Oh no, he lives here now." Rebecca gestured toward the back of the building. "The unit in the back opened up, and he jumped on it." Rebecca's smile broadened.

"That's great," Daniel said, genuinely surprised.

"And very convenient for obvious reasons," Rebecca added with a knowing look.

"It's so good to see you again, Rebecca, really. You've always been one of my favorites," Daniel said sincerely as he relaxed into the reality of why he had driven in to begin with.

"Likewise," Rebecca replied with a soft smile.

Before leaving, Daniel made one final request, "Please don't tell him I was here, okay? I promise I'll come back. I want to surprise him."

Rebecca nodded and promised to keep it a secret. "Don't text him or anything, just…" Daniel reiterated, knowing Brent would never let him live it down if he didn't return.

"As long as you promise you're coming back later today," Rebecca added. "It's so good to see you, Daniel. Brent is going to be thrilled," Rebecca repeated, hoping to brighten his mood.

She nodded, swallowing back strong emotion, shaking her head softly as she watched Daniel turn and step out the door.

*****

Brent Evans, once a strong, healthy, and vibrant man, was now confined to a wheelchair. Still clearly fit and in shape, his balding head was shaved down to the skull, but the intensity with which he leaned forward was familiar.

Brent had really liked Dr. Kaufel. He was the first straight therapist Brent had sought, mostly because gay men predominantly populated his practice. Charlie had found Kaufel for Brent, as only Charlie could. But now, Kaufel, who had helped Brent through the worst of it, suddenly seemed to be turning into the enemy. Was it because he was straight? Brent wondered. Exasperated, Brent leaned forward even more. "I told you. I wanted it! I don't know how to explain it, but I wanted it! I really wanted it!"

"Except you were thirteen years old," Dr. Kaufel said sternly, raising his eyebrows at Brent's declaration.

Brent sighed, leaning back in his wheelchair with frustration. He wiped his forehead with the back of his hand, his fingers brushing against the stubble on his scalp. "I was actually twelve. It was just before my thirteenth birthday," he corrected.

"Right, not even a teenager yet." Dr Kaufel refuted this. "And you said he was forty-something?"

Brent could only stare at him, numb from the exchange. "I don't know how old he was. He was my best friend's dad. How old would a twelve-year-old kid's dad be?"

Dr. Kaufel nodded. Taking a slow, deep, measured breath, he considered his next words carefully.

Brent continued. "I don't know how to get you to understand that I did want it to happen. I mean, what part of this don't you understand?" Brent replied, fighting to keep his frustration from boiling over.

Dr. Kaufel leaned forward, his eyes filled with concern. "You were a child, and he was an adult. No matter how much you think you wanted it, you were still a child, and he was an adult. Those are just facts, Brent," Kaufel asserted, his voice steady and calm.

Brent nodded, his eyes filling with tears. He looked down at his hands, his fingers clenched into fists. "It was my first exposure to anything that felt amazing, sexually. That's what it was for me. I loved it! I was thrilled that it happened. And I remain thrilled about it to this day." Brent's voice was barely audible, barely above a whisper.

"But you said you'd been experimenting with girls," Dr. Kauffel prompted.

"With one girl, who was also older than me," Brent responded.

"How much older?" Dr. Kauffel asked.

"I don't know, a year or two, maybe three," Brent answered.

"And you liked it," Dr. Kauffel followed up.

"I did. It was fun and felt good, except it was nowhere near as exciting. What part of this don't you understand? And I don't understand what this has to do with my current situation," Brent said with increasing frustration.

Dr. Kauffel watched as the clock behind Brent ticked up to the hour. "Are we done?" Brent asked.

"Unfortunately," Dr. Kauffel replied with a nod.

Brent could only smile to himself as his exasperation melted into defeat. "Okay then," Brent acquiesced.

"Brent, I know you're well aware there are all kinds of hormones involved in sex and love and romance and—" Dr. Kauffel began.

"My current situation is so completely different," Brent interrupted. "That's what I'm trying to understand. I brought it up because this situation I'm in now is so different. I was hoping you would help me with *this* part!"

"Except that what started it is the same. I want you to consider this between now and our next session. According to what you've told me, the event that ignited it is almost identical," Dr. Kauffel explained.

"I guess." Brent conceded.

Dr. Kauffel sat back, searching the silence between them. "Maybe we should book something sooner," Dr. Kauffel suggested.

"No, I'm fine. I can go for a week," Brent replied.

"You're sure?" Dr. Kauffel asked.

"Yes. I'm sure," Brent confirmed.

"Okay, if you need me sooner, don't hesitate to call. I'll clear a spot for you," Dr. Kaufel reassured.

"I'll be fine, really. I mean, it's not like I haven't been thinking about this for the past year. Now is just the first time I've brought it up, and I'm beginning to ask myself why I brought it up." Brent couldn't mask his defensiveness.

"Okay, good. See you next week," Dr. Kaufel said with a smile.

The silence between them was palpable as Brent expertly made his way out of the office, down the ramp, and into his SUV, a marvel of ingenuity and modern technology that allowed a paraplegic to maneuver so much in the world around him, let alone drive. As Brent maneuvered his wheelchair up the mechanical ramp and into his vehicle, he started wondering. Why had he brought up this topic? He had spent a year avoiding it, but suddenly, it was all he could think about. He shook his head as he secured his travel wheelchair into the driving position and maneuvered his vehicle out of its parking space and into traffic.

*****

Across town, the Charles River gleamed under the late afternoon sun, its surface rippling with the steady strokes of oars slicing through the water. Keith Chambers, dressed in a faded, sweat-stained T-shirt with sleeves long torn away, moved with the practiced grace of an athlete as he secured his shell to the dock. The quiet splash of water echoed around him as other rowers glided past, the rhythmic pull of their oars creating a steady hum in the background.

Keith wiped the sweat from his brow, causing his tousled hair to stick to his forehead in damp strands. His chiseled jaw clenched as he tightened the final knot, ensuring the shell wouldn't drift. His movements were efficient and precise; a man who was as comfortable on the water as he was anywhere else. With a sigh, he straightened and made his way toward the bike rack, where his well-worn bicycle leaned lazily against the weathered wood of the boathouse.

Having recently turned thirty-one, Keith Chambers' handsome, chiseled features were strikingly more pronounced than those of his twin sister. Both he and Marty shared his iconic bone structure and classic Roman features.

It was no wonder the popular press kept anointing him as their chosen one. Even though his family was entrenched in state and local politics, Keith had somehow managed to avoid the brunt of it. However, he was still living the life of a reluctant celebrity, constantly ducking the press at every turn.

He'd become a lawyer by default. None of it had been easy. It was with a huge breath of relief for everyone that he eventually passed the bar. It wasn't that he was dumb. After all, he had graduated with honors from Princeton University. It was just that he found most of it totally and utterly dull. Once he passed the bar in Massachusetts, he quickly passed it in three neighboring states, more to prove to himself that he could do it than anything else.

Though naturally charming and approachable, Keith's ideas about how to bring authenticity into politics were in constant conflict with his entire family, who were masters of the game. Each one, in their own way, seemed to undermine him in public, particularly Marty. Older than him by mere minutes, she, in her own evocative and persuasive way, dismissed him as merely a pretty face: the poster boy of their prominent, internationally recognized family.

Rounding the corner onto the esplanade, Keith noticed the first of the paparazzi, or was it simply that they had noticed him? With his head down, he thrust harder on the pedal.

Just as Daniel was about to cross the bike path, a skateboarder shot past, nearly colliding with him, causing him to jump directly into Keith's path. Keith swerved at the very last moment to avoid both Daniel and the skateboarder, his wheels kicking up a spray of gravel as he passed.

"Sorry, man!" Keith called back toward Daniel. His voice was strained but friendly.

Daniel barely nodded in response, too distracted to process the close call. What neither of them knew was that the moment had been captured; a rapid succession of camera flashes as a photographer nearby caught the scene from the perfect angle.

Keith's strong jawline, beads of sweat dotting his forehead, and Daniel's face, a mass of conflict and discord right beside him, an image that froze them both in time, their faces side by side. Together.

As the sun began to dip lower, the familiar chaos of the Beacon Hill market greeted Daniel as he pushed through the growing crowd of late afternoon shoppers. The narrow aisles were packed with people, their baskets brimming with fresh vegetables and herbs. The air was filled with the earthy smell of produce: eggplants, bell peppers, and bundles of kale lined the wooden crates stacked high along the walls.

Daniel balanced a bundle of leafy greens in one arm while pulling a newspaper off the stand with his free hand. The bold headline: Governor Elizabeth Chambers Proposes Tough Stand on Crime caught his eye. Beneath the governor's photo was an elegant woman with striking features, her hair perfectly styled in silver-streaked waves. She exemplified poise and authority.

His eyes drifted to the magazine rack beside the newspaper, and there, staring back at him, was that man on the bicycle. However, Daniel's mind was too lost in his own tumultuous afternoon even to begin to make the connection.

America's Most Eligible Bachelor, the caption beneath his photo declared. Keith's face, a handsome blend of ruggedness and charm, was plastered across the glossy cover, his casual smirk catching the attention of every passerby.

Daniel quickly placed the newspaper back on the stand next to the glossy magazine cover featuring Keith. He then shifted his attention to the grocer ringing up his items. As the transaction concluded, he gathered his bags and stepped out into the cool evening air.

*****

Across town, Sophie Bieltran stood in front of her loft, fumbling through her oversized pockets, searching for her keys amidst the chaos of her art supplies and Post-its. Her sun-streaked brunette hair hung loosely around her shoulders. Remnants of clay were embedded in her fingernails, evidence of a long day at the pottery wheel. With a sigh of frustration, she juggled the stack of Post-its and a portfolio, trying to make sense of the clutter in her pockets.

Her eyes then drifted toward the wall, where Keith's bicycle was propped, still dusted with dirt from the river path. A knowing smile tugged at the corners of her lips as she leaned her head back, shaking it in half-amused resignation.

Keith appeared from around the corner, still in the same sweat-soaked clothes and breathing heavily from the ride. He didn't say a word; instead, he buried his face in Sophie's neck while pulling her close with his arms encircling her. The post-its and portfolio slipped from her hands, forgotten on the floor as she melted into his embrace. Keith's fingers found the keys in her pocket. With a deft motion, he unlocked the door. The sound of the deadbolt clicking open echoed softly as they slipped inside. The door closed quietly behind them.

*****

As Brent approached the handicap-accessible parking spot, he felt relieved that no one else had taken it. Unofficially, the neighborhood recognized it as Brent's, so they guarded it fiercely. Occasionally, someone in need would reach it before him, but that wasn't the case today.

As Brent backed in, he spotted a familiar face. Could it be? Excitedly, Brent shifted his SUV into park. Then he checked and rechecked everything. He unlocked his wheelchair, maneuvered it out of the driver's position, and down the mechanical ramp, deftly navigating onto the sidewalk. As the ramp folded into the vehicle and the SUV door closed and locked, he sat looking up at Daniel.

"Dude," Brent said, his voice filled with surprise.

Both fought the flood of tears that neither was going to allow.

"Fuck! Where have you been? Why have you not returned any of my phone calls?" Brent asked, his frustration barely hidden.

Daniel sheepishly hid behind the contents of his grocery bag. "Are you cooking me dinner?" Brent added, breaking the tension.

"Well, I haven't eaten, have you?" Daniel responded quietly.

"Hey, I'll take an Eiman-cooked meal over anything, even if it's not your mother's." Brent's smile broadened.

As Brent wheeled himself up the ramp, he tossed the keys to Daniel, who opened the door. As Daniel held the door open for Brent, the reality of the situation suddenly dawned on him. "You're in trouble, aren't you?" Brent asked, his tone becoming serious.

"I don't know," Daniel replied hesitantly. "I hope not."

"Of course you are. Just once, I'd like to believe you're stopping by, just to see me. Would that be too much to ask?" Brent said, half-joking but with concern.

"I'm a terrible person. I'm a terrible friend," said Daniel guiltily.

"No, no, no, no! You're the best kind of friend anybody could have. And I've missed you. We've all really, really missed you. And it's great to see you!" Brent responded with warmth. "Come on in."

"Thank you!" Daniel said, finally smiling.

*****

Later that night, in a grand hotel in the heart of downtown, its ornate facade, arched windows, and intricate carvings spoke of a bygone era of luxury. As he pulled his truck up to the valet, Keith could see the imposing marble columns flanking the entrance and the doorman.

Grabbing the claim ticket from the valet, he felt the cool air as a welcome change. Straightening his suit jacket, he walked towards the entrance, the polished leather of his shoes clicking against the marble steps. The doorman offered a polite nod as he opened the door, ushering Keith into the opulent lobby.

The sheik fixtures were bathed in light from crystal chandeliers, and modern, full-pile area carpets highlighted the rich mahogany furniture surrounding them. Guests milled about: some lounging in comfortable armchairs while others conversed near the grand piano that graced one corner. The air held a subtle fragrance of fresh flowers, and soft classical music provided a sophisticated ambiance.

Keith navigated the hallways, his path adorned with framed artwork and antique mirrors. Bustling hotel staff ensured everything was in perfect order, their movements testifying to practiced efficiency. As he approached the ballroom, the murmur of conversation and the clinking of glasses grew louder.

The ballroom was a grand spectacle: high ceilings with intricate moldings, large windows draped in luxurious fabric, and chandeliers shining even brighter. Round tables, covered in white linens and adorned with elegant centerpieces, were scattered throughout the space. The city's elite mingled within, their voices creating a gentle whirr punctuated by occasional laughter.

Keith walked through the room with practiced ease, offering firm handshakes and well-rehearsed smiles. He exchanged pleasantries with influential donors and local politicians alike. The conversation flowed: recent court cases, upcoming elections, and city planning developments were all carefully curated topics to support the expected image.

Across the room, a woman with long hair made her entrance, drawing the attention of many. Dressed in an elegant emerald green gown that hugged her figure perfectly, she moved with effortless grace. Her brunette hair was styled in loose waves that fell over her shoulders, beautifully framing her face. Her subtle makeup was flawless, accentuating her striking features: a pair of deep blue eyes that seemed to sparkle with lively intelligence and naturally full lips highlighted simply with shimmering lip gloss.

She arrived fashionably late, her entrance causing a noticeable stir among the guests. Heads turned, and conversations paused as she made her way forward. She greeted acquaintances with warm smiles and light touches, her presence magnetic and inviting. Her shoes, a pair of silver stilettos, added a touch of sparkle and completed her look.

Spotting Keith across the room, she made her way toward him. Her path was deliberate yet unhurried, allowing her to engage with several more people along the way. She paused briefly to exchange a few words with a distinguished-looking older gentleman, her laughter ringing softly before continuing. Her arrival at Keith's side was seamless, as if they had rehearsed it countless times. Together, they formed a striking pair, commanding the attention of everyone around them. She slipped her arm through his, signaling their unity to the watching crowd.

"Keith, darling," she said, her voice smooth and pleasant, "Senator Evans wants to discuss the upcoming fundraiser. Let's go say hello."

Keith smiled down at her, his eyes reflecting a mixture of affection and relief. "Of course, Ashley," he replied, guiding her through the crowd toward the senator.

Keith felt a subtle shift in the room's energy as Ashley joined him, her presence amplifying his own. Her role extended beyond being Keith's partner; she was a key player in the social structure that held their world together. Her background was one of privilege and expectation, much like Keith's. Growing up in a family entrenched in business and philanthropy, she learned the art of charm and influence early. Her presence at events like these was not just expected but essential.

Keith followed her lead, feeling guilty about the emotional distance he maintained in their relationship. He admired her ability to manage these social events. Yet, it increasingly felt like a carefully scripted performance for both of them.

Ashley was seamless in her interactions. Each conversation blended genuine interest with strategic networking, demonstrating how she could make every guest feel valued, seen, and heard, an art form Keith seriously appreciated but never fully mastered himself. As they approached Senator Evans, Ashley's practiced smile returned, ready to engage in a conversation that was as much about flattery as about strategic positioning.

"Senator Evans, it's wonderful to see you again," she said, extending her hand in greeting. "Keith and I have been looking forward to catching up with you."

The senator returned her smile, clearly pleased by her attention. "Ashley, always a pleasure. And Keith, good to see you, too."

As the dinner dragged on, Keith found his mind wandering back to the cases on his desk, the issues he truly cared about. The room echoed with conversation, laughter, and the clinking of glasses and silverware, creating a background symphony. The disparity between the polished surface of his public life and his unfulfilled ambitions grew clearer with each passing minute. He glanced at Ashley, who was effortlessly charming a group of business executives, her laughter light and engaging.

At one point, Ashley glanced back at Keith, her eyes locking with his for a brief moment. She gave him a reassuring smile that spoke volumes about her understanding of his unspoken struggles. Keith returned the smile, though it felt strained, and took a sip of his drink, attempting to refocus.

The floral arrangements on each table were meticulously designed, with the scent of roses and lilies blending harmoniously with the aroma of the gourmet dishes being served. Noticing the bounty around him, Keith felt as if he were merely an observer in his own life. After what felt like an eternity, the dinner finally concluded. Keith and Ashley made their rounds, saying goodbye to various attendees and promising to follow up on commitments and initiatives. Firm handshakes and polite nods accompanied the farewells.

As the valet pulled Keith's truck up, Ashley linked her arm through his, her touch light yet possessive.

"You were wonderful tonight, Keith," she said.

"Thanks, Ash," he replied, trying to match her enthusiasm. "You too. Look, Her Royal Highness has beckoned me for some reason. And I'm going fishing this weekend, and I need to get my dad's fishing pole. Do you want to come with me and say hello, or should I drop you off?"

"No, I'll come with you. I'd love to see everyone!"

The drive to the Chambers' mansion in Dover was filled with a comfortable silence. The city's skyline glistened in the black of an impending night. The streets, which had been bustling with activity and pedestrians hurrying along the sidewalks earlier in the day, had slowed to a crawl as evening approached. Keith's thoughts drifted to the afternoon he'd had with Sophie. She was like an addiction to him. Something about her no-holds-barred approach to sex was increasingly something he was unable to get enough of.

He was also grateful for Ashley's presence in his life. Although a force in her own right, she always seemed completely content, simply sitting beside him, no matter what they were doing. Keith tried to mask the turmoil in his thoughts as they drifted back to that afternoon and the events that led him, yet again, into the arms of Sophie Bieltran.

The afternoon had passed. A flurry of activity: reviewing briefs, preparing for upcoming court appearances, and mentoring a few junior associates who, for reasons he could never understand, continually sought his advice. Despite the pressure and demands, there were moments of genuine hope. Fleeting glimpses of the impact he hoped to make one day. But none of it, on any level, seemed to satisfy him.

"Keith, can you take a look at this?" one of the junior associates asked, handing over a thick file.

"Sure," Keith replied, thinking he'd rather stick needles in his eyes, but saying, "Let's take a look." Flipping through the pages and feigning interest, Keith interjected, "This file looks good, but make sure to cross-reference these statutes. It'll strengthen your argument."

"Thanks, Keith. I'll get on it right away."

Keith completed his final tasks as the sun began its descent in the late afternoon. He leaned back in his chair, stretching his arms and savoring the brief, quiet moment. He had decided to take the shell out. Sophie liked him wet and sweaty; something Keith always found to be both kinky and hot. He'd checked his phone, confirming her whereabouts and availability. There was that familiar mix of anticipation and resignation. His day had been filled with the usual blend of expectations and responsibilities. Yet, underneath it all, there was a growing sense of restlessness, a yearning for something more. He couldn't help but wonder how much longer he could maintain the balancing act.

He glanced over at Ashley. Her head leaned back against the headrest, her eyes closed. The streetlamps illuminated her flawless skin. With her subtle makeup and a hint of lip gloss, she was quietly radiant.

Wouldn't it be nice to have it all? Keith thought to himself as he turned his attention back to the familiar roadway.

*****

Daniel sat in utter fascination, staring over at Brent. Brent had never opened up to him like this before. It was as unsettling for Daniel as it was captivating. As Brent finished his thought, Daniel hung on every word.

"How is it I've known you all this time and never heard this story?" Daniel couldn't mask his shock.

"Well, it's not something I stand on the rooftop and shout out to everyone." Brent countered.

"Still." Daniel could only shake his head.

"The thing is, because my original wet dreams were about girls and I had a handful of encounters with girls, my therapist keeps alluding to something about the whole experience with my friend's dad as hijacking what may have been my," gesturing with air quotes, "'normal sexual development' and expression with girls.

I contend that I'm not really interested in girls at all because the whole thing with my friend's dad was way beyond exciting for me. It was not even close to anything I was experiencing with girls. What went down with my friend's dad felt normal and 'right.' If that experience hadn't happened, I would never have known that I was gay. Or it may have taken me years to find out because I am, without a doubt, gay. I mean, yeah, I didn't know until that moment, but once it happened, there was no doubt in my mind about what I was attracted to and why. Are you following this?"

"Sort of." Daniel only wanted to show support for Brent. "But it is a little shocking. I mean, you know, your friend's dad! That is shocking."

"Yeah, well." Brent was now feeling like maybe he'd shared too much. "Did you have wet dreams when you were a kid?"

Daniel shrugged, "Yeah, of course."

"About boys or girls?" Brent pushed.

"My wet dreams were about water."

"Water?" Brent shot back as a hint of a smile slipped onto his face.

Daniel clarified, "My grandparents had a pool. And that pool had water jets. And somehow, one lazy afternoon, they hit me in the right spot at the right time, and…"

Brent's grin widened, "In your grandparents' pool?"

"Yup, over and over again. As much as I possibly could. From that point forward, I developed this relationship with showers, hot tub jets, pools, chlorine, and so on. Anything and everything having to do with streams of water."

Brent was now laughing out loud. "That's crazy."

"I found it to be very effective and relatively clean," Daniel concluded.

Both laughed out loud.

"So, when did you realize you were gay?" Brent prodded further.

"Andrew."

"No way! Andrew, was your first experience with another dude?"

"Andrew was my first experience with another anybody."

"No way!" Brent really couldn't believe it.

"Yeah, for sure," Daniel assured him.

"Wow." Brent could only shake his head.

"Why do you ask?" Daniel leaned in, intrigued.

"How did you…how did it start with the two of you?" Brent leaned in, equally intrigued.

"One morning, he asked me to cuddle with him, and it seemed like a good idea. It was cold outside, and I liked the way he smelled, especially in the morning." Daniel shrugged. "It just went from there. To this day, it's a mystery to me." Daniel concluded, shaking his head.

It wasn't a mystery to Brent, who offered, "Andrew said he knew the moment he encountered you, that you were the one for him. He always used to say that being with you felt like home to him. That you gave his life meaning."

Daniel could only shake his head. "I really don't get it, Brent. To this day, I just don't get it."

"Dude, you're fucking gorgeous. You always have been. And you're even more beautiful on the inside than you are on the outside. And you don't think you are. You, honest to God, don't realize how special you are."

"Whatever." Daniel genuinely didn't get it.

Brent was adamant. "See, like that. You have no idea how extraordinary you are, Daniel. Really!"

"I know how much trouble I am, that I know. Speaking of which," Daniel tried to maneuver the conversation onto why he'd driven in.

Brent could only shake his head. Daniel circled back. "Anyway, you're way better looking than I am. Dexter, too; hell, Dexter's better looking *and* sexier than all of us put together. And Andrew…Andrew adored Dexter. They adored each other!"

"Dexter's also straight," Brent interjected. "About as straight as a man can ever possibly be."

"Well, they were way more in love with each other than Andrew ever was with me. Trust me, I know."

"No, Daniel. It wasn't like that. What they had was something entirely different. But you? You were his heart. You were his soul. You were his everything. You meant more to Andrew than anyone ever could. I saw it. Felt it. We all did, including Dexter and Marty."

Daniel could only shake his head. This memory of Andrew hit him even more intensely than the earlier photos had. Brent regretted bringing it up. However, there was an elephant in the room, one that Brent firmly believed Daniel needed to stop avoiding.

Realizing this was neither the time nor the place, Brent decided to drop it all and began clearing the table.

Daniel silently joined him as if it were something they had done every night together, their entire lives. The two worked in sync, clearing everything, wiping the counters, and then sitting back down at the now clean table, not saying a word to each other until Brent offered, "Tea?"

Daniel nodded, and Brent turned on the kettle, preparing the teacups before maneuvering back to the matter at hand.

"The kid. Tell me about the kid. I already know you're in trouble, so lay it on me."

"He's, you know, a wallflower. Tries to keep his head down and stay invisible to as many people as possible. But today, after class, he was just... there. Standing in front of me. Struggling with something." Daniel shook his head, still trying to make sense of it. "And I don't know... he started to remind me of myself. My own fucked-up, dysfunctional childhood. And I just... I wanted to help him. So, I put my hands on his shoulders, just to make sure he knew... he had my full attention."

"So, you touched him." Brent was merely stating the obvious.

"Reassuringly. Yes, I reassuringly put my hands on his shoulders." Daniel verified.

"Uninvited." Again, it was more of a statement from Brent than a question.

"Well, I guess, but..." Daniel felt himself becoming defensive.

Brent could only shake his head.

"It worked," Daniel said, emphasizing the point. "He really responded. It seemed to reassure him enough that he basically asked me if I was gay."

"To which you replied?" This time, Brent asked the question.

"Well, at first, I didn't say anything. I just suddenly realized I probably shouldn't have my hands on his shoulders. So I pulled them back, kind of abruptly. And not long after that, he ran out of the room, mumbling apologies without saying much of anything."

Brent nodded his understanding.

Daniel continued, "After he left, I noticed there were kids in the schoolyard right outside my window."

Brent could only imagine what was coming.

"You know, with their phones, etc., etc." Daniel started to collapse into himself before offering, "All I wanted to do was help him. Really." Daniel was trying not to come off as defensive, even though he was starting to sound that way.

"I believe you." Brent nodded across to Daniel.

The two stared at each other across the silence until Brent offered, "So this is what I want you to do: Go to the principal's office tomorrow and tell her the entire story. Start to finish; every bit of it. Don't leave anything out. Ask her what she thinks you should do. First thing. Go directly to her office first thing tomorrow morning."

"Sure, except she's a he." Off Brent's confused look, Daniel clarified, "Mr. Knight is the principal. He's a *he.*"

"Okay, well, that's probably better," Brent said, nodding.

"I haven't, you know. I haven't told 'them' or anybody else about, you know, myself… or my past, or anything. I've been trying to keep a low profile."

Before Brent could answer, Daniel jumped in, "I began as a substitute, which eventually led to…"

"They know, Daniel." Brent cut him off gently, watching his face. "Trust me," Brent said, more firmly, "they know."

"Leominster's a pretty quiet town, Brent."

"It's quiet, and it's blue-collar. But, they still know. They wouldn't offer you a full-time position without vetting you. Not these days."

"Sometimes I just really hate my life, you know?" Daniel's feelings of remorse and frustration were beginning to intensify again. "I was just starting to find a flow. I'm good at teaching, Brent."

"I don't doubt that for one second, Daniel. But you are who you are."

Daniel was suddenly defensive now. "What's that supposed to mean?"

"Look, there's a Chambers event on Friday evening. I want you to come with us. I think you need to be reminded of who you really are."

"Who I really am?" Hurt started to seep into Daniel's defensiveness.

"Yes, Daniel, who you really are. Charlie's going to be there, along with Marty. She's been worried sick about you. We've all been really worried about you. You need to come back to your roots."

"Maybe teaching is my roots. Maybe this is who I really am. I'm doing really well these days, Brent. At least I was doing really well." Daniel shook his head in defeat.

"You're Daniel Eiman, Daniel. That's who you are. You're Daniel Eiman." Brent couldn't have added more affection or admiration to what he was saying, even if Daniel couldn't see it for himself. "You can't run forever, Daniel," Brent concluded.

"I'm not running, Brent!" Daniel countered. Then, almost in a whisper, "I'm not running."

Brent stared across the table at Daniel lovingly, compassionately, and knowingly.

"Okay, I'll consider it, but don't get your expectations too high." Daniel was offering an olive branch. "I want to be away from it all, you know, Brent? I'm sorry, I still need to be away from it all."

"Quite frankly, Daniel, it doesn't sound like you're away from it... at all." Again, Brent was loving yet, at the same time, as direct as he could be.

Lifting their tea to their lips, the two stared at each other until Daniel broke the silence. "Okay, different subject, please. What else is new?"

"Where do I begin?" Brent smiled broadly at Daniel.

"It has been too long. God, I miss you." Daniel smiled back.

"Yes, it has." Brent nodded, more to himself than to Daniel. "And I miss you, too. More than you can ever imagine. We all do."

*****

The Chambers' Dover mansion family room buzzed with quiet commotion. As Keith and Ashley stepped in, Mr. Chambers slowly rose from his leather chair, groaning softly.

At the same time, Keith's older brother William offered brisk handshakes and kisses to Governor Chambers, Marty, and Ashley before making his exit.

Without missing a beat, Governor Chambers intercepted Keith, slipping an arm around his waist and steering him out of earshot. Her tone shifted the moment they were alone.

"Keith," she said, measured and low. "I want to talk to you about Swampscott."

Keith instinctively pulled back, slipping into an all-too-familiar defensive posture, bracing for what he knew was coming next.

She continued, undeterred. "Look, Marty's got a knack for these things. And she's older than you."

"By what, seven minutes?" Keith replied dryly.

"Three, actually." The irony was not lost on Keith as she pressed on. "You're personable. Very personable. People like you. And you like them."

Keith glanced down, shaking his head slowly, uncertain whether it was a compliment or a trap.

"These matters, especially around healthcare, are complicated. And controversial." Her brow folded delicately, like origami laced with warning.

"I can be diplomatic," Keith offered. "Just as diplomatic as Marty. Just give me a chance. I'll do it quietly. No one needs to know."

Governor Chambers shook her head, concern lingering behind her eyes like an unmoving shadow. "Marty's completely on your side. I hear it in her voice. But she has a sharp sense of how to handle these situations. You need to follow her lead. It doesn't look good if she has to clean up after you've gone ahead and... blundered through."

"Blundered through?" Keith couldn't believe it.

"You know exactly what I'm saying." Governor Chambers interjected.

"No, actually, I don't." Keith was becoming increasingly confrontational.

"Please just follow Marty's lead." Governor Chambers pleaded in a steady voice, conveying a concern that was more a mother's than a governor's.

"So, is this why you summoned me here tonight?" Keith didn't even try to mask his frustration.

"No, actually," Governor Chambers subtly signaled across the room to her husband, who made his way over to them.

Mr. Chambers slid up beside Keith, fishing through his jacket pocket. He cast a glance toward Ashley, confirming she was distracted. Then, with practiced subtlety, he guided Keith out of view. Governor Chambers caught the motion, and in an unspoken accord, joined them, forming a quiet huddle around him.

"How are things going with you and Ashley?" Mr. Chambers asked, leaning in.

"Good... great. Why?" Keith replied, stealing a glance toward Ashley, then briefly looking down at the floor.

When he looked back up, Mr. Chambers opened his hand discreetly. Nestled inside an open ring box was a stunning diamond, brilliant, even under the muted light. Keith's eyes widened at the sight of it: 270 points of sparkle housed in a setting that was bold, but unmistakably outdated.

Governor Chambers stepped in beside her husband, her expression warm and expectant, pride radiating from every line of her face.

"You'll have to have it reset, of course," Governor Chambers offered, her eyes twinkling with motherly affection.

Keith could only meet Governor Chambers' gaze in shock as his heart started racing.

"You don't want to marry Ashley?" she pressed gently.

"No... I mean, Mom...really?" Keith turned to Mr. Chambers, searching his face for backup. "Dad...?" The moment hit like a sucker punch. Keith's breath caught. He grabbed the ring box, snapped it shut with a click, and shoved it into his pocket, his movements sharp, almost reflexive.

When he looked up, his parents were waiting. "Of course, I want to marry Ashley. I just...want it to be on my terms. I need it to be on my terms."

The air was thick with silence, laden with words left unsaid.

"Then make it on your terms, darling," Governor Chambers encouraged, her voice filled with warmth. "Just sooner, better than later, please."

Governor Chambers reassuringly squeezed Keith's free hand, then stepped away to bid farewell to the rest of her children.

Keith looked down and shook his head. When he looked up, Mr. Chambers affectionately ruffled Keith's hair, adding, "It'll be good for you to settle down, Keith. It's time." Mr. Chambers gave Keith a reassuring nod before stepping away.

Keith watched Governor Chambers across the room, working with her own children with the poise and charm she employed with her high-paying donors.

Night fell over the Chambers' driveway like an anvil. Ashley sat quietly in the passenger seat of Keith's truck as he stowed a fishing rod in the back. When he climbed in beside her, his face said nothing. His eyes said everything.

"What did they say?" Ashley asked, her voice cautious but curious.

"She just wanted to talk. About Swampscott," Keith muttered, gripping the steering wheel. "She wants Marty to step in. Handle it all."

Ashley frowned. "You're an easy target, Keith. These groups know you'll listen. Sometimes... I think you let your idealism get the best of you."

Keith's laugh was short and bitter. "My idealism? Right. That's it. I'm just an idealist." The sarcasm hit harder than he intended.

Ashley winced slightly, then softened. "I didn't mean it like that. I think your idealism is great. You should follow it. Really. I just wonder... how do you even begin to qualify what you're finding?"

Keith stared out the windshield. "There are mounds of evidence, Ashley. Mountains. It's just" He cut himself off, jaw tightening. "You know what? Forget it."

The silence that followed filled every crevice of the truck. When Ashley gently put a hand on Keith's arm, he didn't flinch, but he didn't lean into it either. He just shook his head slowly, as if trying to shake off something he couldn't name.

Then, without saying a word, he started the engine, shifted into gear, and drove off into the dark roads of Dover.

*****

Just three days later, in Amherst, Mrs. Eiman, striking in her sixties and somehow seeming younger, moved gracefully around her kitchen. Her movements were precise, almost balletic, as she retrieved plates from cabinets and food from the fridge like a seasoned performer executing a well-rehearsed routine.

Charlie Atwood stood at the counter while Brent, seated in his travel chair, smiled up at her. "Mrs. Eiman, don't, really. We don't have time," Brent urged, his voice tinged with urgency.

"Yeah, you know us, Mrs. Eiman. Always on the go," Charlie said with a grin. "We're just going to collect him and get out of your hair."

Mrs. Eiman shot them a scrutinizing look as she continued to pull even more food from the refrigerator.

"Alright, how about we satisfy this urge with a cup of coffee?" Brent suggested, glancing at Charlie.

"Yeah, how about a cup of coffee?" Charlie echoed, joining in the playful banter.

"It's so good to see you both. How long has it been… three years?" Mrs. Eiman asked, her eyes moving between them. "Definitely not since Daniel got back from

Georgetown," she added, then nodded toward Brent's chair with a smile. "You've gotten pretty skilled with that thing."

Brent answered with a flourish, spinning and weaving through the kitchen with ease. His playful maneuvering earned cheers from Charlie and a delighted laugh from Mrs. Eiman.

Just then, Daniel shuffled in, yawning, hair tousled from sleep, still fumbling with the buttons on his jeans.

"Look who's here!" Mrs. Eiman beamed.

Daniel rubbed his eyes, groggy.

"Dude!" Charlie shouted, pumping Daniel's hand before planting a quick, wet kiss on his lips and pulling him into a hug. Daniel stood stiffly, caught off guard.

"Charlie, you are the queerest straight man I've ever met," Daniel muttered, wiping his mouth but finally smiling as he surrendered to the chaos.

"Daniel! Be nice," Mrs. Eiman chided, clearly amused.

"I'm excited to see you, too, man. Been a while," Charlie grinned. "What can I say?"

Daniel's gaze moved from Charlie to his mother, then to Brent, warmth creeping across his face. He turned toward Brent. "You know I'm not coming with you, right?"

"It's just one night, Daniel. One night," Brent coaxed.

Daniel shook his head but couldn't suppress the smile rising despite himself. The familiarity, the comfort, settled around him like a blanket.

Mrs. Eiman, pouring coffee, spoke more to herself than to anyone else. "How long's it been since they've been up here? Too long."

Brent and Charlie grabbed their cups as anticipation stirred in the room.

"You'll be needing your tux," Brent said casually, a mischievous twinkle in his eye.

"I'm not going anywhere that requires a tux, dude." Daniel shook his head again, his voice edging toward rebellion, even as his smile stayed.

*****

The Newbury Boston ballroom shimmered with energy, a jewel box of old money and new ambition. Boston's well-heeled elite milled about, draped in jewels, tailored suits, polished shoes, and tuxedos. Soft light from the chandeliers glinted off cut crystal and polished silverware, as low murmurs of laughter and conversation rippled through the vast, gilded space. It was the unmistakable hum of people who had never doubted their place at the top.

Near the heart of it all stood Marty Chambers, magnetic and radiant, holding court with the ease of someone born to command attention. Her laughter rang out, light, precise, practiced, but it was her eyes that gave her away: a glint of calculation danced just beneath their surface. She was in the middle of a story, her fingers sketching the air as she spoke, each gesture choreographed yet effortless.

"So there they are," she said, "eyes locked on me, probably counting the diamonds on my pumps and just waiting for a slip." Her tone was sweetly self-deprecating, but the smile curled with something steelier. "I know exactly what's going through their heads: 'How about hot tax shelters in Latin America?' Because obviously, that's the sort of thing someone like me must be all about." She paused. The corners of her lips twitched with mischief. "If any of them could formulate an actual question, I'd give them an answer worth listening to."

Laughter broke from the crowd: genuine, indulgent, impressed. They were hooked.

But just then, something shifted. Marty's gaze, mid-sentence, snagged on movement across the room. Three familiar figures were threading their way through the crowd: Brent, Charlie... and, her breath caught, could it be, Daniel Eiman.

Her blue eyes widened. A flash of surprise passed through them, followed by something softer, more profound, more challenging to name. "Oh my Lord," she whispered, just loud enough for those near her to catch the reverence in her voice. "Could it possibly be?"

For a moment, she seemed to forget her story entirely. Then, catching herself before her captivated audience could notice, her smile returned, bigger, warmer, a calculated bloom of charm. "Excuse me, please."

She moved with purpose, shoulders squared, stride assured, cutting across the floor like she still owned every room Daniel Eiman ever walked into. When she reached him, she didn't hesitate. Her hand found his elbow, firm but affectionate, as if grounding herself in something lost and suddenly recovered.

"Daniel Eiman!" she proclaimed, her voice rising as she looked from Daniel to Brent, then back again with a pointed, knowing glint in her eyes. "You devil," she continued, wagging a finger at Brent. "Where did you find him?"

She stepped back, her eyes sweeping over Daniel as though she were seeing him for the first time. Her gaze traveled from his shoes, lingered on his jacket, and finally settled on his face, a smile playing on her lips as if to say, "I approve."

"Welcome back," she said, her voice softer, her expression filled with a warmth that bordered on protectiveness.

Daniel's shoulders tensed slightly, his faint smile fading almost imperceptibly into a frown. He glanced away briefly, ran a hand through his hair, and then met her gaze with a defiant half-smile. "I'm not back, Marty. Just visiting," he replied, his voice firm but not unfriendly.

In response, Marty reached out and pinched his cheek playfully as if he were a mischievous child and not a full-grown man.

"Ouch!" Daniel exclaimed, pulling back slightly, even though he couldn't completely conceal the amusement sparkling in his eyes.

"You look so good," she said, ignoring his mild resistance. Her expression softened as she added, "So, I heard you were last spotted in Leominster." She pretended to be puzzled, her brow creasing as she studied his face, her voice carrying a hint of playful teasing. "What on earth are you doing in Leominster?"

"Getting into trouble, you can be assured of that," Charlie interjected, his voice teasing but tinged with a hint of seriousness.

Before Daniel could voice any objections, Marty enveloped him in a warm, lingering embrace, gently kissing him on both cheeks. The gesture was light yet intimate, exuding an unspoken warmth that felt oddly maternal. She pulled back, still studying his face as if searching for a part of him that had been left behind or lost. "God, I've missed you."

Charlie, watching the exchange, shook his head with a fond smile, and then shrugged.

Marty, Brent, and Charlie then launched into a litany of shared memories, their gestures and laughter aimed at Daniel as they recalled their years of history together. Inside pranks and inside jokes. Of long nights and hard days. Daniel shifted uncomfortably, rubbing the back of his neck as he glanced between the three of them, trying to hide the faint blush creeping up his cheeks.

"Seriously, what are you doing in Leominster, Daniel?" Marty really wanted to know.

"I'm teaching... English," Daniel said, his voice flat but honest, as though he expected them to laugh him off.

Marty arched an eyebrow, her lips twitching in barely concealed amusement. "As in English Composition? The class you, yourself, had to take three times, just to pass?"

Charlie laughed loudly, pointing at Daniel as he joined in the tease. "Yeah, I remember that! You had to take English Comp three times!"

Daniel's expression soured. "Literature. I'm teaching English Literature." Daniel leaned toward Charlie, his voice lowering, his words clipped. "Something you know nothing about." Daniel straightened, squaring his shoulders as though reclaiming his dignity. "And besides, I had to drop out of those Comp courses."

Charlie cocked his head, his grin widening. "Yeah, because you were failing them!"

With a huff, Daniel threw his hands up, turned on his heel, and stepped away from the group, muttering as he went, "I didn't come all the way out here to be harassed and insulted."

As the three watched Daniel waltz off, a trace of concern crept into Marty's face. She turned to Charlie, lips pressed in thought.

"Should we go get him?" she asked softly, not entirely sure he'd be okay.

Charlie shrugged, glancing in Daniel's direction. "Nah, let him go. He'll be back..." His tone was casual, unconcerned.

Marty sighed, her eyes lingering on the space where Daniel had disappeared into the crowd. She crossed her arms, fingers tapping absently against her sleeve as a crease of worry settled between her brows.

"Well," she murmured, almost to herself, "he's not exactly back in the saddle yet, right? Maybe we should go easy on him."

Brent nodded, watching her closely, his expression softening. "Exactly," he said, his voice low and full of warmth.

Charlie, sensing the need to ease the tension, sidled up to Marty with a teasing grin, his eyes glinting with mischief.

"So, a junior Congresswoman now, huh? Just like Mommy... Tell me, are you going to be Governor, too?"

Marty's gaze remained fixed on the path Daniel had disappeared through before turning back to Charlie. Her expression shifted to one of playful deflection. Then she leaned closer, her voice dropping to a whisper as her eyes sparkled with ambition.

"Well, there's talk of Washington now, you know," she said, her voice almost conspiratorial.

Charlie's eyes widened, and he let out a low, impressed whistle. Beside him, Brent raised an eyebrow, his face lighting up with genuine surprise. Marty leaned in closer, glancing around as if to ensure that no one else could overhear. "You didn't hear it from me," she added, her tone becoming a near whisper, "and it's not official."

Charlie, still absorbing her words, shook his head in amazement, his mouth curving into a half-smile of disbelief. "So... does that mean you're going to become Governor?"

Marty offered a nonchalant shrug, but her eyes shone with determination. "Maybe later," she replied, the words carrying a subtle weight as though she were revealing a carefully guarded plan.

Meanwhile, in the plush, dark, floor-to-ceiling, deep forest green marble and gold-gilded bathroom, Keith stood alone at one of the sinks. He gripped the edge of the counter as he leaned forward, his face inches from the mirror. It was a reality check of sorts. He needed to convince himself to return to the evening and the guests.

From his periphery, he saw the glint of the opulent fixtures, each surface polished to a flawless sheen. Dim lighting softened the room's lavishness, casting gentle shadows that blurred the sharp lines of the counters and mirrors. The faint sound of water trickling from a faucet was the only noise, echoing in the stillness of the vast space.

He splashed cold water on his face, droplets clinging to his skin as he straightened, wiping his hands across his damp cheeks in frustration. With his brow creased in concentration, he mumbled under his breath, his words barely discernible and laced with sarcastic bitterness.

"So, this is your Golden Boy... yes, yes, he went to Princeton... and yes, you should have lunch with him... but if you really want to get anything done, you should talk to his sister."

He let out a soft, humorless chuckle and shook his head, staring at his reflection with a blend of frustration and disdain.

The silence was interrupted by the creak of a stall door, followed by the flush of a toilet. Keith glanced upward.

It took him a moment to see Daniel stepping out of one of the stalls, desperately wanting to but unable to go unnoticed.

The two men regarded each other through the mirror, taking each other in with cautious curiosity.

"Sorry... didn't mean to interrupt," Daniel said, drying his hands on a nearby towel. "Rough night?"

Keith said nothing, focusing intently on rinsing and drying his own hands. His face gave little away, except perhaps the hope that whoever this guy was, he'd take the hint and disappear.

It slowly dawned on Daniel; he knew this guy. But from where? He searched Keith's eyes through the mirror, trying to place the face. A spark of recognition lit up inside him. He snapped his fingers, hoping the noise would shake the name loose. "Wait a minute… you're" He snapped again. "Shit. "Do I know you?"

Keith straightened, finished drying his hands, and, after a quick glance, turned to face him.

"No," he said flatly.

Daniel arched an eyebrow, more amused than offended. "Are you always this friendly… or just a Republican?"

Keith's eyes narrowed. "I don't know. Are you always this nosy, or just an asshole?" He brushed past Daniel, his shoulder grazing his as he made for the door.

Daniel watched him go, oddly entertained. He reached for a paper towel, then called out: "Hey, the world's full of shit. Somebody's got to get rid of it."

As the door closed behind Keith, Daniel caught his own reflection in the mirror and smirked. "Fucking Republicans."

Back in the grand ballroom, the festivities had swelled into full bloom. Laughter rolled beneath the music like a second melody, rising and falling with the rhythm of clinking glasses and easy conversation. Boston's social elite moved through the golden-lit space with an almost choreographed elegance: old money brushing shoulders with political power, legacy and ambition mingling freely over cocktails and polite smiles.

Marty, the Governor, and Mr. Chambers navigated the crowd with practiced ease, their expressions gracious, their body language fluid. They paused here and there, gripping hands, sharing knowing nods, exchanging pleasantries that masked deeper calculations. They weren't just hosting a party; they were reinforcing a dynasty.

At the far end of the room, Ashley stood apart. Alone, but not uneasy. Her posture was impeccable: chin high, shoulders set with the quiet confidence of someone raised to command attention without having to chase it. She scanned the room with a measured gaze, not quite searching, but evaluating. Her expression was composed, almost impassive, yet her eyes moved with intention; discerning, weighing, deciding.

She held her glass with delicate precision, tilting it just enough to catch the ambient light. The chandelier's reflection danced across the rim, and for a moment, she seemed lost in it; thoughtful, suspended. A flick of color, a burst of crystal, a beat of stillness in the swirl of everything around her.

The crowd parted as a man in a hand-tailored suit approached her, his smile charming as he gave her a slight nod. He was one of the investment types, the kind of man who wore his wealth as casually as his cologne.

"Good evening, Ms. Ashley Cox," he greeted her, his voice low and smooth, with a practiced elegance in its tone.

Ashley looked at him with a courteous smile, her eyes briefly scanning him with a glimmer of familiarity. "Good evening, Karl. It's a pleasure to see you."

Karl returned her smile, his eyes gleaming with interest as he leaned in slightly. "I didn't want to leave you stranded here all by yourself," he said, his tone almost conspiratorial.

Ashley let out a soft laugh, glancing around the bustling room with a resigned expression. "Sometimes I love these things," she said, her voice tinged with faint irony, "and sometimes I'm just not in the mood. Is it obvious?" Then she winked at him, "I hope not."

She forced a smile, lifting her glass in a half-toast as she nodded toward his group of friends. "But it looks like you're having fun."

Karl's eyes gleamed as he tipped his glass in her direction, his smile widening. "I am now."

Ashley smiled, reaching out to touch his arm lightly, a gesture of acknowledgment, though her gaze remained cool.

"Thank you, Karl. You're sweet to say that," she murmured.

Karl seemed emboldened by Ashley's touch. He straightened, adopting a tone of casual braggadocio. "You know," he began, his voice carrying a hint of pride, "I just had the Ferrari retooled."

Ashley's eyes lit up with a spark of interest as she glanced up at him, her gaze becoming more focused. "Did you?" she asked, her voice taking on a note of genuine curiosity.

Karl nodded, leaning in slightly as though letting her in on a secret. "I'd love to take you for a spin."

Ashley smiled wider, her eyes glinting with the excitement she knew he wanted to see. "That sounds delightful," she replied in an airy yet inviting tone.

Karl grinned; his confidence bolstered. "May I call you?" he asked, his tone smooth, almost a challenge.

"Of course," Ashley replied with a demure smile.

Just then, a figure slipped in alongside Ashley. Keith wrapped his arm around her waist, placing a hand on the small of her back. His expression was now friendly and completely welcoming. Keith acknowledged Karl with a polite nod.

"Hey, Karl," he said, his voice steady and unassuming. "How are you?"

Karl's confident demeanor wavered as he turned to shake Keith's hand, his smile tightening ever so slightly. "Good, thanks, Keith," he said, his voice noticeably more subdued.

Beside him, Ashley shifted. A small smile curved at the corners of her lips as she subtly angled her body toward Keith. Her hand lingered on his arm, fingers grazing the sleeve of his jacket, light, but unmistakably possessive.

Karl noticed. Their familiarity suddenly became clear and undeniable. A trace of discomfort passed across his face. He straightened, adjusting his stance, suddenly more aware of the space between them. Still, he didn't back off. There was no ring on her finger yet.

"Well..." he said, managing a polite smile, though the ease in his posture had slipped, muted by Keith's calm, unshakable presence. "I, uh, don't have your number," Karl added, turning his full attention back to Ashley. His voice carried a trace of forced ease, barely masking the awkward hope beneath it as he tried to recover his earlier confidence.

Ashley's eyes sparkled mischievously as she tilted her head, her smile widening. "I'm listed," she replied smoothly. "Ashley Cox Designs on Newbury." Her voice was breezy but detached, as if offering him a small favor he hadn't quite earned.

"Right... right, of course," Karl murmured, nodding quickly. The atmosphere between them had shifted unmistakably, and his confidence visibly dampened. A faint flush crept up his neck as he stepped back, conceding the moment. He forced a smile, giving Keith a tight nod before stepping away.

Keith watched as Karl faded into the crowd, his gaze steady, his jaw tight. There was no shift in his expression, but something behind his eyes held firm; measured, resolved. Ashley's smile softened. She slipped her arm through his, and together they moved toward the dais where the Chambers were gathering, an elegant, composed pair cutting a quiet path through the ballroom's glittering chaos.

Ashley stopped here and there along the way to acknowledge guests. She was a pro at it. Keith was always happy to have her by his side.

The lights dimmed slightly, signaling a shift in the evening's festivities as the crowd quieted, murmuring in anticipation.

Ashley and Keith crossed the dais to join the rest of the family. A matron with the poised authority of old money stepped up to the microphone. She tapped it once, and the soft feedback drew eyes from every corner of the room as guests turned toward the stage.

The woman cleared her throat, her voice ringing out with practiced elegance.

"Ladies and gentlemen, without further ado, it is with great pleasure that I present to you our hostess for this evening, our own Congresswoman-elect, Ms. Marty Chambers."

The room erupted in applause, swelling with admiration as cameras flashed. All eyes turned to the dais, where Marty stood at the center: calm, luminous, and unshakably composed. At her side, the Governor and Mr. Chambers wore expressions of measured pride. Keith and Ashley stepped in beside them, their practiced poise revealing just how well they knew this world.

Across the room, Daniel turned, his eyes catching sight of the family assembling up front. His face flashed recognition as his expression became more intense. He leaned slightly toward Charlie.

"I'll be a son of a bitch," Daniel muttered under his breath.

Charlie turned, puzzled. "What?"

"That's Keith Chambers." Daniel's tone was low, edged with something: disbelief, maybe, or something more challenging to name. Something that settled in as he really looked.

Charlie rolled his eyes. "Duh…"

Daniel didn't look away. "I've just never seen him in person before," he murmured. "He looks… different."

Charlie shrugged. "No, he doesn't. He looks precisely the same."

Beside them, Brent leaned forward, glancing between the two. "As what?"

Charlie waved it off. "I don't know. As he does in print?"

Brent frowned. "What are you guys talking about?"

Daniel's gaze stayed on the dais. "He's not going into politics, is he?"

Brent shook his head slowly. "Keith? Not directly, no."

Charlie snorted. "Though God knows he's dumb enough to."

Daniel shot Charlie a sharp look, quiet but cutting. Then he turned to Brent, almost as if asking for something he couldn't say outright.

Brent held his gaze, steady and calm. "Daniel," he said, "Charlie's not going to change. You'll have to accept him as he is."

Unbothered, Charlie laughed and looked back toward the dais, where Marty had begun to speak. "Marty's all about healthcare now, and Keith's got that whole 'truth in medicine' thing wedged up his ass. I mean, come on; it doesn't take a rocket scientist to see where this is going. Or why?"

Daniel's eyes narrowed as he turned back to Keith. His expression held still, but beneath it, something was shifting; an almost imperceptible mix of curiosity, wariness, and something more private started to sink in. Disappointment, maybe. Or a recognition he hadn't wanted to see.

"He's an anti-vaxxer," Charlie said, continuing. The tone was mocking, but the edge in his voice made it clear he wasn't entirely joking.

Brent sighed, trying to soften the moment. "He's not anti-vax, Charlie. He's pro-truth in medicine."

"Yeah. *Anti-vax*," Charlie snapped back.

Daniel glanced at Brent, eyebrows raised. "Well, that sounds... controversial." Then, adding under his breath, "I wonder how Marty deals with that."

Charlie slapped Daniel on the back, grinning. "Yeah, right up your alley, bud. Go get him!"

Brent shook his head, a trace of a smile forming, tempered by something quieter. "Look, he's smart. And sincere. And he actually does know what he's talking about. The problem is, nobody's listening."

Charlie let out a short, bitter laugh. "Please. He's a Chambers and he's good-looking. That alone is enough to keep him on the cover of every glossy in America."

Charlie looked back toward the dais, where Keith stood beside Ashley. Something tightened in his gaze. Gesturing toward Ashley, "And that should be worth something, certainly."

Daniel studied Charlie, trying to parse the shift in tone; just enough resentment to notice, just enough truth to sting.

Charlie didn't look away. "Seriously, the guy needs to get a life." He then gestured once again toward Ashley. "Although he does have *that* going for him. And *that* would be life enough for me."

"Yeah, too bad you're so short and ugly and hairy," Daniel said, forcing a smile in Charlie's direction.

Charlie smirked, leaning in. "Yeah, well, at least I've got a big dick. Bigger than yours. And last I heard, you like hairy men. The hairier the better."

Daniel let out a dry chuckle, shaking his head. "Keep telling yourself that, Charlie."

Not missing a beat Charlie shot back, "You're just jealous."

"Right," Daniel called over his shoulder as he stepped away, already halfway out of the exchange before it ended. He moved toward the front of the room, not from purpose but from a quiet need to move.

Brent watched him go, then turned back to Charlie, seizing the lull. "Tell me about Kaufel, Charlie."

"What's there to tell?" Charlie shot back.

"How did you find him? What's his deal?" Brent clarified.

"Who's the dude that helped you convert your SUV?"

"I can't remember his name, something with an S.?"

"Yeah, well, he told me about him. Eddie. I think his name was Eddie. Why?"

"I don't know. We're getting into shark-infested waters. I'm just trying to make sense of why I'm there."

"Shark-infested waters? Could you be just a little bit more specific, maybe?" Charlie could only shake his head.

Brent wasn't humored.

Charlie elaborated, "According to Eddie, it was all one-night stands until he saw Kaufel. Somehow, Kaufel cured him; he's now happily married to that orthopedic surgeon. I've sent three other gay men to him. Two are in stable, healthy relationships. You're the third."

"Did you see him?" Brent prodded further.

"Yeah, for a while. It didn't seem to work as well for me," Charlie clarified.

"Because?"

"Because I'm not looking for romance."

"Everybody's looking for romance, Charlie."

"Not me."

The two watched silently as Daniel weaved his way to the front of the room, his eyes fixed ahead as if searching for something, or someone, among the crowd of guests. Charlie and Brent then turned to each other, their faces showing a mix of amusement and triumph.

"Now that we've hooked him, I'm ready to get the fuck out of here," Charlie said, clapping a hand on Brent's shoulder while gently pushing his wheelchair toward the ballroom entrance.

"We're not leaving him behind," Brent contested.

Charlie smirked and retorted, "He'll find us when he needs to."

The ballroom pulsed with energy: glasses clinking, silverware chiming, bursts of laughter spiraling upward beneath the glittering chandeliers. The live quartet murmured jazz standards from a corner of the room, barely audible beneath the swell of conversation.

Keith moved through the crowd toward Marty and Dexter, his posture relaxed but his eyes scanning. As he approached, he saw the guy from the bathroom standing just beyond Marty, effortlessly charming a small group of well-dressed patrons. Daniel's smile was easy, his body language smooth, and one of the more refined women had burst into laughter as she lightly brushed his shoulder.

Keith frowned. *What the hell could be so funny?*

He reached Marty's side, offering a tired but warm smile. "I don't know how you do this, Marty," he said under his breath. "I really don't."

Marty turned to him, bright and composed. "I like people," she said, then smirked. "And also, what happened to your tie?" She reached up and adjusted it herself with sisterly precision, tugging it slightly straighter. Though they were born just minutes apart, Marty had always claimed the role of the older sibling through sheer will.

There," she said, smoothing the knot and giving it a light pat. "Now you don't look like you're trying to escape." After a beat, she asked the obvious, "Where's Ashley?"

"She bailed. Too tired."

"And you let her leave early?" Marty teased.

Keith shrugged, "I'm going fishing this weekend. She's not into it. Probably needs a break."

Before Keith could finish, Daniel turned and joined them, instantly shifting the energy of the small group. His arrival was subtle, but Keith felt it immediately, like an invisible thread pulling tight.

Their eyes locked.

Keith's expression shifted from wary to hostile in an instant. Daniel, noting it, kept his voice light. "He's having a bad night," he said to Marty, gesturing toward Keith.

Marty blinked, completely caught off guard.

Keith's stare stayed fixed on Daniel, his face becoming colder and even more unyielding.

"Gosh," Daniel went on, just enough to needle. "Could it possibly have gotten worse?"

Keith stepped forward. "Yeah," he said, quiet and tight. "It just did."

The charm Keith had worn so easily earlier now had an edge, cooler, defensive. But Daniel didn't rise to meet it. He stood steady, trying, truly trying, to understand what about him had gotten under Keith's skin so fast.

Marty, sensing the temperature shift, placed a light hand on Keith's arm, then one on Daniel's shoulder; an old reflex from years of diplomacy. "I don't think you two have ever officially met," she said, her voice brightening with effort.

She smiled, wider than necessary, deliberately sunny. "Keith, this is Daniel Eiman. My dear, dear friend Daniel Eiman."

Daniel extended a hand, calm on the surface, though a trace of something unreadable lingered in his eyes: curiosity, maybe. Or restraint. All he wanted now was to ease the tension, step off whatever wire they'd both landed on.

"Nice to meet you, Keith," he said evenly. "Daniel."

Keith paused, a beat too long to be polite. When he finally reached out, his grip was firm, too firm. He held on just long enough to make the message clear before letting go. There was something about Daniel that unsettled him, though he didn't know exactly what or why.

"Keith," he said. "Nice to finally meet you, too. I guess."

Marty forced a laugh, stepping between them once again and placing a hand on each of their arms. "Okay. There we go," she said brightly, a hint of forced cheer in her voice. "Now we're all friends."

Marty's husband, Dexter, had turned to join them just in time to catch the tail end of the exchange. Keith turned slightly, silently acknowledging Dexter, happy for the interlude, expecting the usual detached nod or perfunctory handshake from his brother-in-law.

But the moment Dexter realized it was Daniel Eiman standing before him, his expression shifted, his whole demeanor softening. Then, much to everyone's surprise, but especially Keith's, he pulled Daniel into a full, unhesitating bear hug. "Dude," Dexter said, his voice thick. "Goddamn."

Daniel's arms went around Dexter without hesitation. "He Dex."

For a long moment, neither of them let go.

Keith stood there, his jaw dropping in disbelief. Dexter never hugged, *not like that*. Not even family got that kind of embrace from Dexter. *Who the hell was this guy, anyway?*

Dexter finally pulled back, but his hands remained on Daniel's shoulders. "Damn, you're looking good, Dude."

Daniel smiled back. "Thank you. So are you."

Keith stared across at them, stunned. "Seriously?" He hadn't meant to speak, but the word slipped out before he could catch it.

Dexter nodded without hesitation. "Oh yeah. Columbia swim team. These guys saved my frigging life."

Then, without apology, Dexter pulled Daniel into another hug; tighter this time, longer. There was something deeper in it now, something raw and unspoken that hung in the air between them. "I miss you, man," Dexter said, his voice dropping into something rough and unguarded.

Daniel's reply caught on the edge of his breath. "I miss you, too, Dex."

Keith didn't move. He watched, slack-jawed, as his brother-in-law, someone he'd known for years to be charming but contained, became suddenly unrecognizable. Affectionate. Vulnerable. Open. And at the center of it all stood Daniel, like he'd always been there.

The intimacy of it struck something in Keith he didn't want to name. So, he pivoted. "Columbia..." he said coolly.

Daniel turned to him. Both he and Dexter nodded. "Yes, Columbia."

Keith arched a brow. "Is that where they taught you to harass strangers in public bathrooms?"

The room went still. The tension snapped taut.

Marty gasped, loud and sharp. "What?" She turned, her eyes narrowing as they landed on Daniel.

Daniel's face flushed, but he managed to keep his composure. "He was... I was just—"

"Never mind," Marty cut in, raising a hand. Her voice was quick and direct. "I don't think I want to know."

Keith leaned back, arms folded, his eyes locked on Daniel. There was a faint twitch at the corner of his mouth as though he'd scored something. A small, silent win, maybe.

Daniel met his stare: calm, unflinching. There was no anger in him, only a quiet searching, as if trying to trace the fault line he'd stepped on without meaning to. "A lot going on there, yeah, buddy?" he said softly.

Keith didn't respond. Didn't move.

But then Dexter stepped in, almost like he'd been waiting. He angled slightly toward Daniel, his tone easy, but his words sharp with truth. "Ignore him. He's defensive around anyone who actually knows me."

Daniel chuckled, quiet, contained, but the sound of it landed like a spark in dry brush. It wasn't smug. It was lived-in. Familiar. And it only made Keith feel further from whatever world these two clearly shared.

*****

In Cambridge, Brent parked in his familiar spot as he went through the ritual of getting out of his SUV. A light in his front office illuminated Charlie inside.

Charlie made his way to the easy chair and waited as Brent opened the door and slid inside, tossing his keys onto the corner table.

"So, what's going on with Kaufel?" Charlie asked, genuinely curious.

"It's a long story, Dude." Brent's voice was laced with sarcasm.

"I've got plenty of time." Charlie opened his arms and waited.

"Something happened to me when I was, like, you know, young. With my best friend's dad. And Kaufel's trying to tell me that..."

"So, you were molested." Charlie blurted it out, more a statement than a question.

"Well, it doesn't feel like I was molested." Brent was even more defensive than he was with Kaufel.

"Except that you were."

Brent wheeled through the room, tidying up as he went. "Okay, I was molested. Are you happy? End of conversation."

"What happened?" Charlie wasn't letting it go.

"Dude, really?" Brent turned and faced Charlie full-on.

"Did you go looking for it, or did it find you?" Charlie sat up in the chair deliberately.

"I don't know. Maybe a little of both?" Brent shrugged, his exasperation growing.

"Come on, dude." Charlie wasn't giving up. "You started it!"

"You know, Charlie, it's been a long ass day and night, and I'm exhausted. Help me turn this couch out for when Daniel gets back."

"Just...I want the details."

"No, you don't."

"Yes, I do."

"Well, I'm tired of talking about it."

Off Charlie's look, Brent continued, "I'm actually sick and tired of talking about it."

Raising his arms in defense, Charlie shook his head. "Okay, man, whatever."

"Why did you stop seeing him?" Brent prodded further.

"Kaufel?" Charlie asked, though he already knew. Being difficult had become his default, and provoking Brent was sport for Charlie, especially in moments like these.

"Yeah, Kaufel, asshole! Why'd you stop seeing him?" Brent snapped.

"I told you, I'm not looking for a relationship." Then, catching Brent's growing frustration, Charlie relented. "I went to see what he was about. It's different. Really different. The guy's smart."

"How so?" Brent stopped what he was doing, locking eyes with Charlie. "What makes him different?"

Charlie shrugged, then softened. "Let's just say I saw enough to know you shouldn't stop seeing him. He knows what he's doing, and it's working; I can tell."

Brent shook his head, then gestured toward the couch as he began stripping off the cushions. "Help me with the bed."

Charlie rose slowly and wandered over. He pushed the coffee table aside, nudged Brent's chair just enough to make room, then pulled the sleeper out in one practiced motion. "I'll get to the bottom of this," he said with a small smile. "In the meantime, don't quit." He nodded once, then moved to the side cabinet and began pulling out sheets and pillows.

*****

The crisp night air was imbued with a quiet stillness as Marty, Keith, Daniel, and Dexter, his arm wrapped securely around Marty, strolled through the Public Garden toward Beacon Hill.

The city lights glowed warmly over the park's winding paths and towering trees. The distant sounds of laughter and car horns faintly drifted through the air, mingling with the soft rustle of leaves in the breeze. The Newbury Boston loomed in the background, its lights bright against the dark sky, lending an air of elegance and exclusivity to the surroundings.

Keith walked beside Daniel with his hands shoved into his pockets. His posture was relaxed yet still guarded. Occasionally, he cast a glance at Daniel, suspicion in his eyes that seemed to fade but never quite disappear. Marty walked ahead with Dexter, her laughter ringing out as she regaled Daniel with stories from her latest campaign events, her voice rising and falling in animated excitement.

Finally, Keith broke his self-imposed, unspoken standoff, his voice low as he turned to face Daniel. "So, you're the guy who turned my innocent sister into a total alkie."

Marty overheard him, turning around with a huff of laughter. "Keith! I have complete control over my alcohol," she retorted, her eyes gleaming with mock offense.

Keith raised an eyebrow, giving Daniel a sideways glance. "That was you, right?" he asked, his tone skeptical, though his expression held a hint of amusement. "Are you the one?"

Daniel shrugged, his smile faint. "Have you tried it?" he asked, his tone light but challenging at the same time.

Keith shook his head, a faint smile tugging at his lips despite himself. "No, can't say as I have," he admitted, his tone dry. "But her cabinets are stocked with every flavor of Zwagil known to man."

Daniel grinned, his eyes twinkling with mischief. "So, you've never tried it?"

Keith's smile faltered slightly, though he forced a casual shrug. "Well... I may have tried it once," he said, his voice trailing off as he glanced away. "It didn't work as I recall."

Marty glanced over at Daniel. She knew exactly where to go. Suddenly, they turned and began heading down Beacon Street.

The low hum of conversation filled the cozy bar, punctuated now and then by bursts of laughter from nearby tables. Warm amber light spilled across the polished wood surfaces, catching the gleam of glass and brass. The walls were cluttered with faded photographs, vintage signs, and decades-old memorabilia; each one a story waiting to be told.

Behind the bar, the bartender lined up eight lowball glasses, each shimmering with a different vodka. The crystal clarity of the spirits gave the whole affair a ceremonious air.

Keith, Daniel, Marty, and Dexter settled in at a central table, drawing curious glances from nearby patrons intrigued by the makeshift tasting. Daniel leaned forward, inhaling theatrically from each glass, swirling the liquor as if performing some sacred rite. His eyes twinkled as he looked over at Marty.

"It's so obvious," Daniel declared with a grin, his voice light but certain.

Marty mirrored his expression, lifting her glass with the same exaggerated flourish. "So obvious," she agreed, her smirk laced with affection. Their energy snapped between them like an inside joke too rich to explain.

Keith raised an eyebrow and studied the liquid in his own glass, swirling it with reserved skepticism. He brought it to his nose, sniffed, then took a tentative sip. The vodka hit his tongue with unexpected smoothness, and he blinked, half-surprised.

"Personally, I like tequila," he said, almost sheepishly, as if admitting a minor sin.

Daniel turned toward him, amused. "Noted. Maybe we'll convert you."

"Unlikely." Keith chuckled, but took another sip anyway, more curious this time. As he worked through the line, his movements slowed, thoughtful. He picked up the second-to-last glass, inhaled, and sipped again, then held it in his mouth, considering.

"So… the smoothest, cleanest," he murmured, rolling the flavor over his tongue.

Daniel nodded, leaning in. "No bite. No baggage. Just the flavor."

Keith's eyes lingered on the glass. He set it down gently, then lifted it again, like something fragile and rare. "Given those parameters… There might be one."

Daniel and Marty broke into matching grins and high-fived with gleeful synchronicity. Their shared laughter turned heads across the bar.

Keith turned to the bartender, lifting the glass. "So are the rest of these just garbage?"

The bartender chuckled. "Top of the line. Every one."

Daniel raised his glass ceremoniously. "And what is the name of this revelation?"

The bartender smiled, already anticipating the moment. "Zwagil."

Cheers erupted from nearby tables. Daniel stood, his voice booming: "A shot for everyone!" He turned toward the bartender with mock solemnity. "And put it on Congresswoman Marty Chambers' tab!"

Marty gave him a death stare, half mock, half real, but the corners of her mouth betrayed her. She lifted her glass.

"To Congresswoman Marty Chambers!" Daniel announced, his tone shifting to reverence now. The bar echoed with the toast. Daniel leaned in closer, suddenly quiet, but loud enough for his voice to carry. "So proud of you, Marty. So very proud of you."

She met his gaze, something tender passing between them. "Welcome back, Daniel."

His smile faltered. Just for a second. A hint of pain, which he quickly pushed away.

"I'm not back," he said softly.

Marty didn't flinch. "You can't run forever, Daniel."

Daniel stared into his glass, the hint of a smile tugging at his mouth, more sad than amused. He shook his head slowly, then looked up at her, steady. "Really, Marty? We were having such a nice time."

She reached up and gently tousled his hair. "Yes, Daniel. Really."

Keith watched from just a step away. The sharpness in Daniel's eyes as he sipped, the weight behind Marty's touch, the momentary crack in his composure; it all added up to something unexpected. This guy wasn't the charming provocateur Keith had been ready to dislike. There was something else, something bruised, and startlingly sincere.

For the first time that night, Keith saw it. For the first time, he started to really *see* him.

The cobblestone streets of Louisburg Square were hushed beneath the soft glow of antique streetlamps. The brownstones stood in perfect rows, stately and self-contained, their windows catching the warm amber light and throwing it back like knowing glances. Marty leaned against the wrought-iron railing of her stoop, her posture easy, her cheeks pink from laughter and alcohol. Dexter had already succumbed to the night, slumped on the bottom step, snoring softly in rhythm with the stillness.

Keith and Daniel lingered nearby, a little unsteady, their movements softened by drink and something else, slower and more complex to name. A quiet had settled between them, no longer awkward but full, expectant. Something was unfolding in the space they now shared: tentative, alive, and quietly reaching for more.

Marty steadied herself and pointed at Daniel. Her voice carried a teasing lilt, but there was worry beneath it. "You sure you don't want to spend the night, Daniel? I don't want you driving like this."

Daniel waved her off with the ease of someone used to dismissing concern. "I'm fine. I'll take the train back to Cambridge; crash at Brent's. I've got clothes there anyway."

She turned to Keith, her tone shifting instantly, more stern, more intimate. "And you, don't you even think about getting in a car and driving tonight."

Keith gave a lopsided smile, bracing himself on the railing beside her. "I'm not. Besides, I've still got to find a trailer," he said, then glanced at Daniel, his grin sharpening with mischief. "So, I can meet my destiny with the blues."

Daniel squinted. "Blues?"

Keith mimed a fish swimming. "Bluefish."

Daniel let out a laugh, quick and warm. "Ahhh. Don't you mean so they can meet their destiny with you?"

"In whatever way you want to frame it, Dude."

Marty groaned and rested her forehead briefly against the railing. "You two are a disaster waiting to happen."

Then Keith turned back to Daniel, this time more serious. The grin was still there, but his voice had leveled out. "You want to come?"

Daniel blinked. "Fishing?"

Keith nodded, his eyes not leaving Daniel's.

Daniel paused, head tilted slightly. "I hate fishing."

A beat passed between them.

"But sure," he said, smile returning, slower now. "I'll come."

Marty stepped forward, cutting in before either of them could say more. Her voice was affectionate but edged. "Keith, I'm serious. No driving. And you," she turned to Daniel, narrowing her eyes, "you behave yourself."

Daniel raised both hands in mock surrender. "I always behave myself."

Marty crossed her arms, eyes still on Daniel. "He's dangerous, Keith. Just beware."

Daniel turned to her, feigning innocence, though his eyes never left Keith's. "Do I look dangerous to you?"

"Yes," she cut in, flat and deliberate. Then she turned and faced her brother directly. "Very dangerous." Then, gentler, softer, to both of them: "Stay out of trouble. Both of you."

Daniel gave a lazy half-wave and stepped off the curb, fading into the night. Keith watched him go, the sound of his footsteps lingering in the space he left behind. Then he looked at Marty. As in, really looked at her.

Something in her voice was still hanging there, protective, unresolved. She didn't repeat it. She didn't need to. Keith said nothing. After a moment, he pushed off the railing and followed Daniel.

The Charles River lapped softly at the banks as Keith and Daniel sat side by side on a weathered bench, cups of coffee warming their hands. The river carried the city's reflection, lights scattered like constellations drifting across the water. Couples strolled by now and then, their voices low, their laughter easy and distant.

The silence between Keith and Daniel wasn't awkward, but neither was it entirely peaceful. It was the kind of silence that asked questions.

Eventually, Keith broke it. "So... you took all your electives in the medical college while you were in law school?" His tone was casual, but laced with genuine curiosity, like someone starting to realize he didn't fully understand what he'd always assumed he knew.

Daniel nodded, watching the water. "And you passed the bar in four states but didn't file the paperwork in any of them."

Keith gave a soft laugh. "I filed here. In Massachusetts. Not the others."

Daniel turned slightly toward him. "But you're not practicing."

Keith shrugged, a little too quickly. "They think I am. I let them. Mostly I'm... investigating law, I guess."

Daniel raised an eyebrow. "That sounds exhausting."

Keith's exhale was exaggerated. "It is. In a not very pleasant kind of way."

Daniel studied him more carefully now. "And no politics." It was more a statement than a question.

Keith looked down at his coffee, a humorless smile touching his mouth. "That's a long, slow disaster of a story."

"I've got time," Daniel said, his voice quiet but open.

Keith met his eyes, as if weighing it. Then he spoke. "I've been officially blacklisted. Major media. Minor media. All media. Except the fashion police, of course."

Daniel's expression didn't change, but he was listening now, fully attentive. "Blacklisted?"

Keith nodded. "Literally. Doesn't matter what I say or do. Nothing sticks. Nothing spreads. Anything I care about is met with polite indifference, or worse: silence. I don't know why. I stopped asking."

Daniel sat with it as it settled in. Then, softly: "So you don't really... do anything." He wasn't accusing. He was clarifying.

Keith chuckled softly. "Not anything that matters to me. But at least I'm not running."

That landed – yet again.

Daniel shifted, just enough for Keith to regret having said it, genuinely wishing he could take his words back, but their effect had already taken hold.

Daniel's voice dropped. "I'm not running." He looked Keith square in the eye. "Yeah, I've got shit to work out. But I'm not running."

Keith didn't blink. "What kind of shit?"

Daniel's gaze dropped. He stared at the ground in silence, as if reaching for something just beyond language, something he wasn't ready to share. "Another time," he said softly. Then, more to himself than to Keith, "Another time."

Keith didn't push.

The silence returned, but now it carried weight.

When their eyes finally met again, Daniel's gaze was calm but intent, compassionate and fully present. No longer caught in his own swirl of thought, he let the silence stretch just long enough to show that what he was about to say was something he truly meant. His voice was shaped by something almost reverent, gathering quiet weight as he spoke. "I can't imagine being America's most eligible bachelor. And rich. And a Chambers. Does anyone actually know you for you?"

Keith shook his head. The movement was small, almost reflexive. Then he tilted it slightly, his fingers tracing the rim of his coffee cup. "No. Nobody." His voice was steady now. "Not even my own family."

Daniel nodded. The intensity in his face softened. "I want to meet the real Keith Chambers. How do I get to know the Keith Chambers you are when nobody's watching?"

Keith gave a faint shake of his head, his fingers still circling the cup, as if he needed the motion to stay grounded.

Daniel leaned in, quieter now. "Do you trust me?"

Keith stared at his cup, then looked up, meeting Daniel's eyes. "Exactly how dangerous are you?"

Daniel took a moment to really think about it. The truth came slowly, but he felt compelled to speak it. A smile slipped across his face, slow and subtle. "Well, for you? Probably about as dangerous as anyone could possibly be."

Keith narrowed his eyes. "What's that supposed to mean?"

Daniel shrugged, his smile deepening. "I don't know. Use your imagination."

Keith went quiet again, and Daniel let him. The silence stretched, holding something unspoken between them. Just as Daniel began to accept that his well-meaning plans might not come to fruition, Keith looked up. "I need to be in my office by eleven. Monday morning."

Daniel paused. "You're sure?"

"No," Keith said. "But…"

Daniel smiled. "Gotta love a man who's up for an adventure."

As the clock crept toward morning, Keith sat in the stillness, unsure if this was brilliance or madness, but unwilling to look away.

*****

The first light of dawn spilled across the horizon, casting a golden glow over the untouched beach. Gentle waves lapped at the shore, the ocean stretching out in tranquil blues and soft pinks that melted into the warming sky.

Keith stood alone at the edge of the sand, one hand shielding his eyes from the early glare. His gaze swept across the quiet expanse until it settled on a pile of clothes, tossed carelessly near the dune grass: Daniel's. A solitary marker on the pristine canvas.

Keith squinted toward the water. And there he was.

Far out, Daniel cut through the waves with effortless grace. He rose and dipped with the rhythm of the sea, riding each swell as if it belonged to him. Keith watched, transfixed. A momentary hesitation crossed his face before disappearing.

Without a second thought, he yanked off his shirt, stripped to his boxer briefs, and charged into the surf. The cold bit at his skin, but he barely registered it.

In a rusted sedan parked just above the beach, a man stirred from an awkward sleep. He sat up, stretching, blinking against the sunlight pouring through the cracked windshield. He adjusted the brim of his cap, rubbed his eyes, and looked out toward the water. Something caught his attention.

Just past the shoreline, two figures splashed and tumbled in the surf. Keith and Daniel, bare-skinned and laughing, free of the armor the world usually demanded from them. They chased one another through the water, playful and free, as if the rest of the world didn't exist.

The man reached across the passenger seat for a camera, already fitted with a long telephoto lens. Lifting it to his eye, he adjusted the focus until the scene came into crisp view.

CLICK.

Through the lens, the moment froze: Keith and Daniel mid-laughter, the morning light catching the saltwater in their hair, their faces alive and unguarded. No pretense. No stagecraft. Just joy. Which was now on record.

CLICK, CLICK, CLICK, CLICK, CLICK.

The man's finger tapped rhythmically on the shutter, capturing every moment and carefree smile. He muttered to himself, eyeing the pair with calculated interest as if he had stumbled upon something far more valuable than he could have ever hoped for.

Inside a small beachside shop filled with racks of brightly colored shorts, loose shirts, and beach accessories, Keith handed several bills to the sales clerk. He now wore a new pair of cargo shorts and a light shirt, while his severely wrinkled tuxedo clothes were tucked by his side.

The clerk's eyes moved from Keith to the magazine open on the counter; a full-page spread featuring *America's Most Eligible Bachelor*. Keith's own face stared back, polished and posed, every bit the image of high society.

The clerk looked up, eyes widening in recognition. Keith shifted, offering a tight, uneasy smile.

Before he could say a word, Daniel appeared beside him, holding oversized sunglasses and a floppy sun hat. Without comment, he gently placed the hat on Keith's head and slid the glasses over his eyes, the faintest smirk on his lips.

Just then, another clerk stepped out from the back, his eyes also alighting with recognition.

Daniel scooped the change from the counter and gave Keith a soft shove toward the door. "Come on, mystery man," he murmured, amusement in his voice.

As they slipped outside, Keith exhaled, and Daniel leaned in just enough for their shoulders to touch. "You good?" he asked, voice low, only for Keith.

Keith glanced at him through the tinted lenses and nodded. "Better," he said, quieter still.

They kept walking; Daniel just a step ahead, smiling to himself, and Keith, behind the glasses, trying not to.

In a quiet alley tucked behind the shops, Daniel and Keith crouched low, shielded by a wall of sun-bleached beach murals. The buzz of the town faded behind them, replaced by the hush of their own little pocket of mischief.

Daniel knelt close, dabbing glue on a pair of bushy, fake black eyebrows. His breath was slow and focused as he leaned in, carefully pressing them onto Keith's face. "Hold still," he murmured, their faces only inches apart. His hands were sure, but gentle.

Keith studied him: his concentration, the slight crease between his brows, the way he tilted his head to assess the placement like an artist stepping back from a canvas. Daniel nodded once, satisfied, and held up his phone to show the result.

Keith smirked, catching his reflection. "Jesus."

"Just trust me," Daniel said, already pulling out a tangled black wig. "We're going full incognito here."

Keith chuckled as Daniel slid the wig on, his fingers ruffling the matted dreadlocks into position with surprising tenderness. Then came the beard: thick, absurd, and somehow perfect. Daniel patted everything into place, dusted it with a handful of sand for realism, then stood back and admired his handiwork. "There," he said, arms crossed, grinning. "You look like you've been living in a beach van since '99."

Keith studied his image on the screen, shaking his head in disbelief. "It's... something," he said, but the reluctant smile that tugged at his lips said more.

Daniel handed him sunglasses and a floppy, sun-stained hat. "Okay, here's the deal." He stepped closer, his voice softer now. "Today, I want to hang out with *you*. Not the bachelor. Not the headline. Just Keith Chambers, the real one. No cameras, no suits, no noise. Just you. And I'm going to do the best I can to support all that! Deal?"

Keith looked at him, really looked at him, the weight in his chest shifting. "Deal," he said, slipping on the sunglasses and hat like armor he actually *wanted* to wear. With each piece of the disguise, something let go. He felt lighter. Unburdened. And for reasons he couldn't quite explain, freer than he had in a very long time.

Later, on a makeshift volleyball court lit by the late afternoon sun, the two moved like two kids on summer break. Daniel, now in the oversized sunglasses and floppy hat he'd picked initially out for Keith, tossed the ball up with a shout.

Keith, buried under fake dreadlocks and now streaked with sweat and sand, lunged forward and spiked the ball hard over the net. Cheers erupted around them. Locals clapped. Strangers laughed.

They high-fived, laughing loudly, unfiltered and genuine. And amidst all the noise, Keith quietly forgot to be anyone but himself.

The onlookers, a mix of families, tourists, and fellow beachgoers, cheered them on with growing enthusiasm, swept up in the game's infectious energy. As the ball flew back across the net, Daniel dove to intercept it, his wrists barely grazing the sand as he sent it spiraling back into the air. Keith lunged forward, his body moving with an athleticism that surprised even him, slamming the ball down and securing yet another point for their team.

A roar of applause erupted from the crowd as Daniel clapped Keith on the back, his laughter full of pride.

Pulling Keith out of earshot of the others, Daniel whispered, "Not bad for America's Most Eligible Bachelor," Daniel teased, his grin wide as he watched Keith soak in the applause.

Keith shook his head, a huge smile spreading across his face as he looked around, absorbing the scene: the people, the freedom, the carefree anonymity. For the first time, maybe in forever, he felt like just another face in the crowd. "Not bad at all," he murmured, his voice barely audible over the noise of the cheering crowd.

Still disguised with his fake eyebrows, mustache, beard, and wig, Keith stepped away from the urinal next to Daniel. He scrubbed his hands at the sink, meticulously washing away every trace of sand, salt, and now urine from the day's adventures.

Daniel stepped away from the urinal behind him, skipping the sinks and heading for the door. As Keith caught up with him outside, he raised an eyebrow, his voice dripping with dry humor. "At Princeton, they taught us to wash our hands after we piss."

Daniel grinned and, not missing a beat, replied. "At Columbia, they taught us not to piss on our hands." Keith snorted, shaking his head as he followed Daniel out of the restroom. A faint smirk appeared on Daniel's face. As they stepped back into the sunlight, Keith launched into a litany about uric acid on restaurant mints. Daniel shook his head and waved him off.

As they moved, their steps slowed. Daniel glanced over at Keith, long enough to really see him. Keith noticed, meeting the look with something gentler than before. They didn't speak for a while. But the silence wasn't awkward. It felt earned. Familiar. By the time they reached the corner, their shoulders were close enough to brush. And neither of them moved away.

Keith and Daniel sat across from each other in a cozy, upscale restaurant filled with softly dimmed lights and quiet chatter. Keith, still sporting his outlandish disguise, counted out a generous tip, carefully pushing the check carrier toward the waiter before tucking his wallet back into his pocket. The entire day had softened his usual reserved expression, and he leaned back with a contented sigh. Keith glanced at Daniel, a hint of anticipation in his gaze. "So... what now?"

Daniel opened his mouth to answer, but a pair of servers suddenly approached, each balancing a tray laden with lowball glasses. They set the drinks down one by one, forming a line of glistening glasses in front of Daniel, who blinked in surprise. As the glasses were carefully lined up in front of Daniel, an enthusiastic crowd began to gather around the table, their collective energy lively and expectant. A particularly flamboyant gay man pushed through the small group, his expression lighting up as he caught sight of Daniel.

"Daniel? Daniel Eiman!" he called out, his voice carrying across the restaurant. Daniel's eyes widened slightly as he took in the group gathering around their table, recognizing faces from another chapter of his life.

One of the newcomers, a man with a bright, playful expression, stepped forward. "Daniel? Can it be? Is it really you?" he said, his tone half-incredulous, half-teasing. "Well, I'll be a son of a bitch. Where have you been, girl?"

Before Daniel could answer, another tall, sharply dressed man with a smirk that practically radiated charisma chimed in, "¡Hermana, ¿dónde has estado? Estábamos a punto de llamar a la oficina de personas desaparecidas por ti!"

Keith's gaze darted around, taking in the group with a mixture of confusion and discomfort as more Chelsea Boys approached, each greeting Daniel with exuberant hugs, handshakes, and genuine laughter.

Keith shifted in his seat, visibly tense, as he looked between the band of brothers and Daniel. A Chelsea Boy leaned back, his eyes fixed on Keith, a curious smirk dancing across his face. "¡Vaya, te ves increíble, Daniel!"

He nodded toward Keith, sizing him up.

"Y quién es este?"

"Ahora no es el momento, amigos. En realidad. Ya sabes, en otra ocasión." Daniel shot back.

The small band of gay men stared down at Daniel. Volleying looks between him and Keith. Their smiles broadened mischievously. Daniel wasn't having it. "¡En serio!"

Keith stared across at Daniel. Then up at the sudden growing number of intruders, and then back at Daniel.

Daniel shook his head slowly while Keith observed the restaurant's patrons, realizing that nearly everyone in the establishment seemed to be part of Provincetown's LGBTQ community.

The realization settled over Keith slowly, his discomfort growing as he navigated increasingly knowing glances, along with friendly, approving winks now being sent their way from half the patrons in the restaurant.

Keith burst out of the restaurant, inadvertently slamming the door against the wall, pulling off his wig, and wiping away the remnants of his fake mustache, beard, and eyebrows. Daniel rushed behind, managing to stifle his humor about the whole scenario as he called out, "Dude... wait!"

Keith came to a sudden halt, spinning on his heel with an expression of exasperation. Catching Daniel completely off guard, he collided with Keith, sending both of them stumbling in opposite directions.

Keith's eyes burned with intensity as his voice rose. "Are you out of your mind?" Daniel raised his hands, trying to keep his composure. "What?" he protested, a hint of defensive laughter slipping through. "We're in Provincetown, for crying out loud! We've been in Provincetown all day!"

Keith's voice wavered, his frustration sharp in the strain of it. He took a breath, then another, trying to steady himself. "So? I've been to Provincetown. Lots of times. It doesn't mean I..." He stopped, glancing down at his hands. The wig was in one, the fake mustache, beard, and eyebrows in the other. What had been a disguise was now just a ridiculous handful of props. He looked up, his eyes fierce. "And you think this is funny!"

Daniel could not, no matter how hard he tried, suppress his delight at the sight of it all. "Um, yeah. A little," he said. "I mean, you have to admit..." He stopped himself, suddenly aware of the increasing distress tightening Keith's face.

Around them, a few patrons and passersby started whispering and glancing in their direction, some nudging each other with murmurs of, "Is that Keith Chambers?"

"No way…"

"I think it might be!"

Daniel stepped back, his gaze moving over Keith. Then, hoping to deflect the realization spreading through the steadily growing crowd, he stated the obvious as if it could not possibly be true. "You know, you *do* look like Keith Chambers. Has anyone ever told you that? You look exactly like Keith Chambers."

With a huff of exasperation, Keith stormed off, muttering under his breath as he tried to reattach the wig, eyebrows, and beard. His hands fumbled with the adhesive, his face caught somewhere between embarrassment and fury. Daniel caught up to him, still fighting to keep a straight face. "They're just some guys I knew, Keith," he said, nodding back toward the restaurant. "What's the big deal?"

Keith stopped in his tracks, spinning to face Daniel, his eyes blazing.

"What!?" Daniel opens his arms, more a matter of surrender than anything.

Keith's face flushed crimson. He turned on his heel and stormed off. Daniel moved to follow, but Keith stopped short and spun back, and Daniel slammed into him again. Keith shoved him off, frustration boiling over. "Why didn't you tell me before?" he demanded, his voice tight with something raw and rising. "Now you've gone and ruined everything!"

Daniel's face softened, trying to mask the effects Keith's words were now having on him. Then, defensively, he said, "Tell you what? That I'm gay?" He raised his voice slightly, exasperated. "Alright, I'm gay! Very gay and very out! Marty knows. Dexter knows. Every single human being who's ever heard of me knows! What's the big deal?"

Keith's face was smeared with remnants of glue, sweat, and sand, the wig sliding sideways as if it wanted out of the whole ordeal. He stared at Daniel, wide-eyed and stunned, caught between the effort to stay composed and the rage that refused to let him.

Daniel saw it, the wild mix of humiliation and disbelief. He fought back the impulse to laugh, painfully aware that behind the absurdity of it all was something genuinely fragile for Keith.

In the meantime, Keith's fake mustache was losing its own battle, hanging from one side of his lip like a wet Band-Aid. He pressed it back with a muttered curse, as if sheer will would make it stay. It did not.

Daniel fought with everything he had not to laugh, but it slipped through his eyes, bright and impossible to hide, as Keith unknowingly drifted back toward the edge of the pier.

Even as the sight of him tugged at something tender, Daniel felt warmth rise with the smile he could no longer suppress. Keith was trying so hard to keep himself together, but the whole thing had slipped into that strange space between heartbreaking and hilarious.

"What are you smirking at?" Keith shouted, his voice trembling with fury and indignation.

Daniel swallowed a laugh and reached out, instinctively trying to grab him, but then,

SPLASH.

Keith had taken one step too far and disappeared off the edge of the pier.

Daniel sauntered over and looked down. Keith surfaced, sputtering, the wig and mustache floating beside him like casualties of pride. His soaked face was pure indignation, and for a moment, Daniel could only blink, torn between shock, sympathy, and the ache of genuine affection that overrode it all.

The crowd stirred, concern softening into uneasy laughter and relief. "Dude, are you alright?" someone called out.

Daniel stood at the edge of the pier, his expression calm now, the rush of the moment settling into something simple and real. "He's fine!"

He watched Keith sputtering and pulling himself together, not with pity or amusement, but with quiet acceptance of him, of the night, of everything that had led them to this moment. The air felt different, warmer somehow, even as the breeze turned cool. Nothing would be the same after this, though he could not yet name what had shifted. Only that something had, and that it would matter.

Later, on the beach, Keith sat wrapped in a blanket, shivering, covered in sand. Daniel stood nearby, hands in his pockets, equal parts amused and sympathetic. "You know," he said, "this might be why no one listens to you; you're so damn serious all the time."

Keith's eyes snapped up, sharp. "Wow. Going for the jugular now?" He tapped the face of his watch. "Pretty sure it's still today. Mr. 'I'm going to help you be yourself.'"

Daniel held up his hands, a gesture of acquiescence, his expression softening. "Right. You're right. I'm sorry, that was a cheap shot." He paused, tilting his head as he observed Keith shivering. "But seriously, dude…" Daniel concluded.

Keith glared back, fighting the uncontrollable shivers wracking his body. Daniel smirked, raising an eyebrow. "You should probably take your clothes off."

Keith's glare intensified. "Right! I'll do that right here, right now!"

Daniel shrugged and waved him off. " Okay… freeze. See if I care." He turned and started walking.

Keith hesitated, then clumsily shuffled after him, teeth chattering, blanket wrapped tight like a makeshift toga.

"Unbelievable," he muttered, trailing Daniel with a chorus of shivering gripes and half-cursed complaints. Each step sloshed with soggy indignation, his annoyance growing louder and wetter by the second.

Under the harsh fluorescent lights of a small laundromat, Keith and Daniel sat side by side on a bench. Keith was wrapped in a blanket, his disguise gone: no wig, no beard, no mustache. Just Keith. Recognizable, exposed. Exhausted. People passed outside the windows; some gawking, some whispering. Keith didn't flinch. He stared ahead, face weary but still, the fight in him quieted for now.

Daniel sat silently beside him.

After a long pause, Keith let out a small breath, almost a sigh, but not quite. Then, without turning his head, he asked softly, "What exactly is the Anatomy story?"

Daniel's face softened, his gaze drifting to a distant memory. "She told you the Anatomy story?" he asked, a hint of warmth in his voice.

Keith nodded, shifting slightly to get more comfortable, then settling deeper into the worn, beat-up, weathered leather couch. "It is how you two met, right?"

"Yes," Daniel replied, a soft chuckle escaping as he recalled the details. "It's also how she met your brother-in-law. Did she tell you that?"

"Yup," Keith grinned, leaning back with an almost smug satisfaction. "She owes you for life, doesn't she?"

Daniel chuckled, the sound warm and genuine. "They fit," he said simply.

"They really do," Keith agreed, his eyes momentarily glazing over as he considered the truth of it. Both sat in comfortable silence, wrapped in the easy atmosphere that only comes from recounting shared stories and familiar faces.

A faint smile played on Daniel's lips as he thought out loud, "Too bad they got married during COVID. That's a wedding I would've liked to have attended."

Keith chuckled. "Yeah, it was small. They were planning this massive event, but COVID happened." He smirked. "Saved my father a shitload of cash. I heard he actually offered Dexter fifty grand to elope."

Daniel burst into laughter, shaking his head. "Really?"

"Yup." Keith's laughter grew. "My mother would have shot him; shot both of them, probably! But then COVID came in and saved the day."

"That's hilarious," Daniel chuckled. His eyes still sparkled with amusement when Keith asked, "Would you have come to the wedding?"

Daniel seemed to consider this for a moment, then nodded. "I probably would've. Yeah. For sure. I mean, she's one of my closest friends. Even though we remain at complete political odds. We do share values."

Keith nodded thoughtfully before sighing and shifting slightly in his seat. "Alright, enough of that. Let's talk anatomy."

Daniel's smile broadened as he relaxed into his memories. "I was sitting in my anatomy class, and suddenly, it dawned on me how everything in our bodies just…fits," he said, gesturing as if to capture the enormity of the thought. "Hormones, neurotransmitters, biochemical feedback loops, epigenetic markers, sympathetic and parasympathetic signals… electrical currents, muscle fibers, bones articulating with quiet precision. All these distinct systems, each with its own code, its own rhythm, and somehow, they're in conversation. Constantly. Silently. Miraculously. All of it…fits."

Keith leaned in, paying closer attention, his brow knitting in curiosity.

Daniel's voice grew even softer, almost like he was confiding something he hadn't told anyone before. "And then it hit me: what if the body isn't just a system? What if it's a metaphor for life itself? What if everything, all the time, actually fits? Not just functionally, but… meaningfully. What if beneath the chemistry and chaos, it's completely reflective, and, at some level, rooted in love?"

He glanced at Keith, then away again, as if embarrassed by the word, but unwilling to choose another. "I know it sounds naïve, or maybe even absurd. But the idea overwhelmed me. Like, completely. To this day, I still don't understand why it hit me so hard.

I just remember needing to leave class. I thought I was having some sort of breakdown. Like my mind, my heart, my body; none of it could contain what I'd just come to understand. I honestly thought I might explode right there in class."

Daniel took a moment, the memory seeping back into his skin and bones. He half-laughed, shaking his head as he softly concluded. "I had this vivid image: my guts splattered across the classroom. Like the truth of me had gotten too big for my skin and finally burst out, spraying all over everyone. So, I left."

Keith's expression shifted; curiosity giving way to something closer to awe. "You just... left?"

Daniel nodded.

"Was it a big lecture hall?" Keith was trying to wrap his head around it all.

Daniel shook his head, chuckling at the absurdity of the memory. "No, it was a small classroom. Thirty. Thirty-five of us. But I couldn't stay. I got up and walked out halfway through the class."

Keith's eyebrows rose in surprise. "And why exactly?"

Daniel looked away, his eyes tracing the contours of the brightly lit room. It was as if every bit of dust and dirt left behind by the haphazard cleaning crew held an answer for him. He struggled to find the right words. "I don't know. I really don't. I just felt... like... I had to get out of there before I shattered. It actually felt like my whole body was going to disintegrate or something. Really, it was dire. At least it felt that way to me."

Keith sat quietly, his eyes never leaving Daniel's face, absorbing every word. "From an anatomy class."

"Yeah." As Daniel sank deeper into the memory, his voice softened to barely above a whisper. "Anyway, I got to the quad, and there was Marty, watching me cross with this look of... horror. I thought, 'Is it that obvious?' Am I really falling apart so badly that even strangers know?"

Keith leaned in, captivated. "What happened?"

Daniel's expression grew distant, as if he were back there again, feeling the cool air and seeing Marty's concerned look. "She wouldn't let me pass. She just stepped in front of me and asked, 'Are you alright?' And I looked at her. Really looked at her, and I was, like... 'No, I'm not.'" He laughed softly. "And then she reached out and touched me."

Keith's expression relaxed into an almost reverent gaze as he tried to picture it. "Marty Chambers? My sister, Marty Chambers, genuinely showed concern for a stranger?"

Daniel laughed, shaking his head in disbelief. "Yeah. It shocked me, too. I mean, I knew who she was, obviously, but she didn't know me from a hole in the wall. Yet there she was, reaching out, just... caring. I tried to explain what was going on, but of course, I didn't have words for it."

His smile faded as the memory settled. "And right around that time, Dexter showed up."

Keith laughed, his grin widening as he shook his head. "Dexter?"

Daniel chuckled, nodding. "Yeah, Dexter." He paused, savoring the absurdity of it all.

Daniel's expression once again turned thoughtful as he explained. "As you heard earlier, Dexter and I were on the swim team together. We knew each other, but we weren't exactly friends. I mean, you know Dexter; he's a breeder."

"A breeder?" Keith repeated a hint of confusion in his tone.

Daniel laughed, rolling his eyes. "Yes, a breeder. It's what we… well, what we faggots call straight men who think they're superior to us, just because they sleep with women, and we don't."

"Okay, fair enough," Keith said, chuckling. "But, could you please not use that term?"

"Breeder?" Daniel asked.

"No, faggot!" Keith clarified.

"I am a faggot. We get to call each other faggot. You know, like Dave Chappelle calls his kin…"

Before Daniel could get the N-word out, Keith raised his hands, abruptly stopping him mid-thought. "I find that offensive, too."

"Noted." Daniel smiled as he gently shook his head.

"Thank you." Keith gestured for Daniel to finish his thought.

Daniel grinned as he continued. "Anyway, there I was with Marty, and Dexter showed up. And apparently, he's been smitten with Marty since puberty."

"Really?" Keith leaned forward, clearly intrigued.

"Oh, yeah. Actually, since before puberty. I mean, Dexter didn't share that with us because he never shares details like that. But it came out during one of those heated arguments he and Charlie are always having."

"Charlie? Do you mean the short, hairy fireplug of a guy? That scrappy gorilla guy?"

Daniel burst out laughing. "Yes! That is a perfect description of Charlie. Short, hairy, as scrappy as they come." Daniel shook his head, laughing out loud.

Both men laughed together, the sound filling the laundromat amidst the churning washing machines and the tumbling dryers, creating an almost comforting atmosphere.

Keith, still grinning, asked, "So, what were they arguing about?"

"Anything and everything," Daniel replied, shaking his head. "Always best to keep Charlie and Dexter apart if you want peace."

Keith laughed, then gestured for Daniel to continue the story.

"Well, Dexter apparently told his best friend in grade school that he was going to marry Marty Chambers, that she was the one for him."

"Really?" Keith's eyes widened with genuine surprise.

"Yes, really," Daniel confirmed, a smirk spreading across his face.

"Does she know that?" Keith wondered out loud.

"Oh, she knows," Daniel chuckled. "Trust me, she knows."

Keith shook his head, unable to hold back a grin. "Holy shit!"

"Yeah. So Dexter shows up, and instantly, you can feel it: the connection. Sparks. Right there in the quad, flying between them. Totally palpable. But then Marty, without missing a beat, turns back to me. Looks at Dexter and goes, 'Sorry, but we have to finish this conversation.' And *shoos* him away. Literally!"

Daniel laughed, eyes gleaming with the memory, still entertained by her boldness.

Keith could only shake his head in wonder. "What did Dexter do?"

"Oh, he stood there for a moment, stunned! Utterly stunned. And then he walked away, like a dog with its tail between its legs." Daniel laughed, recalling it all. "Then, halfway across the quad, Dexter turned back, walked right back up to Marty, and asked for her phone number." Daniel laughed, marveling at the memory. "Can you imagine?"

Keith grinned, a mischievous glint in his eyes. "What did she say?"

"She gave it to him!" Daniel said, still reeling from disbelief. "As he walked away, she turned to me and asked, 'Is he safe?'"

Keith burst out laughing. "Did you say yes?"

"Well, first, I asked her, 'Define safe.'"

Daniel leaned back, a smile spreading across his face as he recalled the moment. "So, she asks me, 'He's not a stalker or anything, is he?'"

"How do you know I'm not a stalker?" I shot back. She looked me straight in the eye and replied, 'Honey, really?'" The thought had Keith laughing out loud. Daniel continued, "We both burst out laughing, and that little moment really helped lift my spirits. Somehow, that made me feel better, almost even back to normal."

Daniel took a moment for it to settle in, then said, "I told her, 'He's on the swim team. If he mistreats you, you can find him there, and we'll report him.'" Daniel chuckled, his eyes sparkling with amusement. "Then she asked me, 'How do you know he's on the swim team?' to which I said, 'Because I'm also on the swim team!'"

Keith smirked. "What did she say to that?"

"She said, 'There are some really hot guys on that swim team.'" Daniel mimicked her tone, his grin widening.

Keith raised an eyebrow, chuckling. "And?"

Daniel shrugged, still grinning. "'Yes, indeed, there are,' I said. And then she looked at me and added, 'Yourself included.'" Daniel paused, a slight blush creeping onto his cheeks. "I've always been terrible at receiving compliments, which she picked up on immediately."

Keith laughed. "So, did she ask you to continue your story?"

Daniel nodded, a soft smile playing on his lips. "She did. She really wanted to hear about that anatomy class." He paused, his voice growing more reflective. "But I brushed it off, told her I was fine. Then she handed me her phone and asked for mine.

I put my number in hers, and she did the same. She gave it back, making me promise to call." He let the moment hang, then added with a slight shrug, "Just as I was leaving, I said, 'By the way, I'm gay.'"

Keith chuckled. "Did she ask if Dexter was gay, too?"

"Oh, yeah, she didn't miss a beat!" Daniel laughed. "She was like, 'How about him? Is he gay, too?' I told her, 'Oh no, poor Dexter's about as straight as they come.'" Daniel shook his head, laughing. "Then she was off. But just a few steps away, she stopped, turned back, and asked, 'You're okay, right?'"

"Were you okay?" Keith asked.

Daniel nodded, smiling softly. "'Yes, I'm fine,' I told her. She didn't believe it, asked me again, and then made me promise to call her. I just nodded, and she waltzed off."

Daniel paused, his gaze distant. "That moment… it was… something else."

Daniel shook his head, clearly amused. "So, is that the story she told you?"

Keith shrugged. "Sort of. I mean, she never elaborated on any of those details about Dexter being in love with her since grade school; she only said that you had introduced them and that you were both on the swim team."

"It really was completely out of character for Dexter," Daniel added. "He swears he would never do that; ask a girl for her number. Especially Marty Chambers, of all people."

Keith chuckled. "Why did you think he did?"

Daniel shrugged, smirking. "It's a mystery to all of us. But whatever compelled him, it obviously worked."

Keith chuckled, then leaned back, a glint of curiosity in his eyes. "Alright, now finish the anatomy story. What happened?"

Daniel laughed, his eyes gleaming with playful defiance. "It's one of those things that's just… not explainable."

"Oh, come on!" Keith prodded, nudging Daniel's shoulder.

Daniel shook his head, laughing. "Trust me, it's not that interesting."

Keith grinned, a mischievous glint in his eye. "Okay, so you took all your electives in the medical school?"

"Not all of them, but yeah, most of them. I also studied to be an EMT and shadowed for a while. That sort of stuff." Daniel replied, leaning back with his arms crossed behind his head, an unconscious gesture of surrender.

"But you didn't want to be a doctor?" Keith prodded further.

Daniel shook his head. "Nope. It turns out I didn't want to be an EMT either. But it was fun... those nights in the ambulance. I thought it might be a fun job to do through college. However, I didn't really have the time, and the blood and gore affected me pretty quickly. Still, I learned that I'm good in an emergency."

"How so?" Keith's interest piqued.

"I don't know. The paramedics told me that during emergencies, most people get stressed out and act irrationally, while others become over-focused under pressure. Apparently, I display the characteristics of someone who becomes over-focused under pressure. I think it was a survival mechanism from growing up with four brothers. Go figure."

Keith's brow transformed into a landscape of creases and valleys, etched with curiosity and doubt as he pondered the mystery that Daniel presented. "So why did you major in Poly Sci if you didn't want to be a politician or lawyer?"

Daniel laughed, rolling his eyes. "I just knew I needed to take care of things. People, animals, whatever. I knew that much from an early age." Daniel paused, his expression turning reflective. "But that need was… discouraged by my mother, of course."

Keith raised an eyebrow, settling in with a genuine curiosity. "How so?"

Daniel laughed, a hint of incredulity in his voice. "Oh my God, is this therapy?"

Keith smirked. "No. But I am genuinely interested. Really. I am!"

Daniel exhaled as if blowing away the dust from long-hidden memories. "I must've been four, maybe five, years old and was playing with a doll, probably my cousin's or something. My mother saw me, and the look of horror on her face is something I'll never forget." Daniel shook his head, recalling it all. "She ripped that thing right out of my hands. And that was that."

"Because… it was a doll?" Keith asked, his voice quiet with disbelief.

"I guess," Daniel shrugged. "But it wasn't like I wanted to dress it up or anything. It was more… I wanted to take care of it. I've always had this need to take care of living things. Or anything for that matter. Even if it was a doll."

"Hence, all your electives in medical school," Keith said with a slow nod.

Daniel nodded, sitting forward again, thoughtful. "Exactly. But in my own way. Not that way. I still haven't found it, really. I'm still not sure what I'm looking for, but I love teaching."

Daniel and Keith sat in silence as the weight of the memory settled around both of them like a comfortable blanket.

Daniel studied Keith for a moment, then offered. "Do you ever notice how things sometimes just… get stuck in your craw? Like certain things dig away at you and never seem to let you go?"

"I'm not sure. What do you mean?" Keith asked.

"Like, what's the biggest thing that stands out as a memory when you were five years old?"

"Not playing with dolls." Keith's smile broadened.

"Ha, ha, ha." Then suddenly, Daniel's look started accentuating his seriousness. "Does anything stand out to you?"

Keith looked thoughtful. "At five years old?" Keith clarified. Daniel nodded, "Yes." Keith thought about it and finally offered, "I guess I was mostly learning how to navigate Marty at five years old."

Daniel smirked. "How to navigate Marty?"

Keith laughed, a glimmer of mischief in his eyes. "Yeah. I was this genuinely happy kid, you know? Content with whatever I was doing, until Marty would come in and decide that whatever was making me happy should make her happy, too." Keith abruptly stopped, shaking his head.

Daniel urged him to continue. "Like what?"

"I don't want to throw Marty under the bus."

"Ahhh, come on. Give me some Marty dirt." Daniel leaned in closer to Keith.

"No. Really, it's stupid. Please finish your thoughts. Tell me what's stuck in your craw."

"Well," Daniel sighed, settling into the folds of the couch. "According to this crazy teacher I had in college, around five years old is when children start to explore and develop their natural gifts and talents. If they're lucky, their parents recognize their interest and encourage them."

"Which is basically the opposite of what happens in most cases," Keith interjected.

"Exactly," Daniel agreed. "So, this teacher also said that during puberty, we start to realize for ourselves there's something inside of us motivating us in specific directions."

Keith nodded, hanging on every word.

Daniel continued, "But sometimes, or in some cultures, what we discover about ourselves clashes with how we were raised and conditioned. That definitely happened to me. Did that happen to you?" Daniel asked.

Keith could only shake his head, reflecting. "I don't really remember. I only remember getting into sports at that age: crew in high school. I love rowing to this day. But I don't remember anything like that."

"For me, it was definitely a defining moment of my adolescence," Daniel shared earnestly.

"Hmm." Keith knitted his eyebrows together, pondering. "That's interesting... I'll have to think about it."

"Yeah." Daniel rubbed his chin. "It's just something that's always stuck with me. Because I've spent most of my life trying to figure out what the fuck I'm supposed to be doing."

"Because your parents didn't help with that," Keith remarked knowingly.

"Not just my parents. Nobody did," Daniel replied sadly.

"Well, I can vouch for that," Keith said with a wry smile.

Daniel nodded in appreciation. "So, still no memory of defining moments. Grade school? Puberty?"

"Not really," Keith added, genuinely searching his brain for memory when his face lit up suddenly. "You know, it's funny. Now that I think about it, Ashley..."

"As in Ashley Cox, your girlfriend?" Daniel interrupted, clarifying.

"Yes, as in Ashley Cox, soon to be my fiancée."

Daniel's eyes widened. "Really? Are you engaged? Congratulations!"

"Not yet, but soon," Keith clarified with a grin. "And, thanks."

Daniel's eyes widened with admiration and respect. "Well, congratulations for when it does happen," Daniel added, his voice tinged with awe. "Okay, so go on, Ashley Cox." Daniel gestured for Keith to continue.

As Keith began, a genuine smile spread across his face. "Ashley's mother still loves telling the story. When Ashley was just three or four years old, she confidently declared that she was going to be an interior designer when she grew up. From then on, buying presents for Ashley was a breeze as long as they had something to do with designing things. Especially interiors."

Daniel nodded in understanding, "I can see that."

Keith chuckled at the memory. "But it gets better. When Ashley was eight, her mom had an interior designer over to redo the house. In the middle of it, Ashley interrupts with, 'You're not putting that there, are you?' and 'Mommy, really?' The designer left about an hour later, and Mrs. Cox sat her down and said, 'Okay, Ashley, you design the living room.' So, she did. And her mom used every detail, exactly as she planned it." He shook his head, still amazed by the memory of it all. "She was eight."

"That's incredible," Daniel remarked.

"Right?" Keith said, grinning. "By fourteen, she was already working for design firms in the city. Got into RISD early decision, and the rest is history." He paused, his tone softening with genuine admiration. "She's just naturally gifted. And she absolutely loves it."

Intrigued, Daniel asked, "How does she know what will be trending?"

Keith shrugged, smiling. "She has no idea how she does it; it's all instinct. She'll tell you she doesn't know what's going to trend. She just loves it and trusts it's exactly right for her client."

He shook his head, now genuinely connecting the dots. "Did you ever ask your teacher where his information came from?"

"No." Daniel shrugged. "We all thought he was crazy." Daniel's voice was a gentle murmur, nearly introspective, which stood out against the glaring lights and the constant hum of the washers and dryers in the laundromat. "But this is the kind of stuff that really fascinates me. And it---,"

"Is stuck in your craw." Keith interrupted.

Daniel smiled back, "Exactly!"

A wistful smile played on Keith's lips as he turned to look at Daniel. "I do remember one thing that fascinated me at puberty."

"What was that?"

"Bioremediation." The word hung in the air like a secret, spoken only between them. "Some kid's science project was about microbes eating plastic, and I was like, 'How the hell did you come up with that, Dude?' I mean, I didn't ask him that, but I wanted to know."

"And, what happened?"

"Nothing, nada." Keith's gaze slowly shifted from the memory back to Daniel's. "But I did think we were all going to have a bin in our houses with microbes to eat our plastic. That, of course, never happened. But I thought it was genius."

"So, it's stuck in your craw."

"Yes, it's absolutely stuck in my craw."

"There you have it." Daniel's smile broadened.

The two sat in comfortable silence indoors, oblivious to the passersby, all of whom, in their own way, recognized Keith, including the beach photographer parked in his nearby car, who had been following them all day.

CLICK. CLICK. CLICK.

Keith shook himself from his reverie as Daniel gestured toward the dryer in front of them, which had long ago stopped tumbling. "You think they're ready?" he asked.

"I've got to believe they are," Keith replied.

Soon after they left the laundromat, their arms were filled with their washed, dried, and wrinkled clothes. Keith took in his surroundings. A cool breeze stirred the air, brushing against him with the faint whisper of fall. For the first time in a long while, he felt peaceful, not because anything had changed, but because somehow he had.

"So, what now, Mr. 'let's go find you some anonymity'?" Keith teased.

Daniel grinned mischievously. "It kind of worked."

"Oh, it definitely worked," Keith chuckled. "Until it didn't."

Both men laughed at the irony of their situation. "Well, I don't feel like driving tonight," Keith said, checking his watch. "It's late and I'm exhausted. Do you have any other plans for us?" he asked Daniel.

"Well, now that our cover's been blown, not really. Except for sleep. I'm exhausted, too."

"Beach or motel?"

"Motel. Definitely a motel," Daniel said with a yawn. The weariness in his voice was evident as they made their way to the nearest available motel. Their cover may have been blown, but their bond was stronger than ever.

The drive to nearby Truro was quiet yet comfortable. The narrow road wound through a landscape of rolling dunes and shadowy forest groves, with the car's headlights piercing the encroaching darkness. The rhythmic hum of the engine was the only sound accompanying the subdued atmosphere, a calm undercurrent to the growing connection between them.

By the time they arrived in Truro, the coastal town was bathed in the soft glow of streetlights. The main street was almost deserted, save for the occasional shadowy figure darting into a warmly lit shop or hurrying home. After a brief search, they found a small, weathered inn nestled just off the main road. Its peeling white paint and faint smell of saltwater hinted at years of exposure to the coastal elements; however, its flickering neon 'Vacancy' sign promised shelter.

The interior of the inn exuded a rustic charm that felt welcoming. The friendly innkeeper handed over a hefty brass key attached to a well-worn wooden tag and directed them to a room at the far end of the hallway. The quaintness of the place, set against the backdrop of modern technology, enhanced the overall experience.

The space was simple, featuring two narrow twin beds draped in mismatched quilts. A single bedside lamp cast a warm amber glow across the room's worn furnishings, creating a cocoon of intimacy in contrast to the cool night outside the windows.

As they got ready for bed, handling their belongings and removing their clothes, their movements were synchronized: quiet, deliberate, each instinctively allowing the other room. They moved around the room like partners in an unspoken dance, placing small personal items on the shared nightstand and folding clothing over chairs with unhurried ease. The soft rustle of fabric and muted creak of floorboards created a soothing rhythm, filling the silence without intruding on it.

When the lights were switched off, the room descended into a tranquil darkness, broken only by the faint glow of moonlight streaming through the thin curtains. Lying in their separate beds, they were aware of each other's presence as if it were tangible. The muffled crash of waves on the shore, distant but steady, provided an ambient backdrop to the quiet.

In the stillness, their breaths began to sync, forming a subconscious rhythm that echoed the subtle yet growing connection between them. Without a word, the space between the beds felt smaller, with the divide bridged by an intangible thread of shared experience and growing trust.

As the night deepened, the tranquility of the moment enveloped them both, an unspoken bond settling like a second blanket. Sleep came easily, not as an escape but as a gentle continuation of the companionship silently forging between them.

The late morning sunlight filtered through the expansive glass windows of the roadside diner, casting warm pools of light on the worn, checkered linoleum floor. The air inside carried the mingling scents of frying bacon, sizzling eggs, and freshly brewed coffee, creating a comforting atmosphere of small-town simplicity.

Keith leaned slightly forward; the sleeves of his clean but now completely wrinkled tuxedo shirt were rolled to his elbows. He absentmindedly toyed with the remnants of bacon and eggs on his plate, using his fork to trace patterns in the runny yolk. His face, typically composed and confident, held a hint of pensiveness. He wasn't really speaking to Daniel but more to his plate; his voice was subdued.

"So," Keith began, his tone uncharacteristically reflective, "Marty decided early on that whatever I loved would somehow be something she loved too. I was always being interrupted, yanked out of my little bubble of childhood bliss by Marty swooping in and taking over whatever I was doing."

Daniel, sitting across from him in a booth patched with duct tape, listened intently. "Like erector sets and...?" Daniel's curiosity prompted Keith, drawing him out.

Keith's lips twitched upward briefly in a half-smile. He rested his forearms on the table, his face a picture of genuine interest. "Yeah. Erector sets, books, Play-Doh; you name it. She'd grab it from me, wander off, and inevitably lose interest shortly thereafter. I just learned to move on to something else."

"And your parents let her do that?" Daniel asked, his tone shifting to mild indignation.

"Yeah." Keith sighed, his voice tinged with resignation. "Not only did they let her, they encouraged it. At first, I protested. I'd cry, yell, scream, throw a tantrum, the whole deal. But my mother would step in with this classic line: 'Just let her play with it for a little bit, Keith. She'll give it back to you, won't you, Marty?" He mimicked his mother's gentle tone before pausing, his expression darkening. "Of course, Marty would nod all sweet and innocent before prancing off, destroying my bliss."

"That really sucks," Daniel said, leaning back against the cushioned booth as a calm settled over his face, his expression soft with understanding. "I mean, seriously. That's awful." Then, with a wry grin, he added, "Although... it does kind of fit Marty's personality, doesn't it?"

Keith let out a brief, sarcastic laugh. "Yeah. It does. But she means well. My family is my family, and…"

A sudden interruption shattered the flow of conversation. The waitress, her uniform slightly wrinkled and her name tag crooked on her chest, appeared at the edge of their table. She was a mix of emotions: part annoyed that they were lingering too long at her table, part thrilled to be serving none other than Keith Chambers.

"Excuse me, Mr. Chambers," she said, her tone hesitant yet overly polite. "Will there be anything else for you today?"

Keith looked up and gave her a courteous smile. His keen hazel eyes quickly scanned her name tag before he replied. "First of all, you can call me Keith. And secondly…" He looked over at Daniel, who shook his head, signaling that he didn't need anything else. "I think we're all set, Dawn. Just the check, please."

The waitress nodded, her cheeks flushing slightly as she hurried off. Keith turned back to Daniel, his casual demeanor returning. "Where were we?"

Daniel tilted his head, a playful grin on his face. "I don't remember."

Keith leaned back, letting out a small sigh.

Then his expression darkened, like clouds gathering before a quiet storm. He leaned in, resting his forearms on the table, less a gesture of urgency than of gravity, like he was anchoring himself before wading into deeper waters. "You know, people have all these theories about the 2024 election…"

Daniel's playful demeanor shifted slightly. He raised an eyebrow. "Are you sure you want to go there, Keith? We've been having such a good time."

Keith laughed, a short, hearty chuckle. "Fair enough. But I'll just say this: Bobby Kennedy was the best man for the job."

"As in Robert F. Kennedy, Jr?" Daniel's surprise was evident, his brow shooting upward. "That's not what I expected to hear."

Keith shrugged, his fork slicing through the remains of his eggs. "Yeah. If he had run, I would've voted for him. And apparently, so would about three million other voters. Turns out, a lot of people who voted for Trump may have been trying to assure Bobby Kennedy had a voice," Keith concluded.

"Interesting." Daniel didn't move, but his eyes shifted, narrowing slightly, then softening, listening.

Keith's gaze held his, more hopeful than forceful. "What do you think?" he asked, the question landing gently but deliberately.

Daniel's expression remained neutral. He shrugged, measured, withholding, though something in him was unmistakably leaning in. This glimpse of Keith, unguarded, unexpected, had caught him off guard. Even if what he said was, "Hard to say."

Keith leaned back in the booth, his gaze drifting toward the window. In the parking lot outside, windshields flashed like signal mirrors as the sun caught each one. Beyond the lot, a line of trees shifted gently in the morning breeze.

Inside, the low hum of conversation mingled with the clatter of plates, but Keith wasn't listening. He was wrestling with his thoughts: drawn to say more, but unsure if he should. The ground he was about to cross felt unstable, maybe even dangerous. But something in him kept moving toward it anyway.

"Thank you, Mr. Chambers," Dawn said softly, placing the check on the table. "It was a pleasure serving you." Her return snapped Keith out of his inner battle. Her smile, more composed this time, carried a hint of warmth.

He blinked, then returned the smile, though it landed with a slight awkwardness. "Thanks, Dawn. You've been great."

Before he could reach for the check, Daniel snatched it up with a grin. "I've got this one," he said, waving it just out of reach.

Keith rolled his eyes, straightening up. "Not on a teacher's salary. Hand it over."

"Not a chance." Daniel pulled out his wallet. "You can get the next one."

Keith gave in with a smirk. "Fair enough."

Daniel slid partway out of the booth, then paused. Something in Keith's expression stopped him. He nodded, almost to himself, and sank back into the seat. Whatever was coming, he'd hear it.

Keith felt the shift. He took it as an invitation and leaned forward, his voice low and deliberate. "The thing about RFK Jr.," he began, "is that he's honest. Whether his truth matches ours or not, he's honest. He's a recovering addict. He goes to meetings. Every day. And the ones who make it in the program, the long-timers? They swear by two things: authenticity and rigorous honesty. That's the bedrock."

Daniel listened carefully.

"I trust him," Keith said. "I don't even know why. I just do."

Daniel raised an eyebrow. "He's been caught in some pretty blatant contradictions, Keith. By all accounts, the man often stumbles. Hard."

Keith met his gaze. "According to who? The media? The same media that tells you what to see, how to think, what's real, and what's not? The media is the problem, Daniel. But nobody wants to admit that."

Daniel's tone cooled. "So? All media?"

"Pretty much, yeah. Trust me, I know. Very little is what it appears to be, especially for people like me." Keith's voice was tightening. "And for people like him."

Daniel held back. Then: "Okay, then."

They fell quiet, the space between them charged with unspoken words. Though the silence felt ominous, beneath it lay something more fragile, an offering of support Daniel didn't quite know how to voice.

Keith's shoulders relaxed slightly, and he shifted his weight, interpreting the momentary silence as what could be considered: an opening.

He leaned in with more intent, even as his voice softened. "RFK Jr. is consistent. He's not telling people what to believe; he's saying, be informed. Make your own choices. Not media-fed choices. Real ones. He shows up, takes responsibility. When he screws up, he owns it. Learns from it. Apologizes. Keeps going. He's human."

He paused to let it land.

"I believe him. What I want is a party that speaks the truth. But all I hear is both sides accusing the other of lying. Over and over. Republicans. Democrats. Everyone yelling over everyone else."

Sensing the emerging and strengthening bond, he inched closer to Daniel and continued: "I want a party that speaks the truth. And I think it should be called the white party."

Daniel blinked. "Says the privileged, white," he emphasized, "male millionaire heir to the Chambers throne."

"Marty's the heir, not me," Keith shot back. He leaned across the table, the energy swelling in him now, uncontainable. "White, as in the brilliant, piercing light of truth." His voice was rising. "Our flag is red, white, and blue. We've got a red party. A blue party. But where's the white party? The one grounded in truth. Truth for everyone. Black, brown, red, yellow, indigo; I don't care. Truth is truth. And I want to be part of the party that's willing to search for it, at all costs. I want to choose freely because I'm *informed.* Because this is America! A land where people are aware. A land where people are free. A land where the truth is actually the truth."

By the end, his voice was nearly a shout, his body leaning hard across the table, closing the distance between them, as if the force of his conviction needed somewhere to land.

The diner fell utterly silent. Every face turned toward them: Portuguese tradesmen, blue-collar regulars, white-collar brunchers, a table of older women, a group of hungover teens.

And then, slowly, the teens began to clap.

Daniel sat back, watching in disbelief as, one by one, the entire diner joined in. Clapping. Cheering.

Daniel smiled broadly. And clapped loudest of all.

Keith sat back, the applause washing over him, but his eyes dropped. The heat in his face wasn't pride; it was panic. He felt exposed. He'd crossed a line. One he'd promised his family, *himself,* he never would.

Daniel saw it: something in Keith's face pulling him back, sudden and full of regret: Uncertainty, maybe even shame. So, Daniel clapped, louder, then louder still, moved by something quiet and urgent: the need to steady him, to guide him, to protect him.

When the noise settled, Daniel leaned in with a grin. "I'd vote for you. And so would everyone here."

He gestured broadly, and once again, the room erupted. Cooks. Servers. Strangers. Applauding like something had just been named, a person they hadn't known they believed in.

Daniel's nod was met with Keith's retreat, his eyes going distant as his hand found his wallet, left a crisp hundred on the table for Dawn, and disappeared back into his pocket.

As they quietly slid out of the booth and made their way to the cash register, conversations shifted into resolute support. Heads turned. Some reached out, hands extended, not just to greet Keith, but to touch something they hadn't known they were waiting to see.

Something true.

Something real.

"Thank you, Mr. Chambers," an older woman said softly. "I'll be voting for you, too."

"You're an inspiration!" someone else called out.

Keith shook a few hands, smiled politely, but fading. His charm had dulled and was worn thin by the weight of their attention.

Daniel, trailing behind, paid Dawn quietly. Her fingers brushed his as she returned the change. "Thank you," she said, eyes flicking once more toward Keith.

Keith gave a slight nod, but his usual shine was gone. The spotlight had found him, and it was too much.

As they headed for the door, a final voice called from the diner, "We need more of you, Keith!"

Keith gave a quick wave. But when Daniel caught his eye, the smile was tight. Forced. He leaned in, his voice low, meant only for Daniel. "Trust me," he said. "It's an anomaly. If they knew who I really was, they'd be running for the hills."

Daniel just shook his head, quietly, almost to himself. *What had the Chambers family done to him? And why?*

They finally made it outside, only to be greeted by the flashing lights of paparazzi everywhere. A small crowd had gathered near the parking lot; most were fans, but a few eager reporters shouted questions over the noise.

"Keith, are you working on any new projects?"

"Mr. Chambers, any comment on Swampscott?"

"Who's your friend, Keith?"

Keith lifted his hand, giving a quick nod to the crowd. With a courteous yet assertive smile, he indicated, 'No comment.'

Daniel, caught off guard by the swarm of cameras, leaned closer to Keith as if offering him some unspoken protection. "Okay, this is new. Does this happen a lot?"

"Not always," Keith muttered, unlocking his truck and ducking in. "But often enough."

The two of them climbed into the cab, shutting out the noise and chaos outside. Keith started the engine, the low rumble drowning out the muffled voices and camera clicks. He glanced at Daniel as he pulled out of the parking lot.

"So much for anonymity," Keith said with a wry smile.

Daniel shrugged, his grin unbothered. "It's all good, dude. It's all good."

The truck glided along the narrow road, its tires humming steadily against the asphalt. Ahead, the open roadway stretched on, flanked by dense clusters of trees that occasionally parted to reveal glimpses of sand and sea. The ride back to Boston was bathed in the warm, amber light of the late afternoon sun.

Inside the cab, a quiet calm settled between them, broken only by the soft hum of the engine and the occasional rustle as Daniel shifted in his seat. Keith's hands rested lightly on the wheel, his grip relaxed but sure. His gaze stayed fixed on the horizon. The easy confidence that usually lit his face had given way to something quieter, more introspective. The shifting hues of the sky played across his features as day slipped toward dusk.

Daniel leaned back in the passenger seat, his elbow propped against the door as he gazed out the window. Every so often, Keith glanced over, as if trying to read what was going on behind Daniel's silence. But he didn't ask.

The quiet between them felt earned, like an unspoken agreement between two people who, for once, didn't need to fill the space with words.

The sky deepened into shades of amber and rose as the sun dipped lower, casting long shadows over the road. The world outside seemed to move more slowly, as if time itself were stretching to match their quietude.

Keith finally broke the silence, his voice low and steady. "Where am I taking you? Where's your car?"

Daniel turned his head slightly, blinking as if pulled from a daydream. "Amherst."

Keith glanced at him, one eyebrow raised. "Amherst?"

"Yeah," Daniel said with a faint grin. "Brent and Charlie essentially abducted me. My car is at my mom's place in Amherst. You can leave me at Brent's in Cambridge, and I'll work out the rest from there."

Keith slightly shook his head, a hint of a smile playing on his lips. He glanced at the dashboard clock to check the time. "It's 7:00 PM on a Sunday. I've got until Monday at 11:00 AM." He paused, his voice softening. "Amherst it is."

Daniel leaned forward a bit, his forehead creasing. "Honestly, Keith, you don't need to do this."

Keith shrugged, his tone casual but warm. "I know I don't have to. I want to. Settle in."

Daniel opened his mouth to protest, but something in Keith's calm, matter-of-fact demeanor stopped him. He sank back into his seat, shaking his head with a small, resigned smile.

As the truck veered onto a quieter stretch of Route 3 and headed toward the Mass Pike, the world outside seemed to still even further. The last traces of sunlight vanished, leaving behind a deep indigo sky speckled with early stars. The headlights cast a warm arc ahead, carving a solitary path through the dark.

Keith lowered the volume on the radio until the classic rock became little more than a soft hum. His focus stayed on the road, but his presence filled the cab: steady, grounding.

Daniel stretched his legs and let out a quiet sigh. His gaze drifted toward the horizon, where the faint shimmer of Boston clung to the edge of the sky. A strange, quiet gratitude stirred in him, an unfamiliar sense of calm.

Meanwhile, the headlights of passing cars illuminated the interior of the truck momentarily, casting fleeting silhouettes of the two men.

Keith's thoughts circled back to the diner. Bits of conversation resurfaced. Daniel's easy presence, his laugh, made Keith more aware of the moment's simplicity. And how much he wanted to stay in it.

The rest of the drive passed in silence, comfortable and unspoken, broken only by the hum of the tires and the low rumble of the engine. By the time they reached Amherst, the town was cloaked in stillness: empty streets, porch lights glowing, the hush of a place that had already gone to sleep.

Keith's truck rumbled quietly up the long gravel driveway, its tires crunching over the pebbled surface. A sprawling house slowly came into view. The Eiman estate was a farmhouse that had started small but had grown and been added onto over the decades. Each addition seemed to tell its own story, seamlessly merging into a structure that exuded history and warmth. An outdoor light on the back porch illuminated the yard, casting long shadows across the driveway as if welcoming them.

A sharp bark cut through the air from inside the house. The sound of toenails skittering against the hardwood grew louder, signaling the approach of an enthusiastic greeter. Keith parked beside Daniel's black Saab, which looked like a relic against the backdrop of the well-kept farm. The porch light flicked on, flooding them and everything around them with golden light.

The door creaked open, and a seventy-pound dog, its tail wagging furiously, bounded toward them. The sudden burst of movement startled Keith, who stepped back instinctively. Daniel crouched low, his face lighting up as he rubbed the dog's floppy ears with both hands.

"Jupiter!" Daniel's voice held a playful scolding. The dog quieted momentarily, sitting back on its haunches, only to leap forward again, its tail wagging with uncontainable excitement.

"Such a good boy," Daniel murmured, giving him his complete attention. "Yes. You're such a good boy." Daniel repeated, his voice softening as he rubbed Jupiter's face. Jupiter tried to jump again, but Daniel wagged a finger. "Uh, uh, uh," he warned, and Jupiter settled, his tail still thumping the porch.

Inside the house, Mrs. Eiman bustled about in her cozy kitchen. She glanced up from the counter, her keen eyes catching sight of Keith as he stepped inside.

"Mom, this is Keith."

"It's nice to meet you, Keith." Mrs. Eiman said with a friendly smile. She nonchalantly flipped over the magazine on the counter, hiding the cover that displayed Keith's picture under the headline: America's Most Eligible Bachelor. Without missing a beat, she reached up to the shelf and began to take down soup bowls. "Have you boys had anything to eat?"

Keith opened his mouth to protest. "Oh, thank you so much, Mrs. Eiman, but I really have to leave. "

"You're not going anywhere until you've at least had a bowl of soup," she said firmly, giving the pot a quick stir before turning to the counter and positioning the bowls with an air of practiced efficiency.

Keith cast a sidelong glance at Daniel, who merely shrugged. "There's no saying 'no' to her," Daniel whispered, a smile playing at his lips. "Just take a couple of sips and leave the rest."

Resigned, Keith settled into a chair, his weariness finally catching up to him as he conceded, "I am actually pretty hungry. That late breakfast didn't exactly hold me over here."

Daniel returned the smile as they both devoured the tasty soup and freshly baked bread, which tasted even better than its tempting scent had promised.

Once the snack was finished, Mrs. Eiman gestured toward the stairs and issued an order. "Go make up the guest room for Keith, Daniel."

Keith rose from his seat, hands raised in polite protest. "Oh, no, really, Mrs. Eiman. That's awfully nice of you, but I need to… "

"Nonsense!" She cut him off, gesturing toward the stairs. "You're not getting in a car and driving tonight. Period. Paragraph. The end! Daniel, go make up the guest room!"

Daniel froze mid-step, his gaze darting toward Keith, then back to his mother. Her tone brooked no argument.

Keith sighed, surrendering. "Okay. Thank you, Mrs. Eiman."

As Daniel guided Keith up the creaky back stairs, the house felt alive with history. The faint scent of cedar lingered in the air, blending with the woodsy, musty aroma of the old banister.

The dim light of the hallway above cast shadows that danced along the walls, revealing a dent in the plaster; its outline suspiciously head-shaped.

"That," Daniel explained, gesturing with a playful flourish as they passed, "is where my dad put my brother Johnny's head through the wall. It's been there for thirty years as a reminder: to do what you're told the first time around."

Keith chuckled despite himself, the sound softly echoing in the quiet corridor. As they stepped forward, the hallway opened into a guest suite that felt like a hidden treasure, rivaling the charm of a boutique hotel. A king-sized bed faced a sunken fireplace, its stone hearth aglow with the warm, inviting light of a nearby lamp. Two armchairs flanked the fireplace, their upholstery a bit worn yet exuding comfort. It was as if they were waiting to cradle someone with a good book.

"This is incredible," Keith murmured, taking in the cozy elegance.

Daniel smiled and nodded, then, with casual confidence, rummaged through a linen closet, tossing sheets onto the bed like an artist adding the final touches to a masterpiece.

Keith followed him through a walk-in closet that felt like a secret passageway, leading to a bathroom stocked with all the essentials: fluffy towels and gleaming toiletries lined the shelves. Daniel handed Keith an unopened toothbrush, his eyes twinkling with mischief as he pointed toward a door on the far wall. "Emergency exit," he said with a wry grin. "Her Majesty didn't want guests tracking snow and mud through her house in the winter."

Keith raised an eyebrow, impressed by the thoughtful arrangement. "Well equipped."

Daniel nodded and left, leaving Keith alone in the bathroom to freshen up. The rhythmic sound of water running from the tap was soothing. Back in the bedroom, he found Daniel sprawled on the freshly made bed, fully clothed and already snoring softly.

Keith gently shook Daniel, trying to rouse him. The snoring stopped, but Daniel didn't stir, lost in sleep, peaceful and unaware. He hesitated, weighing his options. Slowly, he began to undress. But when he reached his underwear, he paused, glancing at Daniel's face. Still. Completely still. He sighed, staring down at him, a faint smile tugging at his lips. "Looks like it's lights out," he murmured to no one in particular.

Then he dressed again, piece by piece, and lay down beside Daniel, both of them fully clothed. As he settled in, an unexpected warmth wrapped around him. Quiet. Indescribable.

As night gave way to morning, the resonant chime of a grandfather clock echoed from deep within the expansive farmhouse, softly striking six times. Sunlight streamed through the window, spilling across Daniel and Keith, who lay in the same position. A comforter, now a cocoon around them, had mysteriously been added while they slept.

Keith slowly opened his eyes, focusing. Suddenly realizing that Mrs. Eiman was staring down at him, he bolted upright, his face flushing. Instinctively, he flew out of bed, still fully clothed, his heart racing.

Realizing he was facing an embarrassing male morning dilemma, he quickly pulled the comforter off the bed. He wrapped it around himself to conceal his predicament. "Morning," he mumbled, his voice thick with sleep, as a wave of embarrassment and confusion washed over him.

Daniel lay undisturbed on the bed, fully clothed, with a serene expression on his face. Keith glanced up at Mrs. Eiman, who stood in the doorway, offering a knowing smile. "When he's tired, he sleeps. When he's awake, he doesn't stop moving. His father was that way," she remarked, glancing at the clock. "What time do you need to be back in Boston?"

Keith fought to steady his voice, frantically trying to regain his composure. "Um, I, um... I should probably leave here by seven, seven-thirty."

"Good, then there's time for breakfast. I'll see you downstairs," Mrs. Eiman said, her voice warm and reassuring as she turned to leave.

The kitchen was awash in the golden light of early morning. The scent of freshly brewed coffee wafted through the air. The gentle clatter of pans and the sizzling of eggs created a comforting symphony of domesticity. Keith entered the room, his hair slightly tousled, but his face now composed. He hesitated at the threshold, briefly taken aback by the homeliness of the scene.

Mrs. Eiman turned from the stove, a spatula in hand, and gestured toward the table. "Sit," she commanded warmly. "Breakfast is almost ready."

Keith complied, his movements slower than usual as he processed the unfamiliar sense of ease he felt in the house. "That was..." He gestured vaguely toward the upstairs, trying to find the right words. "We were... I went out like a light. I guess we were pretty tired."

Mrs. Eiman didn't miss a beat as she scooped scrambled eggs onto a plate. "Good that I made you spend the night," she said with a small smile, placing the plate before him. Her gaze momentarily shifted to the overturned magazine displaying 'America's Most Eligible Bachelor' before returning to Keith.

"Yeah, probably," Keith admitted, nodding as he toyed with his fork.

"Coffee?" she asked, holding up the steaming pot.

"Please," he replied gratefully, watching as she poured the dark liquid into a waiting mug. He wrapped his hands around the cup, allowing its warmth to seep into his fingers.

For a moment, the kitchen was quiet except for the occasional scrape of a fork or the hum of the refrigerator. Keith took a bite, the simple, hearty food grounding him. Mrs. Eiman busied herself at the counter, her movements efficient yet unhurried. Her smile deepened.

Later that morning, Keith's truck hummed along the highway as the familiar sign for Storrow Drive came into view. The sprawling estate, the easy conversation, and Mrs. Eiman's considerate generosity stayed with him. For a moment, it felt like he had stepped into a different life, one less polished but somehow more real.

Back in Amherst, sunlight filled the kitchen once more, but this time, it revealed a completely different scene. Daniel stood by the counter, spreading fresh vegetables, fruits, almonds, and sunflower seeds before an industrial-grade juicer. The hum of the machine roared to life as he fed the ingredients into its maw, creating a vibrant, emerald-green liquid.

At the table, Mrs. Eiman, still in her robe, was immersed in her morning ritual: reading the newspaper. She glanced up briefly over her reading glasses. "He's a very nice man," she said, her tone casual but loaded with implication. Daniel didn't look up from the juicer. "He's Keith Chambers, Mom." His voice carried an edge. When she didn't respond, he flicked off the juicer and turned toward her. "The Keith Chambers."

Mrs. Eiman's eyes lifted from the paper, her gaze steady but unimpressed. "Yes, well, he's also a very nice man."

Daniel shook his head, muttering under his breath as he turned back to the juicer. He forcefully shoved a whole apple into the machine, the roar of the blades drowning out any further commentary.

In Boston, Keith jogged along the Charles River Esplanade, the rhythmic thump of his sneakers against the pavement syncing with the steady pulse of his heart. His T-shirt clung to his chest, darkened with sweat, a testament to the vigor of his workout. The crisp morning air filled his lungs, and the sight of rowers cutting through the water brought a rare sense of peace. For a moment, the clutter of his thoughts seemed to dissipate, leaving only the rhythmic cadence of his strides.

*****

Fifty miles away, in Leominster, Daniel entered the principal's office. The space was utilitarian, with a large oak desk dominating the room and framed certificates lining the walls. Mr. Knight, a silver-haired man with a warm but businesslike demeanor, rose from his chair with a broad smile, gesturing for Daniel to sit. The principal's sign on his desk gleamed under the fluorescent light.

In another chair, Mr. Lopez, the science teacher, waited. He rose briefly to shake Daniel's hand. "Thanks for coming, Ben," Daniel said, his tone grateful yet subdued.

Mr. Knight settled into his chair. "So, what's on your mind, Daniel?"

Daniel hesitated, his fingers gripping the armrests of the chair. "Well, I feel like I have to disclose something. And I wanted Ben here... you know, as a witness of sorts. If that's alright."

The principal's demeanor shifted slightly, his smile tightening. "That serious?"

"I hope not," Daniel said with a shrug. "But..."

Knight leaned forward, his expression growing more attentive. "All right, let's hear it."

Daniel shifted uncomfortably, glancing at Mr. Lopez, who gave him a slight nod of encouragement. Taking a deep breath, Daniel began, "I'm not sure how much you know about me, but... "

"Probably more than you want us to know," Mr. Knight interrupted, his voice straightforward yet gentle.

Daniel was taken aback, his eyes widening in surprise. "More than I want you to know?"

"Yes," Mr. Knight said, leaning back slightly. "The internet. Google. Trust me, we know more than you probably want us to know."

"Did you know before I started teaching here?" Daniel asked, attempting to hide his sudden and increasing unease.

"No, not while you were substituting. However, we did conduct a comprehensive investigation and background check before offering you a permanent position. So yes, we knew."

Daniel leaned back in his chair, his back straight and his arms resting on the armrest. He absorbed the information with intense focus, his eyes wide and his eyebrows slightly knitted in concentration. "Do you think the kids' parents know?"

Mr. Lopez chuckled softly, shaking his head across to Mr. Knight. "Daniel, this is Leominster. Everybody knows who you are and where you've come from."

"Really?" Daniel's voice was barely audible as the gravity of the revelation settled in.

"Yes," Mr. Knight said, his tone softening slightly. "But let me be clear: nobody has ever complained about you. Not once. No student has complained about you, nor has any parent."

Daniel's eyebrows knitted together as his voice became increasingly hesitant. "Is somebody about to?"

Mr. Knight shook his head. "Not as far as we know. However, you were the one who scheduled this meeting. Why don't you tell us what's going on?"

Daniel swallowed his nervousness. "It's about Benjamin McCray."

Both men waited, their expressions patient but alert.

Daniel took a deep breath and pressed forward. "The other day, after class, Benjamin approached me. He was visibly nervous. And you know, he's just so shy. I could tell he wanted to say something important, but he was hesitant. So, to encourage him, I..."

Daniel hesitated, shook his head slightly, and dropped his gaze to his lap. Then, gathering himself, he looked up. "I put my hands on his shoulders and leaned in, just trying to help him find the courage, or whatever he needed." He shifted, uneasy with his own vagueness. Then, more directly: "And then, basically, he asked if I was gay."

The room was filled with a silence that felt almost impenetrable as the weight of his confession hung in the air.

"To which you said?" Mr. Knight prompted.

"I didn't say anything," Daniel said, regret threading through his voice. "But I knew I shouldn't have been that close. So I pulled my hands back, too quickly, probably. He was out the door before I could offer anything more."

Mr. Knight nodded slowly, his expression calm but thoughtful. "Is that all?"

Daniel hesitated. "Not quite."

"Go on," Mr. Knight said, leaning forward again.

Daniel pressed his fingers to his temples, brow furrowed. "After he left, I saw some kids in the schoolyard. They might've seen us. And..." He hesitated, lowering his voice. "I think they might've filmed us. Or taken photos."

"Were they holding up their phones?" Mr. Knight asked, his tone steady.

"Maybe. Yeah. Probably," Daniel admitted, his face tightening with concern. "One of them, for sure, was holding up his phone," Daniel concluded, nodding.

Mr. Knight leaned back in his chair, his fingers steepled thoughtfully. "First of all, thank you for coming in. Secondly, don't ever touch a kid, no matter how well-intentioned you are or how you believe they'll respond."

"Yes, of course," Daniel said quickly, nodding. "I completely understand."

"These situations," Mr. Knight continued, "are best approached carefully and, if possible, without physical contact. That said, it's good you brought this to our attention."

Mr. Knight glanced at Mr. Lopez, who nodded in silent agreement as Mr. Knight continued. "Daniel, look, you were offered a position here because you're great with these kids. They love you. We've never had a complaint, and frankly, you're one of the best teachers I've worked with in my thirty-five years as a public school administrator."

Daniel blinked, stunned by the unexpected praise. "Thank you," he said, trying to mask his own insecurity. He wanted to believe the compliment, but his budding confidence was dashed when Mr. Knight reiterated.

"But we cannot ever touch a student. Not in any context. Or for any reason."

Daniel nodded solemnly. "Got it. I completely understand."

Mr. Lopez leaned forward, his tone more serious. "You should also know Benjamin's situation is, how do I say it, complicated. He's one of our high-profile students."

"High-profile?" Daniel repeated the term, lingering awkwardly in the air.

Mr. Knight nodded, his face clouding slightly. "His dad is difficult. And Benjamin… is deeply troubled. He fits the profile of… "

"No," Daniel interrupted, shaking his head. "I cannot imagine that kid ever harming anyone, for any reason. I'm sorry, but I simply cannot."

Mr. Knight sighed. "Unfortunately, those are the exact words people often say about kids that fit the profile."

Knight volleyed a look over to Mr. Lopez, who finished the thought. "That said, in this case, we're more concerned about Benjamin harming himself."

Daniel's jaw tightened as he absorbed the weight of the words. "Is someone counseling him?" he asked, turning to Mr. Lopez. "Maybe you and I could work together and try to help him? Or maybe I could proceed with him and the guidance counselor?"

"Max LeBlanc," Mr. Lopez provided the name Daniel searched his memory for but couldn't find. "That could work," Lopez said. "But there's a further complication."

"What kind of complication?" Daniel pressed.

Mr. Lopez glanced at Mr. Knight before continuing. "Benjamin's dad is severely homophobic. He's also a close childhood friend of Max LeBlanc. They've been joined at the hip since grade school, stayed close through high school, served as best men at each other's weddings; everything. If word gets out that Benjamin is questioning his sexuality, he won't have to kill himself. His dad will do it for him."

"Holy Shit!" Daniel reeled back, feeling as if he'd just been hit out of nowhere.

Mr. Knight and Mr. Lopez locked eyes, their expressions firm and understanding, and gave each other a subtle nod, an unspoken agreement passing between them. With a slight turn of their heads, they redirected their attention back to Daniel, who sat waiting, his eyes darting back and forth between them.

"All right," Mr. Knight said finally. "Let me think about this and figure out the best way forward. In the meantime, do not approach Benjamin, Daniel. Don't encourage him. Just... lay low for now, please."

"Can I at least tell him, yes, I'm gay, and yes, it's going to get better if you just give it a few years?" Daniel inquired, feeling the heavy burden of his emotions. He had to muster every ounce of self-control to hold back the flood of words struggling to escape his throat.

"Yes, you can be honest with him. Just..." Knight hesitated.

Daniel nodded faintly, as if agreeing with a thought he couldn't yet put into words.

Weighing Daniel's inner conflict against the broader picture, Knight continued, choosing his words carefully. "Well, I think you'll know what to do. Just…don't approach him. Let him come to you."

Daniel nodded again, absorbing the weight of it all, his silence thick with emotions too dense to articulate. Whatever fleeting relief the meeting had offered was already fading into impending dread.

"And thank you for coming in, Daniel," Knight concluded. His voice carried the shape of reassurance, yet the restraint within it only deepened the burden of Daniel's raw, unspoken anguish.

Daniel nodded again and shook Mr. Lopez's hand, a silent exchange of gratitude passing between them. Then he turned and left. As he stepped into the hallway and the door shut behind him, he noticed Mr. Lopez and Mr. Knight sharing concerned, uneasy glances.

As he made his way down the corridor towards the exit, the echo of his footsteps broke through the overwhelming thoughts, crowding his mind. The harsh hum of the fluorescent lights overhead only intensified the heavy burden of anxiety, looming above him like an approaching storm.

Pushing open the double doors and stepping outside, the cool air hit his face, a jarring contrast to the suffocating tension inside. He inhaled deeply, trying to clear his mind, yet so many questions remained.

The crisp autumn air carried the faint scent of leaves and damp earth as Daniel walked to his car in the nearly empty school parking lot. He slid into the driver's seat of his old Saab and gripped the steering wheel tightly, the chill of the worn leather biting into his palms. His mind raced, replaying the conversation with Mr. Knight and Mr. Lopez. Every word felt like a stone added to the already absurdly soul-crushing weight pressing on his chest.

Benjamin's nervous face lingered in his memory, and Daniel couldn't shake the feeling that he needed to do more. But how? The advice was clear: lay low. Yet his instincts screamed at him to act.

Daniel let out a sigh as he turned the key in the ignition, causing the Saab to sputter to life. The well-known rumble of the engine oddly comforted him as he drove out of the parking lot and made his way toward Amherst.

*****

At the same time, in Boston, Keith was having a completely different kind of day altogether. He weaved through the crowds on Newbury Street, his bicycle gliding effortlessly along the bustling avenue. The late afternoon sun cast long shadows on the sidewalks, and the storefronts gleamed under their golden rays.

As he approached the yoga center, he saw Ashley leaving with two friends. With her sweatshirt tied casually around her waist and her hair swept into a loose ponytail, she looked gorgeous today.

Keith slowed his pace, making lazy circles with his bike as he watched her from a distance. Her laugh rang out, light and musical, as she chatted animatedly with her companions. One of her friends noticed Keith first, stopping abruptly and nudging Ashley with a sly grin.

Ashley turned, her eyes lighting up when they met Keith's. "Hi," she called, her voice warm and inviting.

Keith grinned and coasted to a stop in front of her. "Hello," he said, his tone playful.

Ashley stepped forward, ignoring the sideways glances from her friends. "What brings you here?"

"Change of plans," Keith said, hopping off his bike and steadying it beside him. "You busy?"

She narrowed her eyes slightly, running through her mental calendar. "Not really. Why did you have something in mind?"

"Maybe." Keith shrugged, behaving more coyly than usual.

All of it was catching Ashley off guard. "Okay, then."

"Okay," Keith repeated. I'm going to ride back to my place, and I'll meet you there.

"Later, girls," Keith called out as he rode off.

"He is *so* sexy," the cuter one murmured as Keith turned the corner off Newbury Street, pedaling toward Commonwealth Ave.

Keith weaved through the foot traffic with ease, his bike gliding between distracted tourists and coffee-toting locals. As he disappeared from view, Ashley turned back to her friends, who were now shaking their heads, part envy, part disbelief.

The taller one leaned in and gently tugged Ashley's arm. "My car's just up the block; I'll give you a ride."

Showered and dressed in a crisp white shirt and khaki pants, Keith stood at his dresser, gazing down at the sparkling 2.78-carat diamond. It looked so much larger in its less ornate, yet equally elegant new setting. With care, he closed the box and placed it in the top drawer of his bureau, hidden between his underwear and a small pile of condoms.

There was a soft knock on his door, followed by a louder one, then the sound of keys turning and locks tumbling as Ashley let herself in. Keith closed the bureau drawer and met her at the door with a smile. "Look at you all clean and showered," Ashley said as she melted into his embrace.

"Hello," Keith murmured, deliberately inhaling her musky scent and kissing her neck.

Ashley pulled back slightly to take in his appearance. "You're in a good mood," she noted.

"Very much so," Keith affirmed as he leaned in to kiss her. Sensing that things might be heating up, Keith maneuvered Ashley back toward his bedroom. "Honey, I need to take a shower." Ashley began to protest.

"No, you don't," Keith assured her.

"Yes, I do," Ashley insisted, trying to wriggle out of his slowly increasing grasp. "It'll just take a second." She murmured as she pulled herself away and headed for the bathroom.

Feeling defeated, Keith sprawled out on his bed, arms and legs stretched wide. In the brief walk from the door, he had partially unbuttoned his shirt and loosened his pants. Stretched out in defeat, debating whether to wait or button up, his landline started ringing. "I'll get it," Ashley called out, picking up the bathroom extension and answering cheerfully, "Hello? Oh, hi...I'm great. How are you? How did you know I was here? Oh, right, of course." Keith could hear her muffled laughter as she closed the bathroom door. "Yes...Yes, I am."

Struggling with intense frustration, Keith refastened his pants, adjusted his shirt, and made his way back to the living room.

*****

Across town, in his Cambridge office, Brent sat across from Charlie with a troubled expression.

"Brent, you need to give me the details," Charlie said firmly.

"I don't know what the details are. That's why I'm asking you!" Brent replied in frustration.

"I know you had an affair with him," Charlie continued.

"We didn't have an affair," Brent clarified. "Unless you consider three...He paused, trying to remember. "Maybe it was four encounters. Two in his office and the other two elsewhere."

"You spent two full weekends together, Dude," Charlie pointed out, "As I recall!"

"One weekend! And were you following me?" Brent asked, taken aback.

"Yes," Charlie admitted without hesitation. "For your own good. And it was two, two weekends!"

"How is snooping around in my private life for my own good?" Brent demanded.

"Well, there are eyewitnesses," Charlie explained. "How do you know I'm not the only one? Is that a subpoena?" Charlie asked, gesturing to the paper Brent was holding.

"It's a summons," Brent revealed, then clarified, "I've been summoned to appear before the medical board."

Charlie was genuinely confused. "For what?"

"I don't know the specifics," Brent replied honestly. "All I know is he's being reviewed for having sexual relations with a patient."

Charlie was taken aback, his mouth agape. "Is he doing this with other patients as well?" he asked in disbelief.

"I have no idea!" Brent snapped back, just as frustrated. "That's why I need you to figure it out." All he could do was roll his eyes and shake his head at Charlie's stubbornness.

*****

The city lights twinkled in the distance as Keith sat across from Ashley in his Back Bay condo. The room glowed softly: candles flickering beside a vase of fresh flowers. Two empty wine glasses sat between them, quiet remnants of a dinner meant to feel more intimate than it was. But Keith's mind had drifted. His gaze was fixed on Ashley's lips, moving, animated, yet her words barely registered.

He stood, carefully collecting the plates, more to end the moment than to clean. Ashley kept talking as he moved through the motions, rinsing and drying, her voice filling the silence he was deliberately preserving.

Later that night, Keith stood outside Sophie Bieltran's loft across town. He knocked once on the heavy metal door. No answer.

Frustrated, he knocked again harder, this time, urgency tightening in his chest.

Finally, the deadbolt clicked, and the door opened just a crack. Sophie appeared cautious.

Keith stepped closer. "Can we talk?" he asked, his voice quieter now. Almost pleading.

Sophie glanced back over her shoulder, then stepped aside to invite him in. Upon entering, he saw a person lounging on the couch, sipping wine. It was difficult to determine whether they were male or a female.

"You need to call before you come over, Keith. You can't just keep showing up like this," Sophie chided him.

Keith ignored her remarks entirely; his eyes focused beyond her shoulder. "What, are you sleeping with him as well now?"

"Her! She's a she!" Sophie corrected him.

"Is she a *she* the way you're a *he*?" Keith snapped, his resentment barely contained. "So what, now you're sleeping with *her* now too?"

"Quit forcing me into your confined, conventional, lame-assed world, you thoughtless, conceited bastard!" Sophie snapped.

Keith stared at her, stunned, then shifted to the androgynous figure beyond her. Something cracked open in him: A surge of confusion, desperation, and hunger.

Without thinking, he stepped forward, grabbed Sophie's face in both hands, and kissed her: fiercely, recklessly. It wasn't gentle. It wasn't clean. It was everything he didn't understand about himself, crashing into her.

Sophie yielded to the kiss, buckling at the knees. They embraced passionately until Keith suddenly pulled away and stormed off down the hall.

Sophie straightened her crumpled blouse and wiped the lingering moisture from her mouth. A moment later, the metal entrance door slammed shut a floor below, Keith's exit echoing through the building. She closed her apartment door with purpose, took a breath, and turned back to her visitor.

The next morning, Keith paused in the entryway of his apartment, undecided. Eventually, he turned and headed to the bedroom. He opened the top drawer of his bureau, rummaging past underwear and personal items until he found the ring box, still tucked beside a pile of condoms.

He opened it. The diamond caught the morning light, dazzling even more than he remembered. For a moment, he just looked at it. Then he closed the box, slipped it into his pocket, grabbed his satchel, and headed out the door.

Later that morning, while sorting papers and checking emails, Keith kept glancing at a small slip of paper with Daniel Eiman's name and number on it. He pulled out the ring box and placed it beside the note, staring back and forth between the two.

He picked up the office phone, started to dial, then stopped, hanging up before the call could connect.

He repeated the motion. Dial. Hang up. Wait.

Finally, after another long hesitation, he let the call go through, just as Ashley walked into his office. Startled, Keith grabbed the ring box and slipped it back into the drawer before she could see.

Keith stood speechless as Ashley's radiant smile greeted him. She had clearly caught him off guard, and there was an awkward moment as Keith struggled to find his bearings.

Holding the phone handset casually by his side, Daniel's muffled voice could be heard softly echoing through, "Hello, you've reached the Eiman residence..."

"Hi," Keith said, trying to mask the unexpected awkwardness he was experiencing.

"Hello," Ashley replied, smiling despite feeling awkward about her seemingly poorly timed entrance. Keith appeared visibly flustered, though she couldn't understand the reason; she had dropped in on him numerous times before. "I was in the area and thought maybe you'd want to grab an early lunch. Are you free?"

Keith stood staring across at her.

"Are you alright? Ashley asked, more than a little taken aback by Keith's unusual unease.

Still holding the phone, Keith blurted back a little too quickly, "No, I mean, yes, I'm fine. I just can't go to lunch right now." Then, as if to convince both her and himself, he added, "I only just got here, not even an hour ago."

Keith pressed on, nodding slightly to himself as if to steady the moment. Suddenly, a faint, muffled blaring rose from the handset at his side. He quickly hung it up, silencing the sound, his eyes never leaving Ashley's.

Ashley looked over at him, trying to grasp the full context of the situation. She then smiled at Keith. "Okay, I guess I'll see you later then."

"Yes, you will," Keith called out after her as she quietly exited, gently closing the door behind her.

A wave of emotion surged through Keith; his mouth went dry, his throat tightened. He struggled to stay composed, reaching for anything to ground him against the sudden rush inside.

Fueled by a fresh surge of resolve, he picked up the phone, fingers trembling as he redialed Daniel's number. He focused, maybe too intently, on the ringing tone, tuning out the hum of the office, unconsciously holding his breath.

Part of him hoped no one would answer.

But this time, he let the call go through, choosing, deliberately, to ignore the knot of anticipation tightening in his chest.

The drive back to Amherst and the Eiman residence passed more quickly than Keith expected. Maybe it was the rhythm of the road, or maybe his thoughts, heavy with things increasingly unresolved, carried him faster than the miles could. When he turned up the driveway, the sight of the house struck him harder than he anticipated. Its large, inviting windows caught the afternoon light, quickening the anticipation rising within him, as though the house itself were alive and waiting.

He parked and stepped out, the gravel crunching under his boots as he made his way toward the side entrance. The late-day sun wrapped the house in a soft, golden hue, lending it a warmth that felt almost human. Before he could knock, the door opened, revealing Mrs. Eiman, who greeted him with a delighted smile.

"Keith!" she exclaimed, stepping aside to let him in. "Lovely to see you again."

Keith gave her a courteous smile and tentatively extended his hand for a handshake. "Thank you, Mrs. Eiman. I hope I'm not imposing."

"Not at all," she said warmly, opening the door wider and leading him inside. The house smelled of fresh bread and something faintly citrusy. The kind of scent that made one feel immediately at home. "Daniel should be here soon. But you know how that goes," She said with a flourish, as Keith followed her into the family sunroom. Three-quarters of it were floor-to-ceiling windows inviting the outside in.

Keith's gaze wandered to the corner patch of wall adjoining the sunroom to the house. It was covered with framed photos, which were a timeline of the Eiman family's life. Keith moved closer, studying them. The photographs depicted the five Eiman boys, primarily engaged in various activities or significant events such as graduations, confirmations, athletic achievements, and weddings.

"Which one is Daniel?" Keith asked, genuinely curious as his eyes scanned the younger faces.

Mrs. Eiman joined him, pointing to a heavyset boy with braces and a shy smile. "That's him, right in the middle."

Keith leaned closer, trying to reconcile the chubby, braces- and glasses-wearing boy in the photo with the man he now knew. "Wow. I wouldn't have guessed. He's really changed."

"That he has," Mrs. Eiman said with a nostalgic smile. "Puberty hit, the braces came off, he switched to contacts, got into swimming, and just like that, he became the strapping young man we all know and love today."

Keith nodded with a slight smile on his face. "That's incredible."

Mrs. Eiman handed him a glass for the bottle of mineral water he now held, which he waved away politely. "Is he usually pretty punctual?" Keith asked, his tone curious but not accusatory. "You said four-ish?"

"Yes. Daniel told me four-ish," she repeated. "It's all right. Why don't you have a seat? I'll get dinner started."

As the afternoon slipped into evening, Keith and Mrs. Eiman sat at the kitchen table, their conversation drifting through family, life, and the Eiman boys. The cozy kitchen came alive with the rhythmic chop of vegetables, the sizzle of meat in a hot pan, and the soft clink of utensils.

To Keith's surprise, he felt himself relax. There was something about her, easygoing, loving, and utterly present, that made it hard not to.

"So," Keith said teasingly, "you filled your backyard with sons trying to have a daughter?"

Mrs. Eiman laughed with a rich, warm sound. "Something like that."

Keith leaned back in his chair, swirling the water in his glass. "Is it true what they say? A son is a son until he takes himself a wife, but a daughter is a daughter all of her life?"

"I'm afraid so," Mrs. Eiman said, her tone tinged with bittersweet fondness. "With all of them?" Keith was asking about Daniel indirectly.

She turned back to the stove, stirring a pot. Her voice grew softer. "Except for Daniel. Who's been long gone, even without a wife."

Keith raised an eyebrow. "Well, he's living here now, isn't he?"

Mrs. Eiman busied herself, her movements brisk but not hurried. "For now."

Keith studied her carefully, sensing a story beneath her words. He hesitated, then decided to push gently. "So, you don't approve of the fact that he…"

"Sleeps with men?" she interrupted, her voice steady.

Keith flushed, his gaze dropping to the floor. "I didn't mean to…"

She waved her hand dismissively, her expression softening. "I just want him to be happy. All mothers want their children to be happy, no matter who they're sleeping with."

Keith considered this for a moment. "You don't think he's happy?"

She sighed, staring out the window as if searching in the darkness for an answer. Then she turned and faced Keith directly. "I don't think a happy man storms around the country smashing his ideas down other people's throats."

Keith frowned, genuinely confused. "I thought he was a schoolteacher."

Mrs. Eiman turned her attention back out the window at the impending darkness, "Where do you think he could be?" she asked, deflecting. At that moment, the sound of crunching gravel and an engine revving closer brought visible relief to her face.

They both turned toward the side window as headlights briefly illuminated the driveway, and the humming car engine came to a stop.

Mrs. Eiman turned to Keith. "Besides, he also has no responsibility. Wife. Children. Mouths to feed. Bodies to clothe. He can afford to be happy."

Moments later, the door swung open, and Daniel burst in, looking harried and more than a little disheveled. His greeting to Keith was hurried, half his attention directed at Jupiter, who had come to life at the sight of him, tail thumping wildly against the floor.

"Daniel, where have you been?" Mrs. Eiman asked, unable to hide her exasperation.

"Mamá, no deberías conducir sin una rueda de repuesto. ¡Me salió un pinchazo! Le espetó," Daniel shot back, throwing his keys onto the table. "Me salió un pinchazo, y por supuesto, tú no tienes una rueda de repuesto. Y por supuesto, mi teléfono se quedó sin batería, y tú... ¡Tú no tienes ni siquiera un cargador de mierda en el coche, tampoco! ¡Quiero decir, qué mierda!"

"Language! Daniel!" Mrs. Eiman's tone was a mix of reprimand and frustration, her eyes narrowing into thin lines.

Keith found the whole situation genuinely entertaining, even as Mrs. Eiman shot Daniel a series of pointed glares from across the room.

"I'm sorry," Daniel groaned, his hands flying up in a gesture of surrender. "But I'm so irritated. Anyway, you've got a spare now..."

Keith tilted his head, his eyebrows knitting into a questioning expression.

"For some reason, I decided to take her car instead of moving it and taking my own. She got a flat. Well, I got a flat in her car. No spare. My cell phone was dead. A fucking nightmare." Daniel delivered the last part with a resigned shake of his head, directing his frustration at the floor before looking back up at Keith.

Daniel softened his tone slightly, almost conspiratorially. "Anyway. You look like you could use a dip in the hot tub, and I for sure need one."

Keith hesitated, caught off guard. "I, ahhh... didn't bring a bathing suit." Keith looked down at his clothed body before concluding, "And I'm kind of, you know, freewheeling, so to speak."

Daniel smiled back. "Got it."

Mrs. Eiman stood at the sink, vigorously scrubbing a plate. Despite her obvious irritation, there was a noticeable sense of relief in the way her shoulders started to ease. "Five boys grew up in this house. I'm sure we can find you a bathing suit somewhere."

Her gaze shifted to Daniel, sharp and purposeful. "Ten minutes." She hesitated briefly, then underscored her point with a gentle yet authoritative nod. "Dinner will be ready in ten minutes."

Daniel smirked, a glint of mischief in his eyes. "Okay, then. We'll have to be quick."

The hot tub shimmered in the impending darkness, its glassy surface reflecting the hues of deepening blue, starting to blanket the evening sky. A gentle breeze rustled the surrounding trees, carrying with it the earthy scent of moss and damp leaves.

Keith let out a deep breath as he folded into the steamy water. The sensation was a balm to his nerves, tension unwinding from his body with each ripple. It amazed him how utterly and totally fulfilling the experience was, as if the seething water itself offered a kind of silent reassurance. He hadn't realized how much he needed this moment of peace, despite enjoying the hours he'd spent getting to know Daniel through the stories of his mother.

Daniel emerged from a deep dunk, water cascading from his hair in glistening rivulets. "I was surprised to hear from you," he said, brushing water from his face.

Keith hesitated, the words forming slower than his usual pace. "Yeah, well, I don't know. A certain sort of pressure is starting to build, and I... I thought I'd come by for some of that Eiman wisdom."

Daniel raised an eyebrow, his lips curving into a wry smile. "Wisdom." He repeated the word, assessing its significance. Then he repeated it, quieter, as if speaking to himself. "Right. Wisdom." His gaze returned to Keith. "If you're coming to me for wisdom, you're in more trouble than you think."

Keith laughed nervously, watching as Daniel slid underwater yet again, cutting through it with a smooth grace. For a brief moment, silence surrounded them, interrupted only by the gentle sound of water lapping against the sides of the wooden tub. "Yeah. I mean, you're intelligent and have compelling ideas." Keith announced more to himself than to the now-submerged Daniel.

When Daniel resurfaced, Keith's voice carried across the water, "What ideas do you storm around the country smashing down other people's throats?"

"What?" Daniel blinked, unsure he'd heard correctly. "Your mother says you… " Daniel squinted across at Keith through water droplets sliding off his head down his face. Keith started to repeat himself until Mrs. Eiman's voice rang out from the house, crisp and piercing, cutting through the moment like a knife, "Daniel."

Daniel rolled his eyes. "Nothing you haven't heard already," he muttered under his breath while running different scenarios through his head as far as what his mother may have told Keith.

As they toweled off and made their way back to the house, the grass felt cool underfoot, the night air settling in with a faint chill.

"So, how's Ashley?" Daniel asked, breaking the silence as they approached the back porch.

Keith hesitated, fiddling with the edge of the towel draped over his shoulder. "She specifically said you storm around the country smashing your ideas down other people's throats."

Daniel stopped in his tracks, eyebrows raised. "She said that?"

"Yes." Keith's tone was matter-of-fact, yet it carried a weight that left Daniel quiet for a beat.

Daniel nodded slowly, then, as if brushing off a thought he didn't want to linger on, turned the conversation back to matters that meant more to him. "Did you give her the ring yet?"

Keith stopped walking, the towel slipping from his grasp. His gaze was fixed on Daniel, unreadable but intense.

"Forget it, Keith!" Daniel said, almost sighing. "It was years ago. She's just... I don't know, my mother."

Back in the kitchen, now dimly lit by the warm glow of overhead lights, the remnants of dinner sat on the counter. The room smelled of roasted vegetables and herbs, still clinging to the quiet of the room. Keith and Daniel settled at the table, its ancient, worn, and weathered surface long cleared of plates and food.

Mrs. Eiman finished up the last of the dishes and glanced at Keith and Daniel with a mix of maternal affection and fatigue. "Good night, boys," she said, wiping her hands on a towel before leaning down to kiss the top of Daniel's head.

"Thank you so much, Mrs. Eiman. Dinner was delicious," Keith called out as she left the room.

She waved a hand over her shoulder in acknowledgment, disappearing down the hallway.

"So, what's going on?" Daniel settled into his seat, savoring the warmth of his tea as he took a sip.

Keith, with a pensive look in his eyes, began to toy with his teacup instead of drinking from it. "The craw thing. I can't stop thinking about all these things stuck in my craw."

Daniel leaned forward, eager for more information. "Like..."

"Well, my grandfather was... look, I'm just going to say it. Crazy." Keith's tone turned somber.

"Your mother's father or your father's father?" Daniel asked.

"My father's father," Keith clarified.

"Crazy, how? Like schizophrenic?"

"Yes. Exactly. Grandpa had schizophrenia. At least so they claimed."

"I had no idea," Daniel said, surprise evident in his voice.

"It's not something we talk about outside our immediate family," Keith explained.

"Got it. So, did he have multiple personalities?"

"No, just craziness. He would say the most outrageous things. He was, of course, convinced that they were all very real."

"Like what kinds of outrageous things?" Daniel chuckled, trying to lighten the mood.

Keith's voice trembled as he recounted the unsettling memories of his childhood. "When I was eight years old, we were having this conversation. Because I knew he was crazy and, you know, because certain things would definitely set him off, I was cautious of how I worded things around him."

Daniel nodded, thoroughly engrossed.

"But then something strange started happening," Keith said, his voice threaded with wonder, and a trace of fear. "He began responding to my feelings before I even had words for them. It wasn't just like he was reading my mind; it was like he could sense the intention behind what I was feeling. Like he was reading my heart. Cutting through all the noise, straight to the truth."

Daniel's eyebrows lifted. "What do you mean?"

"I mean," Keith said, leaning in slightly, "he wasn't just picking up on my thoughts; he was responding to what was underneath them. The motivations. The emotions I hadn't even processed yet. Before I could reframe anything, before I could soften it or hide it, he was already reacting. To what I was thinking, to why I was thinking it, and to how I felt."

He paused, searching Daniel's face.

Daniel nodded deliberately, urging Keith to continue.

"It really freaked me out." Keith laughed nervously. "But it wasn't just me. He could read Marty's heart, mind, and motivations, too."

"Damn!" Daniel was becoming increasingly intrigued.

Keith shook his head. "That's really how I came to realize her motivations toward me. Whenever she tried to take something away from me, he would question her motives and make her feel guilty for trying to steal from me."

"Wow," Daniel murmured, now utterly captivated.

"And then, I started thinking that maybe he wasn't so crazy. Maybe he was reading everybody's hearts, minds, and motivations the same way he was reading mine. I mean, he said some pretty out-there stuff. Everybody avoided him as much as they could, fearing he'd blurt out one of their deepest, darkest desires and ambitions. It was wild. He was crazy. All of it was crazy. But was it?"

Keith stopped for a moment, shaking his head.

Daniel hung on every word, steeped in fascination.

Keith's tone deepened as if telling ghost stories, "Because of this, I started investigating everything he was obsessing about. It turns out at least half of it was true. And then I started thinking that maybe he wasn't crazy after all. I started thinking he maybe was genuinely seeing things and knew things nobody wanted him to see and know."

Keith paused, his eyes searching Daniel's face for understanding.

"Did they lock him up?" Daniel asked incredulously.

"In a mental hospital! Yes, they locked him up." Keith confirmed with a grimace. "But he refused to take his medication because he said it made everything 'foggy' and that he couldn't see things clearly."

"Damn," Daniel muttered, shaking his head in disbelief.

"So many of his stories are still stuck in my head," Keith said with a sigh. "And it doesn't help that my mother always brings up my crazy grandfather whenever she's mad at my dad, who also sometimes says things nobody wants to hear. She'll say, 'The apple doesn't fall far from the tree, does it, George?' And he always shoots back, 'Schizophrenia skips a generation.' But I, of course, overhearing this, can't help but wonder, is this going to happen to me?

Supposedly, in my father's family, it's more prevalent in the males. And I look so much like my grandfather that there are times when I enter the room, and my grandmother actually thinks I am my grandfather."

"You're not a schizophrenic, Keith. I promise you," Daniel reassured him.

"Why am I so obsessed with all this stuff about healthcare and medicine? Or the truth, for that matter? Sometimes it's really crazy stuff. How do you know I'm not making all kinds of shit up? I don't even know. I can't stop thinking about it. It's making me crazy." Keith's voice was suddenly filled with desperation and doubt.

Daniel could only shake his head in response. He had not known Keith for long, but he was sure he wasn't crazy.

"For some reason, when you asked me about things stuck in my craw," Keith continued, "I started remembering all the stuff that's been weighing on my mind and in my heart. And now I cannot stop thinking about them."

"Okay. You have to give me some examples," Daniel urged. "Concrete examples."

"Have you ever seen the movie *Merchants of Doubt*?"

Daniel shook his head in response. "What's it about?"

"I'm not going to say. I want you to watch it and tell me what you think."

Daniel grabbed a pen from the pencil cup behind him in the cupboard and scribbled *Merchants of Doubt* in the margin of a newspaper. "Fair enough. What else?"

"There's a certain pharmaceutical company tried to bring a sweetener to the market," Keith continued, his words spilling out in a rush. "The FDA determined that it was detrimental and denied access, basically ruining the company's reputation"

"Ruining?" Daniel questioned.

"Yeah, pretty much," Keith continued. "Regardless, because the company had spent a fortune trying to bring it to market, they hired a CEO savvy to the process who somehow managed to get it pushed through, even after it had already been denied once."

"Please tell me this is not a fact," Daniel pleaded.

"This is what I don't really know. I don't know if they changed it or pushed through the same failed product. But there's more," Keith said, his tone turning grave.

Not sure he wanted to hear more, Daniel found himself asking, "More to the story, or more things stuck in...?"

"More to the story. That CEO later became a politician and used his political influence during the 9/11 crisis to pass legislation protecting CEOs from liability if it came to light that they knowingly put dangerous products on the market."

"That's incredibly disturbing," Daniel murmured.

"Yeah. It is. It's a piece of information that, for some reason, the media refuses to speak about or to." Keith concluded.

Daniel nodded, absorbing it all. Listening. Waiting.

"My grandfather was a Madison Avenue advertising executive before he had his first major, I don't know, episode." Keith continued.

"Interesting." Daniel nodded for Keith to continue.

"Yeah." Keith nodded further. "The thing that actually set him off was this ad that the Johnson campaign ran called the 'Daisy ad,'" Keith continued, "which they used against Barry Goldwater. Apparently, it was so vivid, visual, and impactful that people to this day think that it's what cost Goldwater the election."

"Did it?" Daniel was genuinely intrigued.

"No, not according to my grandfather. It only ticked Johnson's lead up a little bit. But what it did do was create a false perception in the public's eye that far exceeded the facts. At least according to my grandfather."

Daniel nodded, even as confusion started to settle in. "I'm not sure I'm completely tracking all this."

"My grandfather became obsessed with what did and didn't make it into the media. Including things that did make it in but were quickly, or otherwise removed."

"Like?" Daniel was genuinely interested.

"There's so much, dude. I don't even know where to begin. Really. Just so very much. Including things around COVID.

Daniel let it hang, hesitant to take hold of it, though the heaviness pressing on Keith's heart was impossible to ignore. He leaned back and uncrossed his arms, a small gesture meant to open the space, to invite Keith in.

Keith hesitated, but continued. "An ER doctor in Brooklyn claimed he had found a cure, early in the outbreak. For a day, it was everywhere; YouTube, network news, every outlet you can imagine carried it. Then it vanished. I found others who agreed with him, but they were all shut down or ridiculed. Some were well known, deeply respected. Even now, no one talks about it. It's long buried. But everything around it is significant, including who died and how.

"Jesus." Daniel could only shake his head.

"My grandfather always said, 'whoever controls the media controls the world.' He went to his death saying that."

Again, Daniel waited. He only nodded, only listened. Each detail Keith revealed, every shift, every breath, every subtle turn of tone, pressed more deeply into him, impossible to ignore.

"And then there's all the stuff around JFK's assassination." Sensing a welcome ear in Daniel, Keith continued. "My grandfather swears he saw a movie about JFK's assassination in his youth, depicting the tribulations of over a hundred eyewitnesses who gave detailed accounts to the FBI on multiple shooters."

"I've heard this one before," Daniel remarked, nodding thoughtfully. "That's not new. It's part of the urban legend or conspiracy theories."

"Yeah, well, according to the movie, all of those eyewitnesses mysteriously died within 18 months, even though most of them were young, vital, and healthy; my grandfather swore this film existed, but I can't find anything like it to this day."

"Well, there's the Zapruder film. There are all kinds of controversies around everything having to do with the Kennedy assassination." Daniel interjected.

"This is different. And my grandfather was adamant about it, almost to the point of insanity. My dad remembers him obsessing about it, too. He refused to stop talking about it."

Keith slowly eased into his chair, letting everything settle. The act of saying it aloud loosened something he hadn't realized was wound so tight. As Daniel's quiet attention held, Keith pressed forward.

"Sometimes I notice things that no one else seems to want to talk about. Important things. And the moment I bring them up, it's like I'm dismissed, brushed off. But I can't shake the feeling that what I'm seeing is true, and that it matters."

The silence between them deepened, and in that stillness, Daniel saw something emerging from Keith, something honest and human, fragile and real. It was becoming increasingly difficult for him to ignore.

Daniel waited. Keith went on, his voice drifting into something almost like confession. "All this stuff is stuck in my craw, and I can't get it out. I keep feeling like I'm going to end up like my grandfather. I can't stop thinking about it."

They remained still, apart but connected. As Keith's rawness deepened, Daniel felt a quiet responsibility take hold of him, a need to protect both Keith and what he had inadvertently awakened. "Well, first of all. I feel incredibly guilty for having put this notion of something stuck in your craw into your head."

Keith subtly nodded, smiling. Daniel could only shake his head. "But I'm going to look into all of this and see for myself," Daniel reassured. "What's the name of the company and the CEO turned politician?"

Keith shook his head, more to himself than to Daniel. "I'd rather not say. Just see if you can find it."

"Okay." Daniel's nod was small but full of intent. All he wanted was for Keith to know he was there, completely there. There with the kind of support that came from someplace deep and true.

Keith nodded gratefully.

For a long moment, Daniel said nothing. Then quietly, he asked, "So, is this why you drove all the way out here to see me?"

Shaking his head, Keith replied, "Unfortunately, no."

Daniel waited, unsure if he wanted to hear the real reason. After a moment of silence, Keith continued, "I can't seem to give Ashley the ring. Something's stopping me. I want you to help me give Ashley the ring."

"Okay, sure. How can I help?" Daniel asked, willing to do anything for his new friend.

"I love Ashley. She's been perfect for me. My parents love her; Marty loves her; everybody loves Ashley."

"How did you two meet?"

"She designed Marty and Dexter's beach house, and then after that, Marty had her redo her Louisburg Square brownstone. Her work is stunning."

"That it is," Daniel agreed with a nod.

"So, I hired her to do mine."

"And the rest is history," Daniel concluded with understanding.

"Yes. The rest is history."

"Okay. So, what's the problem, then?" Daniel edged closer, reassuring Keith he was listening and genuinely interested.

Keith took a deep breath before continuing, "So, Ashley's grandmother told her when she was around ten years old that she could do anything she wanted with a boy or man she was interested in. But she should never let him stick his penis up inside of her."

Daniel burst into laughter, utterly flabbergasted by the revelation. "Oh my God! Her grandmother told her that?!"

Keith nodded again, his eyes crinkling at the corners. "That's right. She said Ashley should never let a guy's penis go all the way inside her until she was sure she was going to marry him. And ideally, she should wait until they actually were married."

Daniel's eyebrows shot up so high they nearly reached his hairline. "Her grandmother actually said that to her?"

Keith nodded once more, his expression solemn. "Yes. She told Ashley that when a man's penis hits the cervix, some biochemical reaction occurs in the woman's brain that bonds her to the guy for life."

Daniel's eyes widened further; his gaze fixed on Keith as if he were trying to see if his friend was pulling his leg. "You're kidding, right?"

Keith shook his head. "No, man, I'm dead serious. Ashley believes it, too. She thinks that's why all her friends who slept with complete loser jerks are still stuck with them."

"So, you've never had intercourse with Ashley Cox."

"Correct."

"I cannot believe Ashley Cox is a virgin." Daniel, again, could only shake his head.

"Well, she's that kind of a virgin. And please, don't tell anyone that I told you this."

"Okay. Damn." Daniel smiled, the corners of his lips curling up, "But it's pretty unbelievable!"

Keith shifted uneasily in the chair, his fingers nervously twisting a coaster between them. His eyes flicked up toward the bookcase behind Daniel, lined with books and a forgotten teacup, its dried-out bag clinging to the rim. Finally, he exhaled, the words spilling out like they'd been pressing against his chest for weeks. "I also get the feeling she doesn't like sex. I mean, she's never gone down on me. Not once. And quite frankly, I can't even imagine her going down on me."

Daniel stared at Keith, numbly shaking his head, hoping to hide his shock. Picking up on this, Keith changed course, "Is this freaking you out? I feel like I'm freaking you out."

Daniel leaned forward slightly, resting his elbows on the kitchen table, his expression thoughtful but not judgmental. "Just a little bit, but go on. I want to hear the rest."

Keith shifted again, his cheeks flushing under Daniel's steady gaze. "No. It's alright. We can stop talking about it."

Daniel shook his head slightly, his voice soft yet encouraging. "Keith. Please. Continue. I want to hear this."

Keith ran a hand through his hair, the frustration evident in his movements. "I just get the feeling she's not a huge fan of sex."

Daniel nodded slowly, his face a mask of quiet empathy. "Okay. I could see where that would be frustrating. And it's not a subject you can talk to her about?"

Keith shook his head, 'no.' Daniel then gestured subtly with his hand, signaling for Keith to continue.

"In the meantime," Keith began, his voice dropping to a near whisper, "I've been having very hot sex with this hot girl who is. How do I say this? Becoming a boy."

The words hung in the air between them, thick and charged with tension. Daniel's brow creased, his surprise evident despite his efforts to stay calm. "What!"

Kcith chucklcd ncrvously, the sound hollow in the otherwise serene room. "I can't believe I'm telling you all this."

Daniel sat back, crossing his arms, his expression now one of incredulity mixed with intrigue. "Well, quite frankly, I can't believe it either. But please don't stop."

Keith's eyes searched Daniel's face, looking for any sign of judgment. Finding none, he pressed on. "Can I trust you?

For some reason, I trust you. But can I trust you? I'm suddenly feeling remorseful that I've told you any of this."

Daniel's expression softened, and he nodded. "I feel honored, quite honored, that you do trust me. Really. And yeah, sure, you're talking about stuff that most people are going to tell you is really out there, but…What about this woman who's becoming a man attracts you? Do we call her a he, a she?"

Keith's lips quirked into a small, rueful smile. "I think she considers herself non-binary."

Daniel tilted his head, considering the term. "So, a 'they'?"

"Yeah, I guess. But she's still a 'she' to me, and she's hot. And sexy as fuck. And she likes to have hot, sweaty, dirty sex." Keith let out a laugh, shaking his head. "And I like the way she smells because she doesn't wear any perfume or deodorant or…nothing. It's all just natural. I mean, she's not dirty. She's clean. She is always very clean. But she never wants me to be."

Daniel exhaled softly, giving his head the slightest shake, as if trying to clear the weight of the moment, while keeping his expression open, all compassion and quiet attentiveness.

Keith continued, the tension in his voice giving way to something more confessional. "But get this, she's taking hormones to help her transition, and those hormones are causing her, you know," Keith gestured, what he was unable to speak, "actually to enlarge."

Daniel's eyes widened, his voice rising slightly in pitch. "What!?"

Keith leaned back into his chair, letting the weight of his words settle. "I guess when certain women take testosterone, they grow body hair. However, it's not happening to this girl. Some grow body hair, and for some of them, maybe even most of them, their..." again, Keith gestured what he wouldn't allow himself to say, "grows too. And hers has gotten bigger. A lot bigger. And if I position her the exact right way or sit her on me the exact right way, her enlarged, engorged," Keith gestures, "you know what rubs against me in a way that produces an orgasm, the likes of which I've never experienced before."

"Silence fell between them, thick and charged, as if the room itself were holding its breath. Daniel crossed his arms, tighter, bracing himself. The revelation had left him stunned and completely unsure how to hide it."

"What do you think?" Keith asked, his voice shifting from hesitant to openly vulnerable.

Daniel's mouth opened, then closed. Finally, he managed, "I'm completely dumbfounded. Quite honestly, I don't know what to say."

Keith's lips twitched into a weak smile. "Well, say something."

Daniel let out a breath he hadn't realized he was holding. "So, let me see if I understand this. Your dilemma is that if you marry Ashley, you're never going to have mind-blowing sex for the rest of your life."

"Yeah. Well, that's what I'm afraid of." Keith's voice was low, almost mournful, as he sank deeper into his chair, edging it back against the wall behind him. "I don't know what it is. I just can't seem to pull the trigger."

Daniel nodded slowly, his expression one of reluctant understanding. "And you can't marry this other girl. The hot one that gives you mind-blowing sex?" He paused.

Keith clarified the obvious for Daniel, "The girl who's becoming a boy? You think I should marry the girl who's becoming a boy?"

Realizing the impossibility of such a notion, Daniel conceded, "Right. I guess not."

Daniel leaned back slightly, his hands resting loosely in his lap. He glanced over at Keith, not just thinking, but taking him in. The quiet pulse of nighttime sounds, crickets, and a breeze through the trees, gave the moment a kind of hush. When he finally spoke, his voice was calm, steady, and full of care. "You know, it may turn out that Ashley loves intercourse once she experiences it. That can and does happen. It happens a lot."

Keith nodded slowly, though the doubt in his eyes lingered. "Yes, but what if she doesn't? Do I go through life having sex with someone on the side?"

Daniel raised an eyebrow, a small smile tugging at the corner of his lips. "It wouldn't be the first time."

Keith let out a short, frustrated chuckle and ran a hand through his hair, leaving it a mess. "'I want what Marty and Dexter have, he said, his voice quieter now. 'I want the love and the sex to come from the same person. My parents have it. Marty and Dexter have it too. And I want that, for me.'"

The air hung thick with unspoken words, each word like a weight pulling down the atmosphere. At the same time, both men sat steeped in their own private musings, their gazes penetrating and unwavering. The soft ticking of a nearby grandfather clock seemed to punctuate the quiet. It was Daniel who eventually broke it.

"I'm not trying to change the subject or anything, but Marty and Dexter are suited for each other. Dexter thinks women should rule the world, and Marty wants to rule the world."

Keith laughed lightly, the tension easing just a fraction. "Exactly. My dad thinks that way, too."

"That Marty should rule the world?" Daniel asked, a touch of incredulity in his tone.

"Yes." Keith's agreement was firm, his expression thoughtful. "Well, that women should rule the world. Whether it's my mother or Marty, he agrees with the concept."

"That's not very Republican." Daniel smiled. "I don't think I knew that about Dexter." Daniel pressed; his curiosity piqued.

Keith nodded. "Oh yeah."

"And, of course, Dexter, being the breeder that he is, thinks that his overly-sized penis is a magic wand or something." Daniel continued.

Keith burst out laughing, the tension in the room finally breaking completely. "What? I haven't heard that."

Daniel leaned back, laughing along with him. "Yeah. He's like... I mean... another time."

Their laughter echoed warmly in the room, the heavy atmosphere lifting almost completely. Keith's grin lingered as he gestured for Daniel to continue.

"So, speaking of cervical versus clitoral orgasm," Daniel began, his tone shifting back to a mix of curiosity and amusement, "Charlie and Dexter, who are always at each other's throats, have had endless battles about this one in particular."

"Clitoral versus cervical orgasm?" Keith asked, his eyebrows raised in genuine interest.

"Yes," Daniel confirmed with a knowing nod. "I think they actually hate each other. But they oftentimes find themselves in the same room together, and their conversation always goes to the same place. Speaking of things stuck in one's craw."

Keith smirked, shaking his head. "Yeah, I think I've kind of heard that."

"Yeah. They're both brilliant, clueless straight men. No offense." Daniel's voice carried a playful lilt, though his eyes revealed a hint of exasperation.

"None taken," Keith replied with a grin. "So, what's their argument about?"

"Well," Daniel leaned forward conspiratorially, "Charlie thinks it's unnatural for men to want only one woman."

Keith's eyebrows shot up. "Charlie thinks that?" he repeated, his voice tinged with both amusement and surprise.

Daniel's eyes lit with amusement as he tilted his head slightly, a knowing smile playing at the corner of his mouth. "Oh yes, most definitely," he said, his voice low and rich. "And then, of course, Dexter's whole schtick is that commitment to one woman is everything. Spending time with those two in the same room is like having a live feed of constant entertainment."

Keith's smile broadened. He shifted slightly, leaning in, his curiosity clearly piqued. "How did you meet Charlie, anyway? He seems so… I don't know, different from the rest of you."

Daniel leaned back, thoughtful. The pause felt intentional, like he was weighing how best to explain Charlie. "Charlie has a thing for gay bars," he said at last.

"Straight women go there to relax. No one's hitting on them."

Keith nodded, sliding his chair closer to the table. "I've heard that."

Daniel's mouth curved into a smirk. "Brent, especially back in the day, was a total chick magnet. Eurasian, gorgeous, tall, lean, ripped. Girls flocked to him. But Brent? Gay as they come. He'd get these girls all worked up just by smiling at them. Then there was Charlie, waiting. They'd be drunk, frustrated, and horny, and suddenly, Charlie didn't seem like such a bad idea. He scored. A lot."

Keith chuckled, shaking his head at the absurdity of it all. "That's crazy."

Daniel's grin widened as he continued. "And if he didn't score, he'd start making out with other guys."

Keith stared at him, blinking in disbelief. "What?"

"Yeah," Daniel said with a nonchalant shrug. "If Charlie wasn't scoring, he'd find a guy and start making out with him. And bingo, just like that, girls, thinking he was gay, would want to go home with him."

Keith shook his head, his face a blend of surprise and humor. "That's insane."

"Or maybe it's human nature," Daniel mused, his tone thoughtful as he leaned in to finish. "It's funny because when you were talking about Ashley knowing from childhood that she wanted to be a designer, I thought of Charlie. He's the same way: always knew he wanted to be an investigator. His parents tell stories about him figuring things out as a child with uncanny accuracy."

Keith's forehead was wrinkled with concentration, and a network of lines appeared as he became more engrossed by this newfound understanding of Charlie, someone he was starting to perceive in an entirely new way.

The glow from the overhead light was mirrored in Daniel's eyes as he offered. "Maybe he has schizophrenia, too." Daniel laughed at his own thought.

Keith could only shake his head. "That's not something to joke about."

"Okay." Daniel continued, "Apparently, like with Ashley, there are all these stories. One of them: When Charlie was five, his uncle showed up hours late to Christmas dinner. When they asked where he'd been, he spun some cockamamie tale. And little Charlie, just standing there, speaks up and says, 'No, you weren't. You were with Aunt Alice all afternoon." Daniel let it land before adding, "Aunt Alice was Uncle Charlie's *brother's* wife."

Keith's jaw dropped. He burst out laughing.

Daniel laughed too. "Charlie swears the whole room watched the color drain right out of his uncle's face. The guy kept denying it, blaming a kid's *wild* imagination. But later, Charlie's mom pulled him aside and said, 'You see, honey? This is why you have this special gift.' She actually encouraged it."

"Oh my God!" Keith shook his head, laughing as his laughter faded into a wide grin. "Wow. That's incredible."

"True story," Daniel affirmed, clearly enjoying Keith's reaction. "And over the years, Brent realized Charlie had a gift in this area and began relying heavily on him for insights and advice. Charlie is Brent's investigator. You know that, right?"

"No. I didn't know that." Keith shook his head in wonder, his admiration for Charlie steadily growing. "So that's how Charlie fits into all your lives."

"Exactly," Daniel said, leaning forward. "From time to time, Charlie and Dexter find themselves in the same room, and it's almost guaranteed there's going to be the exact knock-down, drag-out event around male posturing."

Keith's laughter returned. "Alright, so finish. Dexter thinks his dick is a magic wand."

"Yes," Daniel said, grinning. "Although Dexter always refers to it as his cock. And he'll tell you there's a difference."

Keith laughed so hard he had to wipe tears from his eyes. "Yeah. He's got quite the bulge going. Even if you don't notice such things, it's hard to miss," Keith confirmed, shaking his head.

"Exactly," Daniel replied, both of them smiling broadly. "Anyway, Dexter believes that fluids exchanged during intercourse, and only during intercourse, between a man and a woman create a unique calming effect for both parties. An effect that he is adamant can only happen between a man and a woman."

"So, he thinks homosexuality is unnatural?" Keith asked, his tone casual but probing.

Daniel's lips curved into a faint smile, his eyes thoughtful. "You know," he said, leaning back slightly, "he's never actually said that. Not directly. Never even implied it, really. He just once mentioned, very matter-of-factly, that only straight men can honestly calm a woman down. And only and primarily through intercourse." Daniel let the words hang there, more intrigued than offended. "To him, it's not a judgment. It's… how the world works." Daniel's smirk widened into a grin as he nodded across at Keith.

Keith's eyebrow slowly lifted, his eyes widening in surprise and curiosity. His lips curved into a half-smirk, revealing a glint of amusement. "Okay. Go on," he said, gesturing with a lazy wave of his hand for Daniel to continue.

"According to Dexter, one man being truly committed to one woman isn't unnatural; it's supernatural. And the more committed, the more supernatural it gets." Daniel leaned in, "Charlie, on the other hand, has basically become a master, well, *masterful,* at getting women off. Clitoral orgasms are his whole thing now. He swears it's his gift, like that's *his* version of supernatural. Anyway, he and Dex argue about it nonstop. Every time they're in the same room, it's a showdown."

Keith sank back with a half-laugh, shaking his head, unsure whether to crack up or start asking questions.

Daniel chuckled, leaning back, silently chiding himself. "I don't know what's worse, that I actually said all that, or that every word of it is true." He let the moment hang, then pressed on. "Anyway, Dexter, who apparently knew he was going to marry Marty before he even hit puberty, swears that saving his dick for... "

"*Cock*," Keith cut in, a sly grin creeping across his face.

Daniel laughed out loud, "Right. Of course. Saving his *cock* for Marty is what's supernatural and has added to the..." Daniel gestured with air quotes, "'majesty' of their union. He really, deeply, strongly believes this with his whole heart and soul, along with how very special his cock is. And how *very* lucky Marty is that he saved it for her."

Keith could only shake his head.

Daniel continued, "Dexter is so obsessed with the greatness of his cock that he doesn't let anyone else even see it. He says he spent his entire life saving his cock for Marty Chambers. Now that he's married to her, it's sacred."

Keith let out a low whistle, leaning back in his chair, his arms folding across his chest. "That's... specific."

"You don't even know," Daniel continued, his eyes glinting mischievously. "He's never let anyone see it. He's one of those guys who, when you're in a group shower, will literally wash himself inside of his bathing suit or underwear.

Hence, no one catches a glimpse of his 'precious content.' And he always wraps a towel around himself to change. He's got this whole... thing about it."

Keith tilted his head, the corner of his mouth twitching. "Wow. Talk about crazy." He leaned forward slightly, resting his arms on the table, clearly chewing on the thought. "You know what's weird about Dexter? He's kind of like this, as you say, dumb, lumbering jock."

"It was wrong of me to say that because, first of all," Daniel interrupted Keith, sitting up straighter, his tone hoping to deliver clarity as he continued, "he's knock-down, drag-out gorgeous. And sexy as fuck."

Keith laughed, shaking his head. "Fair enough."

"And secondly," Daniel continued, waving off Keith's chuckle, "you don't graduate summa cum laude in engineering from Columbia University if you're dumb."

Keith held up his hands in mock surrender. "Okay, okay! But come on," he argued, "he's not exactly street-smart. You've got to admit that."

Daniel shrugged, letting the statement hang in the air for a moment before answering. "He doesn't have to be," he said finally, his voice calm but firm. "He's married to Marty Chambers. You don't get any more street-smart than Marty Chambers."

Keith nodded slowly, conceding the point. "True," he admitted. "You know, it's funny. Every once in a while,

Marty starts to devolve into this bitter, egotistical, maniacal, power-hungry know-it-all, see you next Tuesday, girl."

Daniel laughed, a sharp, knowing laugh that said he'd experienced the phenomenon more times than he cared to count.

Keith continued, his eyes softening as the memory surfaced. "He'll reach under the table and gently squeeze Marty's thigh. Once. Maybe twice. That's all it takes. And she shifts, like something in her just lets it go. It's beautiful, honestly."

Daniel nodded, his expression softening. "Yeah. Dexter's a king. He's the king of the jungle, and Marty's his lioness. She'll feed him, fuck him, and give him anything he wants because he's protecting her. From herself and from everyone else, at the same time, supporting her in conquering the world. A true king."

Keith sat back. His lips parted slightly in thought. "Wow," he said finally. "That's... an interesting perspective."

Daniel inclined his head, acknowledging the sentiment with a faint smile.

Keith's gaze dropped to his hands, which rested still on the table. "You know," he said slowly, "it's funny. I think my dad does that for my mother, too."

Daniel raised an eyebrow, intrigued. "Yeah?"

"Yeah." Keith's voice dropped a little, becoming more reflective. "He'll never contradict her at the table. Or in front of us. Not ever. Even when she's totally insane, like, ten times worse than Marty insane, if you can believe that. Dad just... lets her. And then, after some of her most insane diatribes, she'll be doing the dishes..."

"Wait." Daniel's eyes widened, cutting him off. "Governor Chambers does the dishes?"

Keith chuckled, nodding. "Oh yeah, sometimes every night. Unless, of course, we have guests. Then she'll tend to the guests and let the staff handle it."

Daniel shook his head, laughing in disbelief. "That's... totally insane."

"She's more than a little bit OCD and likes the dishes cleaned in a particular way. And more importantly, it relaxes her. Sometimes, depending on how stressed she is, it becomes a nightly ritual to help, as she says, 'wash away the day.'"

"That's unbelievable," Daniel said, his voice filled with genuine amazement. He tilted forward a bit, the cozy light overhead creating elongated shadows on his face. His eyes, sparkling with intrigue, stayed locked on Keith as though he were solving a mystery. This gesture only made Keith feel even more at ease.

Keith offered a small, reflective smile. "Anyway, when my mother is, what I would call, misbehaving, my dad lets her. And then, after dinner, when she's alone in the kitchen, he wraps his arms around her, whispers whatever he does into her ear, and usually kisses her afterward. She softens and yields immediately. Half the time, she'll even find us later to apologize."

"Wow," Daniel affirmed, his tone softer now. He sat back in his chair, nodding thoughtfully. "See, he's probably got a magic wand too."

Keith burst into laughter, the sound filling the room with a sense of ease. "Yup, he probably does. I do know that my mother and father also adore each other. Just like Marty and Dexter do."

"Oh, absolutely; Marty and Dexter were made for each other," Daniel said, his voice warm with conviction, a quiet pride threading through his words.

"And you introduced them," Keith added, his tone teasing.

Daniel grinned, leaning back with a look of triumph. "I did, and you can bet your ass I'll never let her forget it!"

Keith laughed out loud, nodding along with him. Then, as if slipping into his thoughts, he spoke more to himself than to Daniel. "Well, that's what I want, Daniel. I want to feel all the love that I have for Ashley and have hot sex, too. I want all of it."

"Ah, so does this mean you have a magic wand too?" Daniel asked, his smile widening into a playful grin.

"Absolutely. I definitely have a magic wand," Keith said with a crooked grin. He leaned back, arms spread just wide enough to tease, but his gaze held steady on Daniel's; less a challenge, more a quiet dare. Realizing Daniel wasn't biting, he conceded, "I know how it sounds… but I'm not kidding."

Daniel nodded, his smile widening. "Okay, then," he said, softly, somewhere between amused and disarmed by all of it. A little embarrassed, and more intrigued than he cared to admit.

He leaned in, tone soft but deliberate. "Like I said… You probably have it all with Ashley. You just don't know it yet. And yeah, maybe you won't be sure until you're married. But I think she's the girl for you, Keith."

Keith offered a subtle nod, his expression pensive. "Maybe you're right."

Daniel stretched and let out a long yawn, breaking the moment of introspection. "I should go to bed."

Rising from his seat, Daniel led Keith to the guest room. The bed had been turned down on the bathroom side, and the room exuded a cozy warmth, with its wooden beams and soft lighting giving it a serene, inviting atmosphere.

Keith took in the surroundings, nodding appreciatively. "What a great room."

"Yeah, it's supposed to be the master bedroom," Daniel explained, his tone softening as he continued. "But after my dad died, my mother couldn't sleep in here anymore. So, it became the guest room. She added the outside door and back stairway after the fact."

Keith turned to him, his voice low with empathy. "Has he been gone long?"

"About ten, eleven years," Daniel said, his eyes dropping. The weight of it still hung in his voice: quiet, but unmistakable.

"I'm so sorry," Keith said sincerely.

"Thank you. I miss him," Daniel said simply, a faint smile tugging at the corner of his lips as he met Keith's gaze.

"So, speaking of your dad, what's with all the Spanish? Was your dad Spanish?" Keith asked, curiosity piqued.

"Mexican. Well, half Mexican," Daniel said with a chuckle. "My father's mother was Mexican. Or I should say she is Mexican. She's still alive."

Keith nodded, gesturing for him to continue.

"Anyway, she's a Mexican woman who hated English-speaking people, even though she fell in love with and married one. She especially hated my mother for taking her precious treasure away from her."

"She hated your mother?" Keith asked, his brow furrowed in confusion.

"Yeah," Daniel said, nodding. "My mother took her one and only son away from her. So, she refused even to acknowledge my mother, let alone speak to her."

Keith smiled, shaking his head in feigned disbelief. "That's wild."

Daniel let out a soft laugh and went on, "My mother didn't want much to do with her, either. But she had her values. One of them was making sure we could all communicate with my grandmother, who only speaks Spanish. So she hired Mexican 'mannies.' "

"Mannies?" Keith interjected, raising an eyebrow.

"Males," Daniel clarified with a grin. "We were all boys, and she wanted us to be influenced by males. So, we had male nannies whom she referred to as mannies."

"Interesting," Keith said, leaning forward slightly. "Go on."

"So, only Spanish in the house, which my father, of course, spoke fluently. English everywhere else."

"Wow, that's amazing. Your grandmother must have loved that," Keith said, clearly impressed.

"Yeah, of course. It didn't make Abulita like my mother any better. Though I think they've gotten used to each other over the years. And there's the fact that it all backfired on my mother. Which, of course, Abulita loves."

"Backfired, how so?" Keith asked, intrigued.

"When we were young and didn't want her to know what we were talking about, we'd just switch to Spanish. Sometimes mid-sentence. We still do sometimes."

Keith laughed out loud, shaking his head. "That's hilarious."

Daniel joined in the laughter. "Sometimes, when I'm flustered, I just start speaking Spanish."

"Like in the restaurant in Provincetown," Keith recalled with a grin.

"Exactly. But those guys are also Latin friends of mine. And then, of course, there are moments like tonight when I'm so angry, I just want to throttle her. So I let loose in Spanish. It usually works. Although she has, over the years, learned to detect when we're swearing. Which she'd rather we not do in any language. Even though she can have the mouth of a sailor herself."

Keith chuckled, shaking his head. "That's amazing."

Daniel nodded, his voice growing softer. "Anyway, I have to go to bed."

"You don't want to stay and keep me company?" Keith asked somewhat sheepishly.

Daniel looked at him, his face composed, almost blank; too still, too careful. "It's a big bed," Keith offered, gesturing toward it. Then, as if needing to justify the moment, he added softly, "I just feel really comfortable right now. I can't remember the last time I felt this good. I don't want it to end."

Daniel didn't answer right away. Maybe he couldn't. But something in his eyes had shifted, just enough to betray what he wouldn't let show. He nodded as if seriously considering the offer before giving Keith a small smile.

"Thank you for hearing me out," Keith said earnestly.

"Oh, for sure. Thank you for sharing it, all," Daniel replied.

Keith opened his arms, and Daniel stepped into them. The two hugged tightly, Keith pulling Daniel closer.

Daniel stepped back, his smile soft. "You probably have to leave before I'm up. So, until the next time."

"Until the next time," Keith echoed. "Goodnight."

"Goodnight." And with that, Daniel slipped out, closing the door behind him.

As Keith stripped, there was a subtle knock at the door. He grabbed his slacks, holding them against himself. "Come in," he called.

Daniel opened the door just enough to duck his head through. "Give Ashley the ring, Keith. I have a feeling it's all going to work out. I'm not Charlie, so I don't know. But she's classy, talented, self-sufficient, beautiful, and she loves you. Give her the ring."

Keith smiled, the warmth of Daniel's words settling over him. "Thanks."

Daniel nodded, smiling back before closing the door behind him.

As Keith headed back to Boston the following morning, he was elated. Even though he felt overwhelmingly vulnerable, having revealed so many of his deepest inner fears to Daniel, he also felt a distinct euphoria coursing through his veins. A euphoria that was unlike anything he had ever felt before.

Throughout his life, everyone had wanted to be friends with Keith. He could never understand why. Now, for the first time, he yearned for someone's friendship in return. For the first time, he felt truly seen and, more than anything, accepted. He knew his ideas were crazy. He knew that nobody cared to hear what he had to say. He knew that, at some level, he was alone in the world and that it was best that he keep things to himself.

He also knew that, for the first time, he dared to show his true self. And it felt good. He felt totally and utterly seen. He felt totally and utterly relieved. Why had Marty kept Daniel from him all this time? Was she afraid that he might take something away from her?

Something about the day seemed lighter.

Something about the day seemed brighter.

For the first time, perhaps in his lifetime, Keith felt a deep, genuine inner peace.

*****

When Daniel came down for breakfast that morning, the house held a hush, broken only by the faint rustle of the newspaper Mrs. Eiman read quietly, accompanied only by the soft drip of the coffee maker. The kitchen was bathed in the golden hush of early sunlight filtering through half-drawn curtains. It smelled of roasted coffee beans and the crisp bite of autumn air drifting in through the open window.

Mrs. Eiman, wrapped in a pale lavender robe, sat in her usual place, her slender fingers curled around a steaming mug. She radiated quiet authority, as if she ruled her domain from that very seat. Her sharp eyes scanned the paper, reading glasses teetering on the edge of her nose.

Daniel entered, his movements precise and focused, gathering vibrant vegetables, fresh fruit, powders, and nuts from the fridge and pantry; each item selected with care, a ritual long refined. The low whirr of the refrigerator filled the silence between them.

The tension in the room was palpable, a silent, simmering undercurrent. It was Daniel who finally broke the heavy quiet, his voice sharp and cutting through the air like a knife. "What?"

Mrs. Eiman didn't look up from her paper immediately. When she did, her expression was one of practiced nonchalance, though her eyes betrayed mild exasperation. "I didn't say anything." Her words were measured deliberately, as though she had rehearsed this line countless times before.

"Well, you're about to," Daniel retorted, his tone bristling with a familiar edge. He slammed a bag of kale onto the counter with more force than necessary. It had become their morning routine: a battle of wills played out in clipped exchanges.

"But I didn't now, did I?" she replied coolly, peering over her glasses. "I can't even read the newspaper in my own kitchen. What is wrong with you?"

"Nothing!" Daniel snapped, the word sharp, clipped, and carrying more than it said.

They lapsed into another bout of silence charged with unspoken, albeit unmistakable, accusations. The rhythmic thud of Daniel's knife slicing through a cucumber broke the stillness. Each slice through the crisp cucumber was swift and exact, the blade gliding smoothly with practiced grace. Yet with every downward motion, the force of his hand sent small splinters flying and left tiny chips on the worn wooden surface.

Mrs. Eiman slowly folded her newspaper, watching Daniel as he forcefully crammed vegetables into the Vitamix. "I haven't seen that spark in you for years, Daniel. Andrew never gave you that spark."

Daniel's hands froze over the blender, the lid poised in mid-air. He turned to face her, his expression a turbulent mix of restrained fury and exasperation. "There's nothing Andrew Steadman could have given me that would have sparked in your eyes. You didn't like him."

"I liked him just fine," Mrs. Eiman countered, her tone calm but pointed. "I didn't like the situation."

Daniel was suddenly consumed by rage. He spun to face her, the words tearing out of him before he could stop them. "Oh, but now you do!?"

Mrs. Eiman leaned back in her chair, crossing her arms - a gesture that was both defensive and defiant. "Look, I know you've suffered a tragedy, Daniel, and it's a big one. But you're thirty-one years old. You have your whole life in front of you."

"Thirty-two!" Daniel shot back abruptly.

"What?" she asked, momentarily thrown.

"I'm thirty-two!"

Mrs. Eiman huffed dramatically as she adjusted her newspaper, her eyes revealing the thoughts she was battling to keep inside. She returned to her reading, though it was evident she wasn't absorbing a single word.

Daniel's frustration flared as he shoved a fistful of spinach into the blender. "Besides, he's straight, Mom." He turned to face her, point-blank. "As in about to be engaged straight."

Mrs. Eiman set her mug down with a firm thud, louder than necessary. "I didn't say he had to be your boyfriend, Daniel. Just be friends. Can't you have a *regular* friend who's a boy?"

Daniel couldn't contain his exasperation. "We are friends! We already are friends! What more do you want?"

Silence fell, sudden and heavy. The only sound was the low hum of the refrigerator, steady and unbothered by the storm between them. She didn't move. Neither did he. The air between them thickened, charged with something that felt perilously close to breaking. It was a standstill, raw and human, and neither knew how to cross it.

Daniel slowly turned back to the counter, gently put the lid back onto the blender, and flicked it to high. The roar filled the kitchen, drowning out her unspoken words and the storm building inside him. He stared at the churning mess of greens and fruit, wishing he could toss the whole morning into the spinning blades and vanish along with it.

The drive to Leominster that morning felt endless. Daniel gripped the steering wheel tightly, his knuckles white against the leather. Outside, the early autumn landscape blurred past, the ground and gutters slowly morphing into a mosaic of fiery reds, burnt oranges, and golden yellows. The impending baron trees seemed to mirror the withering emotions brewing within him.

His thoughts spiraled as he navigated the winding roads. Why had Marty never introduced him to Keith? The question gnawed at him, a persistent itch he couldn't scratch. Andrew would have loved Keith, he mused bitterly. They all would probably have been great friends.

By the time he reached school, the morning periods had passed in a haze. Daniel's afternoon classes, though flying by, felt like a series of disconnected moments. The weight in his chest grew heavier as his last class approached: the one with Benjamin McCray.

Daniel knew he shouldn't do what he was about to. The silent warning looped in his mind, one he couldn't ignore. But he also could no longer bear the sight of Benjamin's sad eyes.

As the bell rang and students filed out of the classroom, Daniel's gaze caught Benjamin's fleeting glance. It was enough.

"Benjamin," he called softly, almost a whisper.

Benjamin stopped, hesitating. His movements were tentative, like a deer caught in the headlights. Daniel's heart ached at the sight of uncertainty etched on Benjamin's face. Once the room was empty, Daniel gave a slight nod.

"I just wanted to let you know, Benjamin, yes. I am gay. And I'm proud to be gay."

For a brief moment, Benjamin glanced upward. Did Daniel detect a glimmer of hope? It was hard to tell. Whatever it was, it appeared sufficient enough to earn a silent nod of gratitude from Benjamin.

Daniel waited.

At last, Benjamin began to nod slowly as if encouraging himself to try. "I've been thinking."

Daniel nodded back, silently encouraging him to continue.

"You know Holden Caulfield? He says everything I'm thinking," Benjamin began, his words tumbling out in a rush. "I mean, I'm thinking about different things, but he just says it. He says all of it. Nobody does that, do they?"

The room seemed to hold its breath. Daniel waited before offering a nod, a small gesture of encouragement he hoped would prompt Benjamin to say more.

Benjamin's voice grew more confident. "I feel like him. I feel like I have to catch everybody from running off the rye."

Daniel's heart ached at the vulnerability in the boy's words. "Yes, Benjamin, I think many of us feel this way at your age."

Benjamin's gaze held Daniel's as he continued, "And I looked up the Jesus Prayer."

A look of surprise flashed across Daniel's face. "You looked it up?"

"It's online. You can find it online," Benjamin explained, his tone tinged with a mix of pride and shyness.

"The actual Jesus Prayer?" Daniel clarified, his voice calm and welcoming.

"Yes. The actual Jesus Prayer." Benjamin's anxiety slowly eased as he found a receptive ear in Daniel. "Lord Jesus Christ, Son of God, have mercy on me, for I am a sinner. Christian mystics repeat it over and over to evoke consciousness."

"Consciousness?" Daniel repeated. "Is that what you're interested in, Benjamin? Consciousness?" Daniel waited while Benjamin collected his thoughts.

Benjamin nodded, more to himself than to Daniel.

Daniel continued to wait until Benjamin finally found his voice again. "I'm always in so much pain, and I keep wondering what I did or what I can do to not be in so much pain." Benjamin shook his head as the last of his words quietly slipped out.

Daniel's heart sank even further as he nodded, more to himself than to Benjamin. He achingly understood.

Silence permeated the room until Benjamin looked up and continued. "I started saying it like they say to say it," Benjamin continued, "and slowly, I started feeling all the things that Franny is feeling. All of them. So, I had to stop."

Listening intently, Daniel nodded. Waited. He wasn't exactly sure what to say or even how to respond.

"Is that the theme you're talking about?" Benjamin asked. "Are Salinger's books about Consciousness?"

"Yes, that is the theme, Benjamin. That is exactly the theme I was looking for. But nobody got it, did they?"

Benjamin shook his head solemnly.

"But you did." Daniel reiterated his admiration, mixed with an almost overwhelming feeling of empathy for Benjamin. "When did you realize this?"

"A while ago," Benjamin answered quietly.

"Why didn't you say something in class?"

"I was waiting for you to tell us. Why didn't you ever tell us?" Benjamin questioned, curiosity mixed with frustration in his voice.

"I don't know," Daniel wondered even to himself. "I guess I felt it would have been better coming from one of you."

Benjamin nodded thoughtfully.

Daniel held himself still as Benjamin wrestled with thoughts he couldn't quite voice. He waited, patient, quiet, though it took effort now to manage the tangle of emotions rising within him.

The silence stretched. Somewhere beyond the walls, Daniel could hear the faint ticking of a clock, the distant echo of kids shouting in the schoolyard. He could almost feel the tension radiating from Benjamin, thick and electric, as the boy searched for words.

Finally, in a voice so quiet it barely reached Daniel, Benjamin spoke.

"None of the men I want to be with, and who want to be with me, will meet me." He looked up, eyes locking with Daniel's. There was something almost pleading in them.

Daniel nodded gently, encouraging. "Because...?"

"Because they're much older than me. And I'm a minor."

Daniel took it in without flinching, careful not to react. His voice, when it came, was steady. "You're not attracted to boys your own age?"

"I don't know how to find them." Benjamin shook his head, gaze falling to his shoes. "I'm ugly. I'm scrawny. My face is covered in zits, and my teeth are crooked. And I'm gonna be bald, like my dad, and like my granddad. And I'm hairy. Like, in all the wrong places. And it just grows back worse when I try to shave it. And nobody my age wants to be with me."

Daniel knew his thoughts should remain inside his head, but he could not bear the weight of what he felt in his heart. He slowly made his way around to the front of the desk, making sure to keep his hands to himself. He also knew he should keep his thoughts to himself, but he simply couldn't.

"I just wish I could wrap my arms around you and hold you close, Benjamin, and somehow make you realize that in just a few years, you're going to fill in," Daniel said softly, looking directly into Benjamin's eyes. "And your skin is going to clear up. Those braces are going to come off. And all of it is going to get better. Personally, I love bald men. I love hairy men, too. The hairier, the balder, the better. There are others your age out here who are attracted to young men just like you. And you will find them."

Tears welled up in Benjamin's eyes. He could only shake his head in total disbelief.

"Do you know of any other boys or girls in school who might be struggling with this?" Daniel asked gently.

Again, Benjamin shook his head.

"Because we can start a small support group," Daniel suggested.

Benjamin now shook his head vigorously. "Nobody can ever know," he whispered, his voice barely audible again. "Nobody can ever, ever know."

Daniel's heart clenched further as he watched Benjamin. He could feel the struggle and could almost taste the weight Benjamin carried, knowing he was different but unable to say it out loud. For a moment, Daniel considered doing what he'd been told: *Wait until Benjamin comes to you.* But it was too late for that. He'd already opened Pandora's box. And now, the silence felt like complicity.

"Benjamin, do you know for sure that you're gay?" Daniel asked gently, hoping his words might offer comfort, or at least a little clarity.

"I have dreams," Benjamin replied, his voice barely above a whisper.

"About other boys?" Daniel asked carefully.

Benjamin shook his head no.

"About girls?" Daniel pressed, already knowing the answer but needing confirmation.

Benjamin shook his head again and then finally managed to mouth the word: "You."

Daniel's eyes locked onto Benjamin's, hoping he had misunderstood him. "Who?" Daniel asked.

"You." This time, Benjamin spoke. "My dreams are about you."

Hearing the words out loud sent a wave of emotions crashing over Daniel like an avalanche. His mind raced, thinking of all the voices that had ever told him how dangerous it was to wear his heart on his sleeve. Yet, he couldn't help but feel everything so intensely at that moment.

Unable to stop himself, he gently and deliberately asked the question he knew would be best left unasked. But he could not hold back. Fearing the worst and hoping for the best, he had to ask, "What kinds of dreams are you having about me, Benjamin?"

In a flash, Benjamin turned and bolted out of the room, leaving Daniel stunned as he watched the classroom door slowly close behind him. Mr. Lopez's concerned face appeared in the doorway moments later. Noticing the distress evident on Daniel's face, he entered the room swiftly.

"What's going on with the McCray kid?" Mr. Lopez asked, his voice calm but urgent.

Daniel shook his head, unable to speak.

Mr. Lopez took a step closer. "Are you okay?"

Daniel opened his mouth, but nothing coherent came. Finally, the words broke out, unfiltered: "If that kid kills himself... I swear to God, I'm going to kill myself."

Mr. Lopez's expression changed instantly: alert, anchoring. He stepped closer, lowering his voice.

"Hey. Hey. Hey!"

"I mean it," Daniel backed away slightly, one hand clutching the edge of a desk for balance. His other hand hovered midair. "If anything happens to that kid..." His voice trailed off. His hands trembled. His chest tightened with a desperation he couldn't name.

Mr. Lopez didn't flinch. He placed a steady hand on Daniel's shoulder, not forceful, just there. "Take a breath. Just one, right now."

Mr. Lopez's eyes never left Daniel's as he reached into his pocket and pulled out a sleek smartphone, swiping through his contacts quickly until he found "Becky" and pressed the call button. His hand on Daniel's shoulder never wavered as the call connected.

"Hey, Hun," Mr. Lopez said into the phone, his eyes never leaving Daniel's face. "I need you to do me a huge favor. Can you pick up the kids from school today? I have a bit of an emergency."

He listened for a moment before responding. "Thanks, love you too."

Hanging up the phone, Mr. Lopez turned back to Daniel with concern in his eyes. "Do we need to bring anyone else in on this?"

Daniel shook his head, unsure of what to do or say. "I don't know... Why does life have to be this fucking hard?"

"Did he say something to you? Can you tell me what happened?" Mr. Lopez asks gently.

Daniel shook his head again and then asked, "Does Becky know?"

"Yes," Mr. Lopez responded calmly. "She's my wife, and she's also friends with Laurie McCray. She'll talk to her and see if we can sort things out."

Daniel nodded slightly, feeling completely overwhelmed by the entire situation. "I feel like such a screw-up. How did I not see this coming?" he sighed.

"Kids are tougher than we give them credit for," Mr. Lopez reassured him. "Benjamin will be fine. I have a good feeling about it."

"Right. Right," Daniel muttered. "Once you convince yourself of that, maybe you can come back and try to convince me, too."

Mr. Lopez gave Daniel an understanding nod before squeezing his shoulder and nudging him toward the door, holding it open as Daniel gathered his leather satchel and numbly followed him into the hallway.

*****

Brent's hands trembled slightly as they rested on the worn armrests of his wheelchair. The synthetic leather was cracked, a web of tiny lines his fingers traced absently, as if searching for answers. The office was quiet but for the faint hum of the air conditioning, which rattled now and then like it wanted in on the conversation.

He drew a long breath, his chest rising and falling in slow waves, each inhale a bid for calm. The door caught his eye. *Just leave*, part of him whispered. He could leave: roll out, say nothing, disappear. But his hands stayed where they were, gripping the chair as if welded there.

Across from him, Dr. Kaufel perched on the edge of his seat, pen poised over a yellow legal pad. Calm, but watchful. There was a stillness to him, but also a sharpness, like he saw too much to be shrugged off.

Bookshelves lined the walls, crammed with weathered volumes and labeled files. Two diplomas, one MD, one PhD, hung behind him. Brent didn't register any of it. He sat quietly, a subtle shake of his head betraying the conflict within. The desk lamp cast a golden glow over the room, soft and warm, in stark contrast to the harsh fluorescence seeping in from the hallway.

The silence between them thickened until Kaufel finally spoke, his voice low and deliberate. "You told me that for months, strapped to a Freedom Bed, completely paralyzed, barely able to do anything but breathe and think... You had an epiphany."

Brent's gaze snapped back to Kaufel, his expression a mixture of irritation and fatigue. His lips pressed into a thin line as he gave Kaufel a look that screamed, *Get to the point already.*

Kaufel, unfazed, flipped through his notes with deliberate care. "You said," he began, reading directly from his notes, "'I realized that I had been an asshole and that a lot in my life needed to change.' You said, 'Everything in my life had to change.'"

Brent shifted in his chair, the wheels squeaking softly against the polished hardwood floor. Low and edged with frustration, his voice cut through the air like a blade. "Right. So, what does that have to do with me and my friend's dad?" His tone sharpened further. "There's nothing about that that I feel needs to change."

Kaufel nodded slowly, his expression one of practiced patience. A brief glimmer appeared in his eyes; perhaps hope or maybe determination. He leaned back slightly, resting his pen against the pad as though giving Brent space to breathe. "I hear you," he said softly, his tone almost soothing. But there was an undercurrent of persistence beneath his words, a refusal to let the moment slip away. "I hear you."

Brent's jaw tightened as he stared at Kaufel, his frustration simmering just below the surface. The room seemed to close in around him, the rattling of the air conditioning growing louder in his ears.

Kaufel tilted his head, studying Brent like a puzzle with a missing piece. Then, breaking the silence again, he asked, "What part of you decided you needed to change, Brent?"

Brent blinked, confusion etched across his face. "What do you mean by what part of me?" He shrugged, his shoulders rising and falling in a gesture of dismissal. "I don't get it."

Kaufel shifted in his seat, sitting upright now, his pen set gently aside. He laced his fingers together and let them hang between his knees, his voice calm but precise. Then he leaned in closer. "What part of you realized something had to change, and what part needed changing?"

Brent let out a sharp exhale, shaking his head. "Okay, what's the point?" His frustration was no longer simmering; it was boiling over now, spilling into his words. He didn't bother to hide it.

Kaufel held his ground, his voice steady and unyielding. "I want you to tell me about this experience with your friend's dad. Again. I want every single detail. While you tell me, I want the part of you that noticed what was going on while you were lying in the Freedom Bed to observe the story as you tell it. Do you understand?"

Brent's face twisted into a grimace, his frustration now mingled with confusion. "No, I don't understand."

"Just give me the facts," Kaufel urged gently. "Tell me what you were experiencing and feeling, and see if, while you're telling me, you can observe it from the part of you that thinks your life needs to change."

Brent let out a bitter laugh, shaking his head as if the absurdity of the situation was too much to bear. "Tell me again why you're so different from every other therapist?"

Kaufel didn't flinch. "This is really frustrating you, isn't it?"

"Ah, yeah!" Brent snapped, his voice rising slightly.

Kaufel glanced at the clock on his desk and sighed. "Well, we're almost out of time. But I want you to really think about this, Brent." His tone softened as he began to bring the session to a close. "Think about it, and we'll pick up from here next time."

Brent's eyes narrowed, his voice laced with defiance. "How do you know I'm coming back?"

Kaufel's lips curled into a warm, knowing smile. "Because you're so close to having a breakthrough here. And the part of you that knows you need to change knows this."

Brent stared at him for a long moment, his face still, guarded. Not blank, just held. Finally, he shook his head, muttering under his breath as he turned his wheelchair toward the door. His movements were deliberate, the wheels squeaking faintly as he maneuvered himself toward the exit.

As Brent reached for the door handle, Kaufel's voice followed, steady and even.

"What makes me different from most therapists," he said, "is that we're not just looking at your *environment*. We're more interested in the part of you that *witnesses* it, not the part that thinks that it *is* it."

Brent hesitated, hand resting on the handle.

"In other words," Kaufel continued, "I focus on the whole of you. Not the scattered parts, but the sum of them. Who's steering the ship, Brent? Which part of you is directing the others? Do you understand?"

Brent didn't look back. His hand remained on the handle, the cool metal grounding him as something inside tightened. The hallway just beyond was quiet, sterile, predictable, almost beckoning. But Kaufel's words, flung across the space behind him: *"Who's steering the ship, Brent?"* landed harder than he cared to admit. He sat motionless for a moment, caught between the urge to flee and something else he couldn't name. Then, he opened the door and wheeled himself out, calm, controlled, and silent.

*****

Governor Elizabeth Chambers sat in her spacious, sunlit office, morning light pouring through the tall, arched windows behind her. She sat beneath the Capitol's great dome, its weightless expanse a constant pressure she'd long since stopped noticing.

Her desk, an imposing slab of mahogany polished to a mirror finish, was cluttered with the tools of her trade: stacks of reports, briefing papers, a steaming cup of Earl Grey tea, and now, a dossier delivered with the utmost discretion.

She leaned back in her high-backed leather chair, the faint creak breaking the stillness. In her hands, she clutched a stack of glossy 8x10 photos. Her brow furrowed as she examined them one by one, each image settling heavier than the last; an accumulating burden she couldn't put down.

The first photograph showed Daniel Eiman: young, intense, standing at the head of a group of demonstrators. His sign was bold, unmistakable in its message: "If Senate Majority Leader Horace West thinks homosexuality is such an abomination, why are known homosexuals working on his staff?!"

She let the photo fall to the desk with a soft slap and picked up the next. Charlie Atwood, face lit with defiance, held a sign high above his head: "Unleashing our power, Leader by Leader, State by State." The crowd around him surged like a wave, their voices frozen mid-chant by the camera's lens. Another image showed a poster in bold block letters: "One United Territory: Unleashing our Power, Leader by Leader, State by State."

Governor Chambers exhaled slowly, her steely composure unwavering. Her sharp eyes carefully rose from the photos to the Special Agent standing rigidly before her desk. His hands were clasped behind his back, his posture as straight as a rod, but a faint sheen of nervousness dampened his forehead. He was awaiting her orders.

"Take care of it, please," she said, her voice low and even, the kind of tone that left no room for debate.

The Special Agent hesitated, his brows knitting together. "How?" he asked cautiously.

The Governor's gaze didn't waver. Her eyes, cold as winter frost, bore through him. "In whatever way you do," she replied curtly, each word clipped and deliberate.

"I guess what I'm asking," the Special Agent clarified, his voice carefully measured, "is, is this the kind of taking care of you want to be kept apprised of?"

For a moment, silence filled the room, thick and heavy. Governor Chambers' expression remained unchanged. She let the question linger between them, her icy stare piercing through any doubt. Then, slowly, she smiled a smile that was all surface, polished and practiced, devoid of warmth. The kind of smile that could make a man's blood run cold. "Just take care of it, please," she repeated, her tone unchanged, her words final.

The Special Agent nodded once, stiffly, and without another word, turned on his heel and exited the room. The soft click of the door closing behind him left her alone once more with the dossier and her thoughts.

Governor Chambers leaned back in her chair, the tension in her shoulders easing slightly. She picked up her phone and dialed an extension. Her voice softened just a touch, though her words remained precise. "Could you please call Keith and ask him to stop by for dinner or dessert this evening? Thank you!"

Moments later, she hung up the phone, her face set with quiet resolve. She turned to the window. Outside, the Daniel Webster statue stood watch over Boston Common, unmoving, unyielding, a reflection of her own steely calm.

That evening, the Chambers family gathered in the grand dining room of the Dover mansion, a space that felt far too large for the small group seated around the long, polished table. The chandelier cast a soft, golden glow, its light catching on crystal glassware and silver cutlery arranged with near-military precision.

Outside, the night was cool and clear, the kind that invited long walks and shared laughter. But inside, the air hung heavy with unspoken tension.

Dinner plates had been cleared, replaced by delicate china saucers holding the last traces of dessert. Silent attendants moved like shadows, refilling coffee cups without a word.

Two place settings remained conspicuously untouched. The chairs beside Dexter and Marty sat empty, their linen napkins still neatly folded. Ashley and Keith hadn't shown up. Everyone knew why. No one said a word.

Governor Chambers sat at the head of the table, her posture regal and her face a mask of calm control. Across from her, Mr. Chambers mirrored her composure, though a hint of discomfort was evident in his eyes. Dexter glanced over at Marty, whose gaze remained fixed on her coffee cup, the silence around them suffocating. The clink of silverware against porcelain was the only sound, a faint, rhythmic reminder of the meal that had come and gone.

*****

Across town in Cambridge, the atmosphere was starkly different. Charlie Atwood slouched at a small kitchen table, cradling a mug of black coffee. The apartment tucked behind Brent's home office was modest but warm: mismatched furniture, a faint trace of incense still clinging to the air. Across from him, Brent sat in his wheelchair by the counter, steeping tea in a chipped mug. The soft hiss of the kettle and the quiet rustle of the tea bag were the only sounds, a fragile prelude to the tension quietly gathering between them.

Charlie broke the silence first, his voice sharp and cutting. "So, what now? You're going to quit? I've never known you to be a quitter, Brent." He spat out the last word.

"You quit!" Brent shot back, his voice rising with indignation.

Charlie leaned forward, his eyes narrowing. "No. I finished. It was mutual. There was nothing more Kaufel could do for me."

Brent shook his head, his frustration palpable.

Charlie pressed on relentlessly. "Don't you want to know what motivated you to seduce your doctor and maybe get him barred from practicing medicine?"

Brent's eyes locked onto Charlie's. "That's what you keep saying. Did you seduce him? Did you or did you not seduce your doctor? Because he is in a shitload of trouble!"

"Charlie, you know you can be such an asshole sometimes," Brent muttered through clenched teeth.

"If it were me," Charlie continued, undeterred, "I would want to know what motivated me to do something so profoundly selfish so that I could be sure and stop myself from doing it again."

Brent rapidly turned to face him and blurted out. "Yeah? Well, fortunately for me, you're not me!"

*****

The following morning dawned crisp and bright, the kind of late autumn day Boston was famous for. Sunlight streamed through the lush autumn foliage, creating a pattern of scattered shadows on the cobblestone roads. Governor Chamber's assistant sat at her desk, her finger hovering over the intercom button.

Governor Chambers' voice, calm but firm, crackled through. "Could you get Keith down here, please?"

The assistant flipped through the Governor's schedule, her manicured nails clicking softly against the paper. "Is there a specific day or time?"

"No," came the Governor's reply. "Just ask him to come down, and we'll make room. As soon as possible, please."

"Very good," the assistant replied smoothly.

"Thank you," Governor Chambers added, her voice trailing off as the line clicked dead.

The assistant jotted a quick note, her pen gliding smoothly over the paper, before reaching for the phone.

Keith was just about to leave for the office when his cell phone buzzed against the edge of the kitchen counter. He glanced down, mid-sip of his coffee, and saw the words GOVERNOR'S OFFICE glaring back at him in all caps. A sigh escaped his lips as he set the mug down, the ceramic softly clinking against the granite. He grabbed the phone, swiping his thumb across the screen.

"Good morning," he said, his tone polite but wary, already bracing himself for whatever was about to come.

He listened intently, his brows knitting together as he glanced at his watch. "When?" he inquired, the word hanging in the air as he rechecked the time, his mind racing to adjust his schedule mentally. Finally, he nodded to himself. "I'll head over right now on my way to work. Thank you." He ended the call with a quick tap, shaking his head as he slipped the phone into his pocket.

Keith grabbed his bag and coat, moving briskly yet deliberately as he headed for the door. The morning sunlight was sharp and golden when he stepped outside, but it did little to ease the knot tightening in his stomach. He knew this wasn't going to be a casual conversation.

As Keith stepped into Governor Chambers' inner office, the solid oak door closed with a click behind him, a familiar wave of tension settling over him. The room was immaculate, almost unnervingly so. Every paper, pen, and object on the Governor's desk remained meticulously arranged. Keith had always found this unsettling. The air smelled faintly of polished wood and the Governor's preferred scent, a mix of lavender and something else, which did little to soften the overwhelming authority the space exuded. The large windows behind the desk framed the sprawling Capitol grounds, with the morning sun casting long, dramatic shadows across the room.

Governor Chambers sat at her desk, her posture as upright and poised as always. The photos and dossier that had been there earlier were gone. Every trace of them was swept away as though they had never existed. She didn't look up as Keith entered, her eyes fixed on something in front of her, though Keith couldn't tell what.

"Are you ignoring invitations purposefully?" she finally said, her voice calm but deliberate, "or are you really just too busy?" Her tone was light, almost conversational, but the edge beneath it was impossible to miss.

Keith stopped a few feet from the desk, standing tall yet guarded. He waited until her eyes finally met his. Her calm gaze bore a weight that made Keith feel as though he were back in high school, being called to explain himself after some minor infraction.

"This is the fourth time in as many weeks, Keith." Her voice remained steady, but there was a subtle shift, a tightening of the words that hinted at her growing irritation. "What's going on?"

Keith hesitated, his jaw tightening as he considered his response. "Well, you don't care much about hearing what I have to say," he said finally, his tone sharp but not raised. "You told me to go through Marty. I've been talking to Marty. I talk to her every day." His lips twitched into a humorless smile. "I'm the good-looking stupid one, remember?"

Governor Chambers leaned back slightly, her eyes fixed on him, calm but assessing. For a moment, she quietly studied him, her silence louder than any words she could have spoken. Then, with a subtle shift, she changed tactics. Her voice softened; her demeanor almost maternal. "Darling…"

Keith shook his head immediately, cutting her off before she could continue. "Oh, darling..." he repeated, his voice dripping with sarcasm. "I certainly know what that means."

Governor Chambers allowed a faint smile to touch her lips, a carefully crafted look of innocence that might have fooled someone who didn't know her as well as Keith did. But Keith wasn't buying it. "Every time you call me darling," Keith said, his voice hardening, "it's because you're about to drop a bomb on me. Okay. Let's have it."

The air between them grew taut, the silence stretching just long enough to become uncomfortable. Then Governor Chambers spoke, her tone shifting back to the measured, authoritative cadence she wielded so well. "I just want to remind you that I am holding a public office, and what you say and do reflects heavily on my… "

Keith cut her off, his voice rising slightly, frustration seeping through his carefully controlled exterior. "I'm thirty-one years old, Mom. And I have a life! And I think that entitles me to…"

Governor Chambers flew to her feet, the sudden movement startling enough to make Keith take a half-step back. "You are entitled to NOTHING!" she snapped, her voice ringing out like a thunderclap in the otherwise quiet office. She stepped around the desk, her heels punctuating the hardwood floor as she approached him.

"You are a Chambers! You've been raised in one of the finest homes in this country; educated in privileged schools! Afforded opportunities and standing that most of your colleagues would sacrifice their lives for! Now, you may not like that very much, but it is a fact! And with it comes a responsibility that I will not have you squander! Do you understand!?"

Keith stood frozen, staring at her in stunned disbelief. The impact of her words struck him like a physical blow, rendering him momentarily speechless. He shook his head slowly, his expression a mix of anger and incredulity.

Governor Chambers seemed to catch herself. Then, her shoulders relaxed slightly. Continuing, she opted to soften her tone. "Please, Keith," she said as she stepped closer.

Slowly. Deliberately. Her voice was quieter now. "You've always been such a good boy. Why start these kinds of antics now?"

Keith stood his ground, his voice low but firm. "What kinds of antics? What kinds of antics am I starting, Mother?"

They faced each other in silence, the tension stretching so tightly it felt as if the room itself might snap.

"Look," Governor Chambers said finally, her voice hardening again. "I want you to pull your life together, and I want you to pull it together today! Do you understand?"

Keith didn't flinch. Instead, he stepped even closer. His face inches from hers. His voice dripped with defiance. "Well, if that means getting married, I wouldn't hold my breath!"

Keith turned on his heel and stormed out. The door slammed behind him with a resounding thud that echoed long after he was gone.

Governor Chambers stood frozen, her fists clenched at her sides. Slowly, she closed her eyes, her face flushed with emotion. She drew a long breath, steadying herself; composure returning by force of will, though it was clear how much it cost her.

Keith's immediate modus operandi would have been to go fuck Sophie Bieltran's brains out. Relieve the pressure. Somehow, do something, anything, to feel better.

But today, he didn't want temporary fixes. He needed something more.

This time, he opted to call Daniel Eiman.

*****

As Daniel's car hummed along the winding roads into Boston, his mind wandered. The trees lining the highway were stripped of their leaves. Autumn was reaching its climax, painting the landscape with vibrant, lush hues. The crisp air carried the faint scent of earth and burning wood as it filtered through his slightly cracked window. For a moment, he let himself relax. The drive was soothing, almost meditative, and he was glad he'd said yes to Keith's invitation, even if it involved something as dreadful as baseball.

Daniel hated baseball. He always had. Everything about it: the slow pacing, the endless innings, and the mind-numbing statistics felt like torture. But Keith sounded like he needed him, and Daniel needed the distraction, so here he was. To his surprise, the drive had been worth it. The game itself was as dull as he'd expected; watching paint dry might have been more engaging, but Keith had been in high spirits. His laughter and energy were contagious, lifting Daniel out of his worries. He had to admit that the Fenway Franks were as good as ever. There was something about cheap stadium hot dogs that felt like a guilty pleasure, especially in Boston.

Later that evening, they arrived at Keith's condo. The living room was dimly lit, creating an atmosphere that felt both intimate and intentional. Pinpoints of warm light cast soft shadows across the sleek furniture. Daniel couldn't help but admire Ashley Cox's impeccable taste. Every piece of furniture and every detail of the decor seemed to belong in a high-end design magazine. It was sophisticated yet livable, truly reflecting Keith's personality.

Keith moved around the room with easy confidence, his movements fluid yet deliberate. He turned on the local rock station, letting the soft hum of guitars and raspy vocals fill the room. The music played low enough to serve as a backdrop, adding a layer of comfort to the space. Keith handed Daniel a beer, the cold bottle pressing into his palm. Daniel took a swig and sank into the plush leather couch.

"So," Keith asked, leaning casually against the edge of the fireplace, his beer dangling from his fingers, "did you watch any of that stuff I told you about?"

Daniel smiled, tilting his head slightly. "I did. I watched every single bit of it."

Keith's brow arched, his lips curving into a playful smirk. "Are you going to keep me in suspense, or…"

"Or what?" Daniel teased back, his smile widening.

"Seriously." Keith's teasing softened into something genuine. He leaned forward slightly, his eyes narrowing in anticipation. "What did you think?"

Daniel set his beer down and leaned back, crossing one leg over the other. "I loved them. I thought they were great."

"And?" Keith pressed, his voice carrying a hint of impatience.

"Do you really want to hear what I have to say?" Daniel asked, his tone half-joking, half-serious.

"Yes. I really want to hear what you have to say. Am I and my grandfather crazy?"

Daniel shook his head, his expression softening. "No, you're not crazy. At least not as far as all these go."

Keith's lips pressed into a thin line as he gave Daniel a skeptical look. "Are you sure? Because I can tell what you're about to tell me."

Daniel raised an eyebrow, intrigued. "Really? Okay, tell me what I'm about to say."

Keith leaned back, crossing his arms. "Well, you're starting to block it now, but something to the effect of... me and cameras."

Daniel laughed, the sound warm and genuine. "So, you're sort of reading my thoughts but not completely."

"No, I'm reading them; I'm just also formulating my response to your thoughts. So, I'm sort of back and forth." Keith shrugged, his smirk returning. "You do know that you are an open book. You know that about yourself, right?"

Daniel nodded, his grin widening. "So, I've been told."

Keith shook his head, chuckling softly. "It's a good quality, Daniel."

"No, it's not!" Daniel shot back. "If you only knew. The reason these things are stuck in your craw, Keith, is because it's what you're meant to do. And you're not an actor, lying to the public, pulling the wool over people's eyes, like those actors in…"

"*Merchants of Doubt*," Keith interrupted him, his tone sharper now.

"Exactly," Daniel nodded. "So, do you want to know what's stuck in my craw?"

Keith nodded silently, his expression shifting into something more serious.

Daniel leaned forward, his voice growing more impassioned with each word. "What's stuck in my craw is all those people at the diner in Truro.

Grumpy old white townies, blue-haired mavens, and the hungover teenagers who were too young to have been drinking in the first place. The schoolgirls, gay men, hell, even the straight men. Cooks, waitresses, all those people cheering for you. For who you are, Keith! For you! For Keith Chambers.

For your passion! For your sensibility. Half of them standing on their feet, cheering, and reaching out, just wanting to touch you; wanting to touch the clothes on your body, knowing that they were in the presence of someone great. And all you wanted to do was crawl under the table and hide."

Keith's hand stalled mid-air, the amber bottle suspended inches from his mouth. His gaze locked onto Daniel as he lowered himself onto the couch opposite him, eyes dilated with shock. "That's what I'm thinking? Is that what your mind is telling you?"

For a moment, the room seemed to hold its breath.

"Then you would be right. That's what's stuck in my craw." Daniel continued, his voice softening but losing none of its intensity. "Things get stuck in our craw for one of two reasons. They either piss us off so much that we cannot let them go, or it's because something deep within us keeps nudging at us, persistently and earnestly, until eventually it's all we think about!

This person you keep rejecting is who you are, Keith. Why aren't you being true to who you are?"

Keith swallowed hard, his throat bobbing as he tried to process Daniel's words. They had struck him like a punch to the gut: brutal, honest, and impossible to ignore.

Daniel leaned back, his gaze never leaving Keith. "All of us know the thing that's pissing us off. Few of us are lucky enough to recognize the gifts that are calling out to us from deep within."

Keith looked away, his hands tightening around the beer bottle. Daniel's words hung in the air, heavy and unyielding. When Keith finally looked back, Daniel's eyes were piercing, cutting through the layers of Keith's defenses.

The room remained still, except for the faint hum of the rock station playing softly in the background. The dim lighting cast long shadows across the modern furniture, enveloping Keith's condo in a warm, intimate glow. The city outside was alive: distant sirens wailing, the low thrum of passing cars, while inside, it felt to Keith as though the world had been reduced to just the two of them.

"This is both for you, Keith," Daniel continued, his voice steady but impassioned. He leaned forward, locking his eyes onto Keith's with an intensity that made Keith want to look away, yet he couldn't. "It's what you're angry about. It also happens to be the thing that's grabbed hold of you and will not let you go. It's both. It's the angry thing you can't let go of. And rightfully so, I might add. And it's the special gifts you have screaming out to you from deep within."

Daniel's words were like a relentless drumbeat, each striking a deep chord within Keith. He shifted uncomfortably, his hands gripping the cool glass of his beer bottle as if it were the only thing grounding him in the moment.

Daniel paused, his jaw tightening as he watched Keith's reaction. Keith's face was a mixture of emotions: confusion, fear, anger, and something else Daniel couldn't quite place. But he didn't let up. He couldn't.

"At some point in time, Keith," Daniel continued, his voice rising slightly, "you're going to have to turn and face it. If you don't, it's going to eat you alive. You were born into a political dynasty, for chrissake! And you're fucking charismatic as hell and smart and authentic and passionate!"

Daniel stopped abruptly, trying to rein in the overwhelming emotions that threatened to overwhelm him. His hands clenched into fists, and for a moment, he was afraid to say another word, fearing that if he did, he might burst into tears. He looked away, fighting desperately to collect himself.

Keith sat frozen, the words echoing in his mind. He wasn't just hearing them, he was feeling them. They hit him in places he didn't even know existed, places he'd spent years trying to bury, years trying to avoid. The silence between them felt heavy, almost unbearable, until finally, Keith found his voice.

"I'm terrified of it," he said at last, his voice cracking under the weight. He leaned back against the couch, eyes lifting to the ceiling, searching for answers in the shifting play of its light and shadow above him.

"All of it terrifies me. The press is already against me. Everyone is; each one will crucify me, say I'm crazy, just like everyone did to my grandfather. And my family? They'll let them.

They'll *help* them." His voice broke again, quieter now. "They'll discredit me with just as much venom as RFK Jr.'s family does him. Maybe more."

Keith's voice trailed off as he shook his head, a bitter laugh escaping his lips. He looked down at his hands, turning the beer bottle over and over as if it were some magic talisman. Daniel watched him, his heart aching for his friend. Keith wasn't just afraid; he was broken, and Daniel could see it in every line of his body, every movement, and every breath.

Daniel leaned forward again, his tone softening but losing none of its urgency. "Just try and manage it, Keith. I'll help you. The people who love you *will* help you. You don't have to go out and run for political office tomorrow. But you do have to manage it.

Start slowly. Marry Ashley. It's the right thing to do. Like you said, she's wired for it. Your family loves her. She'll help you. They'll *all* help you. You just need to be smarter about it."

Keith lifted his gaze to meet Daniel's. For a moment, the world seemed to fall away. Words couldn't convey the depth of what Keith felt for this man sitting across from him. It wasn't just friendship or gratitude; it was something deeper, something he didn't know how to navigate or even name. His lips parted as if to speak, but nothing came out.

Daniel moved closer to Keith, his voice barely above a whisper, filled with significance as it crossed the short distance between them. "*Moral courage is the rarest species of bravery. Rarer even than the physical courage of soldiers in battle or great intelligence. It is the one vital quality required to salvage the world.*"

Keith looked away, his throat tightening. He immediately recognized the truth of Robert F. Kennedy Sr.'s words as so eloquently quoted by Daniel. They burned inside Keith, and he hated how deeply he resonated with them. He hated how Daniel could see him so clearly, cut through all his defenses, and lay him bare. He hated it, but he also needed it. Needed him.

When Keith looked back, Daniel was waiting, his expression patient yet unyielding. This time, it was Keith who broke the silence. "Robert Kennedy was a great man."

"That he was," Daniel agreed, his voice steady, his eyes never leaving Keith's.

"I think he was the best of the Kennedy family," Keith continued, his tone growing firmer. "I don't think he's rolling in his grave because of his namesake. I think he's standing up and cheering him right now."

Daniel nodded, "I agree with you. I think the entire Kennedy family should be ashamed of themselves."

"Yeah. I do, too," Keith said, the words heavy with conviction. He nodded to himself as if solidifying his own thoughts, letting everything sink in.

For a moment, they sat in silence, the only sounds being the faint strumming of a guitar from the radio and the occasional clinking of a bottle against the coffee table. Then, as if on cue, they lifted their beer bottles, clinked them together in a silent toast, and took a long sip.

Keith drained the last of his beer and stood, stretching his arms high above his head. His shirt rode up, revealing a sliver of his stomach, his muscles tightening and flexing with the motions. "I'm exhausted," he announced, his tone casual, but something unspoken lingered beneath the surface. "I'm sorry. No offense, but this whole thing is suddenly exhausting me."

Daniel's gaze rested on Keith's belly longer than he intended and then lifted to meet his eyes, already there, waiting, ready. "Okay. I understand."

Keith and Daniel moved in silent agreement, pulling out the hide-a-bed. Keith yanked off his shirt without hesitation, the fabric landing in a crumpled heap on the floor. He dropped face down onto the pulled-out bed, his voice muffled by the linen. "Will you rub my shoulders?"

Daniel froze, his breath catching. The room seemed to shrink around him, the air thick with unspoken tension.

Keith shifted slightly, maneuvering a hand beneath himself to pop open the button of his jeans. The waistband of his boxers peeked out, the fabric taut against his hips. He easily slid his jeans off, letting them pool on the floor. The sight of him, chiseled back and well-defined obliques drawing attention to the soft, sculpted curve of his glutes, perfectly formed, effortlessly offered, as if he'd never once considered withholding them. The sight was intimate, breathtaking, unguarded, and more than Daniel could bear.

He hesitated, his mind a whirlwind of emotions. His eyes darted from Keith's bare back to the pile of discarded clothes on the floor, then back to Keith's body stretched out on the bed. The faintest sheen of moonlight spilled through the window, casting Keith in a soft, silvery glow. Every line of his body: the curve of his shoulders, the taper of his lats down to his waist, and the subtle rise and fall of his breathing, drew Daniel's attention like gravity.

Keith turned his head slightly, his voice low and muffled by the mattress. "Are you going to rub my shoulders or just stand there?" Daniel exhaled sharply, trying to steady himself. He set his beer on the coffee table; the contact slight, but somehow final. Then he crossed the room and sat beside Keith on the pull-out couch, closer than he'd meant to be. The mattress dipped slightly under his weight, and for a moment, he hesitated again, his hands hovering above Keith's back.

Keith's voice came again, quieter this time. "Please?"

It wasn't the word itself that got to Daniel; it was the vulnerability in Keith's voice. The quiet plea of someone desperate for comfort but too afraid to ask. Daniel swallowed hard and placed his hands on Keith's shoulders. His palms felt warm against Keith's cool skin, the muscles beneath taut with tension.

Daniel kneaded gently, his fingers working into the knots across Keith's shoulders. A low groan escaped Keith as his body melted further into the mattress. "God, that feels amazing," he murmured, voice thick, drowsy, and unfiltered.

Daniel's hands moved with slow precision, thumbs pressing into the tight knots at the base of Keith's neck. The room was silent, aside from the rustle of fabric and Keith's soft, occasional sigh. Daniel tried to steady his thoughts, but the intimacy between them blurred everything else. His hands drifted down, tracing the contours of skin and muscle, the living shape of him. Each touch deepened the quiet pull between them.

Keith shifted slightly, adjusting his position. "Oh my God, that feels amazing," he said, his tone almost dreamy. "You're really good at this."

Daniel said nothing. He just let it happen; his touch steady and certain, even within his uncertainty. He'd known this before, but he hadn't let himself want it for a very long time.

Keith turned his head to the side, cheek resting against the pillow. His eyes opened just enough to find Daniel's face. The smile was small, but full of trust, and it caught Daniel off guard.

His hands faltered. It was a simple gesture, but the way Keith *offered* it: soft, sincere, stitched with everything he couldn't say, hit Daniel harder than he expected. He nodded back, no longer trusting his thoughts, let alone his hands.

Keith shifted again, this time rolling up onto his side. Daniel's hands froze midair as the blanket slipped, revealing more of Keith's chest, and the thick trail of hair descending from his stomach into the waistband of his boxers.

The air between them pulsed, charged, heavy, alive with something unspoken, and undeniable.

Daniel let his gaze fall unwillingly, unready, and yet unable to stop himself. The hard bulge beneath Keith's briefs strained forward, unapologetic, exposed. Daniel drew his hands back, not knowing where to place himself or his feelings. When he finally spoke, his voice was strained, desire and doubt battling for space in his throat. "What's going on, Keith?"

Keith looked away, the apology catching in his throat. "I'm sorry, I…" He ran a hand through his hair, slow and unsure. His arousal pressed upward now, cresting above the waistband, thrusting out onto his stomach; unmistakable now, and no longer hidden. "I don't know what's going on," was all he could manage.

Daniel's gaze sharpened, his brow tightening as he took in the exposed edge of Keith's vulnerability. He didn't mean to speak; it just came out. "Do you have condoms?"

Keith's eyes widened slightly. For a moment, he looked like a deer caught in headlights. "What are we going to do?" he asked, his voice barely above a whisper.

Daniel shook his head and stood up abruptly. "You know what, forget it," he said, his tone sharp with self-reproach. He took a step back, running a hand through his hair as well. "This is… this is a bad idea."

Keith sat up quickly, his movements almost frantic. "No, I'll… I'll be right back." Keith maneuvered off the bed, his bare feet padding softly against the hardwood floor as he disappeared into his bedroom.

Daniel sat back down, this time on the ottoman, his head in his hands. His heart raced, and his mind spun. He knew what was right and what was wrong, but at that moment, he wasn't sure he could trust himself enough to make the distinction. The lines between friendship and something more had blurred, leaving him uncertain about how to navigate it.

A few moments later, Keith returned, a handful of condoms clutched in his hand. He dropped them on the coffee table, where they landed with a soft thud right in front of a framed photo of him and Ashley, her smiling face staring back at him.

Daniel looked from this to Keith, his eyes a swirling pool of emotions, a tempest raging behind a mask of forced calm. Keith stood there for a moment. His shoulders slumped as he took in the scene: the condoms, the photo, Daniel's conflicted expression. He sat down heavily on the edge of the hide-a-bed, shaking his head. "Maybe I'm not quite ready for this after all."

Daniel exhaled slowly, relief washing over him like a warm wave. "I understand," he said, his voice steady but quiet. He leaned back, his body relaxing, just slightly, for the first time in what felt like hours.

The two men sat in silence, their eyes meeting briefly before darting away. The tension in the room dissipated, replaced by something softer, almost tender. Finally, it was Keith who broke the silence.

"I want to rub your back," he said, his voice tentative. "Can I rub your back?"

Daniel looked at Keith, his eyes silently begging for everything to end, wishing desperately for all of it to disappear. "Is that all right?" Keith asked, his tone almost pleading now.

Daniel shook his head, a nervous laugh escaping his lips. "No, probably not... I mean, maybe... Hell, I don't know." He sighed, rubbing the back of his neck. "Just a back rub, though, right?"

"Just a back rub," Keith affirmed, his tone earnest.

Keith's clothes lay in a tangled heap on the floor: shirt, jeans, his outline still faintly visible in the folds. Daniel hesitated, then pulled off his own shirt and let it fall beside the rest. He climbed onto the bed slowly, not with hesitation, but with the weight of something already felt. Something already chosen. He didn't know what would happen next, but it no longer mattered. He was already in it. Entangled beyond denial. Past the point of return.

Keith climbed onto the pull-out, carefully straddling Daniel. His hands moved to Daniel's back, kneading the muscles with surprising skill. "Loosen your pants," Keith said softly, his voice low, almost hypnotic.

Daniel hesitated, then reached under himself to loosen his jeans, exposing the waistband of his Calvin Kleins. The tension in the room shifted once again, but this time, it felt different: softer and less charged.

Keith's face expressed a blend of awe, reverence, and something deeper, something he wasn't ready to name. He closed his eyes for a moment, his hands moving slowly and reverently over Daniel's back. He allowed himself to focus on the sensation of Daniel's skin beneath his palms, gradually converging on Daniel's flesh as uncharted thoughts and feelings entombed him in a sea of crushing recognition. Within moments, not even minutes, Daniel was fast asleep.

Keith continued to touch and rub Daniel's body until sleep overtook him as well. He lay his body alongside Daniel, spooning him, wrapping both arms around him, and pulling him close. Although the sleeping Daniel seemed to welcome Keith's body against his, allowing Keith to maneuver their bodies together for complete and optimal contact, he never seemed to wake up.

As Keith settled in, gently pulling Daniel closer, he drifted off to sleep himself. Moonlight streamed across their bodies, Daniel shirtless, Keith wearing only his boxer briefs. Never had Keith felt this good. Never had Keith felt this safe. Never had Keith slept so peacefully or so deeply.

Hours later, morning sunlight filtered through the window, casting shadows on the walls and furniture, bathing Daniel and Keith in a warm and welcoming glow. Daniel remained sound asleep on the open pull-out bed, his shirt discarded and jeans unbuttoned but still clinging to his frame. Keith lay curled up beside Daniel, gently spooning him, still in just his boxer briefs. On the nearby coffee table, a pair of untouched condoms sat conspicuously, silently witnessing the events of the previous night.

Keith stirred first, blinking slowly as his surroundings came into focus. He stretched slightly, careful not to disturb Daniel. As the memories of the night before rushed back, a small, private smile crept across his lips.

He disentangled himself slowly, sitting up and leaning against the strategically placed sofa cushions. From this new vantage point, he watched Daniel sleep. His features were serene, illuminated by the morning light. Keith stayed like that, perfectly content to watch him sleep, until Daniel's eyelids slowly opened.

"Good morning," Keith greeted warmly, his smile widening as Daniel's eyes met his. "How'd you sleep?"

"Like a baby," Daniel replied, his voice husky with sleep. He glanced down at himself, relieved to see his jeans were still on him, even if unbuttoned. "This is a comfortable sofa bed."

Keith patted the mattress playfully. "Only the best."

"Bacon, eggs, coffee, oatmeal?" Keith offered, stretching as he stood.

Daniel rubbed his eyes and reached for his phone. "What time is it?" he murmured, retrieving it from the pocket of his unbuttoned jeans. "Jesus, ten thirty? How long have you been up?"

"Ten, fifteen minutes. So, what'll it be?" Keith asked again, already heading toward the kitchen.

"Whatever you want," Daniel said, swinging his legs off the sofa bed. He paused to get his bearings. "I'm going to hop in the shower if that's okay."

"Sounds good," Keith called back. "There are fresh towels in the tall closet."

"Awesome," Daniel replied, closing the bathroom door behind him.

As the shower hissed to life, Keith busied himself in the kitchen. He pulled eggs and bacon from the fridge and plates from the cupboard. The scent of brewing coffee filled the air, mingling with the faint aroma of freshly washed, albeit recently slept-in, linens from the sofa bed. He moved with practiced ease, the rhythmic clatter of dishes soothingly counterpointing his thoughts.

In the bathroom, steam swirled around Daniel as he stood under the hot spray, letting the water cascade over his body. After a while, he grabbed the towel he'd draped over the toilet seat, drying himself meticulously before wrapping it around his waist. He examined his reflection in the fogged-up mirror, running a hand through his damp hair. Satisfied, he pulled his underwear from his jeans pocket and pulled them on over his still-damp body.

Just as Daniel reached for the bathroom door, a sudden knock echoed from the front door. Daniel froze, his hand hovering above the handle. Moments later, the knock grew louder, followed by the unmistakable sound of a key tumbling the lock.

Keith, who had been heading back to the living room with two mugs of coffee, stopped in his tracks. His face paled as the door swung open to reveal Ashley standing in the doorway with her keys in hand.

Ashley's gaze swept the room, her eyes narrowing as she took in the scene. Daniel stood at the bathroom door, frozen in place, with wet hair dripping onto his bare chest and down his back. Keith, caught mid-step, balanced two steaming coffee mugs in his hands, his expression one of sheer panic.

Ashley's eyes darted to the unmade hide-a-bed, the pile of shirts, Keith's unmistakable designer jeans among them, and finally to the unopened condoms on the coffee table, directly beneath a framed picture of her and Keith. Then, her gaze shifted to Keith's untouched bed in the adjacent room.

"Ahhh... hey, Ashley," Keith stammered, his voice trembling just enough to catch her off guard. He cleared his throat and forced a smile. "Do you want some breakfast?"

Ashley's face was a storm of emotions, but she managed to formulate a response. "Hi, umm... I don't think I'm very hungry, actually."

Her eyes drifted back to the coffee table, the condoms, and the unmade hide-a-bed, eventually landing on Keith's bed, which she confirmed for herself showed no signs of being slept in. As she contemplated the implications, she paused to gather her thoughts, straightened her posture, and responded to Keith's astonished expression with a polite, albeit somewhat strained, "How was the game?"

Daniel crossed to the pile of clothes, grabbed his shirt, and began pulling it on. He quickly rubbed his damp hair with the towel before hanging it over the edge of the sofa bed. "It was great!" he answered, his tone overly cheerful.

Keith, on the other hand, was visibly flustered. "How was girls' night out?" he countered, his voice totally betraying his nerves.

"It was good. Who won?" Ashley asked innocently, her eyes darting between the two men.

At the same time, Keith blurted out, "Boston," while Daniel confidently answered, "Chicago."

The two exchanged wide-eyed glances, realizing their blunder. In a desperate attempt to recover, they quickly swapped answers, Keith stammering, "Chicago," while Daniel mumbled, "Boston."

Ashley's arms unconsciously folded across her chest as she looked first to Keith, then to Daniel. Then back to Keith before getting out, "I thought they were playing Cleveland."

Daniel and Keith were at a loss, simply gazing at one another without any idea of what to do or say. The tension in the room hung thick in the air, a palpable weight that seemed to press down on all three of them. Ashley's eyes darted back and forth between Keith and Daniel as though she expected one of them to buckle under the stress. Keith cleared his throat awkwardly, his mind scrambling for anything that might defuse the situation, but the silence stretched painfully on.

Daniel spent the rest of the morning driving aimlessly around Cambridge. The city buzzed with the usual morning chaos: honking horns, the chatter of pedestrians, and the occasional sound of a dog barking as it was taken for a walk. His hands gripped the steering wheel tightly, his knuckles white as he searched in vain for a parking spot.

The events of the morning replayed in his mind like a dark and twisted vine, tangled in knots that were impossible for him to unravel. No matter how hard he tried, he couldn't rid his mind of Ashley's voice as she struggled to reject the gravity of the situation unfolding before her.

Finally, he found himself pulling up to Brent's office, a small Colonial-style building nestled between a bike shop and a café. The familiar sight of Brent's van was noticeably absent, and the building appeared quiet, almost deserted. Daniel parked his car and made his way to the front stoop, the cool stone steps serving as a makeshift perch. He sat down, took out his phone, and checked his messages.

Nine unread texts from Marty glared back at him. Each one was more frenetic than the last, culminating in the final message, which screamed in all caps:

MEET ME IN THE PUBLIC GARDEN THIS AFTERNOON AT 2:00 PM SHARP, BY THE SWAN BOATS.

Another terse follow-up followed this: **I DON'T CARE IF YOU'RE ALREADY ALL THE WAY BACK IN AMHERST!**

And then, just a few minutes later: **IF YOU DON'T COME, I'M COMING TO YOU!**

Daniel sighed heavily, leaning against the stone steps of Brent's stoop. The last thing he wanted was to see Marty, especially not while still reeling from the morning's events. He considered simply ignoring her, driving out of town, and leaving all of this behind. But he knew better. Marty wasn't the kind of person one could avoid, not without serious consequences.

When Daniel arrived at the Public Garden, the sight of Marty waiting for him by the swan boats struck him immediately. Her usual poise was overshadowed by a visible anger simmering just beneath the surface. Her arms were crossed tightly, and her foot tapped an impatient rhythm against the stone-cold cement. As Daniel approached, Marty wasted no time closing the distance between them.

"Keith, I could expect this from!" she hissed, her voice low but venomous. "But you, Daniel. You know better!"

Daniel's expression was tight with frustration, his lips drawn into a narrow line. "Know what?" he shot back, his tone sharper than intended. "He gave me a back rub. We passed out on the sofa bed. I didn't even take my pants off. As if it's any business of yours."

Marty's eyes narrowed, her voice dropping to a near whisper, though it carried an edge that cut through the bustling noise of the park. "That's not what Ashley said." She took a step closer, the proximity intensifying her presence.

Daniel's expression darkened. "Oh, really? Was she there? Trust me, nothing happened."

Marty's whisper turned into a low growl. "Well, something is about to... Come on, Daniel!"

Daniel threw his hands up in exasperation. "Did you ever think it might be more complicated than it looks?"

"Did you?" Marty demanded, seizing Daniel's arm and dragging him away from the bustling walkway and inquisitive onlookers. "Do you think, ever in a million years, my mother is going to allow her prodigal son to have an affair with..."

Daniel's patience snapped. "Affair? Is that what we're having, an affair?" His voice rose, drawing glances from a few passersby. "Besides, the Governor doesn't give two shits about..."

Marty's hand moved so fast, she couldn't have stopped it even if she'd tried. It landed squarely across Daniel's face with a sound that echoed across the park. The blow brought tears to both their eyes, but only Daniel's face held the mark.

He staggered back a step, stunned. A few onlookers froze, curiosity sharpening as they reached for their phones. Marty, suddenly aware of the scene she was making, stepped back deliberately, trying to collect herself.

Daniel's anger surged as he closed the distance between them, his voice trembling with rage. "Is that why you never introduced us all these years? Because deep down inside, you knew there was a possibility? Why haven't Keith and I ever met, Marty?"

Marty's voice dropped, but the anger in it hadn't gone; it had only sharpened, darkened with desperation. "Look at how much you've suffered, Daniel. Then quadruple it. Multiply that by ten. That's *half* of what he'll have to go through. You think that's fair to him? You think that's love? Tell me: is that what love looks like to you?"

"Love? Love!? Is that what you think this is, Marty? Love? Daniel's voice cut through the park louder than he meant, loud enough for the growing crowd to hear, though he wished with everything in him that it hadn't. "Well, whatever you think it is, they're still his choices, Marty, not mine. Not mine. Not Ashley's. Not your mother's. And most certainly not yours." He drew a breath, his anger sharp and unrelenting. "If you were any kind of sister at all, you'd help him."

Marty flinched, her lips trembling as she fought back tears. "I *am* helping him," she whispered, voice raw, pulling Daniel a few steps farther from the crowd. "When are you going to live in the real world, Daniel? Instead of out there in the ozone somewhere. Those of us who actually live in the real world, *really* live here, know that people have to make sacrifices. Because in the end, it's the larger picture that counts. Not your pea-brained little life and your pea-brained little ideas." She shook her head, her anger superseding her grief. "Do you ever think five seconds beyond the moment? Do any of you?"

Daniel's fury erupted. "Foolish me. How could I be so bloody stupid? You're right, Marty. I know nothing about sacrifices." He jabbed a finger into her chest. "Not one fucking thing!"

Marty staggered back as if struck, her composure giving way beneath the weight of his words. She reached for him, but Daniel had already turned, walking away, his back closed to her.

Keith's walls seemed to close in further that evening as he arrived at the Chambers' mansion. He timed his visit perfectly, arriving just as dessert was being served and coffee finished. Governor Chambers herself greeted him at the door, her tone crisp and businesslike. "We'll take tea in the family room," she informed her staff, leading the way.

In the family room, Keith's heart sank further at the sight of two suited men standing over a coffee table covered with photographs. Recognizing them as his mother's henchmen, Keith braced himself.

The photos told a story that didn't need words:

Keith and Daniel, body surfing in their underwear.

Daniel, applying Keith's disguise in a Provincetown alley.

Keith and Daniel, playing volleyball.

Keith and Daniel, having dinner surrounded by Chelsea boys.

Keith, sans disguise, dripping with caked sand and water, as Daniel laughed and looked on.

Keith and Daniel, while in the Laundromat.

Keith and Daniel, together in the Truro Diner.

Keith and Daniel,

Keith and Daniel,

Keith and Daniel.

Keith stared down at the photos being methodically dropped, one by one, on the table by the Special Agents. Each glossy image felt heavier than the last. Among them were shots of DANIEL, CHARLIE, and BRENT at various protests.

As Governor and Mr. Chambers approached, Keith's gaze shifted from the photographs. His expression was glacial, the tension in his jaw evident as he spoke, his words clipped and icy. "Yeah. So?"

The silence that followed was deafening.

The more imposing of the two agents finally broke it, his voice measured but firm. "There's an issue that complicates things a bit." With a practiced gesture, the agent handed over a thick docket.

Keith took it cautiously, his fingers tightening around the edges as he flipped it open. Inside was a photograph of Daniel and Benjamin McCray, captured through a classroom window. Daniel's hands rested on Benjamin's shoulders. Their faces were close. The angle made it look as if something unthinkable and unmistakably inappropriate was about to happen. Beside him, the other agent leaned in and held up his phone. A video began to play.

Keith's eyes remained transfixed on the phone, his face a mask of shock and disbelief. The room seemed to close in around him. He looked up, his gaze landing on Governor Chambers, who exchanged a wary glance with her husband. Keith lowered his eyes again, shaking his head slowly. The silence between them grew oppressive, each second stretching out like an eternity.

The docket, the weight of the photograph, felt almost tangible in his hands. The video, damning and precise, cut like a blade, severing the fragile threads of trust and affection that had been forming between them, brutally and without warning. Keith and Daniel's ascent into intimacy had been slow and deliberate. Everything about Daniel, and the world he opened to Keith, had felt exhilarating, expansive, *true*.

In a single moment, it all shattered. Thoughts tore through Keith's mind: their long conversations, the fierce connection, the rare clarity of being seen, entirely, by someone who understood not just who he was, but where he came from. Someone who grasped the constant, shifting terrain he was forced to navigate. The mountains of expectation. The valleys of silent rejection. The unspoken cost of being *him*.

Keith's pulse thundered in his ears, drowning out the faint murmur of voices in the background.

Keith barely registered the Special Agent collecting their documents, or the other grabbing his phone, before they both exited the room. Governor Chambers and her husband stayed behind, silent; their presence was a silent weight pressing down on him.

Keith stood abruptly, his chair scraping against the polished hardwood. He didn't bother with words; there was nothing left to say. Grabbing the docket, he turned on his heel and stormed out, each footfall in the marble hallway striking like a drumbeat of rage.

The brisk evening air struck Keith's face as he stepped outside. The streets were alive with their usual nighttime symphony: the distant hum of traffic, the occasional laughter of passersby, and the rhythmic clatter of the T rolling by in the distance. He shoved his hands deep into his coat pockets, his breath visible in the cool air. He needed an outlet, somewhere to let the storm in his chest settle.

All reality seemed to blur. Keith couldn't remember where he had parked his truck, even though it was right there in the driveway. He couldn't recall the day of the week. He couldn't remember climbing into his truck, backing out of the driveway, and then slipping into traffic.

He couldn't remember how he got to where he was going. He couldn't remember how he knew that Daniel would be there. All he knew was that his feet carried him aimlessly until he found himself standing before a familiar pub, its warm golden light spilling out onto the sidewalk.

A light haze of chatter and the clinking of glasses filled the air, mingling with the faint notes of a blues tune playing on the jukebox in the corner. At a table in the back corner, Daniel, Brent, and Charlie sat amidst the aftermath of their drinks: scattered peanut shells, half-empty beer mugs, and crumpled napkins. Laughter had been their companion moments ago, but now a shadow loomed over their table.

Daniel reclined in his chair, brow furrowed as he stared into his mug, slowly swirling the amber liquid inside. Brent leaned forward, elbows on his knees, fingers occasionally lacing and unlacing. Charlie, usually the group's joker, sat unusually still, his gaze flicking between them, as if waiting for someone to break the silence, to light the match that would bring everything back to life.

Keith stepped inside, the door creaking softly as it swung open. A rush of warmth and the scent of roasted peanuts wrapped around him, briefly anchoring him. He spotted them right away: Daniel, Brent, and Charlie, tucked into a corner near the bar. Taking a breath, he crossed the room, weaving through clusters of patrons and sidestepping a server balancing a tray of pints.

As he approached, Daniel looked up, his expression dampened by the sight. "What's going on?" Daniel said as he watched Keith plant himself at the edge of the table.

"I guess I'd like to hear that from you," Keith muttered, pulling out a chair but not sitting. Around the table, tension gathered, thick with confusion and something far more combustible.

Then Keith's voice rose, cutting through the din; sharp, laced with betrayal. "What ideas do you storm around the country smashing down other people's throats, Daniel?"

The trio turned as one, their expressions shifting from nervous bemusement to startled concern. Keith stood before them, clothes rumpled, his face etched with a raw mix of anguish and fury. He didn't wait for a greeting. He slammed the docket onto the table, its weight landing hard and silencing any objections before they could form.

He flipped the cover open. Top and center was the incriminating photograph of Benjamin and Daniel.

"What the hell is this?" Charlie demanded, his tone a mix of disbelief and irritation as he grabbed the folder.

Daniel leaned in, squinting at the image as if it might rearrange itself. His face drained of color, jaw tightening, lips parting like he was about to speak, then thinking better of it. "It's not what it looks like," he said finally, the disbelief thick in his voice. "It's not..."

Keith didn't wait for an explanation. He turned on his heel and stormed out, the heavy oak door slamming behind him.

Daniel shot to his feet, chasing after him without hesitation.

Keith's footsteps were heavy, his pace erratic as he stormed down the street.

"Keith! Wait!" Daniel's voice called out, strained with urgency.

Keith stopped abruptly, spinning on his heel to face him. "Wait for what? An explanation? Some excuse for this?" His finger jabbed the air, gesturing toward the pub where he'd just left the docket.

Daniel slowed as he approached, his hands held up in a placating gesture. "I'm telling you, it's not what it appears to be."

"Oh, really?" Keith's laugh was bitter, almost a snarl. "Then what is it, Daniel? Because it looks pretty damn clear to me. And there's a video of your entire interaction!"

"Video?!" Look, the kid was struggling," Daniel began, his words halting as he tried to explain. "He needed help. I was only trying to help him."

Keith stepped in, closing the space between them. He jabbed a finger at Daniel's chest, eyes blazing. "By *fucking* him?!" His voice cracked, the venom in it startling even himself.

"What?" Daniel reeled back as though physically struck. "No!"

The intensity of Keith's glare faltered for a moment, replaced by a flash of confusion. He searched Daniel's face, looking for cracks, for tells, for something. However, Daniel's wide eyes held nothing but exasperation.

"You're about to be arraigned for sexual misconduct involving a minor," Keith said finally, his voice softer but no less anguished. "Sexual misconduct with a minor," he repeated before turning and walking away.

Daniel stood frozen in time and space, his now heavy breathing visible in the cold air. Then, helplessly, he called after him, "Keith, please. You know me. You *know* I would never..."

Keith turned abruptly and stepped into Daniel's face. "Fourteen years old, Daniel! Fourteen!" Keith shook his head in utter disbelief, then turned and stormed off into the darkness.

Daniel had paced the streets of Cambridge for what felt like hours, although it may have only been a few minutes. The city appeared indifferent to his turmoil, its usual hustle and bustle continuing unabated.

When he arrived at Brent's office, the building stood like a stark beacon in the dark street, brightly lit from within. The iridescent glow spilling out of the windows gave it the clinical atmosphere of an interrogation room. The sight of Charlie and Brent waiting inside, sitting side by side and poring over a pile of damning visuals, all variations of one theme, only added to the oppressive feeling.

Daniel hesitated at the door, steeling himself before stepping inside. The sharp scent of coffee and paper hit him immediately. Brent and Charlie barely looked up, too focused on the array of images spread out before them. Photographs tracked Keith and Daniel's connection in meticulous detail: Provincetown in every shade, including Keith in disguise, and candid moments of intimacy.

Then, the final blow: the photo of Daniel and Benjamin, taken just outside the classroom. Daniel stared at it, stunned. How a simple gesture: his hands on the boy's shoulders, had turned into *that*, he couldn't fathom.

He was in shock. Speechless, Daniel sank into the chair facing them. The gravity of the situation was palpable, bearing down like a heavy anvil, making the room feel unnervingly still and oppressive. The three of them stared at each other, unspoken accusations and questions lingering in the air like unfinished sentences.

Finally, Daniel broke the silence, his voice strained but defiant. "How did they do that?"

Charlie shrugged, but his expression tightened, like he didn't want to believe it, yet couldn't unsee what was in front of him. Brent leaned back in his chair, closed his eyes, and gave a slow, subtle shake of his head. He wanted to believe otherwise, *needed* to, but the evidence was alarmingly convincing. Even to them, Daniel's guilt felt dangerously close to assured.

"Fucking Leominster," Brent muttered under his breath, rubbing his temples. "Who the hell ever heard of Leominster, anyway? Where the fuck is Leominster?"

"I want to know how they got whatever photo they took. To look like that?" Brent and Charlie stared at Daniel in unison, equally stunned. "I'm telling you. It's not what it appears. That's not even close to what happened."

Brent and Charlie could only stare across at each other. "Charlie, really, see if you can find the original photograph. Someone has to have it."

Brent and Charlie could only shake their heads.

Daniel shook his head further. "Regardless, Keith said, I'm about to be arraigned on charges of sexual misconduct. Sexual misconduct, Brent!" Daniel's voice cracked with exasperation, his frustration boiling over. "Do you fucking believe this?"

Charlie raised an eyebrow, his confusion giving way to something heavier, unease, maybe even fear. "How would he know?" he asked slowly. "How would Keith Chambers even *know* that?"

The question hung in the air, unanswered, bringing with it the unsettling truth: someone, somewhere, wanted this to seem real.

Brent's expression grew more serious as he leaned forward, folding his hands on the table. "What exactly did you do with this kid, Daniel?"

Daniel's eyes snapped to Brent, a flare of anger breaking through his weariness.

"You haven't done anything. You know, with the kid," Brent pressed, his tone tinged with doubt. "Like maybe a mercy fuck, or something like that, maybe?"

Daniel's glare could have cut through steel. "Are you fucking kidding me!?"

Brent held up a hand defensively. "I'm your attorney. I need to know. And if there's even a reasonable question, you have to tell me. Now!"

The room fell silent as Daniel slowly rose to his feet, his movements deliberate and menacing. He kept his gaze locked on Brent, his words cutting through the air like a blade. "Fuck! You!"

Without another word, Daniel stormed out, the door slamming shut behind him, nearly shattering the glass. The echo lingered, amplifying the tension he left in his wake.

Brent and Charlie sat frozen for a moment, exchanging uneasy glances. Finally, Charlie broke the silence, shaking his head in disbelief. "What is his karma? Daniel? He's such a genuinely kind and loving man. Why do people hate him so much?"

Brent leaned back in his chair, exhaling heavily. "I don't know. I really don't know." He pointed to the photograph of Daniel and Benjamin, his finger hovering over the damning image. "But I'll tell you one thing: that's an incredibly incriminating photograph."

Charlie studied Brent, his brow furrowed. "It's the only one, right?" He nodded toward the pile. "There's nothing else. If something *did* happen, wouldn't there be more? More photos? More proof?" He glanced back at the image.

"Honestly, it even looks doctored. AI's changing everything these days, Brent; it *could* be fake." Then, almost to himself: "I need to look into this." Brent didn't answer, his expression grim as he returned his attention to the pile of photos before them.

*****

Keith, wearing the same now even more disheveled clothes, paced the entry stoop of Ashley's brownstone.

Ashley arrived overburdened with sacks of design samples. Keith reached out to help.

Ashley stepped away despite sacks slipping from her grasp and sliding to the ground.

"I'm...he's...it's over." Keith sheepishly offered.

"So, what now?... Do we go back to yesterday? Or the day before yesterday? Or last week? How long has this one been going on, Keith?!" Ashley turned away from Keith's gaze.

"Ashley. It was late. He gave me a back rub. We fell asleep. What difference does it make?" Keith stepped closer, scooping up fallen samples, trying to stuff them into Ashley's overfilled satchels.

"With condoms?" Ashley shot back, yanking the fallen samples from Keith's hands.

Keith could only shake his head.

"You need to think long and hard about this, Keith, and figure out exactly what you want." Ashley's response was as measured as it was determined.

Keith didn't hesitate, not even a bit. "I want you, Ashley."

"Well, you have a very bizarre way of showing it!" Ashley positioned herself between Keith and the door, struggling with her lock as she clumsily tried to insert the key, which inexplicably no longer seemed to fit.

Keith wrapped his hand around Ashley's, guiding it toward the lock. "Keith, please!" Ashley cornered her door, edging Keith out.

A surge of rage rose in Keith before he could stop it. "You know, if you put out a little, Ashley, maybe I wouldn't need to go looking for it elsewhere!"

"What?" She stared at him, stunned, unable to believe what she had just heard.

"Just a minuscule amount," Keith said, his fury hardening into something slower, more deliberate.

"Get out!" Ashley snapped.

Keith blinked, startled by its force. "Just the tiniest bit," he said quietly, as something new stirred beneath the anger, still defiant yet edged with sudden regret.

"I said, get out. I want you *out of my sight.*" Ashley turned back to the door, finally getting it unlocked. She slipped inside without another glance.

Keith stood still for a moment, then slowly backed down the steps, yielding to her words.

The dim porch light cast long shadows over his rumpled form as the door clicked shut behind her. He descended the rest of the stairs with a heavy heart, each footfall more burdened than the last, until he vanished into the dark.

It seemed that every single light was on in Marty's stylish townhouse. The space was impeccably designed, blending voguish sophistication with understated charm. Family portraits and framed photographs lined the walls and tabletops, each image meticulously curated to project a life of connection and success.

Yet the brightness of the lights felt harsh, almost exposing, as if they, too, were interrogating the moment. Keith sat across from Marty, wearing the same crumpled and visibly worn clothes. His posture was hunched, and his gaze was fixed on the rowing calluses on his palms. He picked at them absently, his fingers moving with a nervous energy that betrayed his inner turmoil.

Marty, seated on the sofa opposite him, observed her brother with a mixture of concern and exasperation. "Do you want a beer? Scotch?...oh, that's right, you're a tequila type of guy now." Her tone was light, attempting to puncture the room's suffocating tension.

Keith remained silent, concentrating even more on his calluses as though removing the tough skin might help untangle the complexities of his thoughts. Marty sighed, leaning back into the plush cushions of the sofa. She tried again, her voice softer this time. "Too much sculling?"

Keith's hands stilled. For a moment, it seemed he might say something, but instead he rose abruptly and walked toward the door without a word.

"Keith," Marty called after him, but he didn't stop.

*****

The Leominster Police Station appeared even more menacing than it was meant to be. Looming before Daniel and Brent was the Leominster Police Desk Sergeant, who seemed even more sinister than the desk separating him from the security glass that protected him. Brent rolled his chair forward, his lawyerly demeanor calm yet commanding. "Good morning," he began, his tone professional. "My name is Brent Evans. This is my client, Daniel Eiman. We understand that there is a warrant out for Mr. Eiman's arrest."

*****

The Charles River esplanade unfolded before Keith, resembling a path filled with both limitless potential and past sorrows. The air was brisk, infused with the subtle scent of the river and the earthy fragrance of wet leaves. Keith walked with a heavy gait. His head lowered as if his burdensome thoughts had taken on a tangible form.

In what seemed like mere days but felt like years, he had aged significantly, with the wrinkles around his eyes growing more pronounced and his previously assured stride now faltering. As he moved, the distant sound of laughter pierced through his haze. Two men raced to an unseen finish line, their breaths forming clouds in the cold air. They eased into a walk, playfully circling each other to cool down.

Their laughter rang out, unguarded, pure, as one tackled the other in a spontaneous wrestling match. The tussle ended with one pinning the other to the ground. Then, as if it were the most natural thing in the world, he leaned in and kissed him, a quick peck that softened into something slower, more certain.

Keith stopped short. He watched them walk away, gripped by a strange mix of envy and sorrow. He kept his eyes on them until they disappeared into the crowd, their laughter fading into the ambient hum of the city. Then, abruptly, he turned and walked in the opposite direction, faster now, as if trying to outrun whatever had just broken open inside him.

The heavy outer doors to Sophie Bieltran's loft loomed before Keith, its industrial design stark and unwelcoming. Keith pounded on the metal surface, the sound reverberating through the hallway. Moments later, the door creaked open, revealing Sophie mid-conversation on her cell phone.

Before she could react, Keith grabbed her and, pulling her into the hall, pressed his lips against hers. The kiss was desperate, almost forceful, until Sophie yanked herself away, her eyes blazing with shock and anger. She gave Keith a once-over, her gaze traveling from his disheveled hair to his wrinkled clothes. Then, without a word, she stepped back inside and slammed the door in his face.

Keith stood frozen, staring at the closed door. His breath came in short bursts, each exhale visible in the cold hallway air.

Suddenly, the door flew open. Sophie stepped into his face, eyes narrowed, jabbing a finger into his chest.

"It doesn't matter what team you're batting for, Keith," she said, her voice low and biting. "But you'd better know what *league* you're playing in. Because you might have all the fame and fortune in the world, but you have no grip on reality at all."

The door banged closed again, the noise reverberating through the hallway. Keith had hardly absorbed what she said when the door swung open once more. This time, Sophie extended her hand and seized his testicles, her hold tight enough to make him wince.

"What's driving you there, honey? Huh?" she demanded, her voice dripping with disdain. "What's driving you?"

She released him and stepped back inside, slamming the door one final time. Keith staggered back a step, stunned, hand hovering instinctively at his side. His heart pounded. His chest burned. He stood frozen under the buzz of the fluorescent lights, the sterile hallway pressing in around him; numb, humiliated, and seething.

Weeks later, day had given way to night, and Keith found himself once again parked outside Ashley's brownstone. The yellow Ferrari out front gleamed beneath the streetlights, a glaring monument to everything he was supposed to want. Through the window, he saw her in the kitchen, poised, elegant, handing a steaming mug to Karl, the investment guy from before. They laughed at something, easy and unguarded, the sound muted by glass but deafening to Keith all the same.

He sat in his truck, jaw tight, the brim of his baseball cap casting his face in shadow. The knot in his stomach pulled tighter. He gripped the steering wheel, then let go. Shifted his weight. Looked away. Looked back. A dozen times, he almost turned the key. But he stayed. Stayed and watched, Ashley, Karl, and the life he'd once convinced himself was his, unfolding perfectly without him.

The morning was as gray as it could be. Sweat and river water streamed down Keith's face, soaking into the Columbia T-shirt clinging to his skin. Though the air was cold, a sudden warm front had melted the slush accumulating in the river, giving him a window to row, a break he didn't know he needed. The Charles stretched out before him, vast and indifferent. His shell sliced through it in a steady rhythm, oars rising and falling in perfect sync. Each stroke was clean, powerful, precise; a fleeting escape from the chaos clawing at his chest.

The rising sun painted the sky in violet, orange, and yellow hues, its light ascending behind Boston's skyscrapers and stretching across the water, casting Keith into silhouette. His movements were precise and systematic, resembling a machine engaged in a competition with itself. The perspiration from his exertion created dark patches on his t-shirt and sweatpants, evidence of his relentless pace.

As he neared the river's edge, Keith eased his strokes, letting the shell glide to a gentle stop. He rested the oars across his lap and examined the fresh blisters on his palms. The sting of raw skin anchored him to something real, immediate.

Just beyond, stagehands were battening down the Hatch Shell for the season, their voices a low murmur against the rhythm of early joggers winding through the Esplanade.

He raised one hand to examine the damage, his fingers tracing the angry red welts. The sting was sharp but grounding, beckoning him back to the present.

Keith secured the shell, his arms heavy, every motion slowed by exhaustion. He began dragging it toward his truck, the mud sucking at his boots with each step. Then he stopped, slumped down onto the damp, uneven bank of the Charles. His body sagged, drained, sweat and river water still streaking his face, mixing with the cold air now sinking into his skin. The rhythm of rowing had done nothing to clear his mind. If anything, it had sharpened the noise inside it: memories, regrets, the weight of things he still couldn't name. Now, finally, the chill registered. He was rubbing at the blisters on his palms when a familiar voice broke through the fog.

"Columbia," Marty said, nodding at his soaked T-shirt. "How apropos."

Keith looked up, eyes rimmed red, his face drawn. He tried to smile at the joke, managed a dry shake of the head instead, then turned back toward the river.

Marty sat beside him without asking. Her presence was quiet, steady. No push, no judgment; just *there*, like the faint lapping of the river against the bank. Keith slipped his sleeveless down vest over his chilled torso, shivering now as fatigue gave way to something deeper: a kind of hollow ache he didn't yet know how to fill.

Less than an hour later, Keith found himself once again inside Marty's Louisburg Square townhouse. As the morning sunlight streamed in, it contrasted with the dark, tangled thoughts swirling in his mind. Marty had poured herself a glass of wine and offered Keith a beer. "Marty, it's nine o'clock in the morning," Keith replied.

"So, do you want coffee?" Marty offered.

Keith waved her off with a slight shake of his head and slumped into the corner of her sectional sofa, his elbows resting on his knees and his hands clasped loosely. His hair was unkempt, and the shadows under his eyes were deeper than before, revealing sleepless nights and restless days. He stared blankly at a spot on the floor; his body was present, but his mind was far away.

Marty took the sofa opposite Keith, her legs tucked beneath her as she sipped from her glass. The soft clink of the wineglass against the coffee table broke the silence while she studied Keith with a mixture of concern and resignation.

"You're in love with him, aren't you?" Marty asked, her voice gentle but probing.

Keith's cheeks turned crimson, his brows furrowing tightly. His jaw was set, and his eyes narrowed into slits as he shot a fierce glare at his sister. "You're asking me this now? For real? You're going to ask me this now!? You're a piece of work, Marty, you know that?!" After a brief stare down, Keith pointed across town toward the memory of the fateful morning, toward the memory of unopened condoms. "It's not about that. It's *never* been about that!"

Marty tilted her head, not breaking eye contact. "Not about what?" she pressed. "What do you do with Sophie Bieltran every chance you get?"

Keith let out a bitter laugh, more a huff of air than anything else. "That's over, too," he muttered, looking away.

"Only because she smartened up," Marty shot back, her tone sharper now. She took another sip of her wine, setting the glass down with more force than she intended.

"Nine o'clock in the morning, Marty! It's nine o'clock in the morning!"

Marty took the glass of wine and downed it. Not taking her eyes off Keith the entire time. Keith stifled a sarcastic laugh as he shook his head, a mixture of disbelief and disgust. "You really are a piece of work!"

"Daniel Eiman is a lot of things, Keith, but he's not a child molester!" Marty eventually blurted out.

"Did you see the photos?" Keith countered.

"The photo? The one photo?" Marty offered, "No, I didn't see the one photo."

"How about the video? Did you see that!?" His question hung in the air like a sharp-tipped icicle. "It's pretty goddamn incriminating." Keith could only shake his head. "And the kid *said* he did it! Above and beyond everything else, the kid *says* that Daniel *fucked him*!"

"I don't care what the kid says."

Keith's jaw tightened. He turned to face her, the weight of his emotions beginning to spill over. "How do you know he didn't do it, Marty?" he asked, his voice cracking slightly. "You say it with such conviction! How can you be so sure?"

Marty's expression softened, but her voice was confident as she replied. "*Why are you so sure he did?*"

Keith sprang off the couch, startling both Marty and himself. "Because the kid *said* he did! For chrissake!"

Keith leaned back, staring up at the ceiling and then back at Marty. "What, the kid made it all up? Why on earth would anyone make up such a thing? I mean, it takes a pretty twisted mind to accuse a completely innocent man of!" Marty shot off her couch and headed toward her bar. Keith followed her with his voice, "Don't you think?" Marty swapped her wine glass for a whiskey bottle and poured a neat shot into a tumbler.

"Marty, it's nine o'clock in the morning! Really, what are you doing?"

She turned and faced Keith, bottle and glass in hand, punching him with her words. "I told you Daniel Eiman was trouble, Keith. I told you. Right from the very beginning. I didn't introduce you because Daniel Eiman is trouble."

"Trouble?" Keith repeated, his tone incredulous.

"Yes, trouble," Marty countered, stepping toward him. "You just didn't see it because you didn't want to."

Keith opened his arms to the ceiling as if it held the answers. "What kind of trouble?" he asked her directly. "If it's not child molesting trouble! What kind of trouble!?"

A silent standoff ensued. Neither moved a muscle, their eyes communicating volumes in the absence of speech.

Keith shook his head, caught between sheer frustration and utter disbelief. He let out a dark chuckle and slumped back onto the couch, settling into its corners. "How do you know Daniel, Marty? Why was he *such a close friend of yours*, but I've only ever heard about him? Why? Why haven't I ever met Daniel Eiman? The man who introduced you to your husband? This very, very close friend of yours. And his, apparently!"

Keith stared across at Marty, then, with complete earnestness, asked, "What is it that makes Daniel Eiman so dangerous? I don't get it! You don't want me to have something I want because you want him all to yourself? Is that what it is?"

Marty could only shake her head, now desperately fighting tears.

"What, Marty? What? What aren't you telling me?! Why is Daniel Eiman so fucking dangerous?!"

"It's not that he's dangerous to everyone, Keith. He's only dangerous to people like you. Do you understand? He's especially dangerous to people like you."

"Why?" Keith was now on the edge of the couch. "How is he dangerous to people like me? What does that even mean? Dangerous to people like me?"

Marty took a moment to collect herself. She then seemed to slip deliberately back into her measured self, the self that so resembled their mother. The self that Keith most resented in both of them.

"People like me. What the fuck is that even supposed to mean?" Keith was incredulous.

Marty hesitated, her gaze darting toward a closed closet door in the corner of the room.

After grappling with her thoughts, too many memories, and turmoil, Marty crossed the space and opened the closet door.

Keith watched Marty sift through boxes and stacks of papers until she extracted a black binder. Its cover was frayed at the edges, and faint, nearly indiscernible stains blemished the surface. Were they blood stains? It was hard for Keith to tell.

Marty returned to Keith and gently handed him the black binder, her hand lingering for a moment before letting go. "This," she said quietly, "is what makes Daniel Eiman so dangerous to people like you."

Keith opened the binder, its weight almost symbolic. A stack of yellowed newspaper clippings spilled onto his lap, each a snapshot of a life filled with triumphs and tragedies. Keith's fingers trembled slightly as he picked up the first clipping: a weathered obituary with a black-and-white photograph of a strikingly handsome young man in his twenties. The caption beneath it read:

"Philanthropist Myles Steadman Loses Only Son."

Marty stared at the ceiling, the sharp morning light casting elongated shadows on the walls, her eyes wet but refusing to let the tears fall. The air in the room felt heavy, the kind of heavy that pressed down on your chest and made it hard to breathe.

Keith was immediately transported back to a cold night in rural Virginia, moments replaying like a fragmented dream. Time seemed to stretch and slow. The meeting room, bustling only minutes before, now stood in stark contrast. Tables were dismantled with the clatter of folding legs, and a group of local teens stacked chairs. Their banter about sports echoed faintly, a thin veil of normalcy over the tense atmosphere.

By the door, Daniel stood silently beside Andrew and Charlie, their expressions a mix of anticipation and exhaustion. Harvey lingered a few feet away, still engaged in conversation with the council members. The faint rustle of papers and muted laughter from the teens created a strange juxtaposition to the unspoken tension in the air.

The outer door creaked open, and a gust of cold air swept through. Brent stepped inside, shaking off the chill. "The coast is clear," he said, his voice low but steady. "They seem to be gone."

As Harvey approached, his steps slow and hesitant, Andrew's tone lightened, though it couldn't hide the edge beneath. "Harvey, where's your car?"

Harvey gestured vaguely toward the back of the building, his gaze darting toward the windows as though expecting someone.

Daniel, breaking his quiet demeanor, offered a warm smile. "We'll walk him over there."

Andrew nodded. "I'll pull the truck around front."

Not missing a beat, Brent added, "I'll come with you."

Andrew turned to Daniel with a grin. "Give me your jacket."

Daniel hesitated, pulling the collar tighter around himself. "It's freezing out, dude," he protested, but relented with a sigh, handing it over.

"Exactly," Andrew said, smirking into the jacket. "I'll take that hat too."

Before Daniel could react, Andrew plucked the hat off Daniel's head and removed the black O.U.T. binder from Daniel's grasp. Leaning in close, he whispered for Daniel's ears alone, "Be nice."

Daniel shook his head, watching Andrew and Brent enter the cold. "Turn the heat on full blast," Daniel had called after them.

Harvey, flanked by Daniel and Charlie, watched as Brent and Andrew exited. Charlie pointed at the side wall where the skinheads had been standing, then turned to Harvey. "Who were those guys?"

Never saw them before," Harvey replied, his voice tinged with unease.

Outside, the biting wind tore through the empty parking lot, carrying with it the faint scent of rain-soaked asphalt. Andrew and Brent made their way toward the truck, their footsteps crunching against the gravel-strewn pavement. Most of the vehicles were gone, leaving an eerie silence broken only by the occasional rustle of leaves and the hum of distant traffic.

Andrew squinted at his truck, a vague unease prickling at the back of his neck. Something about the way it sat there under the dim amber glow of the streetlamp felt wrong. As they drew closer, the metallic sheen of wet paint caught his eye, the garish red letters slicing through the night like an open wound.

"Faggots die!"

The words dripped down the side of the truck, their venom still fresh, staining the air with the acrid tang of spray paint. Andrew's breath hitched as he stepped closer, the weight of the message sinking in. Brent's smile faded, his face hardening into a mask of quiet rage.

Andrew reached out, his fingers grazing the paint. It was sticky, still wet, and the smell clung to his skin. His chest tightened as a wave of nausea rolled over him. Before he could react, the air behind him shifted with a sudden whoosh that set his instincts alight.

"Andrew!" Brent's shout was cut off as the attack began.

A blur of movement descended upon them as the shadowy figures of five masked men emerged from the darkness like wraiths. Andrew barely had time to turn before a gloved fist connected with his jaw, sending him stumbling back into the truck. The cold metal bit into his spine as he fought to stay upright.

Brent lunged at one of the attackers, swinging his fists wildly, but he was outnumbered. Two of the men wielded pipes, their brutal arcs finding purchase against flesh and bone with sickening thuds. The others shoved and struck with almost mechanical precision, their grunts of effort mingling with the sounds of flesh colliding and the dull clang of metal against metal.

Andrew and Brent fought back as best they could, their groans of pain punctuating the frenzied chaos. Blood spattered against the ground, mingling with the scattered papers that had spilled from the fallen O.U.T. binder. One of the posters, a map of America marked with colorful clusters of dots, lay crumpled beneath the truck tire, now smeared with streaks of red.

Amid the assault, Andrew's gaze blurred, the world tilting as his knees buckled. His head slammed against the side mirror, causing him to crumple and fall to the ground, his body folding in on itself like a discarded rag doll. Brent lay motionless in a growing pool of blood just beyond him.

The masked men retreated, their footfalls fading into the night as quickly as they had arrived. The echoes of their assault lingered, serving as a ghostly reminder of the violence. Andrew lay slumped against the truck, his cheek pressed against the cold metal, further smearing the wet paint. His breaths were shallow, each one a struggle, each one laced with pain. Inside the makeshift conference room, the thick walls muffled the faint commotion from outside.

Daniel, Harvey, and Charlie had reached the back exit. Their conversation was lighthearted. Daniel's voice was warm and genuine as he turned to Harvey. "You were great up there. How long have you lived here?"

"All my life," Harvey replied with a small, proud smile. "Except for college and medical school."

"Wow," Charlie said, clearly impressed. "They must all be really proud of you here."

Daniel rolled his eyes, but the corners of his mouth twitched upward.

Charlie had reached up and wrapped his arms around Harvey. "We'll get them the next time, buddy. We'll get them the next time."

Before Daniel could respond, the gymnasium doors burst open with a deafening bang. A teenager stumbled in, his face pale, his words tumbling out in frantic gasps.

Daniel didn't need to hear the specifics. His body moved before his mind could catch up, his legs propelling him across the gym and out of the main entrance. The cold night air hit him like a wall, yet he didn't stop. Charlie and Harvey followed close behind, their footsteps echoing in the silence.

The scene outside stopped them dead in their tracks.

Andrew lay crumpled on the ground, his blood pooling beneath him, soaking into the loose papers that fluttered gently in the breeze. Brent was nearby, his chest barely rising, his face pale and drawn. The vivid red of the spray paint on the truck clashed grotesquely with the deeper crimson of blood staining the pavement.

Daniel dropped to his knees beside Andrew, hands trembling as he reached out. His training kicked in, thrusting him into a state of laser focus. He checked for pulses and breathing, moving his hands methodically despite the fear clawing at his chest.

"Andrew," he said urgently, his voice breaking. "Can you hear me? You need to try and stay awake, Andrew."

Andrew's eyelids fluttered, his lips parting as a faint moan escaped. Daniel leaned in closer. "You need to try and stay awake, Andrew, okay?"

"I wasn't mad at you," Andrew choked out, his voice barely audible over the pounding of Daniel's heart.

"What?" Daniel leaned in closer, his voice gripped with emotion.

Andrew's lips moved once more, his words a fading whisper. "I love you. I'm sorry."

"You need to stay awake, Andrew," Daniel implored, his voice rising with both urgency and desperation. "Please, Andrew. Try and stay awake, okay? Please!"

Daniel's chest heaved as the weight of Andrew's limp body pressed against him. He cradled Andrew closer, his trembling hands gripping Andrew's blood-soaked shirt. "Please stay." Daniel pleaded.

"Don't go.

Not here.

Not now."

Around him, the world blurred into a haze of muffled sounds and distorted shapes. The stark reality of the moment seared into his mind like a brand.

Charlie stood nearby, his face pale and streaked with tears. He shook his head as if denying the reality before him. His hands clenched into fists at his sides. "This can't be happening," he muttered, his voice cracking. "This can't be real."

The distant wail of sirens pierced the night, their haunting melody growing louder with each passing second. Blue and red lights emerged from the distance, their approach slicing through the oppressive darkness.

"Please, Andrew. Please stay." Daniel whispered, his voice trembling as he clung to the faintest shred of hope. His hands moved instinctively, applying pressure to the worst of Andrew's wounds, but blood oozed through his fingers no matter how hard he pressed.

Nearby, Brent stirred slightly, his eyelids fluttering open. He groaned, his voice hoarse and strained. "I can't feel my legs," he gasped, panic rising in his tone. "I can't feel anything."

"Don't move!" Daniel barked, snapping out of his grief for a moment to focus on Brent. He turned to Charlie. "Keep him still. Don't let him move a muscle."

Charlie nodded and knelt beside Brent, his voice low and soothing despite the tremor in it. "You're going to be okay, Brent. Just hang in there. Help is almost here."

As the sirens grew louder, a small crowd began to gather. Meeting room helpers and lingering participants stepped cautiously into the parking lot, their faces etched with shock and disbelief. The sight before them, the blood, the crumpled bodies, the graffiti, was a tableau of horror that would be burned into their memories forever.

Andrew's breath caught one last time, his chest lifting gently before going still. His head sank into Daniel's chest, his features softening into an eerie, peaceful stillness.

The sirens blared deafeningly now, their flashing lights casting harsh, oscillating shadows across the scene. Two paramedics and an EMT poured out of the ambulance, moving swiftly and efficiently as they rushed to the injured. Approaching Daniel and Andrew, one paramedic worked quickly to find a pulse in Andrew's neck and check for breathing. The other nudged Daniel to let go of Andrew's body. Daniel didn't want to let go. Wouldn't let go. Couldn't let go.

The paramedics exchanged glances. Knowing there was nothing more they could do, one of them instinctively slid down alongside Daniel, gently cradling his head and pulling him close. Meanwhile, his partner carefully peeled Daniel's arms away from Andrew's now lifeless body.

Daniel slowly stood, his blood-soaked hands trembling as they hovered uselessly by his side.

The paramedic guided Daniel as he stumbled backward, his legs barely able to hold him upright. His chest felt hollow, as if someone had reached in and ripped out the most vital part of him. Charlie was at his side in an instant, steadying him with a firm grip from the other side.

"He's gone, Charlie," Daniel whispered. "Andrew's gone."

Charlie didn't respond; his grief weighed heavily in the silence between them. Around them, the paramedics worked swiftly, stabilizing Brent and gently lifting Andrew's lifeless body onto a stretcher. Bloodied papers and posters fluttered around them, caught in the chaotic whirl of activity.

The flashing lights illuminated the grim scene that assailed the night: the spray-painted slur on the truck, the blood pooled on the pavement, and the silent witnesses standing in a semi-circle, their faces pale and stricken. The world seemed to hold its breath, suspended in the aftermath of a world gone horribly wrong.

Daniel glanced down at his palms, dark stains settling into the grooves of his skin. His chest rose and fell unevenly, each breath a battle against the storm gathering inside him. Despite everything, dread seeped in, slow, unstoppable, until it overwhelmed him completely.

Andrew's final words echoed in his mind, their weight utterly crushing him.

"I wasn't mad at you. I love you. I'm sorry."

Marty remembered how the call had come like a cold, domineering avalanche, shattering the fragile calm she had managed to hold onto. Dexter stared across at her as her face went white. Their drive into rural Virginia stretched out like an endless corridor of silence, the only sounds being the hum of the tires against the asphalt and the occasional rustle of trees lining the road.

Neither of them said a word; the weight of unspoken fears pressed down on them like an oppressive fog. Marty stared out the window for the entire ride to the Arcadian town. The barren landscape streaked past in muted grays and browns. Her mind churned with questions she was too afraid to voice, the stillness between them thick with tension.

What she remembered most vividly from that night was the glaring red letters spelling E M E R G E N C Y atop the small community hospital. The letters seemed to pulsate against the darkened sky, serving as an ominous beacon warning of the tragedy that awaited inside. As Dexter's Land Rover rolled to a stop, he motioned for Marty to go in alone. They locked eyes, silently acknowledging what couldn't be spoken. Nothing had hit Dexter this hard; nothing had prepared him for the emotion that was now slowly overtaking him. The look on his sad face was one that Marty would never forget.

Marty grasped Dexter's arm reassuringly and then slowly maneuvered herself out of the car. She knew he needed time. She knew he needed a moment. She knew their lives would never be the same. Marty approached the waiting figure of Charlie, who stood beneath the harsh fluorescent lights outside the entrance, smoking. There were hugs, quick and tight, but no words were exchanged. The silence carried a gravity that words could not reach.

Inside, the waiting area was eerily quiet, its harsh, sterile lighting casting sharp shadows across the worn linoleum floor. Marty's eyes were immediately drawn to Daniel, sitting alone by the window. He resembled a statue of despair, staring blankly at the darkness beyond the glass. His face, pale and streaked with dried blood, was taut with an agony that seemed to have drained all life from him. Dried blood caked his clothes, arms, and hands, and in his lap rested a disheveled, bloodied black binder that appeared absurdly small and fragile in the vastness of his grief.

In one hand, he clutched a plastic bag, its contents chillingly mundane yet profoundly heartbreaking: the blood-stained clothes that had housed Andrew's body. For a moment that stretched into eternity, Marty stood frozen, the air around her suffocatingly thick. Daniel's gaze eventually shifted, his hollow eyes meeting hers. They were unseeing and distant, as if he were looking through her rather than at her.

Charlie appeared at her side, his presence steadying yet silent. Together, they approached Daniel, the weight of the moment pressing down on them. Daniel's head dropped, his shoulders curling inward as if trying to shield himself from the unbearable reality. Marty moved instinctively, taking the seat beside him. Without hesitation, she pulled him against her chest, her arms wrapping around him like a protective cocoon. Her fingers found their way to his hair, stroking it gently as if the simple act might mend the fractures in his soul. She murmured soft, incomprehensible words, a balm for the unspeakable pain radiating from him.

The ride back to Georgetown had been silent. Just before getting on the freeway, Dexter pulled the car over on the rural road and stopped. Marty looked over at him with questioning eyes. Dexter then quietly asked, "Can you drive, please?" Marty numbly nodded as Dexter shifted the gear into park and applied the brake. As she slid over, Dexter opened the back door and asked Charlie if he could sit in front with Marty.

Without a word, Charlie climbed out, quietly relinquishing the back seat. Dexter slid in without hesitation, his movements deliberate. He gathered Daniel into his arms and held him tightly against his chest, as if anchoring him to something solid in a world that had just come undone. He stroked Daniel's hair, matted with blood, and clung to his forehead as Dexter gently cupped his face, his fingers moving with quiet reverence through the smeared streaks of blood and tears. Daniel didn't resist. He folded into Dexter's embrace, his body giving way completely, as tears began to fall, slow and unchecked, from both their faces.

Marty vividly remembered standing in the doorway of Daniel and Andrew's Georgetown bedroom. The room bore the unmistakable signs of a life interrupted; clothes draped over furniture in careless heaps, the bed unmade and rumpled, still holding the imprint of lives lived and loved in. That morning's paper lay sprawled across the covers, flanked by two half-empty coffee cups on the nightstands. The scene was achingly domestic, a quiet testament to all that had been lost.

A shadow moved through the hall, and Daniel stepped in. His clothes, still stained with Andrew's blood, hung on him like a shroud. The binder dangled from one hand, the other still clutched the plastic bag. His face was hollow, his eyes dull and unfocused as they fixed on the bed. Marty moved to stand beside him, silent and steady. Charlie had offered to stay the night. Dexter had insisted that Daniel come home with them. But Daniel's refusal had been firm. They all knew he shouldn't be alone, yet they also knew him well enough to respect his need for solitude.

As she prepared to leave, Marty reached out and gently slid the binder from his hand. Her fingers lingered for a moment, then she leaned in and kissed his cheek, a soft, grounding gesture. Her lips brushed against the grime of blood, sweat, and tears. Then she turned and walked away, her heart heavy with the knowledge that this was a wound that may never heal.

Keith continued to stare down at the binder open before him. His hands trembled slightly as he turned the pages, each a testament to Andrew's life and work. In his other hand, he held a weathered obituary. Its edges softened from handling. His gaze lingered on the photograph of Andrew. His name emblazoned below with the caption: **Philanthropist Billionaire Myles Steadman loses only son.**

Across the room, Marty approached the liquor cabinet. The glass felt cold and solid in her hand as she poured herself a drink. She swallowed it in three quick gulps, the burn of the alcohol a fleeting distraction from the ache in her chest. She stared at the empty glass for a moment before refilling it. This one went down even faster. Her gaze drifted back to Keith, who remained fixated on the binder, his expression a mixture of sorrow and determination.

In a low voice, Keith murmured, "I have to talk to him."

Marty turned, the glass hovering near her lips. "No, Keith," she replied firmly. "Right now, you need to stay away from him." Her voice trembled, the plea raw and unguarded.

Marty's hand wavered as she poured another drink. Just before bringing it to her lips, she muttered to herself, "I really do have to stop all this drinking." Ignoring her own advice, she poured herself a fourth drink, lifting it to her lips. Just before she drank, she muttered to herself, her tone dripping with self-reproach, "I have to stop all this drinking."

Keith observed Marty intently, his eyes fixed and unflinching. His face was an enigma, a canvas devoid of emotion that left no hint of the thoughts or feelings lying beneath the surface. As he stood to leave, Marty's voice followed him, quieter this time, as though she were speaking more to herself than to him. "You're right. It's becoming a problem."

Marty's voice hung in the air, both fragile and resolute, as Keith paused in the doorway. He observed her intently, noticing how her fingers quivered around the tumbler before she placed it back on the table with a quiet thud. The atmosphere in the room appeared to grow denser as if weighed down by the burden of her soft-spoken revelation.

Keith nodded to himself, a silent acknowledgment of the storm brewing within both of them. He stepped into the icy morning, the air biting at his skin as he tightened his coat. The city's muffled sounds felt distant, blurred by his swirling thoughts.

A week later, Brent swung open the door to his apartment, the scent of coffee greeting Charlie like a bitter welcome. The room bore the stale aroma of sleepless nights and too many tense conversations.

"You're knocking now?" Brent quipped, his tone light but laced with curiosity. "Where's your key?"

Brent maneuvered his wheelchair back slightly. "Why all the secrecy?" Brent continued as he made room for Charlie, who stepped aside to allow Keith Chambers to step around him.

Keith entered, followed by Charlie, who surveyed the room with practiced familiarity. Brent wheeled through, collecting scattered coffee mugs and glasses from surfaces like forgotten relics of a long, exhausting day.

"Coffee?" Brent offered, his tone as casual as the situation allowed.

"You got any beer?" Charlie asked with a smirk. Brent's disapproving glance was immediate, prompting Charlie to backtrack. "Coffee's fine... leaded."

Charlie reached for a cigarette, pulling it from his pocket. Before he could light it, Brent shot him a sharp look. "Not in here, Charlie."

Charlie rolled his eyes and climbed out onto the fire escape; the sharp flick of his lighter echoed through the open window. Keith and Brent exchanged glances, the unspoken words heavy in the silence between them.

Finally, Keith broke it. "I want to help."

Brent raised an eyebrow, his expression somewhere between skepticism and curiosity. "Okay, great! So what? Do you want to be a character witness? How do you want to help?"

"I want to plead the case," Keith stated, his tone steady, almost defiant.

Brent blinked, unable to conceal the disbelief that was evident on his face. "You actually want to try the case?"

Keith nodded. "I'll do it pro bono. You don't have to pay me."

Brent leaned back in his wheelchair, crossing his arms. "Have you talked to Daniel about this?"

Keith shook his head, his gaze unwavering. "No. Could you ask him?"

Brent sighed, his tone warm but deliberate. "Don't you think it would be better coming from you?"

Keith hesitated, the vulnerability showing for the first time. "Yeah," he admitted. "That is… if he'd return any of my texts or phone calls."

Brent nodded, smiling, knowing this was typical of Daniel. He had a hunch to take it further, thinking it wouldn't hurt. Recognizing he might have an ally in Brent, Keith's breathing deepened, and the tightness in his chest slowly began to melt away.

Charlie re-entered the room, brushing ash from his sleeve as he climbed back inside. "So, what's the verdict?" he asked, leaning against the table.

"Charlie, could you step out for a moment?" Brent said, making it clear it wasn't a request.

Charlie glanced back and forth between them, his smirk disappearing. "I just gave you a moment."

"Go for a walk. A long walk." Brent prodded.

Charlie snarled at Brent, his frustration palpable as he glared at him. "Fine," he snapped, throwing up his hands and heading for the door.

Brent wheeled to the desk and dialed the number, one he knew by heart now. The ring echoed through the Eiman house, a sound that felt equal parts hopeful and foreboding.

In the dim living room, Daniel sat slumped in a leather armchair, his head tilted back against the cushion. He didn't want to talk to anyone, and he'd made that clear. The weight of the past two months pressed down on him, heavy and unrelenting.

The phone's insistent ring broke through the silence. Daniel closed his eyes, hoping whoever it was would give up. But Mrs. Eiman, ever the caretaker, answered it with her usual cheerfulness.

"Daniel, it's Brent," her voice called out moments later, soft but insistent.

Daniel reluctantly picked up the extension in the family room. "Brent," he said, his voice weary.

Meanwhile, in Cambridge, Keith sat by an extension, tense and waiting. His anxiety peaked as he heard the click of Daniel picking up. "Daniel," Keith began, his voice steady despite the storm of emotions behind it.

A long silence stretched into eternity. Keith glanced at Brent, who was on a separate extension across the room, displaying an oddly encouraging expression. Gathering his courage, Keith nodded and spoke again, this time with more confidence. "Daniel, it's Keith."

Another silence followed, even heavier than the last. Brent, ever the mediator, interjected. "Daniel, listen to what he has to say, please."

Daniel didn't respond immediately; the sound of his shallow breathing was the only indication that he was still on the line. Keith pressed forward, his voice softer now. "Daniel, I know you're innocent. I don't know what I was thinking before. I want to make this right. I want to represent you, if you'll let me. Is that okay? Will you let me do this? Please?"

The silence returned, stretching longer this time. Keith's heart pounded as he waited, every second feeling like a test of his resolve.

Keith finally broke the quiet again. "It's what I'm passionate about, Daniel," he said, his voice tinged with earnest desperation. "It's the one thing I really, really want to do. Please. Let me do this for you."

Brent and Keith exchanged glances, their respective phones still pressed to their ears. Then, the line went dead. Daniel had hung up.

Brent placed the receiver back with a soft click and turned to Keith. "Well, he didn't say no," he remarked, sounding unexpectedly hopeful, as he reiterated, mostly to reassure himself, "He didn't say no."

Daniel sat alone in the Eiman family room; the stillness around him felt oppressive. His hands clenched the arms of the chair as his mind raced. Without warning, he pounded his fists against the leather ottoman in front of him, the sound reverberating through the room. His frustration spilled over in a guttural groan, but he remained seated, his head falling into his hands.

A week later, Brent's office had come alive. The conference table was a chaotic mess of documents, photographs, and legal books. Brent and Keith sat across from each other, poring over legal briefs with intense focus. The faint scratching of pens and the rustling of paper filled the room as Charlie leaned against the window, watching them with an amused expression.

The intercom beeped, breaking their concentration. Rebecca's cheerful voice came through. "Brent, Daniel is here."

Brent pressed the intercom button, his voice calm. "Send him in, please."

Moments later, the door opened. Daniel stepped inside, his presence instantly commanding the room's attention. His eyes swept over the group before settling on Keith.

"So, you want me to trust you in a courtroom when you've never, ever litigated before," Daniel stated, his voice cutting and edged with doubt.

Keith straightened in his chair, his confidence unwavering. "Moral courage is the," he began.

"Before he could go any further, Daniel cut him off, "Don't!" Daniel's gaze shifted to Brent, who obviously didn't understand the context of the remark, even though he recognized where it came from.

Brent shrugged, offering a faint smile to Daniel. "I don't know why. I just have a good feeling about this. Go figure."

Daniel then eyed Charlie. "I do, too, dude. Go figure."

Daniel's eyes narrowed as they returned to Keith. The room held its collective breath as Daniel studied him, his gaze piercing. Finally, he spoke. "Don't fuck this up."

A smile tugged at the corners of Brent's mouth as he exchanged a knowing look with Keith. It was exactly the answer Brent knew was coming.

A week later, the four occupied almost the same positions around the table. Different clothes, different days, and a different Keith whose demeanor had shifted in a way none of them had seen before or anticipated. His voice was steady, his posture commanding, depicting both confidence and authority. "Okay, Daniel, I'm going to ask you a few questions. I know your answers, but I want to hear them directly from you."

Daniel gave a slight nod. "Okay."

Looking at Charlie for confirmation, Keith turned to Daniel and spoke plainly. "They claim you questioned

Benjamin about his sexual orientation, discovered ambiguity, and made advances, encouraging him to explore his feelings with other men."

Daniel shook his head, his frustration evident. Keith continued, his voice calm but insistent. "You also told him that if there were others, you could arrange to help him with his predicament. That you'd done it before, and you could do it again. Is that what happened?"

Daniel rolled his eyes and sighed. "Yes, in a convoluted sort of way."

Keith frowned. "A convoluted sort of way?"

"Well, he initially approached me," Daniel explained. "But I did tell him; I asked him if he knew of other boys, other kids that were grappling with the same issues."

"Why?" Keith asked.

Daniel turned to Brent, his exasperation clear. "We've been through all this, Brent."

Brent's tone was firm but patient. "Go through it again."

Keith leaned forward. "Was there an attraction between the two of you?"

Daniel's jaw tightened, his frustration boiling over. "Yes," he admitted, his tone clipped. "There was an attraction. I mean, I wasn't attracted to him, but he was—"

Keith waited.

As Daniel shook his head. Keith's expectant eyes bore into Daniel, seeking an explanation. "He was what, Daniel?"

Daniel shook his head, now visibly agitated, struggling with thoughts he could hardly bear to consider, much less articulate. "He mentioned that he was... that he'd had... I'm not sure how to say this."

Keith leaned forward, his tone steady yet firm. "Try the direct way."

Daniel shifted in his seat, discomfort tightening his posture. His voice, tense and uneven, filled the room with a palpable unease. "Just hearing him talk... I couldn't help but care about what he was going through," he said, shaking his head at the memory. "He was struggling. And I... I genuinely felt for him." He paused, working to steady himself.

"He told me he was having dreams about me," Daniel concluded, his voice catching. The memory stopped him cold, like the words themselves had reached out and seized him, suspending everything in midair.

Keith straightened slightly, his pen pausing mid-scribble. "Dreams?" he repeated, requesting clarification.

Daniel only shook his head, his expression torn between frustration and reluctance. But Keith needed clarity, no matter how much it might cost Daniel to say it. The knot in his stomach tightened, but he pressed on, eyes fixed on Daniel's. He needed the truth, needed to *hear* it, even if it broke something open between them.

"What kinds of dreams?"

As Daniel sat in deafening silence, Keith pressed further. "What kinds of dreams was Benjamin McCray having about you, Daniel?"

"*Those* kinds of dreams," Daniel said, his tone sharper than he meant, frustrated, edged with something unspoken. Then, as if trying to steady himself, he repeated it, quieter this time, almost to himself. "Those kinds of dreams."

Keith shuffled his notes, the motion betraying his growing unease. Despite the nerves creeping into his posture, he held Daniel's gaze: steady, determined.

Daniel let out a deep, weary sigh, the weight of the moment pressing on him. "He confided in me," he said, his voice edged with concern, "that he'd been visiting certain websites regularly. Chatting with much older men." He paused, searching for the right words. "I simply suggested... if he was going to explore, maybe it ought to be with someone his own age. Not older men. Other boys."

Daniel gave a slight nod, more to himself than anyone else, as if reaffirming a decision he still believed in, even as doubt crept beneath the surface.

Keith wrestled with everything, attempting to grasp Daniel's perspective and comprehend the situation. However, he felt he still needed additional details. Trying to keep his tone firm but not accusatory, he inquired, "Did he ask you to explore something?"

Daniel shook his head with resignation. "No."

Keith pressed on, though his voice remained deliberate and measured. "So, you just assumed and recommended that if he wanted to explore, it should be with other boys."

Daniel hesitated before nodding. "Yes, although that's not the exact wording I used."

Keith adjusted his posture, his pen poised over his notepad. "What was the exact wording?"

Daniel's forehead creased with intense focus. "I don't remember," he said, his voice laced with frustration.

Keith's resolve and perseverance were evident when he calmly uttered, "Daniel."

"Look, I don't remember!" Daniel snapped, his voice rising with the weight of his emotions. "I wasn't thinking, all right? If I had been thinking, I probably would have told the little fuck to fuck off!" His glare cut across the room, landing squarely on Keith.

The air was taut with tension. Keith consciously softened his posture, his voice low and steady, edged with empathy. "It's going to be a lot worse when you take the stand, Daniel."

Sensing the strain, Brent reached out and placed a hand on Daniel's shoulder. "It's all right," he said gently, his voice a balm. "Everything's going to be all right, Daniel."

Daniel exhaled sharply, his anger collapsing into something quieter: *a deep, throbbing regret.* He lowered his eyes to the table and murmured, mostly to himself, "Why didn't I know better? I should have known better."

*****

The crisp air bit at Marty's cheeks the following day as she stepped into the open space. The faint smell of evergreens and damp earth grounded her. The Public Garden had always been a haven for her, a cherished part of the city she called home. Its proximity to her work and townhouse made it a place of countless moments of reflection and confrontation.

Charlie was already there when she arrived, leaning against a bench with his usual air of casual indifference. He glanced up as she approached, offering a lopsided grin. Marty didn't waste time on pleasantries; she wasn't in the mood today and got straight to the point, her voice firm.

"What did you say to Keith about the night of... the..." she trailed off, searching for the right word.

"Murder?" Charlie interjected bluntly, his gaze unwavering. He always preferred to call it as he saw it.

"Accident," Marty finished, her tone sharp.

"Well," Charlie began, shifting his weight, "Why don't we just call it what it was? A hate crime, though it turns out it probably truly was an accident. A tragic and terrible accident. But that's *not* what I told Keith." Charlie had made an effort to emphasize the word, *'not.'*

Marty waited, her eyes narrowing slightly. "What did you tell him?"

Charlie let the pause linger, a smirk tugging at the corner of his mouth. "I told him that the night Andrew was killed, both he and Daniel had promised Andrew's sister, Maggie, that Andrew would be in attendance at her thirty-fifth birthday party. It was important to Maggie, and they both assured her that Andrew would be at that party, sans Daniel."

Marty frowned, trying to process the information. "That's it? That's all you told him?"

"That's it. That's all I told him," Charlie confirmed with a shrug. "Though there's more to it if you want to hear the rest, but that's all I told Keith."

Marty paused, uncertain if she should delve further. "Do I want to hear the rest?"

Charlie shrugged again, his grin widening. "Up to you, dude."

The Chambers' dining room was dimly lit. The heavy wood paneling and antique furniture lent it a particularly somber air this evening. The table appeared nearly empty, its usual vibrancy muted by the sparse gathering. Governor Chambers sat at the head of the table, her gaze downcast as she absently picked specks of caked salt from her individual shaker. At the table with her were Mr. Chambers, Marty, Dexter, Keith, their oldest sibling, William, and his wife, Jenifer. The rest of the chairs remained conspicuously vacant.

The quiet lingered for a while after the meal had concluded. Keith was the one to shatter the oppressive silence with his clear and pointed voice. "So, it appears as though Daniel Eiman has been framed. Can you imagine that?"

Marty stiffened, pointedly avoiding his gaze. As did everyone else. The words hung heavily in the air, unacknowledged by everyone except Governor Chambers. She met Keith's gaze steadily, her expression calm and composed. "No, honey, I can't," she replied evenly. "It's just awful."

Keith stared at her with unwavering intensity. "Yeah," he said, his voice laced with sarcasm. "I can't imagine it, either."

Governor Chambers looked away first, her composure faltering. Keith stood slowly, his movements deliberate. "Sit down, please, Keith," Governor Chambers ordered, her voice assertive. "I want to talk about these choices you're so intent on making."

Keith remained standing, his eyes narrowing. "What, no 'darling' tonight?" he said mockingly.

Governor Chambers didn't flinch under Keith's glare, though the faintest tightening of her jaw gave away her irritation. Keith's gaze remained fixed on her, unyielding.

"Sit down, please, Keith," she repeated, her voice measured and firm.

Keith remained standing. "Why? So, can we keep playing this game of 'pretend everything's fine'? I'm not interested."

"Things are not fine here, Keith. They are *not* fine! I want to discuss it." Governor Chambers was unrelenting.

"Well, it happens that I don't." Keith countered, "Want to discuss it, that is!"

Governor Chambers met his words with stony silence, her eyes locked on his. Everyone watched as Keith's glare held unyieldingly until, without another word, he turned and stormed out. Moments later, the heavy front door slammed behind him, the sound echoing through the house. Then came the screech of tires on the driveway, sharp and final.

The room fell into a stunned silence. Mr. Chambers, seated across from Governor Chambers, looked at her intently. His gaze, filled with unspoken questions, lingered on her, but she refused to meet it. Instead, her hands went back to the saltshaker, her fingers methodically plucking at invisible grains of salt.

Marty's voice cut through the stillness, quiet but firm. "Daddy, could you excuse us, please?"

Mr. Chambers stood up gradually and pushed his chair back, willingly yielding the room to Marty. One by one, the others followed suit, leaving Marty alone with Governor Chambers in the cavernous dining room. The sound of footsteps faded, replaced by the steady tick-tock of the nearby grandfather clock.

"Mother." Marty's voice was soft at first. Her tone betrayed her with its mix of uncertainty and resolve.

Governor Chambers did not respond. Her attention remained fixed on the salt shaker, her hands continuing their futile task.

"Mother!" Marty repeated, louder this time, her voice cutting through the silence. Governor Chambers eventually lifted her head, locking eyes with her daughter. Her face remained calm and collected, but a fleeting flash of irritation appeared in her eyes.

"How could you?" Marty asked, her words laced with accusation.

Governor Chambers didn't waver. "I think a more appropriate question would be, 'Did I?' Or are you jumping to conclusions too?" Her voice was calm and measured, but there was an edge to it, a challenge.

The silence stretched between them, broken only by the steady tick of the grandfather clock in the entry foyer.

Tick...Tock...Tick...Tock

Marty leaned forward slightly, her intensity growing. "Really?" she pressed.

Governor Chambers held her daughter's gaze, her composure unshaken. "Marty, I have no firsthand knowledge of this," she said firmly. "I found out about it the same way everyone else did. That's the God's honest truth."

Marty's eyes narrowed, her suspicion clear. "Did you ask anybody to... take care of things for you?" she asked, her tone pointed.

Governor Chambers's hands stood still for the first time, her fingers frozen above the saltshaker. She remained motionless, her silent response conveying everything she was not saying.

Marty shook her head, consciously controlling both her thoughts and her breathing. Then, continuing with manufactured calm, "I'll take your silence as a yes," she said, her voice low but resolute. She continued to study her mother's face with amazement and wonder.

"Did you know that both Daniel and Andrew promised Maggie Rogers that Andrew would be at her birthday party the night he was killed?"

Governor Chambers kept her calm demeanor, her eyes narrowing even more intently on the saltshaker she held.

"Yeah," Marty continued, her voice growing sharper. "He wasn't even supposed to be there. They knew for a fact that Andrew was going to be at their party. And that Daniel was going to be at that Virginia town meeting."

Governor Chambers remained silent, though her hands stopped moving completely. Her face was a mask, but her stillness spoke louder than any denial could.

"There's one other fact," Marty said, her voice deliberately slowing on the word. "Something I want you to ponder deeply."

Marty paused, letting the weight of her words settle over the room. "Why do you think Myles Steadman, a billionaire with unlimited resources, never used them to track down and prosecute the people who murdered his son?"

Governor Chambers didn't react at first; her face remained stoic. However, there was a subtle shift in her posture, a tightening of her shoulders that revealed a growing discomfort. Her gaze remained fixed on the center of the table, avoiding Marty's eyes.

"I don't think he meant to kill Daniel," Marty said, her tone quieter now, almost reflective. "I believe they intended to scare him, to do anything possible to drive him away from his precious son."

Her words lingered in the room, but their meaning was unmistakable. Governor Chambers sat still, her hands resting on the table, no longer fidgeting with anything.

"The whole thing, it turns out, truly was a tragic accident," Marty continued, her voice trembling slightly but still firm. "For whatever reason, the final blow propelled Andrew into the side mirror. It struck his temple in exactly the right spot to cause the brain bleed that killed him. He was dead before the paramedics even arrived."

Marty took a steady breath, her eyes locked on her mother. "If Andrew hadn't hit that side mirror, he'd still be alive. The rest of his injuries, while serious, weren't enough to be fatal. It was all a terrible, horrible, tragic accident."

The silence that followed was deafening. Governor Chambers sat motionless, her eyes fixed on the table. Marty's hands trembled slightly as she folded them in her lap, her composure on the brink of cracking.

"Mother," she said softly, the single word carrying the weight of everything left unsaid.

Governor Chambers couldn't respond. She refused to even look up at Marty. The ticking of the grandfather clock continued to fill the void between them.

Marty gently pushed her chair back, every nerve in her body working overtime to stay composed. Without another word, she left the table, her head held high despite the storm of emotions brewing within her. Behind her, Governor Chambers remained at the table, her focus now intently fixed on removing every last grain of salt from the shaker, which she held in both hands, her fingers methodical and tense.

*****

It was the dead of winter as Daniel, Brent, Keith, and Charlie made their way through the throng of people crowded outside the Leominster Courthouse. The atmosphere was heavy with tension. The crowd, divided into two distinct groups on either side of the courthouse steps, hurled insults and shouted provocative remarks at one another.

On one side, religious protesters waved garish signs painted with hateful slogans.

"God punishes the damned."

"God condemns the wicked."

"Faggots take your sickness and disease and go home."

The protesters' chants rose in sharp, discordant bursts, each shout aimed to provoke.

On the opposite side of the steps, human rights demonstrators stood firm, their signs bearing messages of solidarity and hope. The slogans "Equality for All" and "One United Territory" were in high contrast with the vitriol of the group opposing them.

As the four men ascended the courthouse steps, a newswoman stood to the side, preparing for her broadcast. Camera operators and photographers jostled for position, their cameras clicking to life the moment Keith and Daniel came into view.

"Keith! Over here!" one of the reporters shouted, stepping forward. Another called out, "Mr. Chambers! How do you respond to claims that—"

Keith didn't stop. His focus was unshakable as he led the group through the crowd and into the courthouse. The cacophony of voices faded behind them as the heavy courthouse doors closed behind them with a resounding thud.

Inside the Governor's office, Elizabeth Chambers sat at her desk, her eyes scanning the bold headlines of the newspaper in front of her. Beneath the inflammatory title **"GOVERNOR'S SON TAKES A STAND ON SEXUAL DEVIANCE"** was a prominent photograph of Keith, Daniel, and Brent leaving the courthouse.

She looked up from the paper to meet the steely gaze of the Special Agent standing across from her desk.

"The guy's a loose cannon," the special agent offered flatly. "His kid's been lying about his age and frequenting adult dating sites where he's been chatting with older men. We engaged him in a simple, innocuous conversation. That's all. He chatted about being attracted to his teacher. We captured a snap of the chat and showed it to his old man with a copy of the video. That's all we did. There was no money exchanged. Nor any coercion of any kind. Just a simple, innocent chat." He concluded, answering her unspoken question. "The video has been destroyed."

The Leominster courtroom buzzed with an undercurrent of tension as the trial ventured into waters that they knew would be treacherous. Every seat was filled. The crowd comprised teachers, students, and intrigued spectators, including numerous press members with cameras hanging from their necks, while courtroom sketch artists hurriedly completed detailed drawings.

At the defense table, Daniel sat alongside Brent and Keith, their faces set with quiet determination. Behind them, Charlie sat in the front row, his sharp gaze fixed on the proceedings. On the opposite side of the courtroom, Benjamin McCray sat between his parents, his posture willowy and withdrawn despite his height for his age and his long, lanky body. He avoided eye contact, his gaze fixed on the floor. To Benjamin's father's left sat the county prosecutor, Mr. Swarth, a stern older man in a meticulously pressed yet outdated suit.

As the day wore on, the jury, a cross-section of Leominster's residents, watched attentively as Daniel stared out from the witness stand. The courtroom fell silent as Mr. Swarth pretended to read from his notes and stepped forward with a commanding presence.

"Mr. Eiman," Swarth began, his voice smooth but pointed, "were you alone with Benjamin McCray at any point in time?"

Daniel met his gaze steadily. "Yes," he replied. "But only in my classroom."

Swarth's lips curled slightly, his tone growing sharper. "He seems incredibly vulnerable, doesn't he?" He gestured toward Benjamin, whose head remained bowed.

Keith rose immediately. "Objection."

The judge glanced at Swarth with a firm expression on his face. "Sustained. Mr. Swarth, move on, please."

Swarth adjusted his tie, unfazed. "Did you ever touch Benjamin McCray?"

Daniel's voice faltered slightly. "Yes."

"Speak up, please, Mr. Eiman," Swarth said, his tone edged with faux encouragement.

"I may have put my hands on him once," Daniel admitted, his voice barely audible. "I put my hands on his shoulders once."

Swarth narrowed his eyes, his tone growing sharp. "Well, he claims you only sodomized him once! You may have touched his shoulders once, as you then led him…"

Keith shot to his feet. "Objection, Your Honor!"

The judge slammed down his gavel. "Sustained." He turned to the jury, his voice firm. "The jury will disregard that last comment."

Later that afternoon, Governor Chambers sat stiffly in her family's living room. The news played on the television before them, the screen showing footage of Keith and Daniel leaving the courthouse. A newswoman's voice overlaid the images.

"In what proved to be a significant and compelling display of character, Keith Chambers, son of Massachusetts Governor Elizabeth Chambers, spent this afternoon in a courthouse here in Leominster, Massachusetts, defending alleged sex offender Daniel Eiman. The renowned co-founder of the homosexual activist group One United Territory has found himself an easy target for right-wing conservatives who capitalized on the…"

Governor Chambers gazed at the screen with an expressionless face. Across the room, Mr. Chambers watched her intently, his expression serious. When the segment ended, he spoke up, his tone calm yet pointed. "Isn't it interesting how the more we try to control a situation, the more out of control it becomes?"

Governor Chambers snapped her head toward him, her composure breaking. "Shut up, George!"

Mr. Chambers smiled faintly, his calm demeanor unshaken. "Nobody asked for your opinion here!" she snapped again before storming out of the room, the sharp sound of her heels echoing behind her.

Marty and Mr. Chambers exchanged looks, shaking their heads simultaneously. Mr. Chambers broke the silence, his voice carrying a blend of paternal affection and profound insight. "It's a valuable lesson, Marty. Best you learn it now, while the mistakes aren't so costly."

Marty frowned, her voice suspicious. "What's that supposed to mean, Daddy?"

He softly touched her cheek, his smile enigmatic. "Oh, I think you know exactly what it means, my sweet princess." Then, he exited, leaving Marty alone with her thoughts.

The television switched to a different segment. On the screen, the image of Governor Chambers transitioned to a montage of Keith and Daniel at the courthouse, accompanied by the voice of the news anchor overlaying the footage.

"Governor Chambers has remained notably silent on matters related to family values, choosing instead to concentrate on fiscal responsibility and crime. She has not been available for comments. Meanwhile, in other news tonight…"

The same news report played on a much smaller television perched on the counter in the Eiman kitchen. Mrs. Eiman's hands, damp from washing dishes, rested on the sink's edge as she watched intently. As the reporter's words about Governor Chambers lingered in the air, Mrs. Eiman's face, etched with worry, turned back to the sink. Dishes clinked softly while the reporter's voice droned on.

The next day, the courtroom hummed with a subdued energy. It was the same scene, yet it felt different: tenser, heavier.

Keith and Brent sat in their usual spots at the defense table. Charlie remained in the front row of the gallery just behind them. Keith's appearance was strikingly polished. His neatly pressed, hand-tailored suit and commanding posture exuded confidence. A quiet resolve radiated from him. Brent rifled through legal briefs while Charlie leaned back, his sharp eyes observing every detail.

Mr. Chambers, Marty, and Ashley were seated, mid-gallery, among the spectators. Marty's gaze remained fixed on Keith, a mixture of admiration and worry volleying across her face. On the other side of the aisle, Mrs. Eiman sat alone. Her hands were clasped tightly in her lap.

Daniel was once again seated on the witness stand. Mr. Swarth stepped forward, his presence dominating the room once more. Behind him, Benjamin McCray sat between his parents, his shoulders hunched and his eyes avoiding anyone and everyone. The boy's posture appeared even more sheepish today as the weight of the trial increasingly bore down on him.

Swarth slowly handed Daniel a sheet of paper. "Can you identify this, Mr. Eiman?"

Daniel took the paper, his eyes scanning it quickly. His voice was steady as he answered. "It's my reading list."

"Your reading list," Swarth repeated, his voice tinged with disdain. "Not the reading list recommended by the Leominster Board of Education, but your reading list."

Keith shot out of his seat, his tone sharp. "Objection, Your Honor."

The judge nodded. "Sustained."

Swarth continued, undeterred. "I'll rephrase." He gestured to the paper in Daniel's hand. "Could you read the titles, please, Mr. Eiman?"

Daniel paused, glancing quickly at Keith before he complied... "*The Catcher in the Rye, Lord of the Flies, Franny and Zooey, A Separate Peace...*"

Before he could finish, Keith was back on his feet. "Objection, Your Honor! The Leominster school system allows every teacher within the system to determine..."

Swarth cut him off. "Your Honor, I was trying to point out that Mr. Eiman was intent on bringing homoerotic literature to his students with the hope of..."

Keith stepped closer to the judge, his tone rising. "These books are classics! They are taught in every classroom in this..."

Swarth interrupted again, his voice booming. "Not here!" He moved closer to the bench, his words cutting through the room like a blade. "They are not taught here! This is a Christian, God-fearing community!"

Keith's jaw tightened. "Christian? God-fearing?" he repeated, incredulous.

"Yes, Christian, God-fearing," Swarth declared, his voice resonating in the courtroom. He nodded defiantly, emphasizing his words as the room descended into stunned silence.

Keith broke the silence, his voice starting low but growing in intensity. "God-fearing."

Swarth spat back, "Yes, God-fearing! As in, what precisely is sodomy if not the worship of a false god?"

Keith abruptly turned and faced the judge. "Your Honor!" He called out, his frustration barely contained.

The courtroom erupted into murmurs, the tension palpable. Keith stepped forward, his voice cutting through the chaos. "Leominster is not a Christian school, Your Honor. Please inform me if I'm wrong, but it is my understanding that Leominster is a..." He stepped toward Swarth as he finished his thought, "Public school. And I'm sorry, but I don't know of any author more heterosexual than J.D. Salinger."

Swarth immediately shot back, "Yeah, another pedophile!"

"Oh my God, you've got to be kidding me!" Keith blurted out. He then deliberately turned back to the judge via the jury. "This line of questioning is totally inappropriate!"

"I agree! Sustained. Mr. Swarth, control yourself," the judge replied.

Swarth retreated to his table, adjusting his tie. "That will be all. I have no further questions."

As Swarth settled back and Keith returned to the defense table for his notes, Daniel's eyes burned with a fury that knew no bounds. He locked onto Swarth across the courtroom, his voice trembling with barely contained rage. "Do not even presume to think you know the nature or expression of my love, sir!"

Keith turned swiftly. "Daniel," he cautioned, his tone firm yet calm, meeting Daniel's eyes with a quiet plea for control.

But Daniel couldn't stop himself. His voice rose slowly, words spilling out unchecked. "You could not even begin to fathom the nature or expression of my love! Sir!" Daniel's voice echoed in the silent courtroom, cutting through the charged atmosphere.

The judge looked sternly at Daniel, his patience wearing thin. "That will be all, Mr. Eiman."

Daniel ignored the command, his emotions tumbling out like a dam breaking. "Yes, I teach the classics, because they prepare young, vital minds for the real world! Because they expand their horizons and prepare them for life!"

Keith stepped quickly between Daniel and the jury as if to shield them from Daniel's outburst. "Daniel!" he implored, attempting to keep his composure, yet Daniel's anger only intensified.

The judge, now gripping his gavel, raised it to restore order. "Mr. Eiman, I said that is enough!"

Keith shook his head in quiet desperation, knowing Daniel all too well. "Daniel," he pleaded again, softer this time but still firm.

Daniel's voice only sharpened his words, becoming a full-out attack. Fiery, defiant, and unrelenting. "You'd all rather just mold them and manipulate them into these neat little squares that you think you're going to shove into round holes. Well, they are not square. They are round and full-spirited, and you are killing them! What about that commandment, Mr. Swarth? What about thou shalt not kill?"

The judge repeatedly slammed his gavel, but the commotion drowned out his commands. The jury members leaned in, straining to look past Keith, who was doing his best to block their view of Daniel.

Daniel's fury knew no bounds. "You may think you are protecting these children, but indeed you are not!"

Mr. Swarth shot up from his seat, face flushed, eyes blazing. "Our failure to protect our children is *very* clear to us, Mr. Eiman. That's exactly why we're here!" His voice thundered as he stepped toward Daniel, jabbing a finger back toward Benjamin and turning to the jury. "Because we failed to protect them from the likes of *you!*"

The Judge rose and slammed his gavel over and over, harder and harder. "That is enough!" he shouted, his voice strained against the chaos.

The courtroom erupted. Court officers placed their hands on billy clubs, ready for action.

Daniel, held in the suffocating grip of his rage, looked up toward the back of the entry to the room, where something caught his eye, disorienting him instantaneously.

Keith slowly gazed back to the courtroom entrance, wanting to see what had suddenly caused Daniel's demeanor to collapse.

Dexter stood silently at the courtroom entrance, staring across at Daniel, mouth agape, slowly shaking his head.

Daniel's shoulders drooped entirely as his intense anger imploded inward. His head hung low, and his voice became a whisper, almost inaudible. The courtroom fell silent as every eye turned to listen. "Thou shalt not kill does not mean sticking a knife in someone's heart or murdering them in cold blood."

The Judge paused mid-motion. Something in Daniel's delivery gave him pause.

"When you force a child to become something they feel compelled to turn away from or coerce them to act against their deeper inner yearning, you kill their spirit," Daniel said, even softer now. "It's as bad as killing their flesh."

He lowered his head, the weight of regret pressing down, and added quietly, more to himself than anyone, though everyone heard him, "Sometimes... It's worse."

The room remained frozen, the silence dense, the tension thickening with every unspoken thought.

The judge surveyed his courtroom: Mr. Swarth wiped the sweat from his brow; Benjamin McCray trembled, visibly falling apart; the jurors sat on the edge of their seats, their faces a mixture of shock and curiosity.

Keith's attention remained fixed on Dexter, who had reached the row where Marty was seated and squeezed in between her and Ashley. As Marty grasped Dexter's hands in both of hers, Keith was suddenly transported somewhere else.

He shook his head frantically, trying to fend off what was gradually consuming him. But it only intensified until all he noticed was the complete and utter silence of the courtroom.

Dead silence.

The whole courtroom appeared to be fixated on Keith, anticipating his next move. Yet, he remained uncertain about what to do. All he could do was observe his surroundings and experience his emotions, and all of it was horrifying.

At first, he was engulfed by an overwhelming sense of loss, an unimaginable, paralyzing loss, followed by just as unimaginable despair. The despair gradually descended into dread. Complete and utter dread. 'Do they all know?' Keith wondered to himself. 'Do they know what a fuck up I am? Do they know I have no control over my client or this case? Do they know I should never have taken this case on? Does everyone know?'

Feeling utterly defeated, Keith stumbled towards the defendant's table, clutching it tightly like a lifeline keeping him afloat. Once he managed to regain some composure, he gradually lifted his gaze.

Brent leaned in, "Trust yourself, Keith." He whispered to Keith.

"What?" Keith searched Brent's eyes, utterly and genuinely confused.

This time, Brent spoke it out loud: "Trust yourself."

Suddenly, Keith jolted back to present awareness. For no particular reason, he found himself back in the courtroom, in command once more. There were no thoughts or feelings at all, just complete and total conviction. In an instant, Keith realized what needed to be done and pivoted to face the judge.

Realizing he had regained control of his courtroom, the judge was calling out in the meantime. "Perhaps we should take a fifteen-minute recess."

Keith cautiously took a step toward the bench. "Your Honor, if I may. We have just one question. While the moment is upon us."

Mr. Swarth rapidly stood up. "Your honor, I agree." He motioned down to Benjamin McCray, who was clearly devolving into a collapsed emotional state. "I move that we recess!"

The judge glanced from Benjamin to Mr. Swarth, then to Keith, and finally down at Daniel, who now stared at the floor, overwhelmed with remorse. "Phrase your question carefully, Mr. Chambers," he warned, motioning for Keith to proceed.

"Your honor." Mr. Swarth remained standing.

"Sit down, Mr. Swarth."

Keith nodded and approached Daniel cautiously. "Are you all right, Daniel?" he asked gently. Daniel couldn't respond. His gaze remained fixed on the floor, his eyes unseeing and his ears unhearing.

Keith eyed the Judge. "Are you alright to continue, Mr. Eiman?" The Judge asked, looking down at Daniel.

Daniel looked up at the Judge, but neither answered nor gestured a response.

Satisfied, the Judge nodded to himself; then, with a trained eye on Benjamin McCray and one on Daniel, he motioned for Keith to continue.

Keith took a deep breath, lowering his voice. He stepped closer to Daniel. "Did that ever happen to you, Daniel? That someone tried to kill your spirit?"

"Objection!" Mr. Swarth bolted to his feet again.

The Judge's response was immediate. "Overruled"

Keith stepped even closer to Daniel. Then, his voice gentle but insistent, he continued, "How old were you when that happened to you, Daniel?"

Swarth was on his feet again. "Your Honor! I object!"

The judge's voice was sharp now. "If you do not sit down and remain seated, Mr. Swarth, I will hold you in contempt! Do you understand?"

Defeated, Swarth took his seat.

Daniel stared straight ahead, his body tense as if one word would shatter him. Every juror leaned in, their attention locked on him. Across the room, Benjamin McCray's silent unraveling deepened the weight of all of it.

Mr. McCray and Mr. Swarth both grew visibly agitated, their tension amplifying Benjamin's distress. "Your Honor, may I approach the bench, please?" Swarth pleaded.

The judge's voice cut like steel. "No, you may not!"

Swarth stood up and pointed to Benjamin. "But my client..."

Under the judge's steely glare, Mr. Swarth sat back down.

Turning back to Daniel, the judge softened his tone. "Mr. Eiman?" he urged gently. "I want you to answer the question." He gave a subtle nod to Keith, permission to proceed, before shifting his full attention to Benjamin McCray, who was visibly unraveling before him, and before everyone else in the courtroom.

Completely oblivious to anyone else in the room, Keith now stepped even closer to Daniel. His voice dropped to a near whisper, pulling the entire courtroom into the moment's intimacy. "Daniel, is it true that when Benjamin McCray stepped before you and asked for your help, you threw all caution to the wind? You forgot that your lover died in your arms defending gay rights and that, as a teacher in a public school system, others might find your motivations suspect?"

The weight of Keith's words hung in the air, each syllable slipping deeper into the room's collective tension.

Keith's voice softened even more, drawing the courtroom in even further. "Is it true that you threw all caution to the wind to help this young man because you thought someone was killing his spirit... the same way your spirit was killed when you were his age?"

The silence in the courtroom was deafening as Keith grew even quieter. "Daniel, did you think someone was trying to kill Benjamin McCray's..."

Suddenly, Benjamin McCray leaped to his feet, his voice piercing through as he cried out…"I lied! It's all a lie!" He pointed at his father, sobbing uncontrollably now, breath ragged between words. "They made me lie!" he choked out.

Mr. McCray lunged at his son, whacking him across the face full force and throttling him as Mrs. McCray screamed, throwing herself between her husband and Benjamin.

The courtroom erupted into total chaos.

Court officers rushed forward, pulling Mr. McCray off Benjamin as he fought violently against their grasp.

Benjamin sobbed uncontrollably, tears streaming off his face as court officers rushed in, prying him away from his father's wild, flailing fists. "I'm sorry, Mr. Eiman!" he cried, out, his voice slicing through the room like a jagged shard, shattering what little composure the courtroom had left. "I'm sorry!"

The Judge slammed his gavel down repeatedly, shouting over the chaos. "Order! Order! Order in this court!"

As the commotion continued, the judge surveyed the room, his voice steady. "This case is dismissed." He banged his gavel and motioned to the court officers, who were cuffing Mr. McCray and leading him away.

The Judge then purposefully turned and looked down at Daniel. "You are dismissed, Mr. Eiman." Daniel slowly looked up to meet Keith's gaze, but Brent had rushed Keith and was bear-hugging him. Slowly rising and stepping out of the witness stand, he allowed himself to be pulled into their jubilation.

Back in the gallery, Mr. Chambers walked through the excited, noisy crowd, crossing the aisle to intercept Mrs. Eiman as she made her way to the exit. He extended his hand, warm and steady, intercepting her with a genuine smile, "George Chambers."

Mrs. Eiman glanced at him, her confusion momentarily transforming into a courteous smile. She took his hand with both of hers. "I know who you are," she offered before adding, "Nice to meet you, George. Suzanne. Suzanne Eiman."

"Thank you," Mr. Chambers said, his voice filled with sincerity.

Mrs. Eiman tilted her head a bit, her brow creasing. "For what?" she inquired cautiously.

"For raising such an incredible son," he replied without hesitation, his eyes the whole time meeting hers with deep appreciation.

She blinked, clearly taken aback. Then, "Oh, believe me, I did everything in my power to stop him," she said with a faint, almost nervous smile. "Didn't you hear? Some people just can't be held back."

"Thank God for that," Mr. Chambers acknowledged, his tone soft but resolute. "We do the best we can, don't we?"

She looked away, unable to meet his eyes. Mr. Chambers reached out, gently taking her hand and giving it a firm, steady squeeze. His smile widened." Truly, thank you," he said again. He gave a final nod, gratitude expressed more in gesture than words, before turning and merging back into the crowd.

Outside on the courthouse steps, Daniel, Keith, Charlie, and Brent pushed through the throng of journalists, photographers, and press agents. Flashes from cameras and strobes illuminated the afternoon, and questions were hurled from every direction.

Marty, Dexter, Mr. Chambers, and Ashley waited off to the side, their expressions a mix of relief and pride. Ashley, in particular, watched Keith with renewed wonder, love, and overwhelming admiration. She struggled to manage her own emotions amidst the chaos, navigating the press and paparazzi alongside the Chambers family.

As they passed, Keith's eyes locked onto Ashley's. Her smile was warm, encouraging, and filled with love. Something unspoken passed between them. Keith stepped away from the others, moving toward her.

Spectators reached out, brushing against Keith as he navigated through the crowd. He greeted their touches with quiet dignity, his focus unwavering.

That evening, Brent's office was dimly lit. Daniel, Keith, Charlie, and Brent sat around the coffee table, still in the same clothes they had worn in court, now creased and weary from the long day. The air between them was lighter but tinged with exhaustion.

"You should come back, Daniel," Charlie said, his tone uncharacteristically earnest. "There couldn't be a better time for you to step back into the arena."

Daniel leaned back thoughtfully, his expression reflective. "There's nothing quite like finding that spark in a kid and nourishing it, letting it grow," he mused. "Pretty soon, the whole classroom is with you. They want to learn, Charlie. They want to be a part of each other's growth."

Charlie shook his head, unable to suppress a frown. "A way with words," he muttered. "The curse of a born politician."

Daniel chuckled softly, his sincerity evident. "I like teaching, Charlie. It's my calling."

Charlie rolled his eyes, deliberately shaking his head. "You know, Daniel, sometimes you're so full of shit I just want to tear your fucking head off."

The room erupted into laughter, the tension finally breaking entirely.

Daniel wiped a tear of mirth from his eye, looking at Charlie warmly. "I love you, Charlie. You know that? I do. I really, really love you."

"Yeah, yeah, I love you too," Charlie replied, lighting a cigarette and taking a deep drag.

Brent snapped his fingers at Charlie, pointing firmly toward the fire escape. "Not in here!"

Grumbling, Charlie climbed out onto the fire escape, muttering under his breath.

As the night deepened, the group quietly settled into a sense of winding down. Brent started pulling cushions off the couch, gesturing to Daniel. "You need to stay here tonight," he said. "There are a few things we need to go over in the morning."

"Or you can come stay with me," Keith offered quietly.

Daniel glanced between them, his gaze lingering on Keith. After a moment, he moved the cushions and rearranged the furniture to set up the pull-out bed. Keith and Daniel shifted tables and chairs, creating more space. Brent wheeled over to a closet and pulled down pillows and bedding. The three of them worked in tandem, their movements fluid and practiced.

Charlie climbed back in through the window, preparing to leave. Daniel caught his eye. "Thanks, man," he said earnestly. "Really, thank you so much, Charlie."

Charlie smirked as his gaze softened. "I'm not the one you need to thank, Daniel," Charlie said pointedly, directing his attention to Keith.

Keith flushed crimson, ducking his head. When he looked up, everyone was smiling at him. "Kudos, man!" Brent said. "Yeah, kudos," Charlie agreed."

Keith spread his arms wide, welcoming their words, and said, "I couldn't have done it without you." This led to a group hug.

Brent gently steered Charlie toward the door. "We'll give you two some space," he said, calm, steady, and unmistakably intentional.

Before leaving, Charlie grabbed Keith's hand and pumped it firmly. "They're wrong about you, Keith Chambers. You're awesome. Freaking awesome. And smart. You're actually very smart."

Keith grinned and shook his head, amused by the compliment's double-edged nature.

After nudging Charlie out the door, Brent gave Keith one final, silent nod, a gesture of trust, of understanding, then turned and disappeared down the hallway.

Keith and Daniel were left alone, standing in the quiet, staring at each other. Silence lingered in the air, dense with unvoiced feelings. Where to begin?

Finally, Keith spoke up, his voice calm and soft, "Are you okay?"

Daniel gave a subtle nod, his eyes dropping to the floor, as if trying to avoid the full weight of Keith's gaze. "Yeah," he said softly. "Thanks for asking."

Keith stayed still, eyes fixed on Daniel, observing each of his subtle expressions. "I want you to tell me what happened the night Andrew died." Keith gently nudged.

Daniel could only shake his head. "I don't really remember; it's all still very much a blur to me. There were these skinheads and…"

"No," Keith gently cut him off, "I mean, after."

Daniel gazed across at Keith, his mind awash with a multitude of thoughts and feelings.

"Marty told me that it was the night Andrew died, that she realized she was going to marry Dexter." Keith clarified further, "She said she knew that night that Dexter was the man to be the father of her children."

Daniel nodded as memories flooded in. After taking a long, slow, deep, deliberate breath, he recounted the story. "Shortly after we left the hospital, Dexter pulled the car over and asked Marty to drive. He then gently asked Charlie to get in the front seat with Marty, which he did. Then Dexter slid into the back with me, wrapped his arms around me, and held me tight all the way back to Georgetown."

"Wow." Keith was amazed.

"Yeah." Daniel nodded.

"That's so unlike him," Keith added.

"That it is." Daniel reiterated.

"What happened with you today when you saw Dexter enter the courtroom?" Keith prodded.

Daniel shook his head, struggling to manage the flood of emotions that threatened to overtake him.

"Something shifted when you saw Dexter in the back of the room." Keith clarified, "What was it?"

Daniel nodded, his mind swirling, unsure where to even begin. "I tend to talk too much," he murmured. "Andrew and Dexter were always on me to think before I spoke. Just as I was in the midst of basically shooting my mouth off, Dexter arrived. And…" Daniel shook his head and shrugged. "I just figured it may be a sign that I should stop talking." Daniel nodded, more to himself than to Keith, retreating inward as the weight of the afternoon returned.

Keith nodded, more to himself than Daniel, and continued thinking out loud. "It's always Dexter who is grounding Marty. He's the solid one. But today, for the first time ever, it felt like Marty was grounding him."

Daniel nodded, his eyes never leaving Keith's, though it was clear he was fighting back strong emotion. Still, Keith pressed on. "It was Marty who took Dexter's hands into hers, not the other way around." Sensing how his words were affecting Daniel, Keith fell silent, afraid that saying more might undo them both.

Daniel sank onto the edge of the hide-a-bed, the motion itself carrying more weight than the words that followed.

"Andrew and Dexter were best friends," Daniel reflected. "Two men cut out of the exact same mold. I mean, Dexter came from abject poverty, and Andrew came from the most elite of the elite. But they knew and understood each other without ever having to say a word. They knew and understood each other to their very core."

Keith took it all in with quiet fascination, seeing his brother-in-law not as he had long understood him, but as he might truly be.

Daniel continued, "The truth is, I think we comforted each other that night. Yes, it was him holding me. Trying to pull me out of this unfathomably dark and despairing abyss. But at some level, I think we comforted each other."

Keith pulled a nearby chair and sat in front of him, taking in Daniel's presence. As he inched nearer, he could feel Daniel's pain moving through him, brushing against his own. He steadied himself, knowing he had to make room for both, without letting it consume either one of them. "Well, somehow, I felt like I was transported there today. I don't know how it happened, and it completely freaked me out."

"Transported there? Transported where?" Daniel asked.

"To that night. To that parking lot." Keith shook his head. "To you."

Daniel's face softened, a small shift that carried both recognition and ache.

"I remember thinking: Why is Marty comforting Dexter? I know he likes you." Keith was thinking out loud.

"Tolerates me." Daniel's face remained calm, though his eyes revealed the complicated tenderness that had always defined Dexter for him.

"Okay, tolerates you." A faint smile touched Keith's face before he sank back into the weight of what was surfacing. "I know he tolerates you. But what struck me today was how she was comforting him, and then, all at once, I was having this visceral experience of... I thought it was you. But maybe it was him."

Keith shook his head at the memory. Daniel waited, as Keith's distress seemed to move through the space between them.

"Maybe it was both of you. I don't know. It's like I felt your anguish and your despair as Andrew," Keith shrugged, not sure how to say it, "died in your arms. He literally died in your arms, didn't he?"

Daniel slowly nodded. For a moment, he said nothing, the effort to steady himself visible only in the faint shift of his expression, the quiet tightening around his eyes as he fought not to be pulled back to that moment.

Caught between the ache of needing to protect Daniel and the ache of his own truth, Keith gave way as the words tumbled out. "Well, I could feel it, and it completely overtook me. And then suddenly, I realized I was starting to have what felt like a psychotic break. Right there in the courtroom in front of everybody."

Daniel nodded and leaned in, his own pain receding briefly beneath the fragility of Keith's unraveling. "I walked over to Brent, basically begging him to help me. He told me to trust myself." Keith shook his head softly, still marveling. "Can you imagine?

"He said that to you?" Daniel asked, the question carrying both wonder and something closer to awe.

"Yes." Keith nodded, a smile appearing on his face. "He said, 'Trust yourself, Keith.' And then, suddenly, it was no longer about me. It was all about you. And it wasn't even about winning or losing the case. It was about somehow getting you safely off that witness stand."

Daniel looked at Keith, his eyes welling with emotion. "All I could think about was everything you've suffered and how I could get you off that witness stand safely."

Daniel stared at Keith, overwhelmed by the quiet astonishment of being seen, and shaken by how much it mattered.

Gesturing as he explained, Keith continued, "Cross my heart and swear to God, all I wanted to do was get the room to see you as I see you. To somehow get them to have a taste of who you really are."

Daniel shook his head slowly, a quiet sorrow settling over him as he took it all in.

"I just wanted to take care of you. To take care of the situation," Keith said, his voice dropping to an almost reverent whisper.

"That's crazy," Daniel breathed, the rawness in his voice giving way to something almost fragile. He shook his head, eyes bright with a realization that seemed to lay him bare.

"It is, isn't it? Crazy! Do you think it's part of my genetic affliction?" Keith chuckled, shaking his head. "I did seriously think I was having a psychotic break of some kind. It felt like I was... literally about to have a nervous breakdown. Right there in the courtroom in front of God and everybody. It scared the shit out of me."

Daniel, followed by Keith, burst into laughter, the tension easing but the closeness holding fast. "I'm sorry," Daniel managed, "I don't mean to..."

"Is that what happens with schizophrenics?" Keith asked, entirely sincere, even as the smile lingered on his face.

"Maybe. I don't know." Daniel let out a soft chuckle that faded as quickly as it came. He leaned closer to Keith, his voice low and full of compassion. "But can we stop thinking of this as your affliction and maybe call it your genius?"

"I don't want that kind of genius," Keith said sincerely as his smile slipped off his face. "Seriously, I never want that to happen to me again."

As the emotional temperature transitioned, the air between them shifted. Keith leaned in a little closer to Daniel. A quiet settled between them, something both fragile and very alive.

Keith shifted, suddenly awkward and insecure.

Daniel waited, not just holding the space that was becoming increasingly more sacred to him, but really beginning to see the full spectrum of what this beautiful, complicated man was made of.

Keith lingered on Daniel's face, his eyes tracing something he could no longer hide. The words came slowly, drawn from a place deeper than thought. "Might there be a time when you could let someone else in, Daniel?"

Daniel looked across at him, his eyes tired yet full of love and compassion as Keith pressed on. "I know I will never, ever be able to replace Andrew. I will never, ever try to replace Andrew. But might there be a time when you and I could let this become something more? Really come to know each other in every way?"

Daniel's gaze drifted behind Keith to the posters on the walls, which were blown-up photographs of him, Brent, Charlie, and Andrew at various rallies and events. One image, a large poster of the four of them on the steps of the White House, caught his attention. His focus shifted to a smaller picture nearby: a candid shot of him and Andrew, their faces alight with laughter and warmth.

Daniel's shoulders sank. When he finally lifted his eyes, Keith knew what was coming. "I cannot go through that again, Keith," Daniel said, his voice cracking. "I'm sorry. I cannot love or lose like that ever again..." He drew a slow breath. "It wouldn't be fair to you." Then, almost in a whisper, more to himself than to Keith, "I'm sorry."

Keith's face tightened as he absorbed Daniel's words. He nodded, his expression a blend of understanding and pain. "I get it," Keith said softly, though his voice faltered. After a moment, he added, "But I want you to know that I do love you, Daniel Eiman. As God is my witness, I have never loved like this in my whole life."

The words hung in the air, raw and unguarded.

"Not ever," Keith said, his voice punctuating his sincerity.

Keith composed himself, took a calming breath, and stood up, pausing to look down at Daniel for a moment longer. With purposeful strides, he walked to the door. Just before exiting, he turned back one last time, meeting Daniel's gaze. "Goodnight, Daniel Eiman," he said softly, his words hanging in the air. As the door slowly closed behind him, Daniel's voice trailed after him, just above a whisper, "Goodnight, Keith Chambers."

The moment the heavy door clicked shut, Brent's wheelchair emerged from the shadows. He had heard everything.

The heavy outer door closed with a dull finality, and Keith's footsteps faded down the steps into the night. Only then did Daniel find his voice.

It sounded less like he was addressing Brent and more like he was speaking into the room itself, yet Brent absorbed every word as if they were meant for him alone.

"When I was a kid growing up in that insane household, I used to fantasize that my father was like this: super-spiritual angel, or something. One of the Dominion's fiercest warriors. The kind whose sole purpose was to protect *me*. I used to pretend that I was his favorite, most precious son. That he adored me. Really, truly adored me. Adored me above and beyond anyone else, even my mother."

Brent smiled softly as he settled himself directly across from Daniel. "That sounds wonderful."

"It was. It was my great escape." Daniel shook his head softly, almost in wonder. "I'd forgotten all about that until this afternoon."

Brent stayed quiet, listening.

"Andrew really adored me, Brent. I felt like he adored me. Even more than I ever imagined my father did, or even could." A gentle smile touched Daniel's eyes as he allowed himself to bask in the memory.

"That he did..." Brent nodded, first to himself, then to Daniel. "That he did."

Daniel shook his head, fighting back tears that clouded his eyes. "I never understood why. I mean, I adored him too, but...Those first four years with Andrew were pure bliss for me. I never imagined I could be that happy."

Daniel shook his head again. "He was the one who suggested that I become an activist. Did you know that? It was his idea."

Brent nodded once, steady and sure, and waited, certain more was coming.

"Suddenly, I was getting all this attention. And it felt amazing. It felt incredible. I craved it. I threw myself into cause after cause. One after another. Savoring all the attention I never received as a kid. I was intoxicated by it."

Brent nodded.

And waited.

"Honestly? I don't think people *should* 'out' themselves, Brent. I've never thought it was the right thing to do. I also don't believe we should be storming around the country smashing our ideas down other people's throats. I don't think that helps our cause. If anything, it hurts us! Andrew was right. It all became bigger than I was. I wasn't fighting my own causes, Brent; I was fighting everyone else's."

Brent didn't want to speak, but he had to. "It was six, almost seven years ago, Daniel. Times were different back then. We were all doing what we thought was right."

"I didn't believe in it, Brent." Daniel's eyes dropped to Brent's still legs, the sight deepening his sadness. "I didn't believe in it then, and I don't believe in it now. We shouldn't have been there that night."

Daniel shook his head, sifting through the past as he had so many times before, desperately trying to find the *why;* trying to pinpoint the exact moment in his life when he chose anything else over Andrew. "And why didn't we leave right away? As soon as we knew Harvey wasn't going to 'out' himself, why didn't we all leave?"

"We were all there of our own accord, Daniel," Brent said gently. "You didn't make us stay. We wanted to stay. Every one of us."

Daniel's voice grew quieter, but more urgent. "If I had insisted that we leave, would you have all stayed?"

Brent locked his wheelchair and carefully moved himself out of it onto the pull-out next to Daniel. Wrapping an arm around him, he pleaded, "Please don't do this to yourself, Daniel. Please don't."

Tears began streaming down Daniel's face. "We shouldn't have been there, Brent," he whispered, more to himself than to Brent. "We should not have been there."

Brent drew Daniel closer, letting the weight of it all settle as he fought not to be swept into it himself. His hand gently pressed at the back of Daniel's neck, anchoring him. He waited, breathing for them both, until the room was quiet. His hand stayed warm and steady, as if promising Daniel he was not alone, until he felt the storm begin to ease.

Daniel finally pulled back just enough to meet Brent's eyes, his voice small, almost as if it belonged to someone else. "Do you think they'll let me go back to teaching?"

"They have to, Daniel," Brent said, steady, a defiant edge in his voice. "You were acquitted. Completely exonerated.

They either put you back or they pay you. With back pay for every day you've been gone, either way."

Daniel nodded, a glimmer of hope beginning to crack open inside him.

"Which reminds me," Brent said, careful with his tone. "We got a call this afternoon from one of your students."

Daniel's eyebrows shot up. "One of *my* students?"

"Yeah. Mark, something or other, called right after today's proceedings wrapped up."

"Mark Slate?"

Brent nodded, "Yeah, I think that's his name."

"What did he want?"

"Well, he said he always knew you were innocent and wanted to congratulate us. And then he mentioned something about *praying* or something. Is he, like, a religious type?" Brent gestured to the conference table, pointing to a Post-it note front and center.

Daniel shot off the pull-out and snatched up the note.

Brent eased himself back into his wheelchair, looking up as Daniel unfolded it. "What does it say?"

Daniel stared down at the Post-it, reading Rebecca's flawless script out loud. "Tell him it's about the," Daniel hesitated, the words catching before he was able to force out, "Jesus Prayer."

"Yeah, that's what I thought it said!" Brent shot back. "Were you praying with these kids? I never took you to be the praying type, Daniel!"

"No." Daniel's rebuke was instant and firm. "Salinger. *Franny and Zooey.* Surely, you've read *Franny and Zooey?*"

"Yeah, in high school. Or maybe college." Brent frowned. "What about it?"

Daniel offered a faint, weary smile and shook his head. "It's too complicated even to begin to explain." The very idea of putting it into words felt like more than he could handle.

Brent studied Daniel. Hovering just above him, he somehow appeared smaller despite his height. "Could you try, please?" Brent asked, firm but not unkind. Then his tone softened. "Because he wants to meet with you."

Daniel sank back onto the pull-out. "Mark Slate wants to meet with me?" The bare fact of it seemed to weigh on him.

"Yes," Brent said slowly, as if he was still figuring it out himself. "And it has something to do with the Jesus Prayer. I mean, seriously, dude?"

Daniel took a breath, searching his memory. "During our whole, I don't know what you would call it, *exchange,* Benjamin McCray mentioned that he wanted to know what he did, or what he had to do to not be in so much pain."

"So, you told him to *pray?*" Brent asked, caught between disbelief and incredulity.

"No!" Daniel snapped.

Brent's expression hardened, frustration overshadowing any compassion he might have had. "So, if you weren't praying with them, what exactly were you doing?"

"I was *teaching them literature!*" Daniel shot back. "English *literature!*

Brent sat back, aware that the right words wouldn't come, no matter how hard he tried.

Daniel searched for his own, still fitting the pieces together in his mind. "Why do you think Salinger stopped publishing?"

Brent shrugged. "Jeez, I don't know, Daniel. Maybe because *The Catcher in the Rye* made him millions of dollars, and he never needed to publish again!" He let out a short, incredulous laugh. "Or maybe the answer is, 'Who fucking cares?'"

"I do!" Daniel shot back at Brent, simultaneously, flying to his feet, jamming a finger toward himself. "I care!!"

For a heartbeat that felt like it lasted forever, even the air seemed to stand still. The words echoed inside Daniel's chest, too sharp to take back. Too true to regret.

The rush of emotion had surprised him. But suddenly, it had nothing to do with Salinger at all. It was about Andrew and Keith; it was about the quiet shattering of his own soul as everything he had ever tried to hold back came rushing out of him.

"Some literature, most literature, simply entertains or distracts us. *Great* literature transforms us. It makes us better, Brent. It is timeless, even if it doesn't belong to its own time. Except in the case of Salinger, who, it turns out, *was right on time.* And seems to still be *on time* even to this day."

"It's just…nobody was listening. Nobody truly understood! Nobody really cared. What if that's why he stopped publishing? Because nobody got it. Nobody. Not the high-flying critics in their ivory towers in New York. Not the Ivy League colleges he so often referred to, including Columbia, by the way. Not even one of the tens of thousands of high school teachers teaching Salinger across the country."

Daniel fell silent, the words hanging in the air like smoke. "Nobody gets it."

"Can you please tell me what this thing is that nobody, *including me*, seems to understand?" Brent shifted in his chair, the movement sharp, his frown deepening. There was a challenge in his voice, and also a dare.

"I think you all should figure it out. I don't understand why no one can. It's all right there. Salinger reveals the wound in *Catcher,* exposes it further in *Franny and Zooey,* while also providing the salve. Full circle." He drew in a slow breath, letting the words settle before adding, softer now, "It's all right there."

Brent felt his frustration rise. He still didn't understand what Daniel was driving at. And the passion behind the words struck him like a live wire. It left him restless, gnawing at the edges of his certainty. "So, tell me what all of this has to do with the Jesus Prayer?"

"*Everything.* It has everything to do with the Jesus Prayer, Brent. With *that kind* of praying." Daniel's voice softened, the fight draining out of him as he sank back onto the edge of the pull-out. "That's the brilliance of allegory. It draws us in, stirs us to think, but only if we care enough to look. But how many of us really care?"

Brent sat frozen in space, his mind blank, words refusing to come.

"Benjamin cared. But I never go to explore it with him," Daniel said quietly. "Everything got in the way." His gaze drifted, almost inward. "Life got in the way. Like it always does."

Brent nodded slowly. He didn't fully grasp what Daniel was saying, but he could feel the gravity behind it, and that was enough. "Well, maybe this Mark Slate kid cares, too."

Daniel's shoulders sank. "Maybe," he whispered, quietly slipping back into himself.

Brent hesitated, then added softly, "So, what do you want to do about him?"

As the silence stretched, Daniel's thoughts tumbled over one another, gathering speed until he could no longer hold them back. "I didn't have a homophobic father. I had the opposite. When my father was in the house, all the abuse stopped. He wouldn't allow it. He protected me. I think in his own way, he protected all of us. Who's protecting Benjamin McCray?" Daniel shook his head, letting himself sink into memories that felt equal parts ache and solace.

Desperate to shake it off, Daniel forced himself to look up. Brent's eyes were warm, compassionate. "I had it, Brent," he said, the words catching in his throat. "I had everything. More than I ever imagined possible."

"Including four brothers." Brent offered it with a half smile, trying to lighten what had become unbearable, even if he could not quite help himself.

Daniel paused, as though steadying himself on the thought, before letting a crooked smile slip. "I was talking about Andrew, you dip wit!"

"Well, four brothers would have been everything for me," Brent said, completely serious.

"It was a war zone, dude. Trust me, you wouldn't have liked it."

"No, *trust me*. I would have *loved it*!" Brent shot back, a grin tugging at the corner of his mouth.

Daniel's lips curved despite himself, the tension cracking for just a moment.

"I'm sorry, but your brothers are gorgeous," Brent said.

Daniel rolled his eyes, but his smile lingered.

"Did you ever see any of them naked?" Brent asked, unable to stop himself.

Daniel just stared at him. "Really?"

Brent didn't hesitate, "Yes, really."

Daniel took a moment, then answered flatly. "The three of us in the middle shared a bedroom until I went to college. So yes, we saw each other naked."

"Your older middle brother never went to college?" Brent was genuinely curious. Of all Daniel's brothers, Seth was the one he was most attracted to.

Daniel's tone softened with reluctant fondness. "Seth went to Amherst. Which, of course, he rode his bike to."

Brent's grin widened. "Like everything? Did you get to see everything?"

Daniel hesitated. He knew the waters were dark and treacherous, but there was a point he wanted to make. "We all woke up with morning wood, dude. And half the time went to bed with it. Especially at that age. So yes, we saw everything."

Brent hesitated, curiosity tightening with embarrassment and vulnerability, raw desire simmering just beneath. It was impossible to ignore. When he finally spoke, it was more a disbelieving statement than a question. "And it didn't turn you on."

Daniel sat with it for a long moment, letting the weight of the words settle before he spoke, calm but edged. "They were my brothers, Brent." He shook his head, the dryness in his tone betraying the strain underneath. "What the hell?"

"Not even a little?" Brent pressed.

"No!" Daniel's voice stayed controlled, but every trace of softness was gone. "Not at all." He forced a small smile onto his face, but it didn't reach his eyes. "So, your friend's dad wasn't enough? You'd have gone after your brothers, too?"

"First of all, my friend's dad came after me." Brent's grin lingered, but the seriousness beneath it was unmistakable. "I was willing, sure, but he did approach me. And I didn't have any brothers to go after. It's just a fantasy, dude!" His grin faded as his voice softened, vulnerable and earnest. "Cut me a break, will you?"

"Well, I'm sorry to disappoint you, but that definitely would not have happened with any of my brothers. I guarantee it. They're straighter than Dexter, hard as that might be to believe."

Brent's smile broadened. "You don't know that."

"Oh yeah, I do." Daniel shot back, his tone clipped, though his smile widened almost against his will. "God, Brent, you really are something else! I'm sorry, but you are."

"Hey, it is a lot of people's fantasy." Brent's tone carried a spark of defiance.

Daniel didn't raise his voice, but there was no mistaking the firmness in it. "Yeah, well, maybe you should use that imagination of yours for something a little more constructive, if not realistic."

"Like having my father adore me?" Brent shot back, the flash of defense betraying more than he meant to.

"Yes, exactly!" Daniel said it softly, but the intensity in his eyes made it land hard. "Like having *someone* adore you."

The air thickened between them, an unspoken challenge hanging there.

Daniel's next words were quiet but unshakable, as though guarding something that mattered deeply. "At least I knew what it would feel like when Andrew came along. And Andrew was way beyond anything I could ever have even imagined." He gestured sharply. "And not because he stuck his hands down my pants."

Brent's face fell. For a moment, he had no defense, no ready grin to hide behind, only the raw weight of the entire conversation pressing in on him.

Daniel hadn't meant for it to land so hard. He immediately softened, his voice losing its edge but not its resolve. "Look, I'm not judging you, Brent. And I'm not saying anything you did was wrong or shouldn't have happened. I get that it helped you, I do. I just think there may be more to it all than you realize."

Brent nodded slowly, the fight easing out of him. "You might be right. I mean, I was *mostly joking*, dude, but..." He let out a long breath. "You might be right."

"Sorry, man. It's just... that's a lot to joke about..." Daniel's voice was quieter now, but there was a steadiness in it.

"Well, someone's got to talk about it, because it happens a lot more than you think!" Brent shot back, the edge in his voice surprising even him. Then, softer, as though clarifying more than defending himself, he added, "And it is a lot of people's fantasy."

Daniel shook his head, not in dismissal but as if to clear the heaviness pressing on him. He stared down at his hands, letting the silence stretch, then looked up with a mix of compassion and weary frustration, as though he wanted to move them past this but could not quite find the words.

"I'm sorry, but it is, Daniel," Brent said it again, quieter now, but with the same intent.

The silence stretched between them, grave and unmoving, as if it belonged to a place where words were rarely spoken. At last, Brent conceded, his tone careful, "In the meantime, what do you want to do about this Slate kid?"

Daniel's fragility surged again, a wave of emotion rising so fast it nearly unmoored him. He blinked hard, pressing his knuckles to his eyes, trying to hold himself together through sheer force. When the word finally left him, "Mark," it was as though he had reached back into something he had tried not to touch. It hung there, suspended, the weight of it pressing down between them.

"Yes, what do you want to do about Mark Slate?"

"There have to be at least five adults there. Maybe six or seven. And maybe one or two of the teachers from the school," Daniel shot back.

"And if he doesn't agree?" Brent asked, his mind already working out how to make it happen.

"Then we're not going to meet!" Daniel was adamant.

"Don't you think that's a bit extreme?" Brent's voice was calm but weighted, protective of Daniel yet carrying the quiet conviction that this needed to be done for Daniel's sake and for the kid's.

"No. Not at all." Daniel's tone was edged, his frustration breaking through even as he tried to hold his ground.

"Okay, buddy." Beneath Brent's words lingered a quiet understanding that seemed to settle the space between them.

Daniel could only shake his head. "Why does life have to be this hard? It just seems so unbearable sometimes." The question seemed to hollow the room, and before he could stop it, the tears were back, pressing relentlessly against his eyes.

Brent moved without thinking, slipping out of the wheelchair and back to Daniel's side in one smooth, certain motion. It felt almost reverent, as if closing the distance between them might stitch something back together. Never had he been more aware of how much care Daniel's heart required, or of how fiercely he needed to protect it. "We are going to get through this, Daniel," he said, his voice quiet but unwavering. "All of us. We are all going to get through all of it."

Daniel looked up, his gaze drifting across the posters on the walls before settling on the door through which, just over an hour earlier, Keith had disappeared. As if seized by the sheer incomprehensibility of it all, he whispered, more to himself than to Brent, "Keith Chambers."

Daniel slowly looked up to find Brent's waiting, compassionate eyes. "Can you even imagine it?"

"Yes." Brent didn't hesitate. "Yes, I can imagine it. And I think you should, too."

Daniel's response was immediate and final. "No! I cannot go through that again, Brent. I can never, ever go through that again. I still haven't gotten through the first one."

Brent searched Daniel's eyes, feeling the heavy weight of it all settle over him.

Daniel's tears started to fall, the weight of everything bearing down on him: The death of Andrew, Benjamin McCray, the trial, and Keith. Every cause Daniel had carried, even the ones he never wanted and those he never should have. All of it pressed in on him until it came crashing down, crushing him where he sat. "I'm sorry, Brent." His body began to tremble as he said it again, softer this time, as the words tore their way out of him. "I'm so sorry."

Brent's own breath caught, his vision blurring as tears filled his eyes. He pulled Daniel close and held him, steady and unyielding, as though he could shoulder even a fraction of the weight threatening to swallow him whole.

"Okay. Apology accepted." Brent's voice was barely above a whisper as he pulled Daniel closer, his hand gentle in Daniel's hair, his words quiet and steady. He drew Daniel fully against him, his breath hitching as a wave of feeling crested inside. When he spoke again, it was almost a plea, raw and breaking. "Apology accepted."

Daniel collapsed into the warm, welcoming strength of Brent's arms, a steady presence unyielding against his unraveling, as he slowly started sobbing.

Brent drew Daniel as close as he could, cradling him as if he were the most fragile thing in the world, because to Brent, in that moment, he was. He pressed a trembling kiss to the top of Daniel's head, his breath catching before he whispered into his hair, his voice raw and unguarded, "Thank you, Daniel… Thank you."

Tears cascaded off Brent's face as he pulled Daniel even closer, and for the first time since that horrible night, Daniel gave way to his grief, fully, openly, unabashedly, and without restraint.

*****

In the Chambers' kitchen, the door from the dining room swung open. Governor Chambers stood at the sink, washing dishes. Her hands moved with mechanical precision, scrubbing the same plate repeatedly. Although her behavior was not unusual, it was clear she needed space and time.

Mr. Chambers moved behind his wife, maintaining a silent presence. He maneuvered closer, wrapped both arms around her waist, and pulled her close. Leaning in, he spoke softly into her ear, "He's becoming an awful lot like you."

Governor Chambers straightened a bit, her voice steady yet quivering with emotion. "He's nothing like me," she said, her hands stilled in the soapy water. "He's exactly like you. He always has been. Exactly like you."

Mr. Chambers smiled and kissed the back of her neck. "I'll take that as a compliment," he replied gently. "But I also think he's starting to act a lot like you."

Governor Chambers shook her head, fighting back tears. "I didn't mean for this to happen," she whispered, her voice cracking.

"I know you didn't, my sweet," Mr. Chambers replied, soothing her. "But it's all worked out now, hasn't it?"

She choked back her emotions and leaned back into his embrace. "I just don't want to find him bloody and beaten in a parking lot somewhere," she said, battling tears she refused to let flow.

"Shhh," Mr. Chambers murmured, his voice a gentle mantra. "Shhh, shhh, shhh. It's okay."

Governor Chambers turned in his arms, burying her face in his chest. "So now you're going to tell me you approve of this," she said, her words muffled.

Mr. Chambers didn't hesitate. "I approve of him," he said firmly. "I truly do. I approve of him."

He kissed the top of her head and held her close as she surrendered to his embrace. "Keith will do the right thing, Liz. He has always and only done the right thing."

Unable to suppress the flood of tears that slowly overtook her, Governor Chambers melted into her husband's hold as he whispered soft reassurances into her hair.

*****

Brent rolled into Kaufel's office, morning light pooling across the floor. He was usually an afternoon appointment. Not today. Today, he needed Kaufel.

Kaufel's tone was calm, steady. "So, a breakthrough."

Brent's throat tightened as he swallowed nervously. "Yes," he managed, the word catching slightly before tumbling out. "I had a breakthrough."

Kaufel gave a slight wrist gesture for Brent to elaborate, settling back into his chair: a master of his craft at work.

Brent hesitated momentarily, his eyes lingering on the framed certificates on the walls before finding Kaufel's calm, attentive gaze. Taking a deep breath, he began, his words heavy with recollection.

"It started that night at my friend's place. His dad was in the kitchen, getting water from the fridge. I'd seen him naked at the gym plenty of times. Something about this night was different. Maybe it was the summer heat. Maybe it was the way he wiped his mouth, the way he looked at me. It flipped a switch. My vision tunneled. My loins tingled. My breath hitched. The surge came hard and fast, a tremor I couldn't name then, only feel."

"Because he was naked in the kitchen," Kaufel interjected, his tone probing, devoid of judgment, but curious nonetheless.

Brent pressed on, "He wiped his mouth and placed the glass on the counter. We never broke eye contact. Some switch flipped inside me. I was floored by him. Not just his insanely sexy body and rugged good looks. But his calm, physical confidence. The way he owned the room. It completely devastated me. It was impossible not to want him, even if I had no idea what that even meant."

Kaufel leaned forward, his interest evident but restrained, like a chess player pondering their next move. "And then?"

Brent's gaze drifted to the floor, his words tentative, as though testing their weight. "He just kept staring at me. And then a surge, out of nowhere. I couldn't breathe."

Kaufel nodded slowly, the motion deliberate. "And," he said, his voice soft but steady, inviting Brent to continue.

The room seemed to fade around Brent as he relived the moment. His voice trembled slightly as he continued. "He approached, pace unhurried, eyes holding mine. The air was thick with heat, but a cold slid through me, and the shaking started; I was shivering uncontrollably, unable to make it stop."

Kaufel tilted his head slightly, one hand resting on his knee, his gaze steady and unflinching: a quiet invitation to go on.

"I can't recall the particulars. I only remember the surge. It was sudden. All-consuming. I felt intensely aware and very alive."

Kaufel nodded again, his expression unwavering. "Okay," he prompted gently.

Never breaking eye contact, Brent continued, his voice gaining momentum as he delved deeper into the memory, "He pulled me off the couch and into his muscular, hairy body. Heat, weight, his heavy breathing, his pungent scent, and then the rush. It was over almost before I understood what was happening, my underwear and shorts saturated with cum."

The words hung in the air. The silence was punctuated only by the faint rumble of traffic outside. Kaufel nodded in understanding, his expression unchanged.

Brent's voice softened as he continued, the weight of his recollections pulling him deeper into the moment. "It was all pure pleasure. Layered. Insistent. He never once looked away."

Kaufel tilted his head slightly, his gaze sharpening as he asked, "And you never looked away?"

"No. Insane. I never looked away." He touched a finger to his mouth, 'Shhh,' and guided me toward the half bath. The fan hummed, the tile cooled the air, and the fluorescent glare hit hard. My breath stayed high, a tremor running through me like a live wire."

"He undressed me there, controlled, methodical. I froze. Then he took the mess in my underwear and smeared it across himself. I remember seeing him then, totally aroused and leaking. Then he finished himself off, into the sink."

"In front of you," Kaufel clarified, his tone as steady as ever.

"Oh yeah," Brent said, nodding with a strange mix of embarrassment and nostalgia. "Right in front of me. Then he moved with the same precision as before. Soap, water, the hiss of the tap. He rinsed the shorts and underwear, wrung them out, and pulled them back on me, still damp. A finger to his lips; "Shhh," he whispered once more, and then headed back up the stairs."

Brent paused, exhaling sharply like he'd just cracked open a pressure valve. "I went back to the couch. Everything came in waves. Breath, thought, then the loop again. I kept trying to shake it, but the charge wouldn't dissipate. It had complete control of me. I must've jerked off three more times trying to make it stop, to get it out of my system. But it wouldn't go down. I was still hard. Still completely lit up.

I couldn't stop replaying it, what had happened, and how it happened. And how insanely turned on I was."

Kaufel's eyes didn't waver as he absorbed Brent's words. Brent shook his head as if to clear it.

"Okay. Did you feel violated?" Kaufel prompted, his tone inviting.

Brent could only shake his head. "No. Not. At. All."

Kaufel nodded. Waited. It was he who broke the silence. "And the epiphany?"

"The epiphany," Brent began slowly, "came later. It was this: those were the exact feelings I had that day in my doctor's office. The same sudden, overpowering rush, out of nowhere. Exactly the same."

Kaufel reclined a bit, a look of understanding on his face. "Do you mean the intense sexual attraction?" he asked.

"Yes. The overwhelming, almost intoxicating surge," Brent confirmed, nodding. "I wasn't shivering, but it took my breath away. And then I caught myself wondering, 'Is he aroused?'"

Brent continued slowly, reexperiencing it in his mind's eye. "Because his erection arches back toward his belly, it isn't obvious. I couldn't see it, but I sensed it. I could feel the energy of his arousal, even though I couldn't see it."

"Because it felt the same way as your friend's dad," Kaufel verified, his voice cutting through the haze of Brent's memory like a guiding light.

"Exactly." Brent swallowed. "With my doctor, he stopped me, pulled my hand back. He tried to thwart it. But I wanted it and I kept reaching. His mind may have been saying no, but his body was screaming yes."

The confession hung heavily in the room. Kaufel remained composed, nodding slightly to encourage Brent to continue.

"He kept trying to stop me," Brent said, his voice breaking under the strain of the memory. "He kept yanking my hand away. But then... then he gave in. And once I got my mouth on him, he pulled me up again, hugged me, and just held me."

"Hugged you?" Kaufel asked, his tone gentle, probing.

"Yeah. Tight." Brent nodded, his voice softer now, tinged with vulnerability. "He held me so tight. I guess he was trying to stop whatever was about to happen."

"But something had shifted. The feelings were still overwhelming, just...different. I didn't want the act anymore. I wanted what was happening while he held me. I wanted everything that was suddenly opening up inside of me. All these feelings that were somewhat distant but at the same time suddenly, seemingly, new to me."

The room seemed to shrink as Brent spoke, the walls of Kaufel's office closing in around the intimate, heavy conversation. "I pressed into his warmth. He smelled like himself: clean, human. He kept rubbing my scalp and back, steadily, like breathing. All sounds and distractions vanished. What was left was a fierce, settling tenderness that felt a lot like love."

Kaufel nodded slowly, offering Brent space without pressure, presence without intrusion."

Brent's eyes went distant. "Then his lips found mine," he said softly. "We kissed, and the world dissolved. Everything slipped out of frame. What remained was the sheer rightness of it all."

The faint hum of an air conditioner filled the silence between his words, a quiet backdrop to the flood of emotion in the room.

Brent shifted in his chair, his hands fidgeting as though trying to release the tension. "The next thing I remember is him reaching the end, while inside of me," he said, breath catching. "And it landed deeper than my body. It felt more like rapture than a release."

Kaufel nodded, his eyes calm yet piercing as they held Brent's gaze. His hands rested lightly on the armrests of his chair, a picture of patient attentiveness.

Brent continued, his voice faltering. "Then it was like before. He cleaned us up, calm and exact, and sent me on my way. I went home blissed out, convinced something in me had come back online. I was so excited to see him again, but the next appointment had me assigned to a different doctor.

The words lingered in the air, heavy with disappointment and unresolved longing.

Kaufel nodded again, his face revealing no judgment, only a quiet understanding. "And how did you handle that?"

Brent exhaled sharply, his frustration evident. "I didn't. I went on Grindr, trying to recreate what I had felt with him. I met three different guys. Two my age and one older, closer to his age."

"And?" Kaufel prompted, his voice gentle, his body language open.

Brent shook his head, his hands running across the stubble of his shaved head as if trying to rid himself of the memories. "Nothing. Nada. It was terrible. It was worse every time. The last one was the worst of them all."

Kaufel tilted his head a bit, his brow creasing with curiosity. "What makes you say that?"

Brent's voice became tense. "Because everything with my doctor was different. It wasn't just the act. Not sex. Not lust. Deeper. I suddenly needed something I couldn't find with them. Something I only seemed to be able to find with him." He paused, taking a deep breath before continuing.

"I called my doctor and begged to see him, not for sex, but because I needed to understand what was happening to me. I promised I'd respect his boundaries. I just needed a neurological read on what I was feeling. He's my neurologist. You know that, right?"

"Yes." Kaufel's lips curved slightly in a faint, knowing smile. "Did he agree to meet you?"

Brent nodded, his voice growing quieter. "He begrudgingly agreed to meet with me. And... it all happened again."

"What happened again?" Kaufel's tone was patient, inviting Brent to articulate his thoughts.

Brent's gaze dropped to his hands, now clenched in his lap. "We ended up... basically, getting it on again: The same thing."

"There was hugging, kissing... and that same overwhelming feeling. Only this time, it felt even deeper, like it was reaching some part of me I didn't even know had been waiting."

Kaufel leaned forward slightly, his interest piqued. "And then it stopped?" he asked, seeking clarity.

Brent's eyes grew distant as he nodded, lost in the memories. "We stole a final weekend. Two days that somehow held a lifetime. We spoke about everything. Who he was at home, who he is at work, and what meaning looked like to him. The closeness surprised me. It felt nearly spiritual, and I don't say that lightly."

Brent's voice trailed off as he relived the moments all over again.

"And then, on the afternoon we were supposed to return to Boston, we shared our third and final encounter. For me, it was the most incredible experience of them all."

Kaufel waited patiently for Brent to continue, prompting him with a simple, silent question.

"The epiphany," Brent began slowly, each word chosen with care. "What I felt for my friend's dad might have been nothing more than raw, undeniable lust, and maybe more his doing than mine. But it takes two to take." He drew a slow breath before continuing. "With my doctor, though... it was different. Something quieter. Deeper. Something that felt a lot closer to love.

After all those months of him helping me, really seeing me, helping me piece my life back together, it became a bond I didn't expect." Brent pressed on. "Maybe it was a bond he didn't expect either. It felt... loving. It felt deeply, profoundly loving," Brent said quietly. "I felt like he loved me. Not just physically, but in a real, whole way. And I... I loved him back. I really did."

Kaufel nodded in understanding.

"Yes. It started as lust. If that's what you've been waiting for me to admit, then fine, you're right. But where it went... that was something else entirely." Brent paused, searching for words that could do the shift justice. "It's hard to describe. The best I can say is this: It became something real. It turned into something that really mattered." Then softly, more to himself: "Like what it might feel like to be truly adored."

"Yes," Kaufel agreed with a gentle nod. "I believe you're right."

Brent finally sat back in his wheelchair, fully absorbed. The magnitude of it struck him in a single, undeniable rush. "I can't help but wonder, is that how healthy sex starts? You know, with all the love?"

Kaufel nodded with a small smile, clearly impressed by what they'd reached together. "For some, yes," he said quietly. "For the lucky ones."

Overwhelmed with gratitude, Brent leaned toward Kaufel and said, "Thank you so much for everything. Thank you for being patient with me."

"It was my pleasure. Truly," Kaufel replied.

These were the moments that made all the challenges of his profession worth it for Kaufel; a reminder of why he had chosen this path.

"I don't mean to pry," Brent said, "but do you ever get attracted to your patients?" He couldn't help asking.

"Yes. Absolutely," Kaufel said with a small smile. "It doesn't happen often, but it does happen from time to time."

"And?" Brent asked, half-joking, half-prying.

"And I have absolute boundaries I do not cross. For any reason," Kaufel said.

Brent's face was thoughtful and sincere as he asked, "You think it was wrong of my friend's dad to approach me, don't you?"

Kaufel's response was measured and neutral. "Well, there are laws. And it is against the law. So, from that point of view, yes."

Brent nodded in understanding, though his eyes held a hint of conflict. "It all helped me so much, though. It did."

Kaufel's gaze softened as he chose his words. "It may also have introduced you to a hormonal storm that isn't exactly conducive to healthy explorations of sexuality and love."

Brent's forehead creased. "What are you trying to say?"

The older man continued, slow and deliberate. "When something is taboo or breaks norms and laws, it can trigger cortisol and adrenaline on top of the usual serotonin, dopamine, oxytocin. Layers that would otherwise come naturally with sexual and romantic intimacy."

Brent nodded thoughtfully.

"A hormonal mix that can feel, as you said, 'intoxicating.'" Kaufel concluded.

Brent nodded again as the feeling returned to him. "And at his son's wedding," Kaufel pressed on, "you said your friend's dad profusely apologized for his actions." He waited.

"Yeah. He did. I told him I loved it." Brent reiterated, "I told him that he saved my fucking life, and there was nothing to apologize for. He just kept saying how sorry he was." Brent nodded.

"So, whether or not I think it's wrong, or you think otherwise," Kaufel clarified, "it clearly felt wrong to him."

Brent nodded, taking it in. "Sex..." He paused. "It suddenly seems like such a complicated arena."

Kaufel nodded. "You also said that your wet dreams before this happened with your friend's dad were about women." He waited for clarification.

Brent chuckled. "One girl. And my teacher. But honestly? Neither of them had that... spark. What's wild is they were all over me in the dream, but in real life? Nothing. Not even close."

Kaufel nodded thoughtfully. "Still, it might suggest there's some part of you that's genuinely open to the opposite sex."

Brent shook his head, firm. "Maybe. But like I said, no spark. And besides, women hate men these days. I'm glad I'm gay!" He glanced at Kaufel, half-expecting a challenge.

None came.

"Really! They're exhausting," Brent added, more to himself now. "All the drama. All the games. I'm honestly relieved I'm not attracted to them."

"Not anymore," Kaufel clarified.

"Not at all!" Brent was emphatic. "Thank God for my friend's dad. Seriously."

"Sexuality can be very, as you said, very complicated." Kaufel offered. "Although this is somewhat unorthodox, I just want to plant this bee in your bonnet."

Kaufel waited for confirmation from Brent to continue. "I had the exact opposite experience of you. During puberty, I couldn't touch a girl's breast without prematurely ejaculating. Forget about getting my private parts anywhere near theirs. Some girls I'd start to unbutton their blouse, and I'd be ejaculating."

Brent laughed out loud. "Really?"

Kaufel smiled broadly. "Yes. Really! I experimented with boys, one in particular, who was my older brother's friend. Who also turned out to be gay."

"Really?" Brent couldn't believe it.

"Yes. But for me, it was about learning how to contain myself. I wasn't at all interested in him sexually. Not even a little, except for where things went and how to get it to happen. I had to close my eyes and pretend he was a girl even to get aroused. He was a great teacher, though." Kaufel smiled at the memory.

"How old was he?" Brent sought confirmation.

"Two grades ahead of me in school. We were pretty close to the same age. And I was very aware that I was not nearly as interested in him as he seemed to be in me. But through it all, if not because of all of it, I learned how to contain myself with women. I remain deeply grateful to him and better off for having had the experience."

"That is so interesting. Thank you for sharing it." Brent was sincere.

"Normally, I wouldn't. Ever. But for some reason, it seems appropriate here, today." Kaufel yielded.

"Well, thank you so much." Brent nodded.

"Also, I want you to know my wife is incredible," Kaufel continued, his voice warming the room. He leaned back, a fond smile touching his lips, as if painting her in careful strokes. "She doesn't hate men at all. She adores them. She adores me. She adores our son. She adores men. She adores life and living!"

Brent watched him closely, noting the quiet light in Kaufel's face. "She's kind and yielding, but strong. Soft, but knowing. Vulnerable, honest, real." His voice fell, almost reverent. "She's never manipulated me. Not once. And she's been a remarkable role model for our daughters. One of whom is a total tomboy. More boyish than any boy in our entire household. But she's proud to be a girl. Wants to be just like her mom. Maybe she'll end up the best of both of us."

There was a pause, the room held by a gentle hum. Kaufel's gaze drifted, perhaps to a particular memory. When he spoke again, it was with a simple certainty. "She's everything I think a woman should be. Which is why I married her."

Brent's smile was genuine, his admiration clear. "I'm so glad to hear that. Is she a stay-at-home mom?"

Kaufel chuckled softly and sat a little straighter. "No, she's a pediatrician. A very successful one." Pride rose in his voice. "A pediatrician who puts her own kids first. And always will."

Brent nodded thoughtfully, gears turning. The balance Kaufel described sounded almost too good to be true: ambition and devotion in harmony. "That sounds... amazing," he said, a hint of longing in his voice.

"It is," Kaufel said, steady and grateful. "But it's not just what she does. It's who she is. I don't take that for granted."

The room went quiet for a moment as his words settled. After a beat, Kaufel went on. "You know, some men, and many women, aren't as interested in sex as you or I might be."

Brent nodded, urging him to continue.

"And then there are some men who have sex with as many women, or men, or both, as possible and don't think anything of it," Kaufel said, tone neutral, almost clinical, with a flicker of amusement. "Some people smoke, drink, eat junk food their whole lives, have as much sex as they possibly can, and still live happily past over a hundred."

"Like Charlie!" Brent said, lighting up.

"Exactly!" Kaufel laughed softly. "Charlie loves everything about his life. He thrives, smoking, drinking, and having sex with as many women as possible. And he loves his work."

"And he's insanely talented at it," Brent added, with clear admiration in his voice.

"There's no conflict for people like Charlie," Kaufel said, leaning forward as if to underline the rarity. "His witness and his experiencer line up. Seamless. He's rare."

Brent's expression shifted with a touch of self-awareness. "Unlike me, who has huge conflict."

Kaufel nodded slowly. "Me as well," he said, his candor softening the moment. "Other people have immovable moral codes and suffer for it immeasurably. It's what makes life interesting, right?"

Brent tilted his head; the lines on his forehead eased. "That does describe Charlie to a T. He's happy. And gifted. I really admire him."

A pause opened between them. Brent's voice dropped, a hint of vulnerability showing. "I'm so glad you're my therapist. I wanted to quit so many times."

Kaufel's expression warmed with unmistakable pride. "But you stayed with it, didn't you?" he said, the tone like a parent watching a child persevere.

"I did," Brent said, a little proud himself. He glanced at his watch and laughed. "Oh my God, we've gone over."

Kaufel waved it off with a reassuring smile. "Yes, it's on me. I felt you might need the time, and I wanted to be sure we got through it."

Brent's gratitude was plain. "Thank you so much."

"You're welcome," Kaufel said, the smile softening. "It's moments like this that remind me why I do what I do."

Brent nodded, settling further into his chair, as if the session had grounded him more than he expected. He hesitated. "In the next session, we have to talk more about my doctor."

Kaufel nodded, calm and steady. "We'll get to that. One step at a time."

Brent nodded again, a faint smile crossing his lips. "I wish I could tell him how sorry I am and how much he gave me. I'm pretty sure I messed up his life. It really was all my fault."

Kaufel's expression softened further, his voice quiet but firm. "We'll try to get clarity on that, too. It's all good, Brent. It's all terrific."

Brent exhaled deeply, his shoulders loosening. "Thank you. For everything."

"You're welcome," Kaufel replied, his gaze warm and steady. "Take care, and we'll pick up where we left off."

Brent nodded, a glimmer of hope in his eyes as he turned to leave. The door clicked shut softly behind him, the room settling into a quiet, albeit completely fulfilling calm once more.

*****

The Eiman family sunroom was alive with golden morning light, far brighter than Keith remembered. The first time he visited, the afternoon sun softened the room. However, today, beams of light streamed through the large windows, dancing across every surface and illuminating the numerous photos that filled the space. Each frame seemed to tell a story, and in nearly every picture that included him, Daniel's infectious smile radiated a warmth that seemed to belong only to him.

Keith sat in a cushioned chair, holding a green glass bottle of mineral water. He examined the label idly, its foreign name still unrecognizable. Across from him, Mrs. Eiman sipped her tea from a delicate porcelain cup. Her posture was relaxed yet regal. She looked over the rim of her cup, her eyes gentle yet perceptive. "He's in Cambridge," she said, setting the cup down on a small side table. "With Brent and the boys. It's good for him. It's where he belongs."

Keith nodded slowly, his gaze momentarily shifting to a photo on a nearby shelf. "I've seen him a couple of times," he admitted. "He seems pretty happy."

Mrs. Eiman's lips curved into a soft smile that held both pride and sorrow. Despite their nearly daily insufferable exchanges, she genuinely missed her son. "So, when's the big date?" she asked, deftly changing the subject.

Keith blinked, momentarily thrown by the shift. "Not sure," he said, recovering quickly. "Late summer, early fall."

Her smile brightened as she placed her hands delicately in her lap. "That's wonderful. Congratulations. Ashley is a wonderful girl. I'm sure the two of you will have a beautiful life together."

Keith leaned forward slightly, his sincerity evident. "You'll be invited, so please come! My dad's a big fan of yours."

The compliment seemed to catch her off guard for a moment, but then her smile widened. "That's very sweet of you. Thank you."

Keith hesitated before speaking again. "Yeah, I was in the area. I wanted to be sure to come by and say hello."

Mrs. Eiman tilted her head slightly, her eyes softening as she regarded him. "That was a very bold thing you did for my son," she said, her voice carrying an understated weight.

Keith chuckled. The sound was nervous and self-deprecating. "Yeah, I wasn't entirely thinking very clearly. I think if I had been, I would have been too terrified to take it all on. It seems a lot bolder to me now, after the fact."

They shared a laugh, the tension in the room easing as their smiles mirrored each other.

"Matters of the heart seldom involve clear thinking," she said, her tone becoming reflective. "Which is why I think Daniel's always in so much trouble. His heart is too big for his own good. He can't seem to get away from it. I don't think he wants to."

Keith shifted in his seat, his fingers absentmindedly peeling the label off his bottle. When he looked up, he found her watching him, her expression kind yet firm. "In the end, it doesn't really matter, Keith. What matters most are all those other things: love, family, and living the life you're born to live. Daniel does as Daniel will and must do. And so now must you."

Keith's gaze drifted to a photo just above her head. In it, Daniel was surrounded by his four brothers, all appearing stoic and serious. Daniel, however, stood out, his bright smile illuminating the entire image. It was impossible not to feel the joy and individuality radiating from him.

*****

The engagement celebration was yet another grand Chambers family event, one of many that Keith had come to tolerate rather than enjoy. However, this one felt heavier; it was for him and Ashley. There was no escaping it. Attendance wasn't optional.

Keith's truck pulled into the circular driveway at Star Market. Ashley popped out, her long evening gown shimmering under the streetlights. She looked stunning, with the heirloom diamond on her finger catching the light and refracting it into a brilliant display. The new, understated setting made the stone seem even more significant, symbolizing their impending union. Keith stayed in the truck as she walked toward the entrance, adjusting his tie absentmindedly.

His attention was drawn away by an argument unfolding across Boylston Street. Two men in their thirties stood close together, their voices raised. Although Keith couldn't make out their words, the tension between them was palpable.

The taller man gestured emphatically, his tone firm yet not aggressive. The stockier man shoved him away, his movements sharp and defensive. The taller man hesitated briefly before stepping forward again, blocking the other from leaving. His presence remained steady, and his movements were deliberate as he attempted to defuse the situation.

Passersby began to take notice, some pausing to watch while others hurried past with uneasy glances. Keith couldn't tear his eyes away as the scene drew him in further and further. The taller man said something in a low, even voice, and the stockier man seemed to falter. The tension shifted. Slowly, the shorter man's body sagged, leaning into the embrace of the taller man.

Keith's breath caught as he realized what he was witnessing. The taller man wrapped his arms around his companion, holding him tightly. Then, in a tender, unguarded moment, he tilted his head and kissed him. Their movements were slow, deliberate, and filled with quiet intimacy. Without a word, they turned and walked away together, their steps perfectly in sync.

"Keith?" Ashley's voice startled him. She had returned with a small shopping bag in hand and was sliding into the passenger seat.

Keith's focus drifted to Ashley, almost in a daze. "Yeah?" he replied, forcing himself to put the truck in gear. The engine rumbled as they pulled onto Boylston Street.

In the rearview mirror, Keith watched the two men walking away, their silhouettes disappearing into the night.

Keith drove in silence, his thoughts lingering on the scene he had just witnessed. Something about the two men stirred a quiet ache deep within him that he couldn't quite name. It wasn't just the kiss that stayed with him; it was the way the taller man held his partner, the way they moved together as if the world around them didn't exist.

Keith's grip on the steering wheel tightened as he glanced at Ashley out of the corner of his eye. She was flipping through her phone. Her expression relaxed, entirely unaware of the moment he had just experienced. The diamond on her finger caught the light with every slight movement of her hand, a stark reminder of the life they were building together, a life Keith was not entirely sure he belonged in.

The Newbury Boston stood tall and imposing, its familiar elegance masking the increasing discomfort Keith was experiencing as they arrived. He had always preferred the understated luxury of this venue. Though the Ritz-Carlton Hotel company had long since sold its interest, Ritz-Carlton's original attention to detail and quality still inhabited its bones. Tonight, however, its grandeur only heightened his sense of detachment.

Inside, the ballroom buzzed with activity. Guests in formal attire mingled, glasses of champagne in hand, as their laughter and chatter filled the space. Keith stood among them, with Ashley on one side and Marty and Dexter on the other. Ashley's diamond sparkled beneath the crystal chandeliers, drawing admiring glances from everyone who approached.

The tailored suits. The champagne smiles; the practiced certainty of people who'd never had to question the script. Keith's gaze slid past them, lost in the memory of two men on a street corner: unguarded and achingly genuine.

A supporter approached, draping an arm around both Keith and Marty. His voice boomed with enthusiasm. "The Lioness is at it again," he declared, directing the comment to Marty. "You Chambers' always get what you want, don't you?"

"That we do!" Marty replied, her smile dazzling. She turned to Keith, her grin widening. "That we do," she reiterated.

Keith felt a faint smile tug at his lips, but it didn't reach his eyes. The noise of the room seemed to fade as he looked around, taking it all in. Marty was radiant and confident. Dexter was steady and strong. His parents, nieces, nephews, and cousins formed a sea of faces filled with expectation, pride, and patronizing approval: The image of perfection, a family that always seemed to get it right.

His gaze drifted back to Ashley, who was chatting with another guest, her laughter light and melodic. The diamond on her finger sparkled brilliantly, symbolizing their future together. Yet instead of feeling pride or joy, Keith felt an overwhelming weight pressing down on him, a suffocating sense of duty that left no room for authenticity.

Marty's smile faltered as she noticed the change in Keith's expression. "What?" she asked, her voice laced with concern.

Keith turned toward Marty, his movements slow and deliberate. "Excuse me," he said softly, then shifted his full attention to Ashley. It wasn't a rebellion. It wasn't even a decision. It was a remembering of something he'd never allowed himself to want, until now. Taking both her hands in his, he looked into her eyes, his voice gentle but steady. "I'm leaving, Ashley. I'm sorry, but I have to leave."

Ashley blinked, her brows knitting together in confusion. "What do you mean?" she asked, her voice wavering.

Keith's gaze didn't waver. "You're an amazing woman," he said, his tone filled with genuine admiration. "You're going to make somebody an amazing wife." Leaning in, Keith kissed her forehead, then her cheeks, and finally gave her a gentle kiss on the lips, lingering for just a moment before stepping back.

"Keith..." Ashley's voice cracked as she reached out, but he was already walking away.

Marty, Ashley, and Dexter watched in stunned silence as Keith exited the hall. The sound of laughter and clinking glasses seemed distant now, a backdrop to the confusion and concern etched across their faces. "Where's he going?" Marty asked, her voice barely concealing her worry.

"I don't know," Ashley whispered, her eyes fixed on the door Keith had just exited through. Her fingers instinctively moved to the diamond on her left hand, twisting it slowly as if searching for answers in its brilliance.

"Is he coming back?" Marty asked, her voice hesitant.

More to herself, Ashley murmured, "I don't think so."

Ashley, Marty, and Dexter stood staring long after Keith had left the banquet hall.

The night air was crisp and biting as Keith crossed the Public Garden, then Charles Street, entering and crossing Boston Common. The park's pathways glistened beneath the faint glow of streetlights, the slick pavement reflecting the amber light like a mirror.

Bundled pedestrians hurried past, their breath visible in the cold; however, Keith strode through in his tuxedo, oblivious to the chill. He had left his truck behind with the valet, unwilling to risk anyone stopping him or asking questions he couldn't answer. His mind raced as he walked, each step echoing with clarity and confusion alike. The life he had built with Ashley, the expectations of his family, the image of success: everything seemed to blur into one another.

The underground sign indicating the T's arrival at Harvard Square came into view after just a few stops on the Red Line. The familiar streets, dotted with late-night cafes and bookstores, felt more vibrant than the gilded halls of The Newbury Boston. Brent's windows shone brightly, like a beacon calling him home.

Keith approached the door hesitantly, his heart pounding. Brent wheeled into view behind the glass, his face a mix of surprise and understanding. He opened the door, pausing briefly before pulling it wider to let Keith inside.

Keith stepped in, his tuxedo crisp against the cozy clutter of the office. Daniel, lying on the pull-out couch, sat up immediately. He didn't even attempt to hide his surprise as his eyes locked onto Keith.

Without a word, Brent grabbed a large overcoat from the rack, draped it over his lap, and wheeled past them, exiting into the night without so much as a greeting. The door clicked softly behind him, leaving Keith and Daniel alone.

Keith stood motionless, staring across the room at Daniel. The pull-out couch creaked softly as Daniel shifted under Keith's intense gaze, his expression a mixture of curiosity and caution. The shrill ring of Brent's landline suddenly broke the charged silence between them. Both men startled slightly, their focus snapping to the desk where the ancient answering machine clicked on with a mechanical whirl.

Brent's familiar voice filled the room. "You've reached the law offices of Brent Evans. We're unable to speak with you in person right at this moment. Please leave as detailed a message as you'd like. Don't forget your contact info."

The beep was followed by Charlie's unmistakable tone, teasing and irreverent. "Daniel, pick up the phone... Come on, man; I know you're there! It's true, isn't it? You lost your job."

Keith's brow shot up, his expression a mixture of surprise and disbelief. He looked back at Daniel, who rolled his eyes and shrugged lightly. "Charlie," Daniel said, the hint of a smirk tugging at the corners of his mouth.

Keith couldn't help but smile. Followed by a frown, "You lost your job?" he asked, incredulous.

Daniel sighed, maneuvering himself to the edge of the hide-a-bed. "They didn't technically fire me," he explained with a calm yet resigned tone. Rising slowly, he added, "They gave me an option. But you know... It's cancel culture, and suddenly, all kinds of parents don't want their kids taught by a...," Daniel signaled, "child molester," his voice carried the weight of exhaustion.

"You were exonerated!" Keith exclaimed, his voice rising in indignation. "Completely exonerated and acquitted!"

"Yeah, but you know. It's Leominster," Daniel replied, shrugging again.

"Meaning?" Keith's voice was sharp with frustration.

"Meaning it's very blue-collar and kind of red," Daniel explained with a wry smile.

Keith's face darkened, his jaw tightening. "Those frigging idiots," he muttered, his anger palpable. "They don't know what they're losing."

Daniel laughed softly, a bitter edge to the sound. "A lot of trouble, actually. That's what they're losing: a lot of trouble."

Keith's gaze swept the room, his expression determined. "Where's your stuff?" he asked abruptly, already scanning the space.

Daniel blinked. "Why?"

Keith didn't answer; instead, he stepped toward the closet and pulled the door open. "Because you're coming home with me," he finally declared matter-of-factly, rifling through the contents.

"I don't think that's a good idea, Keith," Daniel protested.

"I don't care what you think, Daniel," Keith shot back, his voice firm. He turned back to the room, resuming his search for Daniel's belongings. "Help me," he ordered, kicking the edge of the pull-out couch for emphasis, which startled Daniel, who took a step back. "Where's your suitcase?" Keith commanded.

Daniel hesitated, watching Keith with a mix of bemusement and apprehension. "And Ashley's...?" he began cautiously. "Isn't tonight your engagement party?"

Keith froze for a moment before turning to face Daniel, his expression unwavering. "Ashley is going to make someone an incredible wife," Keith said evenly. "Just not me."

Daniel's eyes widened slightly, his concern evident. "Keith..." he began, but Keith had already moved into the adjacent room, where an open suitcase lay on the floor. He grabbed a toothbrush and other supplies from the office bathroom, tossing them into the suitcase before snapping it shut.

"Aren't you cold?" Daniel asked, noting Keith's lack of a coat.

"No. Why are you?" Keith replied absently, still focused on his task.

Daniel frowned. "No, but you were just outside. It's like twelve degrees out."

"Well then, bring a coat," Keith retorted with a shrug, his tone matter-of-fact.

Daniel stared at him, his astonishment growing by the second. "Keith," he said, slowly inching closer to him, "what are you doing?"

Keith straightened, his eyes locked onto Daniel's. When he spoke, his voice was steady: gentler now, but no less assured. "I am in love with you, Daniel Eiman. And I need you. I don't know what that's going to look like, or where it's going to lead. But I do know this much: you're going to have to deal with it. Because I'm not leaving here without you."

"Maybe you don't have a choice, Keith!" Daniel countered, his voice rising with frustration.

Keith ignored him, grabbing Daniel's suitcase and reopening it to toss in more clothes. "I'm a Chambers," he said simply. "And we Chambers always get what we want."

Daniel watched him, stunned. "What about what I want?" he demanded.

Keith paused, meeting Daniel's gaze with unwavering resolve. "I don't care what you want," he said plainly.

Daniel blinked, trying to process the words. "You don't care what I want?" he repeated, his voice tinged with disbelief.

Keith glanced around the room, his eyes landing on the posters covering the walls. Activist slogans and historic events stared back at him: Stonewall, the March on Washington, and countless reminders of battles fought and won. He turned back to Daniel, his voice calm but firm. "Seriously. I thought about it all the way over here. I don't care what you want."

Daniel's eyes darted to the posters as well, his mind racing. He searched for the right words to halt the whirlwind unfolding before him, but nothing came.

Before he could say more, Keith closed the distance between them, grabbing Daniel's face with both hands and kissing him, softly at first, then with growing intensity. Keith's kiss deepened, his hands cradling Daniel's face with a mixture of urgency and tenderness.

Daniel froze for a moment, completely caught off guard, his mind scrambling to process what was happening. But then Keith's lips pressed harder, and the flood of sudden emotion overwhelmed Daniel's resistance.

Keith pulled back just enough to search Daniel's eyes, his breath heavy and his gaze filled with determination. There was no hesitation when he leaned in again, this time with even more intensity, as though he were trying to convey in one instant everything he would never be able to find the words to say.

Daniel's hands instinctively rose to Keith's chest, but instead of pushing him away, they lingered there, gripping the fabric of his tuxedo. His breath came in short gasps between kisses as Keith's passion consumed him. The pull-out couch creaked beneath them as they tumbled onto it, their movements becoming increasingly frenzied.

Shirts were tugged overhead and tossed carelessly to the floor. Shoes were kicked off in hurried motions, landing in opposite corners of the room. Keith's hands moved to

Daniel's belt, fumbling with the buckle as he continued to press kisses along Daniel's neck and jawline.

"Keith, wait," Daniel managed to gasp, his voice strained. He tried to pull away, but Keith's arms wrapped around him tightly, refusing to let him go.

"Don't," Keith murmured, his voice low and desperate. "Don't overthink this, Daniel."

"I'm not," Daniel insisted, his hands pressing against Keith's shoulders. "But we need to… "

Keith silenced any further protest with another kiss, his lips cutting off Daniel's objections. Daniel's resolve faltered as the intensity of the moment swept him up once more. Keith's hands roamed over his back, pulling him closer until no space remained between them.

For a brief moment, Daniel tried once more to pull away, but Keith's hold on him only tightened. "Keith, listen to me," he began, but his words were lost as Keith kissed him again, this time slower. Intentional. Undeniable.

It was as though time had stopped, the room fading away until only the two of them remained. Their movements grew more synchronized, their breaths mingling as they gave in to the overwhelming attraction neither one of them was ever going to be able to deny.

Meanwhile, the banquet hall had quieted considerably back at The Newbury, Boston. Guests continued to trickle out, offering their best wishes to Ashley and expressing concern for Keith's abrupt departure.

"Well, I hope he feels better soon," one woman offered kindly, patting Ashley's hand before leaving. "Such a sudden illness can't be ignored."

Ashley forced a polite smile, nodding along as the guest walked away. Next to her, Marty and Dexter stood in tense silence, exchanging glances as they tried to process what was happening.

Marty's patience snapped first. She turned to Dexter, her expression sharp. "Don't look at me," Dexter said quickly, holding up his hands in defense. "I don't know where he went!"

Ashley remained quiet, her eyes fixed on the doorway that Keith had exited through just over an hour ago. She absently twisted the diamond ring on her finger, which made her thoughts chaotic.

"He is coming back, Ashley!" Marty said, her voice unusually soft but still firm, as if trying to convince herself.

Ashley shook her head, barely speaking above a whisper. "Clearly, he's not, Marty!"

Dexter shifted uncomfortably, glancing between the two women. "Should I... what do you want me to do?"

Marty exhaled sharply, folding her arms. "I need this like I need another hole in my head." She nodded toward the waiter wheeling away the portable bar. "Get me another drink."

Dexter raised his hands, gesturing to the stripped-down setup. "The bar's closed."

"Then go to the corner and buy me a bottle," Marty snapped.

As Dexter reluctantly moved to comply, she slipped her arm through Ashley's. Her tone softened as she said, "We'll figure this out, sweetie. Everything's going to be fine."

Ashley could only shake her head as the humiliation mixed with rage building inside her was starting to become palpable.

Back in Brent's Cambridge office, the energy had shifted entirely. Keith rolled off Daniel, both of them now naked save socks, breathless, sweaty, and flushed. The room was warm, and their clothes were scattered across the floor. Keith lay on his back, staring up at the ceiling as a tear slipped from the corner of his eye.

"That was unbelievable," Keith said quietly, his voice filled with awe. "Un-fucking believable. Who knew?"

Daniel shook his head, his expression a mix of euphoria and disbelief. He propped himself up on one elbow, glancing at Keith. "You're insane," Daniel muttered, though his tone held no venom.

Keith sat up slowly, his hands brushing over his face as he tried to collect himself. He began searching for his clothes, pulling on items without much thought as to whether they were his or Daniel's. The two of them passed shirts and pants back and forth, their movements awkward yet tinged with a lingering intimacy.

As Keith fastened his tuxedo shirt, he leaned in to kiss Daniel again, unable to resist. His lips found Daniel's, who murmured between kisses, "Marty's never going to forgive me for this. Or you. She's never going to forgive you, either!"

"She'll get over it," Keith said confidently, reaching for his tuxedo jacket.

"No, she won't," Daniel insisted, pulling back slightly. "Keith, do you even know your own sister?"

Keith silenced him with another kiss, his hands cupping Daniel's face. "Shhh," he whispered. "No thinking. No more talking."

"Keith—"

"Shhh... shhhh... shhhh…" Keith continued, his voice soft as he kissed Daniel once more.

Keith couldn't stop kissing Daniel, even as they fumbled with their scattered clothes. Each kiss was purposeful, as if he were trying to imprint the moment in his memory. Finally, Keith managed to pull his tuxedo jacket back on, smoothing the fabric as he grabbed Daniel's suitcase and nudged him toward the door.

Daniel hesitated, glancing back at the disheveled pull-out couch: the space that had, for a time, been his refuge. "Keith," he said, nodding toward the bed. "Shouldn't we... tidy up a bit?"

"We'll come back in the morning," Keith replied without hesitation. Then, catching Daniel's hesitation, he added more gently, "I promise."

Daniel's silence spoke volumes. His gaze was quiet, questioning, and firm. Keith met it without flinching. He stepped closer, his voice steady, grounded. "I know exactly what I'm doing, Daniel." He answered the unspoken protest with calm certainty. "You're coming home with me. Now. End of story."

Daniel stared at him, eyes welling. Keith couldn't tell if the tears were frustration or, like his own, pure elation. Maybe both. It didn't matter. Setting the suitcase down, Keith placed his hands deliberately on Daniel's shoulders.

His voice dropped lower, but his conviction didn't waver. "Marty'll be pissed. Ashley will survive. But this?" he searched Daniel's eyes: "you and me? This is real. And I'm done pretending that it isn't."

Daniel let out a breath, his shoulders sinking. He looked down at the suitcase as Keith slowly lifted it again. "This... kind of terrifies me," he whispered.

Keith's grin came instantly: warm, unshakable. "Good." He nodded once, then his smile softened, deepening into something tender: laced with longing, devotion, maybe even awe. "It kind of terrifies me, too." It wasn't just an invitation; it was a vow. Quiet. Honest. Defiant. Then he opened the door, glanced back, and gestured. "Let's go."

Back at The Newbury Boston, the banquet hall was empty. The once-lively room now held only a few staff members clearing tables and stacking chairs. Marty stood with her arms crossed, her expression a mix of irritation and disbelief as she watched Dexter return empty-handed. "The liquor store was closed," Dexter said, shrugging apologetically.

Marty groaned, pinching the bridge of her nose. "Of course it was," she muttered. She glanced at Ashley, who sat nearby, her shoulders slumped and her hand still fidgeting with the diamond ring on her finger.

Marty softened, sitting down next to Ashley and looping her arm through hers. "We'll figure this out," she said, her voice quieter now. "Everything's going to be fine."

Ashley looked up at her, her eyes red-rimmed but determined. "Oh, no, sweet thing. This is over! This is most definitely over. There will not be another chance. Not ever. Never." Ashley resolutely stood up and walked away, shaking her head as she went.

Marty stared after her and then eyed Dexter. "Stop looking at me like that, Marty. Seriously, you're starting to piss me off!"

Marty could only shake her head.

The streets of Boston Common glistened under the faint glow of streetlights as Keith and Daniel emerged from the Park Street Red Line station. Keith carried Daniel's suitcase effortlessly. His tuxedo jacket flared slightly as a chilly gust of wind swept through them. Daniel walked beside him, shaking his head as if trying to make sense of everything that was now happening.

"The thing is," Keith began, his tone sincere and unguarded, "Ashley placates me. She's not interested in me at all. It's like talking to a wall. She stares at me blankly, like she's desperately trying to comprehend what I'm saying. She's as bad as the rest of them."

The air around them thickened, seemingly charged with electricity, as Daniel's concerned gaze met Keith's fiery glare, "Keith..."

Keith cut him off, his voice rising with passion. "It's death by a thousand cuts! Don't get me wrong, she has a lot to offer. She's just, not...you."

Daniel hesitated in his stride, processing Keith's words as his mind raced. He began to notice more and more the people surrounding them, the inquisitive looks. A wave of camera flashes gradually surged as a few paparazzi started to recognize the treasure they had stumbled upon.

"Keith, maybe you should, you know, quiet down a little bit," Daniel urged, his voice low and tense. He tried to create some distance between them, but Keith was undeterred.

"And also," Keith continued, oblivious to the growing crowd, "I'm sorry, but that was the best fucking sex I've ever had in my whole life."

Daniel's eyes widened as he glanced around nervously, now acutely aware of the growing crowd. "Keith, seriously… " he started, pointing out the growing crowd of people to him. Keith barreled on, utterly unfazed.

"The best!" Keith repeated, his voice full of conviction. "The very best!"

The flashes grew brighter. An increasing number of onlookers began pulling out their phones to capture the scene unfolding before them. Daniel tried once more to step away, but Keith reached out and pulled him even closer.

"Stop!" Daniel hissed, his voice urgent. "Don't you see what's happening?" Daniel deliberately gestured to the growing crowd.

Keith paused, glancing around at the crowd. For a moment, he seemed to consider Daniel's warning. Then, with daring defiance, he dropped the suitcase, cupped Daniel's face in both hands, and kissed him deeply.

Flashbulbs erupted in a frenzy, turning night into day. The murmurs of the crowd swelled into a roar as more onlookers stopped to watch. Daniel stiffened at first, his instincts screaming at him to pull away, but Keith's grip was firm and unrelenting. The kiss lingered, meaningful and unrestrained. When Keith finally pulled back, his forehead rested against Daniel's, their breaths mingling in the cold air.

"I'm not hiding anymore, Dude," Keith whispered, his voice resolute. "I'm sorry. I'm not. And neither are you." He then replanted his lips firmly onto Daniel's, passionate, fearless, and free, for the whole world to see.

*****

The following morning, the Chambers household was unusually quiet. Governor and Mr. Chambers sat at the dining room table, staring across at each other. The staff's attempts to set the table and serve breakfast remained at bay.

Instead of china and silverware, the dining room table was covered with newspapers and tabloids. Nearly every front page featured the same image: Keith and Daniel locked in a kiss, passionate, defiant, and unmistakably public, with Boston Common and the State House as their dramatic backdrop.

Governor Chambers fixed her gaze on the array of newspapers and magazines spread out before her, her expression a mask of inscrutable calm.

Mr. Chambers leaned back in his chair, his hands neatly folded in his lap. "It is what it is, Elizabeth," Mr. Chambers said finally, his tone calm but firm. "It is what it is."

Governor Chambers sighed, "Close the drapes, please, George," she said softly.

He obliged, drawing the drapes on the ceaselessly rising tide of news vans and reporters outside, leaving them alone in the quiet, dim hush of their dining room.

Thank you for reading Entitlement

If your journey through these pages has stirred questions of consciousness, authenticity, or the quiet call to come home to yourself, I invite you to explore *Becoming Authentically M.Y.S.E.L.F.*

www.becomingauthenticallymyself.com

It is a living journey in mindfulness and self-realization, twenty-two steps toward uncovering and embodying the authority of your truest self.

If what most moved you were the human questions, about love and sex, truth and illusion, belonging and resistance, you can continue that conversation.

www.brandenblinnnarrativefiction.com

There you'll find reflections, reader dialogues, and spaces to explore the themes *Entitlement* opens: the courage to see clearly, to feel deeply, and to live honestly in a complicated world.

Character Reference

Keith Chambers (Protagonist)

Daniel Eiman (Deuteragonist)

Andrew Steadman – Daniel's college lover

Brent Evans – Daniel's attorney, close friend, and college teammate of Daniel, Dexter, and Andrew

Marty Chambers – Keith's twin sister, a close friend of Daniel, Brent, Andrew, and Charlie, married to Dexter

Charlie Atwood – Brent's investigator and close friend of Daniel, Brent, Andrew, Dexter, and Marty

Governor Chambers (Antagonist) – Keith and Marty's mother

Mrs. Eiman – Daniel's mother

Mr. Chambers – Keith and Marty's father

Dexter Louis – Marty's husband. A close friend and college teammate of Daniel, Brent, Andrew, and, by default, Charlie

Benjamin McCray – Daniel's vulnerable student

Ashley Cox – Keith's fiancée

Sophie Bieltran – Keith's primary distraction

Mr. Swarth (Antagonist) – A political operative

Mark Slate – A student of Daniel's and a story catalyst

Made in the USA
Las Vegas, NV
07 December 2025

35901081R00246